On the morning of her thirteenth birthday, Fryda of Clan Waegmunding—daughter of Weohstan and jewel of King Beowulf's eye—wanted only one good kill.

She wished for a sturdy arrow shot straight and true, the rending of flesh under her knife, and the tang of hot blood sending curls of steam into the chill air.

In the pre-dawn darkness, she wriggled her way into trousers pilfered from the laundry the day before. The icy glimmer of stars peeped through the smoke-hole cut into the roof as she pulled on a roughspun tunic and fastened a leather belt around her childishly slim waist. *Good*, she thought. No one else in the household would stir for another hour at least.

She gathered her wild, butter-coloured curls into thick braids and wound them around her head, hoping the pins would hold, and slid a short *seax*—a sharp, tapered hunting dagger—under her belt. For a moment she considered fetching Theow from his pallet in the kitchens and asking if he wanted to come with her.

As Theow's name hovered in her mind, she felt a small frisson shimmer up her spine. Her breath quickened, the hairs on her arms stood up, and her young body woke in ways she did not entirely understand. She nearly surrendered to the rush of temptation that tugged her towards the kitchens, but did not want to risk Theow receiving credit for her hunt. A warrior gets credit for his kills.

Her kills, she thought. Or at least, one kill to prove her prowess at the hunt. One wolf pelt to hang in the mead-hall and call her own.

SHIELD MAIDEN

SHARON EMMERICHS

REDHOOK

Redhook Books/Orbit
Hachette Book Group
1290 Avenue of the Americas
New York, NY 10104
hachettebookgroup.com

First U.S. Edition: October 2023
Originally published in the U.K. by Head of Zeus Ltd,
part of Bloomsbury Publishing Plc, in February 2023

Redhook is an imprint of Orbit, a division of Hachette Book Group.
The Redhook name and logo are trademarks of Hachette Book Group, Inc.

The publisher is not responsible for websites (or their content)
that are not owned by the publisher.

The Hachette Speakers Bureau provides a wide range of authors for speaking events. To find out more, go to hachettespeakersbureau.com or email HachetteSpeakers@hbgusa.com.

Redhook books may be purchased in bulk for business, educational, or promotional use. For information, please contact your local bookseller or the Hachette Book Group Special Markets Department at special.markets@hbgusa.com.

Library of Congress Control Number: 2023931916

ISBNs: 9780316566919 (trade paperback), 9780316566926 (ebook)

Printed in the United States of America

LSC-C

Printing 1, 2023

For every girl and woman who wants to be a shield maiden

Author's Note

At the back of this book, you will find a glossary with pronunciations and definitions of character names and Old English words that appear in this story. However, if you prefer to either make up your own pronunciations or just blip over the words you don't know, this author has no objection whatsoever.

Happy reading!

~ Sharon

Précis

The Old English poem *Beowulf* (produced somewhere between 975 and 1015 CE) recounts the tale of the superhuman hero-turned-king Beowulf, who fights and kills three monsters: Grendel, who kept eating people in Denmark; Grendel's mother, who wanted revenge for her son's death; and a dragon, who destroyed Beowulf's village in the fiftieth year of his reign in Geatland. Beowulf demonstrates superpowers during his battles —feats of great strength, and the ability to hold his breath underwater for hours, for example.

This novel concerns the last battle, with the dragon. The original poem tells us that an unnamed slave, who had been exiled from his master's house, found a secret way into a dragon's lair filled with treasure. He steals a goblet, which wakes the dragon, who rains havoc and fire down upon the land. This is the story of that slave, and the woman who loved, inspired, and believed in him.

THE GEATS

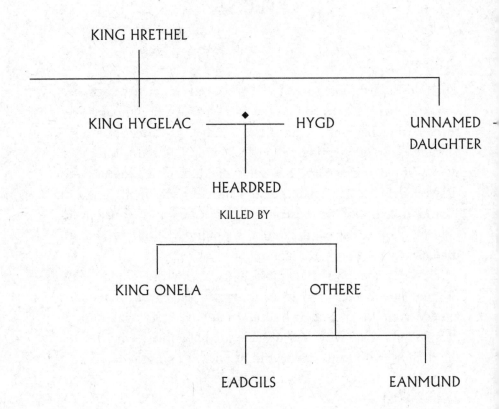

KING HRETHEL

KING HYGELAC ──── ◆ ──── HYGD   UNNAMED
                                     DAUGHTER

HEARDRED

KILLED BY

KING ONELA   OTHERE

EADGILS   EANMUND

THE SWEDES

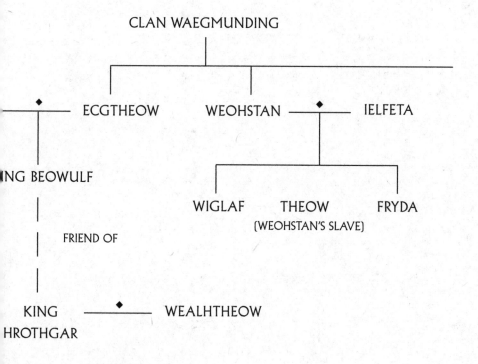

CLAN WAEGMUNDING

ECGTHEOW   WEOHSTAN ———— IELFETA

NG BEOWULF

WIGLAF   THEOW   FRYDA
              (WEOHSTAN'S SLAVE)

FRIEND OF

KING   ———————   WEALHTHEOW
HROTHGAR

UNFERTH
HROTHGAR'S THANE

THE DANES

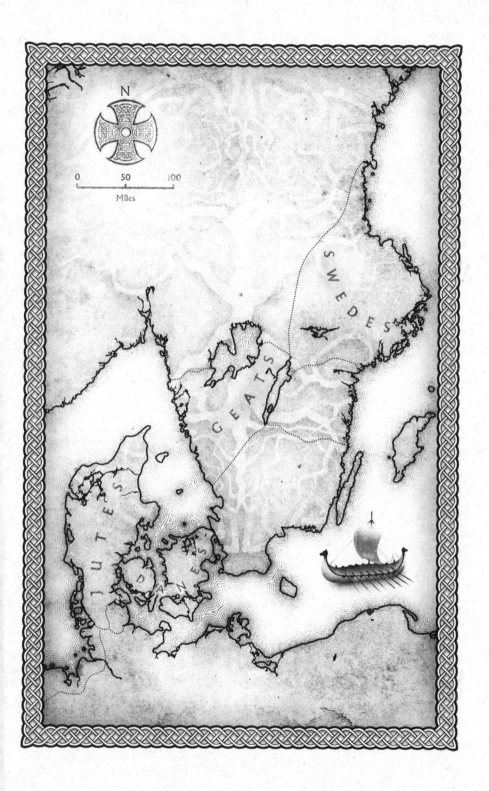

PART I

Prologue

Geatland, in the year 987 CE

On the morning of her thirteenth birthday, Fryda of Clan Waegmunding—daughter of Weohstan and jewel of King Beowulf's eye—wanted only one good kill. She wished for a sturdy arrow shot straight and true, the rending of flesh under her knife, and the tang of hot blood sending curls of steam into the chill air.

In the pre-dawn darkness, she wriggled her way into trousers pilfered from the laundry the day before. The icy glimmer of stars peeped through the smoke-hole cut into the roof as she pulled on a roughspun tunic and fastened a leather belt around her childishly slim waist. *Good*, she thought. No one else in the household would stir for another hour at least.

She gathered her wild, butter-coloured curls into thick braids and wound them around her head, hoping the pins would hold, and slid a short *seax*—a sharp, tapered hunting dagger—under her belt. For a moment she considered fetching Theow from his pallet in the kitchens and asking if he wanted to come with her.

As Theow's name hovered in her mind, she felt a small frisson shimmer up her spine. Her breath quickened, the hairs on her arms stood up, and her young body woke in ways she did not entirely understand. She nearly surrendered to the rush of temptation that tugged her towards the kitchens, but did not want to risk Theow receiving credit for her hunt. A warrior gets credit for his kills.

Her kills, she thought. Or at least, one kill to prove her prowess at the hunt. One wolf pelt to hang in the mead-hall and call her own.

She grabbed her bow and a quiver of arrows from her wooden chest and crept from the building, trying to be as silent as possible. In the early morning hush, every step, every breath sounded unnaturally loud, and she startled at each rustle and distant birdcall. Her breath misted in the late autumn air, but the nights were not yet cold enough to freeze the dew that pearled on the grass, making everything smell fresh and green.

Fryda made her way towards the western wall, stealing through the *burh* as quietly as she could. In the hovering darkness of the far-northern autumn, the structures resembled a sprawling village rather than a walled estate. Warm, reddish earthen walls rose in square and rectangular blocks, adorned by thatched, timbered roofs and arched windows set with real glass, sparkling like gemstones. Wooden structures hunkered in rows around an ancient standing stone. The air smelled like salt and brine, and she could hear the distant thunder of waves crashing against the rocky shore.

She nodded to the guards stationed at the gate and they let her pass without question. She had no doubt they would report her early morning exit from the *burh* to her father, but by that time —she hoped—she would have a fine wolf pelt to placate him.

Fryda padded through a wooded grove outside the stronghold wall, avoiding rustling leaves and noisy twigs. Soon her boots were soaked through and a chill pebbled her skin, but she did not think about turning back. Shield maidens did not stop fighting because of damp feet.

She scanned the ground as she moved, alert for any sign of the beast that had plagued the *burh*'s hunters since summer's end. After several cold, breathless moments she spotted the paw prints of an enormous wolf in some soft mud and steadily tracked them westward. They led her out of the woods to the bare, wind-ravaged meadows along the edge of the cliff. Elation filled her, making her feel as if she floated above the ground. She was going to find the wolf. She would find it and kill it and her father would finally see her as a worthy shield maiden. He would finally let her...

Her thoughts rattled out of her head as the earth beneath her shuddered and jerked. Fryda gasped as she staggered, trying to keep her feet. A terrifying roar filled her ears—a sound so monumental she thought Woden himself must have made it. Certainly no wolf could produce such a clamour.

The ground shifted sideways and violently flung her into the grass. A sharp report echoed across the sky, as if the very fabric of the air cracked and tore. The meadow undulated beneath her as though suddenly turned to water, and Fryda clutched the long grass in her fists. The coarse blades tore in her grip as the earth tried to shake her off, like a flea in a dog's fur.

The great cracks and rumblings became deafening, and Fryda sobbed in terror. The ground lurched, and then...disappeared.

For one breath she lay on solid, if tumultuous, ground and the next she plummeted downwards. A scream tore from her throat and she clawed with frantic hands for anything to break her fall.

Something grabbed her by the wrist, and for one breathless moment she thought Woden had indeed stretched out a hand to save her. But when a lightning bolt of pain shot from her hand down to her shoulder, Fryda understood why the clan revered the All-Father as the god of madness as well as death. She screamed again as her hand became fire and flames licked through her arm, her shoulder, and into her chest. She blinked against the sparks dancing across her vision and wondered if disobedience to her father had truly brought about the end of the world.

The violence of the earthquake had hollowed out a deep, deep chasm in the earth and she'd managed to jam her hand into a narrow crack in the wall. Fryda stared at the shards of white bone jutting from her ruined skin, the wells of shocking red blood running down her arm. It dripped from her fingers onto her neck, her face, into her clothing, and fear rushed to fill the spaces of her body left empty by leaking blood and protruding bone. She clutched the wall with her good hand while her feet scrabbled against the rock, trying to find purchase. But every movement caused great flowers of pain to bloom in her hand and chest, and she realized the fall had separated the bones of her arm completely from her shoulder.

Time began acting strangely. She had no idea how long she hung there, drowning in agony and hoping she would soon die. Eventually the darkness of night crept into her bones. Her throat burned with thirst and screams. Her eyes grew dim; her body shook with cold and weakness. Her arm and shoulder had gone numb hours before, but her hand seethed with pain from the bones piercing her skin and from the rock that kept her trapped like a rabbit in a snare. She screamed again, her voice feeble and wounded, and heard an answering music rise from the bottom of the chasm, a tinkling like bells or chimes.

It wasn't real, of course. She knew that now. Once night had claimed the land, she had fallen into a kind of delirium wherein she heard and saw things from the wrong side of reality. Strange phantasms from her life that could not possibly exist in this place and time hovered around her, like the scent of Hild's delicious mushroom soup, or the tang of the ground galls the hunters used for tanning skins. Perhaps the visions, the scents, the music were heralds of her death. If so, she welcomed them.

The torment from her trapped hand writhed through her body like a living thing. The hours since the earthquake had not acted as a balm for her pain. She thought, as she had a thousand times since she fell, about the hunting knife tucked in her belt.

She whimpered. Her hand, with all its torn flesh and broken bones, had swollen so rapidly she could not budge it from its rocky prison. But she could wrap her belt around her arm; tighten it. Take the knife and...

A gust of wind from the sea snaked through the chasm and buffeted her against the cliff wall.

Fryda screamed in earnest as her broken wrist twisted and the bones ground together. She fumbled for the *seax* at her waist, but her fingers faltered as the darkness closed in on her, and she gratefully succumbed to her fate.

Awareness

Deep in her cave, buried under a massive pile of treasure, Fýrdraca, Fire-Dragon, shifts. She feels the touch of gold and silver slide against her scales. For a moment she almost wakes, but something catches her and drags her back down into nightmare, like a drowning victim caught in an intractable undertow.

Not a nameless something. An ancient curse.

Fýrdraca struggles against the dark magic that binds her and the earth trembles at her strength and power.

The gold and treasure are her prison as well as her saviour. She reaches out, longing again to be free, to stretch her wings and fly. From her nightmares she lashes out at the barrier keeping her from the winds and clouds, and the ground shakes again. A sound like a thunderclap reverberates through the cave and this time the land cracks, fractures into long, deep fissures of jagged rock and stone. The earth-barrier between her precious gold and the sky breaks, splits, and for the first time in centuries the sun reaches in with gentle, trailing fingers and caresses her blighted treasure, like the touch from a long-lost lover. It brings warmth and light and...a noise. A sound never before heard from within her nightmare prison. Something small and insignificant. Not of gold or silver, no, nor of gems or pearls, but of flesh and bone and blood. Something scared. Something hurt.

Something human. A girl-child.

The pitiful sound diverts the flow of her memories. She remembers the Lone Survivor standing upon the promontory, *clutching a large and ancient goblet in both hands and keening, anguish twisting his face into something monstrous. The goblet seemed forged from legend, crafted in gold and silver and myth. Intricately embossed hunting scenes curved around the bowl and stem, and gems glowed in the raging firelight, reflecting the charred corpses of the Lone Survivor's kin, strewn across the land while the remains of his stronghold burned behind him. Fýrdraca again feels his heart shrivel and tear in his chest, where it seeps pain like a suppurated wound. His body curls around it, as if to protect a malignant birth that would forever curse him... and her.*

One

Geatland, seven years later, in the year 994 CE

"**A**rms up! Keep your stance strong!"

Fryda awkwardly lifted her elbows, and the practice spear she wielded wobbled in her tenuous grip. She couldn't get her clawed, twisted fingers all the way around the shaft, but she attacked anyway. Hild blocked it and the force of the blow knocked Fryda off balance, and onto her behind. The crude spear fell from her hand.

Instantly her dress and shift were soaked with early morning dew.

Bollocks.

She looked at Hild, with her bare feet and her old kitchen work tunic, and could not suppress a smile. Hild stood with her stave still raised, her expression worried and her dark brown skin a sharp contrast to the knee-high yellow grasses in the meadow behind the forge where they held their secret practices. The field stretched to the edge of the cliff that dropped to meet the shore and the sea, and a narrow set of steps carved into the cliff face wound down to Weohstan's fleet of longships. The field hosted the clan's festivals and ceremonial rituals, weddings, and competitions. The clanspeople burned their dead and paid homage to their gods, Woden and Frige, there—but for most of the year the wild expanse of grass lay empty and fallow.

A perfect place for forbidden fighting practice.

From her very first memory, Fryda had wanted only one thing. When she was four years old, she announced to her family she planned to become a shield maiden when she grew up.

Her father said no and told her to never speak such nonsense again.

On her tenth birthday, Weohstan caught Fryda and Theow—his own slave, no less—sparring in the field behind the forge. Her father's canny eye had immediately noted the smoothness of her movements and the dancing lightness of her feet—indications that this was far from the first time they had practised with the rough wooden swords the blacksmith had carved for them. Incandescent with rage, her father had burned the blades, forbidden her friendship with Theow, and shut her in her room for the rest of the day. She had cried, alone and hungry, while the people of Eceweall celebrated her birth with a grand feast in the mead-hall.

Her thoughts dodged around her disastrous attempt at a hunt when she was thirteen and, without thinking, she pulled the sleeve of her tunic over the ruin that used to be her left hand.

Now, at twenty years of age, she had learned discretion, if not obedience. Her dream of becoming a shield maiden had died that night in the chasm, but she could not seem to stop working towards it anyway.

"Are you all right, my lady?" Hild asked, her chest heaving. Her black hair fell in long braids to her waist and her too-thin frame was sleek and well muscled. Fryda frowned at Hild's bony wrists and prominent collarbones and vowed to speak again to Moire about increasing food rations for the entire kitchen staff.

"What did I say about your stance, Sunbeam?"

Fryda looked up to see Bryce standing over her, his arms crossed over his massive chest and his braided beard quivering with annoyance. She drew her mangled hand against her body and couldn't quite meet Bryce's gaze.

"I can't get a good grip on it," she mumbled.

Hild lowered her wooden stave and Fryda flinched away from her sympathetic look.

Bryce helped her to her feet. His blacksmith's hands, rough with old burns and scars, caught on the nap of her tunic. "Look," he said as he reached out to peel the sleeve from her hand. Fryda shuddered at the sight of her canted wrist and twisted fingers. She never looked at her hand if she could avoid it. "You don't have to grip it with both hands. Use your right hand for force and your left for direction and balance."

He handed her the practice spear. Bryce's face had no doubt been handsome in his youth, but age and experience had etched deep lines and grooves into his skin, and something or someone had broken his nose at least once. Fryda squinted at it. *Probably twice.* Though years had turned his hair the colour of iron, his physique had never diminished. The man's thighs were tree trunks, and half a lifetime of working the hammer and anvil had corded his arms with hard, curved muscle.

"Like this." Bryce positioned her right hand around the spear and gently moved her left so her twisted fingers anchored the weapon rather than gripped it. To her surprise, it felt a great deal more stable.

"I'm sorry about that, my lady," Hild said, and Fryda huffed. In all the years they had been friends, she had not convinced Hild to address her informally. Fryda was the lord's daughter and Hild an indentured servant in her father's household. It would be dangerous, Hild had once told her, to forget that.

"Not your fault, Hild," Fryda said. Bryce gave her hip one last nudge and she finally adjusted her stance.

"Try that," he told her.

Hild again raised her spear. This time when their weapons clashed, Fryda maintained her grip and deflected Hild's blow without mishap.

"That's more like it!" Bryce bellowed. His broad grin made

the early summer sun seem suddenly brighter. "You're learning now. Once more, but this time you attack and Hild defends."

Fryda readied her spear, taking care to position both hands correctly, and looked at her friend. Hild nodded, and Fryda leapt.

As she reached the apex of her jump, arms held high and a warrior shout in her throat, an odd sensation shivered through her body, as if hot blood were replaced by a trickle of cool water. Her breath seemed to fill her entire body and her senses sharpened to crystalline clarity. The trickle suddenly swelled into a flood and she gasped, for the water carried strength within it. Her muscles became smooth and supple and her body obeyed her every command. Without thinking, she tucked the spear under her left arm, holding it with her right hand and pinning it against her side, and twisted her body. The spear, aimed at Hild's chest, cut through the air with deadly precision.

Hild managed to raise her own weapon to divert the blow, but it knocked her off her feet and flung her backwards into the tall grass. Fryda landed with perfect balance, spun the wooden stave with a flourish, and drove it into the ground.

Bryce and Hild stared at her, mouths open. The chirps of birds and shrill song of insects sounded loud in their silence. Fryda blinked.

"What?" she asked.

Before they could answer, her newfound strength deserted her. "Whoop," she said, suddenly dizzy and disoriented. She staggered to one side, her limbs heavy and her head floating, as if stuffed full of fledgling goose feathers. Her left hand cramped and the old, familiar ache flooded her wrist once more.

Hild got to her feet as Bryce ran to Fryda. "Are you all right, my lady?" she asked, sounding breathless.

"I'm…oop…I'm fine," Fryda said as Bryce put a steadying arm around her shoulders. Her legs trembled and her entire body hummed, as if a thousand tiny wings fluttered under her skin. "That felt so strange. Are *you* all right? I didn't mean to hit you so hard."

"I'm fine." Hild dropped her spear and shook out her hands. "That was quite a wallop you gave me, though."

"It was indeed." Bryce took Fryda's shoulders and held her at arm's length, his eyes roving over her for signs of injury. She submitted to his inspection without complaint. The feathers and tiny wings were slowly dissipating, leaving behind nothing more than fatigue and confusion. "How did you do that?" Bryce asked, finally convinced she wasn't hurt.

Fryda shrugged. How could she possibly describe what had happened or what she'd felt? Bryce and Hild would think her mind touched.

"I guess I had the best teacher," she said, a bit of cheek creeping into her tone.

"Mmm." Bryce let her go. He slanted a glance at the sky. The sun, which rose early in the summer, had climbed above the horizon. "Best get back now, loves. The hall will be stirring soon."

Hild groaned. "Moire will have us working all day and all through the night, what with the king's feast beginning tonight." She scrubbed a hand through her thick, braided hair.

"Thank you for coming out this morning," Fryda said, clasping Hild's forearm. "Especially with…" She gestured to Hild's torso, which she had nearly bludgeoned. Woden's beard. What had got into her?

Hild gave her a sardonic look. "These mornings are the only way I can get through my days sometimes," she said. "I still have sixteen years of service before I gain my freedom, and Moire is going to squeeze every last bit of work out of me she can."

"Sixteen?" Bryce looked confused. "I thought your parents were indentured for only eight years when they came here. And that was fifteen years ago."

Fryda's mouth twisted as she released Hild's arm. "When

they died, my father added twelve years to Hild's indenture, in addition to the original contract."

"That's...why did he do that?"

Hild crossed her arms. "He said it was compensation for the cost of raising me. I was just a child, after all."

"Raising you." Fryda wanted to spit. "My father dumped you in the kitchen when you were four years old and never thought about you again. And since when do we expect payment for helping raise a child?"

"To raise clan children, no." Hild gave her a level look. "But we were outsiders, and indentured as well."

Fryda flushed. Only at times like this did she realize how sheltered her whole life had been. Her father and brother kept from her the ugly truths and realities of life, and she ended up looking foolish and ignorant as a result. She had worked hard in recent years to shed her naivety, but moments like this showed how far she had yet to go.

"It's outrageous. I still hope to find a way to help you buy your freedom." Fryda wiped her sweaty face on her dress and pulled her sleeve over her hand again.

Hild made a dismissive noise. "Don't fuss yourself about it, my lady," she said. "After all, my family started out as Roman slaves, but my parents managed to buy and work their own land. I plan to honour them and do the same once I've worked off my debt."

Bryce picked up the training spears and rested them on his shoulder. "I remember your parents," he told Hild. "Good people. And they loved you." He tapped a finger under Hild's chin. "They would be so proud of you now."

"Yes, and imagine when you become a shield maiden," Fryda said with a smile.

Hild rolled her eyes. "Oh, yes, your father will definitely allow an African kitchen servant to join his elite band of warrior women."

"Ah. No need to worry about that," Fryda told her, bouncing

up and down on her toes. "He doesn't choose or approve the shield maidens. The warriors are Olaf's responsibility, and once I'm established as lady of the house, he will listen to my recommendations."

"And will you be recommending yourself to him?" Bryce asked. His eyes were sombre as he regarded her.

Fryda yanked on her sleeve.

"I will not," she said, and she could hear the flat, expressionless tenor of her voice.

"But Fryda." Hild uncrossed her arms and touched Fryda's shoulder. "It's always been your dream."

Fryda looked at her left hand, still hidden from view in her sleeve. She remembered her father's mocking laughter seven years before as she'd lain in her bed, weak from pain and fever, and told him she still wished to be a shield maiden.

"Don't be ridiculous," he'd said. For the first time in her thirteen-year-old memory he looked pale and shaken.

A healer-woman had tipped a cup to her lips and Fryda reflexively swallowed. The *dwale* had a bitter taste that even the added honey and verbena couldn't cover, but the potion quickly calmed the unbearable throbbing in her hand and shoulder. Her vision grew fuzzy, though her father's anger remained starkly sharp and clear.

"Not 'diculous," she'd murmured, her words as slurred as her mind. "Gonna be a warrior. Shield maiden."

Weohstan glared down at her, and despite the potent pain medication, Fryda knew she would never forget his cruel words.

"I think your...deformity...puts to rest any lingering notions you might still have about that."

She'd even wondered more than once since then if Weohstan had directed the healers to let her hand heal wrong to put an end to her dreaming.

"Dreams can change," she told Hild, coming back to the present.

Bryce looked as if he wanted to argue with her, but Hild stepped forward and nodded towards the longhouse. "Theow's coming," she said.

Fryda's undisciplined heart lurched as she turned to look. A jewel on display, the longhouse sat at the highest point on the great hill and was the centre of all life in the stronghold. At the front and back of the thickly thatched roof, intricate carvings of fantastical creatures—dragons, griffons, sea monsters—graced the wooden supports. Ivy grew up around the walls, curling green tendrils making intricate designs. The main door, set into an elaborately carved arch, was fashioned from hardwood planks and stood over twenty feet high. A tall man with flame-red hair had emerged through the doorway and strode towards them.

Theow was the only person other than Bryce and Hild who knew about Fryda's early morning training sessions, so it was not fear that made her breath catch and her blood rush. Hild looked sideways at her and smirked. Theow came around the corner of the forge and jogged up to join them.

He had a slender and wiry build—all bone and sinew and ropy strength, earned through years of toil and labour. His shock of thick red hair made him seem crafted of fire, but his face could have been chiselled from pure, white marble. His features were all planes and shadows, fine lines and hollows. A scattering of freckles dusted his nose and cheeks, and she wondered—not for the first time—if he had them anywhere else on his body.

Looking at him, she realized she seldom noticed the twisted red and white scar that marked his face from his right eye to the patch of bare scalp over his ear. He'd clearly suffered a terrible burn as a child, though she knew he could not remember how it had happened. Her chest ached as she thought about how much the wound must have pained him, but her mouth went dry as she studied him—a riot of beauty caressed by the fingers of dawn.

Fryda became uncomfortably aware of her own fingers, twisted and bent at strange angles, the odd angle of her wrist, the bulge of bone at the base of her thumb. She did not want Theow to look at her deformity, though she knew he'd seen it many times before.

She couldn't remember much about her rescue from the gorge, or the painful days of healing that followed, but she vividly remembered Theow's reaction when he saw the mangled, bloody mess that used to be her hand and wrist.

"Fryda," he'd said. "Your hand. Your hand. Your poor hand." Over and over, like a prayer to the gods. She had taken one glance at her hand and turned her head away, unable to look at the twisted mess of blood and bone. Theow, however, had stayed with her as the healers had tried to piece her back together, like one of the wooden puzzles Bryce made for the clan's children.

Even so, as Theow approached her now from the longhouse, she slid her left hand under her right arm, hiding it from view.

Theow's eyes flicked down at the movement, and then back up to her eyes. His glances were always full of stories, untold and secret, and she wondered if he would ever share them with her again. When they had been children and they could laugh and play together without censure, he would sometimes tell her stories, but she often could not catch their meanings. Half his words came out in his native language, which she remembered as lilting and lovely and sounding like music, and the other half in her own harsh, Geatish tongue.

But as time passed, the stories stopped. They dried up like the language of his forgotten childhood, and if he ever crafted new ones in his adopted tongue, he kept them locked behind those eyes.

Theow nodded to Bryce and Hild, but focused on Fryda. "A messenger just arrived," he said. "The king is on his way and should arrive later this morning."

Hild's eyes became huge. "Oh no," she said, and broke into a run towards the kitchens.

"Don't worry," Theow assured Fryda. "Moire hasn't noticed her absence yet. We got word in the kitchens the king was expected soon, and she roused everyone and has been in a frenzy ever since."

"What about you?" Fryda asked. "Won't Moire notice you're gone?"

Theow smiled. "She sent some boys to the storage cave to fetch mead and supplies," he said. "I snuck out with them and came right here. If she wants to know where I was, I'll tell her I went to the cave with the others."

"The stronghold will be in an uproar," Fryda said, her good hand fluttering. "We've been waiting for the king's arrival for *days*. I was starting to worry he'd miss his own feast tonight."

Theow chuckled. "I doubt that would interrupt the festivities."

"Did you see Wiglaf, or my father?"

"No. I've seen no one else."

"Good. Then I haven't been missed, either." She huffed. "Not that I ever am, really, but I'll have a lot to do today."

Theow frowned and looked as if he wanted to disagree with her, but did not speak. He just gazed at her with those eyes full of stories.

"I…um."

Theow blinked. "What?"

Fryda groaned to herself. *Why must I be so awkward around him?* From the corner of her eye, she saw Bryce shake his head and look at the ground. She had the distinct impression he was trying not to laugh.

Fryda cleared her throat as her cheeks burned. "I wanted to ask if instead of working in the kitchens, you'd rather serve in the mead-hall tonight? To see the king?"

Theow was silent for a long moment—long enough for Fryda

to wish for another crevice to open underneath her and swallow her whole.

"I would be happy to serve," he said at last. He leaned towards her a few inches. "But not so I can see the king."

Fryda swallowed. "You'll need clothes," she blurted.

Theow raised his eyebrows. "I...usually wear clothes."

Bryce rubbed his forehead with one hand.

Fryda coughed. "Sorry. I mean, you'll need to see Eadith for some new clothes. Father won't want to see holes and patches." She looked at Bryce, then back to Theow. "Well. I'll see you tonight."

And she fled.

★ ★ ★

Theow watched Fryda walk away with her determined little steps, her back straight and clinging to what was left of her dignity. He smiled.

She wanted him in the mead-hall tonight. With her.

He heard Bryce clear his throat as the blacksmith came to stand beside him. "You'll be needing a belt and something to fasten it with to go with your fancy new clothes. Come on. I've got what you need at the forge."

"Yes," Theow said absently, still watching Fryda. "Yes. Belt."

Bryce snorted and gave Theow a shove towards the forge. "Woden's beard, lad," he muttered. "Your head is stuffed with straw today."

Theow could not deny the charge.

"Do they never feed you in those kitchens, lad?" the blacksmith asked a short time later. "I could wrap this belt around you twice and still have enough leather left over to cover an axe handle."

"Not enough, Bryce." Theow laughed. "Never enough."

The forge was one of Theow's favourite places and the

huge, grizzled blacksmith one of his few friends. Theow could not remember his real father, the man who had sired him and presumably cared for him before he was stolen and sold into slavery, but over the years he had come to look on the gruff blacksmith as a kind of father figure in his life. He was the man Theow went to with his problems, and he was the person he asked for advice.

Bryce glanced at Theow, eyed him critically, and turned to search through a chest of brooches, clasps, buckles, and other odds and ends, trying to find something suitable.

The forge had a broad, airy feel with open, waist-high walls and a ceiling of wide, slatted timbers under its covering of thatch. An enormous, petrified tree stump dominated the room, smooth and polished to serve as an anvil. A squat, round oven hunkered in the corner like a miniature hut. Scraps of iron, metal, and wood shavings covered the floor. Tools and a staggering array of items Bryce had forged over the years littered every surface, giving the room the look of a disorganized market stall. Armour, buckles, jewellery, tableware, cloak and dress fastenings, locks with keys, hinges, nails—and, of course, weapons—filled the room.

The chief of Bryce's weapons, a huge two-handed sword, hung above the glowing hearth. The sword drew Theow's eye every time he entered the smithy. Forged from iron, it had an elegant hilt that curved above and below the polished wooden grip. Carvings adorned the pommel—trailing leaves, sheaves of wheat and fantastical birds in elegant, sweeping lines—while the crossguard echoed these images in tiny, delicate shapes. Patterns, like runes, had been etched into the flat sides of the broad blade, but he could make no sense or meaning of them. The blade looked ancient, and Theow always wondered if those markings held the key to a lost language, or perhaps they were a spell to ward off evil.

As a boy Theow had once asked Bryce if he could hold

the sword and look at the etched markings on the blade. The blacksmith's curt response had left such an impression that Theow had never asked again.

Bryce held up a gold filigreed buckle set with red and blue glass. He shook his head. "Too elaborate," he said, and placed it back into the chest. It never failed to amaze Theow that a man with Bryce's bulging muscles and scarred, rough hands could produce such lovely and delicate work.

"What do you think Moire will say about you serving in the mead-hall?" Bryce asked, pawing through the chest. "She likes to keep you hidden in the kitchens as much as possible, doesn't she?"

Theow laughed and nodded. "It's the scar. And the hair, of course," he said. "I think Moire considers red hair a personal affront and an embarrassment to the clan."

Bryce chose another buckle and put it up to Theow's waist. "Too big," he muttered and continued searching.

Theow scratched the puckered scar over his ear. "She won't be happy about it," he said, "but she would never go against Fryda's orders."

Bryce looked up at him again, his expression neutral. "Indeed."

"Though I do wonder why she did it. Fryda. Think of me, I mean. For the mead-hall."

"Mmm. Here we go." Bryce straightened up, a simple bronze clasp in his hands. "Come here."

Theow moved to stand in front of him. "Do you think she does?" he blurted. "Think of me, I mean?"

Bryce wrapped the belt around his tunic at the waist and folded the loose ends over each other. "I can't say," he said, his voice noncommittal. "She doesn't always tell me what she thinks."

"Does…does she ever talk about me?" Theow had no idea what possessed him to ask, but he found he could not breathe until Bryce answered him.

"Theow." The blacksmith fastened the belt with the bronze buckle. He sat back and surveyed the results. "These are questions you ought to ask *her*, not me. Besides, we don't talk of such things. We're usually too busy practising."

A surge of envy for the blacksmith hit Theow.

Bryce clapped Theow on the shoulder. "There. You're ready to go."

Theow did not move. "Bryce…" he said and stopped.

"I know, lad." Bryce's eyes were warm and sympathetic. "But a lord's daughter is beyond the reach of a slave. You know that. You've always known that."

Theow gave him a wry grin. "Well, I have no memory of my family or where I came from. I could have been born a prince for all we know."

For one moment, the blacksmith's expression reflected a confusing array of emotions, as if haunted by a painful memory or guilt. Theow had seen that look on Bryce's face many times before. That soft air of devastation would often flash through his eyes over the years, but just as quickly, the expression shifted to an impish grin. "Just enjoy yourself tonight. Not too much!" He pointed a finger at Theow. "Don't get yourself in trouble."

"I won't. There isn't really any trouble I can get into."

And he knew *that* for a lie as soon as he spoke it.

"Watch yourself around Weohstan, lad," Bryce warned, as if he could sense the direction of Theow's thoughts. "Don't let him catch you even breathing too near his daughter. He would have you hacked to pieces and fed to the sea monsters."

Yes, indeed, Theow thought as his spirits plummeted into his stomach. *That trouble.*

"I know it's hard, lad." Bryce gave Theow's shoulder a friendly shake.

"Will you be at the feast?" Theow asked.

"No. The feast is for warriors, not blacksmiths."

"You were a warrior, Bryce, before you came to Eceweall,"

Theow said. "I'm sure you would be welcome. And you would get to see the king."

"No." The word was hard and sharp. "I have no desire to see the king." Bryce's mouth thinned.

"All right," Theow said.

Bryce shifted, still scowling. "Why does he even come here?" he asked, putting away his box of buckles. "Why doesn't he hold his celebration in his own *burh*?"

"Lord Weohstan wanted to honour his kinsman by holding the celebration here," Theow said.

"Of course," Bryce muttered. "*Of course* he would be kin to the king." Still grumbling and shaking his head, he walked to the hearth and started pumping the bellows to heat the coals that would stoke the forge-fires.

"Thank you for the buckle." Theow suppressed his curiosity. "I'll bring it back after the feast is over."

Bryce waved a hand. "Keep it. Consider it a gift." His face lost its hard-edged anger and he smiled at Theow.

Theow frowned. "I don't know…"

"Keep it, lad, and tell Eadith to make sure she gives you a suit of clothes that does it justice." Again, something like guilt crossed his features, and the blacksmith turned away.

Theow fingered the bronze buckle. It was not the first gift Bryce had given him that came with such a look. Bryce always denied it when pressed. *It's just your imagination, Theow*, he'd say, and then change the subject. Theow had amassed a small treasure trove of trinkets, from little toy horses and wrought-iron warriors to brooch clasps, a comb for his thick, unruly hair, and a small bronze box to keep it all in.

"Thank you," Theow said. "I'll come tell you all about the celebration in the morning."

"You'll be sleeping off the pleasures of the feast in the morning." Bryce gave him a brief shove. Theow tried not to fall over and had to lean against the table to keep his balance. "Or at least you should be. Now go. I don't want Moire coming here looking for you." He gave a dramatic shudder and Theow laughed.

Theow left the forge. He rubbed his temple where a pulse throbbed under the twisted scar, and made his way to the longhouse and the woman who awaited him there.

Magic

The sleeping dragon twitches again, and a shower of riches sings to her its glorious music. For a moment it pulls her from memory and she once more loses herself in its strange song as it speaks to her in a language only dragons can understand.

Gold—the lifeblood of dragons and source of all their magic. The Lone Survivor and his kind had for generations ripped it from the mountains and hills and drained dry the veins of the earth that sustained her and her kin. The humans hoarded it, gathered it in massive structures and caves, away from the sun. And one by one the dragons had died, for few men know dragons cannot live without gold to sustain them. Gold runs through their blood, a strange alchemy that combines the body, the air and the earth, and distils it into an energy unique to dragonkind.

The humans call it magic.

As if the word calls forth the powers from ancient gold and dragon-blood, Fýrdraca feels a small burst of raw, unchecked magic flash through the ether. It startles her so much she nearly wakes, nearly slips the shackles of the Lone Survivor's curse, but it tendrils into her soul and still anchors her to nightmare.

The fire-dragon probes the source of the magic with her sixth sense that is not quite scent and not quite vision but something between the two. She does not know what she will find, but never expects the jolt of recognition from the creature who let the magic escape. She touches the mind of a human, the girl who *leaked her life out on the rocks above her cavern seven years before.*

Ancient warrior magic hums through the girl, no longer a child, out of tune with the treasure-song and hovering in the dragon's mind like a swarm of angry wasps. Fýrdraca has not felt such magic in centuries—not since all her kin died out. The girl possesses a dragon-strength magic that heats a warrior's blood and allows him—or in this case, her—great feats of fortitude, strength, and courage.

No wonder the little thing managed to survive her torment.

And in the distance, but moving ever closer, comes a fainter, older, answering pulse of power—like the echo of a father's heartbeat against the child at his breast.

Something comes, and magic burgeons and dies like the ebb and flow of the tide with its approach. Fýrdraca feels the Lone Survivor's curse swell and gather itself in response.

Two

"Weohstan!"

Fryda jumped, startled by the booming voice echoing across the early morning emptiness of the mead-hall. She clutched the full pitcher awkwardly to her chest and some mead slopped onto her dress. *Better that*, she thought, dabbing at her front, than on her father's priceless tapestry, laid out on a wide trestle table for cleaning. The longhouse had an air of waiting, of anticipation for the first of three feasts to take place later in the evening, and the still air shattered against the thunderous voice.

King Beowulf stood in the centre of the long, narrow room next to the raised fire pit, fists on his hips and feet apart as if daring anyone to move him. He must have stood over seven feet tall by the old Roman measurements, and his long, braided hair and beard, once the colour of honey and amber, had turned snowy white. His chest was as broad as a standing stone, his hands as big as dinner plates, and his keen blue eyes snapped with energy as they scanned the mead-hall looking for the master of the house—Fryda's father, Lord Weohstan.

"Uncle Beowulf!" Fryda exclaimed, putting the pitcher down on one of the low benches that edged the hall and wiping her hands on her skirt. She tucked her left hand into her sleeve. The king's eyes found her and brightened with delight.

"Fryda! My sweet girl," he bellowed and stretched his arms out to her. She ran into them and felt herself lifted from the ground in a rib-crushing, loving grip. She winced, but hugged him back.

"Why did you not tell us when you were coming?" Fryda said, her voice muffled against his massive chest. The king laughed and lowered her back to earth. "Most of the other dignitaries have already arrived," she continued, straightening her crumpled dress. "We expected you days ago. If I'd known when you planned to be here, I would have asked my father to greet you at the gate with the guards and some of our more important guests."

"Ah, nonsense," Beowulf said, swiping an enormous hand over her hair as if she were a small child. A few pins sprang loose from her heavy braids and fell to the floor. "I came a few days late to avoid such things."

Fryda gave him a stern look. "You gave Hrothgar more notice than you gave us," she accused. Since she was a babe she'd heard the stories of Beowulf's unannounced landing on the Danish King's shores, and how Hrothgar's warriors had nearly skewered him with their spears.

"I was younger then. Give an old man leave to inconvenience his family." He looked around the mead-hall. "So where is the old goat?"

"I am here, my king."

Weohstan strode into the mead-hall, exuding the arrogance and confidence with which he did everything in his life. Fryda stiffened, glancing down at herself to make sure her dress was straight, that her maid had fastened her brooch clasps evenly, and had properly knotted her belt. She had not yet bathed after her practice with Bryce, and the spilled mead had stained her bodice, but she hoped her father would not notice. A wayward strand of hair fell across her face and she pushed it away. She never could tame her wild mane—curls burst from her braids and refused to yield to pins or combs. Her father hated it. She suspected it violated his sense of order and decorum.

Beowulf made a frustrated noise. "After all these years, Weohstan, you can't call me by my given name? We are blood, after all, and we've been friends since we were boys."

Weohstan's lips flattened. "You are my king," he said, and stopped before him, reaching out an arm. Beowulf clasped it and the two men held to each other with something between ceremony and affection. Next to the king, Fryda's father looked diminished...deflated. Weohstan had kept his warrior's body well into his later years, but he had neither Beowulf's height nor breadth—nor his charismatic presence. Weohstan rarely smiled. His eyes, flat as dark, unpolished topaz, never twinkled. His back could teach the mighty ash tree straightness, and his speech always sounded clipped and precise—all of which made him as unreachable as a ripe berry in winter.

Weohstan stepped back and shot Fryda a sharp look. "You should have sent for me as soon as the king arrived," he said. His voice, tight and repressive, pricked her like a thorn. Fryda had long since given up trying to navigate the brambly undergrowth that led to her father's heart. Her failures had only ever broken hers.

"Leave off, Weohstan, I just got here," Beowulf said, releasing Weohstan's forearm. "And where is the young lord? I haven't seen Wiglaf in years. He was out with the longships when last I came."

Fryda didn't think it possible for her father's lips to get any thinner, but he proved her wrong. "He is here," Weohstan said. "No doubt he is spending the afternoon in the company of his cup and some improper young woman. He will appear when it suits him."

Beowulf laughed and threw his arm around Fryda. He gave her an affectionate squeeze that lifted her off her feet again. "Ah, youth!" he bellowed, and Fryda winced as her ears popped. "I'm glad to hear Wiglaf seems to be enjoying his." Fryda grunted as the king set her back on her feet with a *thump*.

King Beowulf's attentions to her unfortunately drew her father's notice, and he frowned as he looked her over.

"What have you been up to, girl?" he demanded.

Fryda froze. "I..."

"You're all sweaty and..." Weohstan reached out and plucked a piece of grass from her hair. His disapproval was as thick as a fog rolling in from the sea.

She searched her mind for an excuse. "Um. I was in the kitchens," she said, "checking on the feast. It was quite warm."

She hoped Moire would not tell him otherwise and reveal her lie.

"Indeed?" Weohstan flicked the piece of grass from his fingers. "Well, I look forward to seeing in which dish this grass will grace our table tonight."

Fryda looked at the floor.

King Beowulf came to her rescue, a gleeful glint in his eyes. "So, tell me. Who has arrived so far?" he asked. "And who were the earliest arrivals hoping to curry favour before their rivals could get here?"

Weohstan brushed one grey-streaked black braid over his shoulder. "The first arrival was Lord Ansten from Sweden," he said, "followed closely by Lord Rawald and King Eadgils."

"Eadgils?" Beowulf sobered. "Eadgils, the Swedish king, is here?"

"He is." Weohstan's voice betrayed nothing.

"How strange." Beowulf shook his head as if to jar something loose from his memory. "Did he come alone?"

"King Eadgils has no wife or children," Weohstan said.

"No, no, I mean without his guards, or soldiers, or a retinue."

Weohstan raised one eyebrow. "No. He arrived with a full honour guard like all the other dignitaries. Why do you ask?"

Beowulf stroked his beard. "I have reports that Eadgils' guards and soldiers were seen marching north to determine what this upstart Olaf Tryggvason is up to in Norway. I had assumed

Eadgils was with them." He cast a sharp eye on Weohstan. "And considering the history between you two, it surprises me that he would deign to set foot in your house. I always thought he wouldn't stop to piss on you if your beard were on fire."

Fryda blinked. She knew enough from watching her father conduct business to understand that such irregularities often meant trouble. When reports and reality didn't match, it usually meant someone, somewhere, has lied.

"He came to honour you." Weohstan's voice had the disapproving, repressive tone Fryda knew all too well.

Beowulf boomed out a laugh and clapped him on the shoulder. "Eadgils knows you and I are friends and kin. All things considered, I don't think he'd stop to piss on me, either."

Weohstan remained silent for a moment before he said, "I don't like this. I'll find out what my scouts have to say."

"I'm sure it's nothing," Beowulf said, waving his hand. "Eadgils must have changed his plans, or the news went awry somehow before it reached my ears."

"Eadgils said nothing to me about this when we exchanged news. And in truth, I was surprised to see him." Weohstan paused, frowning. "I don't like surprises."

"Then you're going to hate the feast tonight," Beowulf said with a laugh. "I have several planned for you."

Weohstan scowled. "I don't like irregularities. I am responsible for your safety."

Beowulf chuckled and winked at Fryda. "Usually I'm the one who says that."

Fryda smiled back. "Your only responsibility while you are here is to enjoy yourself," she said. "After fifty years as king, you've earned the right to be celebrated."

Beowulf grinned and kissed the top of her head. "I would never disobey one of your orders, sweet girl," he said.

Weohstan cut her a look and Fryda banished the smile from her face.

"I'm going to post a few of my warriors as guard while you are here," Weohstan said.

Beowulf grunted. "I brought my own guards, Weohstan."

"I'll hear no argument." Weohstan glared at the king. "While you are in my house, you will enjoy my protection."

The king scowled. "Weohstan, what do you think Eadgils can do to me? He must be coming on eighty years old and he's as big around as one of my thighs."

"You may laugh yourself to your grave, my king," Weohstan said, "but you shall not do it under my roof."

Beowulf sighed gustily. "Weohstan, you're as much fun as Grendel at a party."

"Come, my king," her father said, ignoring the comment. "We will visit Olaf, my chief warrior, and then I will show you to your rooms myself. No doubt you will want to rest before the feast tonight."

"That I do," Beowulf said, and stretched out his back. Fryda's eyes widened as she heard a loud *pop* and the king laughed. "These old bones don't travel as well as they used to." With a final fond smile at Fryda, Beowulf turned and left the longhouse. Her father did not look at her at all as he followed the king out through the door.

★ ★ ★

Hild entered the mead-hall from the kitchen entrance, carrying water and rags, just in time to hear a great masculine bellow and see Fryda nearly spill mead all over the tapestry she needed to clean. She watched as Fryda fumbled with the pitcher, her deformed hand making it difficult to hold upright. A swell of sympathy rolled through Hild's chest, but she quickly banished it. Lady Fryda would not welcome pity from her—or anyone.

Then Hild saw the king.

She stopped abruptly, the water in her bowl mimicking Fryda's pitcher and wetting the front of her dress. She melted back into the shadows, watching as Beowulf greeted first Lady Fryda and then Weohstan. She could not hear their words, but the Lord of Eceweall appeared perturbed by their conversation while the King of Geatland found humour in whatever upset him.

She waited until Lord Weohstan and the king left the mead-hall before she emerged from hiding and made her way to Lady Fryda, who stood beside the trestle table and the tapestry.

Hild noted the sadness in Fryda's storm-grey eyes and the tension in her shoulders. Not an uncommon consequence of speaking with her father, she thought. Memories of her own parents had faded over the years. A famine had forced them to give up their land and sell themselves into indentured servitude, but she knew that, despite their hardships, they had been fonder of her than Weohstan was of his children.

She set the bowl on the table and Fryda looked at her.

"Hild." She smiled, the sadness falling away. "How lovely to see you."

"My lady." She dunked the rags into the water and smiled. "Good day to you."

Fryda clasped Hild's arm. "Are you all right?" she asked. "You know, from where I hit you this morning?"

Hild rubbed her chest, remembering the mighty blow Fryda had dealt her. She could not fathom how such a tiny frame could house such strength.

"I'm fine, my lady," Hild reassured her. She would *not* tell Fryda she was sore.

"Do you need help with anything?"

"Not at all." Hild began to sponge the tapestry, dabbing at the thin fabric and delicate threading with a careful hand. "But thank you, my lady. You'll have your own hands full soon enough."

She leaned over the trestle table and applied her cloth to the tapestry, her motions both delicate and sure. As she cleaned, she studied the exquisite crewel-work threads depicting a fraught battle in which Weohstan and Beowulf had fought together, years before. Yellow-threaded men riding red and blue-stitched horses hurled spears at each other over embroidered bodies piled on the ground between them. Hild wondered what capricious whim of the gods had resulted in the value men placed on war.

Fryda noticed her interest. "This depicts the battle Father and the king fought against Onela, the tyrant who usurped the throne of Sweden," she said, tracing a finger over a fine, delicate thread. To Hild, it looked as if Weohstan and Beowulf were fighting each other, standing on opposite sides of the slain.

Hild poked Fryda's hand away from the tapestry. "My lady, if you damage this tapestry you, not I, will have to answer to your father."

Fryda snatched her hand back. "All right, all right," she laughed. She waggled her finger at Hild. "You know, the king thinks it's perfectly right for people to call each other by their given names. I heard him say so."

"Well, the next time I see him, I'll be sure to call him 'Beo' and see how he reacts."

Fryda sputtered a laugh. "Please don't do that. I merely meant I wish you would call me by my given name." Her voice became small and a little hurt. "Why won't you call me by my name, Hild? Do you not consider me your friend?"

Hild's heart twisted in her breast. "Oh, my lady. Of course I do. We practically grew up together. But…" She wracked her mind, trying to find the words that would help Fryda understand. "When we were about ten or eleven years old, Moire overheard me telling one of the other girls about something you'd said. I don't even remember what it was. Anyway, Moire heard me refer to you by your given name and the next thing I knew, she'd slapped me so hard across my face I saw sparks."

Fryda looked horrified.

Hild still remembered her own shock at the blow. "She informed me I was disrespectful, and that if someone else in the household heard me talk about you that way, I could be exiled from the *burh* and left in the wilderness to die."

Fryda's mouth fell open. "Exiled?" she sputtered.

"Obviously Moire was exaggerating, trying to frighten me into better behaviour," Hild said. "But it was effective. I always knew it was better to sacrifice the intimacy of names if it meant I could stay here with you and be your friend."

Fryda's eyes became bright with tears. "Oh," she said. She seemed to reach for other words, but could not find them. Instead, she walked over and took Hild into a snug embrace.

Hild started with surprise, but relaxed and returned the hug.

"I'm so sorry, Hild," Fryda said, her voice muffled against her neck. "You know I've spoken to Father about Moire many times, but nothing seems to change." She straightened with a determined look. "Once I become lady of the house and can take on more responsibility, I promise there will be some changes."

"I know," Hild assured her. She pulled back and smiled at her friend. "Moire terrified all the children with stories of exile and the monsters that would eat us if we misbehaved. It's just difficult to overcome a lifetime of fear."

Fryda looked thoughtful. "All right," she said. "I'll stop asking. Maybe one day, you'll feel comfortable enough to use my name with me. And if that day happens, I promise, you will not be exiled." She stepped back and shook out her dress. "I'd best get back to work. There's still so much to do before tonight."

Hild knew the rest of the guests would soon assemble in the mead-hall to celebrate the fiftieth year of King Beowulf's reign, and tonight, at long last, Fryda would take her place as lady of the house.

No wonder she was a bundle of nerves and emotion.

Fryda picked up the pitcher of mead with her good hand and braced it against her chest. She moved towards the alcove that housed the head table and the lord's elaborate seat atop a raised dais. As Hild watched, a flash of copper-red caught her eye.

Leaning against a broad wooden support column, half-hidden in shadow and out of reach of the light from the circular iron candelabra suspended from the rafters, stood Theow. He did not move, but watched Fryda with green eyes flecked with gold, like sunshine breaking through a canopy of forest leaves.

Fryda stopped and Hild heard her breath catch. She smiled and looked at the tapestry, pretending to be absorbed in her task. Theow so rarely left the kitchens that it must have startled Fryda when he appeared like this—silent, beautiful, watchful. His threadbare clothing was ragged and stained, and his hair fell across his forehead in lank, shaggy locks. He had a smudge of soot on one cheek, but Fryda did not seem to notice. They stared at each other across the mead-hall, still as carvings, until finally Theow stepped back and disappeared through the servants' doorway.

Hild heard Fryda sigh, and though there were a great many things she wanted to say, she kept them to herself. She had watched these two circle each other for years, and she had faith that one day they would stop and settle themselves into stillness with each other.

In the meantime, she had tapestries to clean and bread to bake, herbs to gather and preparations to see to. She would do what she could to make everything perfect for her lady tonight.

Revenge

When Fýrdraca departed her homeland, she winged her way through deserts and plains, over tundra and oceans, searching for the gold that would save and redeem her kin. After many long, arduous travels, and on the brink of death herself, she had scented gold and spied its glimmer like a beacon on the horizon. Feeling an answering brightness in her blood, she wrapped her wings around the wind and flew towards her salvation.

The glow from the buried treasure guided her like a small sun, and soon she found herself hovering over a settlement built of rock and stone, wood and straw. It teemed with people and hunkered over a trove of treasure buried deep within a hollow cave, like a mother protecting her unborn child. The scent of gold aroused her anger for those who had torn it from the earth and stolen it from the dragons. And so, with her remaining strength, she gathered her breath and lay waste to the village with fire and smoke.

Fýrdraca gloried in the screams of fear and anguish, and afterwards in the silence of death. With her firebreath she cleansed the world of those who sacrificed her kin for their greed. She brought down every last man, woman, and child with her flame, and watched as their structures burned and buried their bodies.

Consumed by her great need, she peeled away the earth's skin in one swift stroke of her great obsidian talons, like skinning an apple with a battleaxe. The first caress of gold against her coal-black scales felt like mother love. Her life thread—which *had been flickering like a fragment of fire on a candle wick—anchored within her breast, and she knew then she would live.*

She did not know how long she lay there before the Lone Survivor returned to his stronghold to find it ravaged by fire, his kith and kin dead. She heard his cries first—great, wordless howls of grief that shook her from the thrall of treasure-song. She raised her head and looked upon his sorrow.

She saw a man, a hunter, bow slung low across his back. He held the reins of his horse, and a newly killed stag lay draped across its saddle. His pain was so great, so open, she could step right into it. She'd known, then, that he would somehow be her undoing.

Just as she knows now that the girl—the little human with her fierce battle-magic—will be her saviour.

Three

Hild slid a thick slab of dough into the clay oven with a scarred wooden paddle and wiped her face with her sleeve. The kitchens had reached a peak of frenzied activity now that word of King Beowulf's arrival had reached them, and Hild had barely had a moment to breathe since she'd returned from cleaning the tapestries in the longhouse that morning.

Everything vibrated with energy and noise, and the scents of roasting meat, herbs, and freshly baked barley bread perfumed the air. A whole wild boar, cleaned and spitted, crackled over an open flame as fat dripped into the fire, causing puffs of smoke to waft through the hole in the ceiling. Women plucked game birds—snow-white geese and drab, brown grouse—careful to save the feathers that would later fill the family's mattresses. Others skinned deer, butchered lambs, and peeled apricots for stew. Bulgar wheat in ale with red, purple, and yellow carrots baked in low clay ovens while soup bubbled in the fireplace, rich with leeks, mushrooms, and spring onions. Large baskets of mussels and oysters awaited boiling in great pots, and an array of cheeses, nuts, and summer fruits were heaped onto platters.

Hild was checking on the bread when a pained shout surfaced above the general noise. It took her a moment to identify the shouter as Toland, a young lad tasked with basting the roasting meats with rendered fat.

Moire, the kitchen-keeper of about forty or so years, stormed towards the boy. A lifetime of labour paired with a nasty disposition had given her a hard, surly look. A perpetual slick of perspiration shone across her forehead accompanied by the stench of grease, sour sweat, and wood smoke. Moire grabbed Toland's arm and examined his hand.

Hild winced when she saw it. Toland's skin was bright red and beginning to blister. The boy tried to be brave as he held back his tears.

"Toland!" Hild put a supporting arm around him. "What happened?"

"Looks like he ladled boiling hot fat over his hand rather than over the boar," Moire grumbled, turning the offending hand over with a rough twist. "This will need treatment." She skewered Hild with a glare. "He'll need a draught of white poppy from the stillroom. Bring it here, fast as you can."

Hild lowered her eyes and nodded. She wiped her hands on her skirt and hurried from the kitchens.

The *burh* hummed with activity as she walked down the hill towards the green. She passed Bryce's forge, which sat at the easternmost tip of the promontory and overlooked the narrow strip of rocky beach that led to the longships moored offshore. Far to the west, a long, curved stone wall protected the *burh* from landside invasion, spanning the headland from edge to edge. Within the wall stood the main *burh*, with the longhouse, the forge, and the kitchens situated at the top of a high hill. Beyond that, the farmsteads stretched out for miles and miles, with their pastures of sheep and fields of wheat, barley, and vegetables.

At the bottom of the hill lay the green, dotted with wooden houses and engraved with neatly raked gravel paths. An ancient menhir endured at the centre of the green, as it had for centuries. Tall, rough-hewn, blue-grey rock, it was the last remnant of what had been a stone circle long before any people had permanently settled in the area. The warriors' barracks lined the western edge of the green by the gate, and men guarded every entrance at the wall day and night. No army had ever managed to breach them.

The stillroom was housed in an old outbuilding near the green, and it was Hild's pride and joy. Her favourite memories as a child were the scent of a stillroom and the sound of her mother's voice talking about the medicinal properties of plants and herbs. Weohstan had authorized a plot of land for her use, and there she grew everything she needed—white poppy, verbena, foxglove, basil, nettle, feverfew, coriander, betony, chervil, mugwort—and she used the stillroom to make her tinctures and potions.

As soon as she entered the small wattle-and-daub stillroom, however, she knew something was wrong. Things were not as she'd left them. Several bundles of dried herbs had been knocked from where they hung, and her little pots and jars were scattered across the simple wooden table. All her neatly organized medicines were jumbled together and…Woden's beard, some of them were missing.

Hild did a quick inventory and her spirits plunged as she realized that several bottles of white poppy syrup were missing. *Oh no.*

She counted again, hoping she had been mistaken. But no. Oh, Lady Fryda would be so heartbroken when she heard about this.

Hild mixed a dose from the remaining white poppy syrup with mead for Toland and put a few of the stoppered bottles in her belt pouch. She snatched up a pot of burn salve made from charred goat dung, boiled and pounded wheat stalks, and butter. As she hurried back to the kitchens, she promised herself she'd talk to Bryce about crafting a lock for the stillroom door.

★ ★ ★

When Theow returned to the kitchens, he picked up a stack of dirty dishes from the table and took them to the large wooden tub. No one accosted him for being late, so he washed his way through the enormous pile, his memory playing the music of Fryda's voice through his mind as he worked.

He had almost finished the last dish when a resonant *clang* startled him out of his daydreams, and he looked up. He saw Moire whack one of the scullery maids with her wooden spoon as she screamed vulgarities, with spittle flying from her mouth. The hapless girl ducked and tried to pick up the heavy pot of cooked grain she had dropped.

Just then, Hild entered the kitchen. She scanned the room, found Moire, and made her way across the room to her. Theow saw her hold out a cup and a small pot. Moire stopped beating the girl, tossed aside the spoon, and took the offerings. She hurried away, and Hild leaned down to help the crying girl to her feet.

"It's all right," he heard her say as he placed the last clean plate on the pile. "I'll help you clean it up." She caught Theow's eye and gave the girl's arm a squeeze. "I have to talk to Theow first, though. Sit for a moment. Drink some water. You'll be fine." Hild patted her on the shoulder and made her way over to Theow.

"Everything all right?" he asked. She looked troubled. Upset, even. Hild had been his friend for many years, even though she was a bonded servant and he a slave. She would eventually pay off her debt and earn her freedom and he…would not. They were the only two workers in the household who were not Britons, however, and they shared the bond of the outsider.

She opened her mouth to answer him, but then noticed two young women nearby watching them.

Well, watching him. They did that quite a lot, to his eternal mortification.

Hild closed her mouth. She fixed a smile on her face and said, "Hey, Theow. I have riddle for you. Listen carefully, now." Her false smile shifted to a genuine grin and her eyes began to twinkle as the listeners leaned in. Theow groaned to himself.

"Here it is. Are you ready? 'Splendidly I hang by a man's thigh, under the master's cloak. In front is a hole. I am stiff and hard; I have a goodly place. What am I?' " Hild raised an eyebrow as the eavesdroppers gasped, and then giggled.

Theow huffed a low laugh. It was one of Hild's favourite pastimes to try to make him blush by reciting dirty riddles. She'd never done it in front of other people before, though.

"I don't know," he said.

Hild rolled her eyes at him. "You don't even want to guess? It hangs by a man's thigh, Theow!"

Despite himself, his face flushed red and he silently cursed his fair skin. The girls giggled again, their cheeks pink and their young eyes knowing.

Hild laughed. "It's a key, Theow…a key! What did *you* think it was to turn your face that colour?"

Theow shook his head and she, after a quick glance around the kitchen, made a shooing gesture towards his giggly admirers.

"You lot, off you go. You've work to do, and you don't want me telling Mistress Moire you've been idle now, do you?"

Theow stared at Hild as the young women scattered. "You wouldn't actually tell on them, would you?"

"Of course not. I just need to talk to you in private and I didn't want them following us. Come on. Moire will be busy for a while tending to Toland's hand."

She grabbed Theow's arm and pulled him outside. "What happened to Toland's hand?" he asked, bewildered.

She did not answer as they ducked around the forge and walked into the tall grass. Hild stopped and turned to face him. Men, women, and children rushed about the *burh* in preparation for the king's celebration, and the meadow was the one place they could be certain not to be overheard.

"Where were you this morning?" he asked before she could speak.

Hild gave him a sly look. "Cleaning the tapestries in the longhouse. You didn't see me?"

Theow blinked. He hadn't seen her. He had only seen Fryda.

Hild chuckled. "Ah, I see." She gave his shoulder a small shove. "Your attention was focused elsewhere, eh?"

He could not deny it. He rubbed his scar, expecting her to laugh at his blush, but she did not.

"Theow." Her voice was gentle. She clasped his arm. "Do you want to tell me about it?"

He did and he didn't. "Nothing to tell, really," he muttered. "Nothing you don't already know, anyway."

Hild squeezed his arm. "I know."

Theow knew she did. They had been children when she'd first asked him about his feelings for Weohstan's daughter, and finding Hild understanding and sympathetic, he had confided in her many times over the ensuing years.

"Theow." The change in her voice drew his attention back to her. "I need to tell you something. Something strange."

Theow raised his eyebrows. "What is it?"

"After I finished cleaning the tapestries, Mistress Moire asked me to mix a draught and fetch some medicine for Toland, who had burned his hand."

"That's not so strange." Theow rubbed his scar. "Toland is always injuring himself somehow."

"No, it's not that." Even though they were alone, Hild's voice dropped to a whisper and her forehead creased with anxiety. "When I went to the stillroom to mix the potion, I noticed someone had been there. Some things were moved, the herbs and bottles were in disarray. And some things were missing."

Theow frowned. That was odd. Anyone had the right to ask for medicines from the stillroom. There was no reason to steal anything. "What was missing?" he asked.

"About half our stock of white poppy syrup. Plus some verbena and honey."

Theow's heart sank. "Have you told anyone else?"

"No." Hild's braids whipped across her shoulders as she

emphatically shook her head. "I didn't want to be blamed for the theft. And besides…"

Anger burned like acid in his throat and he swallowed. "I know. It was probably Wiglaf."

"Yes."

The young lord's not infrequent indulgences, usually partaken after a run-in with his father, were the household's most poorly kept secret. No one knew if Wiglaf's fondness for drinking mead doctored with a few drops of opium and some verbena and honey to mask the bitter taste was the cause or the consequence of Weohstan's frustrations with his son, but everyone knew Wiglaf's habits offended his father's sense of honour and duty.

And it upset Fryda, which was enough to make Theow want to punch Wiglaf in his smug, self-righteous face.

As if he didn't have reasons enough already.

"Theow." Hild put a hand on his forearm. "I am also worried that Mistress Moire will accuse you of stealing the white poppy."

Theow's jaw clenched and he tried to relax. Hild was right. Any time anything went missing in the *burh*, Moire blamed him first.

"I cleaned up the mess and tried to make it look like nothing had happened," Hild whispered. "But as soon as she does the inventory…"

Theow swore. "You need to tell Lady Fryda. She trusts you, and she'll know neither of us would steal anything. She'll know what to do."

Hild nodded. "I will. I also brought the white poppy syrup away with me, just in case the thief comes back for the rest of it."

"Good thinking. What are you going to tell Moire?"

Hild passed a hand over her tired face. "I don't know, Theow. If I can speak to Lady Fryda soon, maybe she can find the stolen bottles and replace them before anyone finds out."

"Yes, I think that's best." Theow glanced at the longhouse. "We'd best get back. Moire won't tarry over Toland for long."

They slipped back into the kitchens just in time. Theow picked up his first silver goblet to polish just as Moire came storming back into the kitchens, and he breathed a silent sigh of relief as she passed him by without comment.

Treasure

Fýrdraca feels them both…the woman-warrior with her heart of fire and her echo with his faded dragon-magic cooled by the passing of years. He had been strong in his youth; she could feel it—but the girl would be much stronger.

In times long past, before the first scop *told the first story, dragons and humankind lived together, sharing everything of this world—including its magic. All magic was born of dragonkind, but they could bestow it upon worthy mortals, great heroes who fought to protect the dragons from harm. But one by one, these great men and women fell to the one enemy they could not defeat —their mortality. And as they died, one by one, men and women greedy for power and glory came to destroy the dragons, whether by stealing the gold and gems from the earth or in fraught battles between humans and dragonkind.*

As the dragons died, so did their magic, until it became nothing but the stuff of myth and legend. But every once in a great while, a child would be born…a descendant of those who had guarded the dragons and their magic, and a scrap of that magic would be born within them. A gift bestowed by the last surviving dragons. These babies grew to become great kings and queens, heroes and warriors, men and women with such gifts they appeared mightier than mortals, though lesser than the gods.

Fýrdraca knows this warrior-woman, this one fated to break the Lone Survivor's curse is one such mortal.

The dragon shifts and turns within her gilded prison, seeking the dreams that only gold—this cursed gold—can give her. Her movement disturbs the delicate balance of the treasure hoard that covers her, and an ancient goblet—forged in gold and silver by a son of giants and carved with an intricate forest hunting scene—tips and rolls down the pile, coming to rest in a narrow shaft of broken light.

Four

Bryce watched the *burh* come alive with activity as morning gave way to early afternoon, and a dark melancholy settled in his chest, as it always did in such moments. He lived in the *burh* but existed on its edges, outside the social bonds which made the clan a collective unit. It gave him no comfort to know his feelings of exile were self-imposed. He thought of Theow and his anxious questions about Fryda, about Beowulf. About Bryce himself. And, as he always did when faced with unthinkable things, Bryce turned to his work for comfort and distraction. He lit the fires in the hearth and pumped the bellows until his muscles burned, as if he could force the guilt to escape his body, along with the sweat that soaked his clothes.

But no. He could not free himself so easily. He never would. So he forced it back down, away from the surface of his thoughts, as if he could somehow manage to keep his darkest secrets hidden even from himself.

For a time, he lost himself in his work, in the rhythm of the hammer and the anvil, the glow of flame, the showers of sparks. His mind quieted and his thoughts became hollow, as hard metal turned malleable under his hands. He worked as if he wielded the power of the elements by will alone. All that mattered was the searing heat of the fire, the feel of iron and bronze changing its shape and meaning beneath his hammer, the hiss of cooling water against blood-red metal. All he needed was the roar of his muscles as he used them to flex and force the ore into the form and function of his choosing.

Bryce did not know how long he worked, but when he finally resurfaced and the world once again pressed against him, insisting upon his attention, the sun had advanced some distance across the sky. Bryce laid down his hammer and gave a mighty stretch, rolling his head back and forth to loosen the muscles in his neck. A soft noise, like a sigh, made him look to the doorway.

"Now that's a sight I never tire of." Eadith, leaning against the wooden doorframe, gave him an appreciative smile.

Bryce blinked. "How long have you been there?"

"Long enough to know you've more on your mind than blacksmithing." Eadith pushed herself off the doorframe and entered the forge proper. "You looked like you wished to trade places with your creations. As if you felt you deserved to be beaten under your hammer."

Bryce cursed to himself and he heard Eadith chuckle. The woman always saw right through him. "What do you want?" he grumbled, turning away from her.

He heard her approach, but did not turn around. He stiffened as her hands landed on his back…gentle, always gentle…and she slid her arms around his waist.

"Woman, I am drenched in sweat and covered with soot," he said. However, he could not stop himself from clasping his enormous hands over her small, gnarled ones as they settled against his stomach.

"And I smell like piss and lye from the laundry," she answered, her voice calm and reasonable. "But I don't hear you complaining about that." Bryce felt her rub her face against his back and a strange feeling crept over him, a kind of cracked and broken tenderness that for a moment eased the sorrow in his breast.

She was the only one who could cast light into his shadows.

He turned in the circle of her arms and looked at her. She raised her face to him, and he reached out a finger to brush an errant wisp of silvery hair from her eyes. She smiled again and he pulled her close, her body thin and bony but still fitting against him as if she belonged there. Her eyes overflowed with affection for him, and though he would forever feel undeserving of it, he leaned down and kissed her.

He lost track years ago of how many times they had made love. Hundreds…perhaps thousands, from the time he came to Eceweall a raw, broken young man who had lost everything, through all the times Eadith—then merely an under-servant in the home she now ran—had tried to put him back together.

Every move, every sound, every touch was comforting and familiar. Much had changed over the decades—Eadith's pale hair was now more silver than gold and Bryce's black locks had turned iron-grey. Their bodies had shifted in shape, his frame becoming thick with muscle while Eadith's youthful curves had waned and flattened, making her more angular than voluptuous these days. Work and many frigid winters had roughened their hands and etched deep lines on their faces.

But this…this had not changed.

Her touch from those rough hands at once eased him and wakened his hunger, his need for contact, for connection. Her hands, as they knowingly roved over his body, made him feel human once more, and even though she did smell of piss and lye, his fingers echoed hers as she peeled him out of his clothes. Their bodies merged joyfully, knowing where their secret pleasures lay. Knowing exactly how to release them. And for a few precious minutes or hours, Eadith managed to banish the ghosts that haunted him.

Afterwards they lay together, spent and out of breath. This part, too, felt familiar and comfortable.

Bryce looked at the woman in his arms and chuckled.

"What?" Eadith asked. She trailed her fingertips up and down his forearm.

"Now I smell like piss and lye, and you are covered in sweat and soot." He rubbed at a smudge on her shoulder that had migrated from his body to hers.

Eadith laughed. "A small price to pay."

Bryce squeezed her gently. "Eadith. Why are you here?"

She gave him a playful glare. "Is this not reason enough?"

He swept his fingers down her cheek. "It is a delightful reason, certainly. But it is not the reason you came."

Eadith sighed and moved out of his arms, turning to look at him. "I wanted to tell you King Beowulf has arrived."

His entire body went tense, like a harp string under a tuning key, and he knew Eadith felt it.

"Hild saw him talking with Fryda and Weohstan in the longhouse this morning," she continued. "I wanted to warn you."

"I thank you, but I already knew. Theow came this morning to tell us the king was expected today." Bryce tried to relax, but his mind was now as jittery as his body had been. "It's not like I didn't know he was coming. This is his celebration, after all."

He released Eadith, stood, and gathered up their discarded clothing. As they shook off the intimacy of the moment, they made no protestations of love or affection. In fact, Bryce had never given her words of love in all the years they'd known each other. He had never spoken to her of marriage and they had never shared a bed for more than a few hours. They had never even slept in each other's company. He wondered sometimes if that hurt her, if she wanted those things from him. But she had never asked for them, nor made him feel she expected them. He suspected that she loved him, and he did love her in his own way, but she knew him well enough to understand he simply could not give her those words. They belonged forever to another.

Eadith made no move to dress herself. "Bryce." Her voice was soft, but it thundered through Bryce's ears like the surf breaking on the shore.

"Don't." They'd had this conversation too many times already. He saw no benefit in having it again.

Eadith stood, clutching her clothing to her. "Bryce." He heard the underlying urgency in his name.

"We are not talking about this."

"The king is right here." Eadith pointed in the direction of the longhouse. "You should talk to him, if you won't talk to me."

"I'm not going to talk to him, Eadith." All the good working at the forge had done for his mind, the languorous satisfaction making love with Eadith had given his body, evaporated. "In fact, I'm going to take great care to avoid the king at all costs."

"You stubborn old fool." Eadith slipped her shift over her head. "You'd rather wallow in uncertainty than face your past and actually get answers to the questions that still plague you, even after all these years."

Bryce tugged on a boot and gave her a considering look. "There are worse things than not knowing."

"You always say that." He could hear the affection in her voice, even under her frustration.

"That's because it's always true."

Eadith sighed, but thankfully dropped the subject. She started picking hairpins up from the floor where he had flung them.

Bryce looked for his other boot. "Did Theow come to see you?" he asked.

Eadith grinned. "Of course he did. You sent him to me. Don't worry, I made him presentable enough."

She paused and he saw that look in her eye. The one that meant she was again going to prod his emotional bruises. "When are you going to tell him?" she asked.

"Soon." He looked under his bench, and then the table. Where was his bloody boot? "I have to talk to Weohstan first."

"And when will you do that?" Eadith leaned to one side, grabbed his boot from the floor and handed it to him.

"After the celebrations are over and the king has left the *burh*."

"Will you promise me?" She placed her hand flat against his

chest. His heartbeat rebounded against her palm. "You carry too many secrets, Bryce. It's not good for you."

Bryce didn't meet her eyes. He knew she was right—he had just thought the same thing earlier that day. But that did not mean he was ready to reveal them to the world. "I have no secrets. They aren't secrets if another person knows about them." He gave her a speaking look. "And you know all my secrets."

"Sometimes I wonder."

Before he could answer, there was a shout from outside. Eadith looked at Bryce with concern. "I'll go look," she said, and hurried from the forge.

She returned before he got his other boot on. "It's Olaf," she said. "I think you'd better come."

He glanced up at her, and she shook her head, reading the question in his eyes. "The king is nowhere in sight."

Bryce pulled the second boot on and scrubbed his hand through his beard. "Right," he said, stood, and walked out into the summer sunshine towards the longhouse. Eadith joined him and walked at his side.

Coming out of the forge always made Bryce feel like a chick emerging from a new-cracked egg. He stepped from his dark enclosure filled with heat and shaping and creation into a windswept world with a sky so huge he could scarcely comprehend it. Anything seemed possible in such a world, from love and redemption to danger and death, and such vastness made him want to scuttle back into the close but safe little space made for him alone.

As he and Eadith approached the longhouse, Bryce spied two of Weohstan's elite warriors—Olaf, a tall, handsome man with dark blond hair, and Bjorn, a young Geat who showed brilliant promise on the battlefield and wore the elaborately embossed leather belt of the *gedriht*, Weohstan's oath-sworn band of prized warriors. Olaf, a Dane who had come to Geatland to fight in the wars with Sweden many years ago, had stayed when Weohstan offered him the position of commander of the *gedriht*. Facing Olaf stood Fægebeorn, an archer who was decidedly *not* one of Eċeweall's *gedriht* fighters, and who was clearly furious about something.

Olaf stood with his arms crossed. He was not a young man, though he had fewer years than Bryce. His blond braids and beard were still untouched by grey and his face, scarred as it was from his many battles and raids, remained unlined. He stood solid as a rock, unmoving in the face of Fægebeorn's wrath.

"...can't believe this," Fægebeorn shouted as Bryce and Eadith approached the two men. "It's the king's fiftieth anniversary feast. You *must* let me prove myself before the king!"

"Fægebeorn." Olaf's scowl told Bryce this wasn't the first time he'd tried to reason with the angry archer and that he was nearing the end of his patience. "I will not change clan law for you. You had your chance to prove yourself and you failed."

"I did not fail!" Fægebeorn's rage burst the boundaries of his control. "I was cheated of my chance."

"You had the same chance as all the others who put themselves to the test, Fægebeorn," Olaf snapped. "It's time you faced the facts. You will never be one of the *gedriht*."

"And I witnessed the trials," Bjorn said. He was a handsome young man with brown braids and the beginning of a warrior's beard. "Fægebeorn mistakes ingenuity and sound strategy for cheating."

"Problem?" Bryce kept his voice mild as he and Eadith paused, as if they had just been out for a walk in the afternoon sun.

"No." Olaf's tone brooked no contradiction.

Fægebeorn contradicted anyway. "Yes!" He turned to Bryce and did a double take. He clearly had not expected to explain himself to a blacksmith. But he could not resist the temptation to complain to a potentially sympathetic ear.

"I was obstructed during the *gedriht* trials," Fægebeorn

complained. "One of the other fighters cheated and wounded my leg."

"What you call 'cheating,' I call 'superior skill,'" Olaf said. He met Bryce's gaze and rolled his eyes. "You were bested, and that was your second and final trial."

Bryce clapped Fægebeorn on the shoulder. "I wouldn't fret about it," he said. "The *burh* needs men at the walls and fighters and hunters just as much as we need the *gedriht*. There are no unimportant jobs here."

Fægebeorn's lip lifted in a snarl, transforming his face from furious to feral, and he twitched Bryce's hand away. "And what would you know, blacksmith? Your mind is full of metal."

"And fire," Eadith said with a wink at Olaf. "Don't forget fire."

Fægebeorn growled and Bryce eased his body in front of Eadith, ready to protect her in case the incensed warrior forgot himself. He felt more than saw her small, amused smile.

"Fægebeorn, that's enough." Olaf had a natural gift of command, and when he spoke, he expected others to listen. "You'll have your chance to impress the king in the regular sparring matches and feats of strength at the feast tonight. But you will not be amongst the *gedriht*. Now get out of my face before I change my mind about even that."

Fægebeorn glared at all four of them, hesitating with his hand on his bow as if tempted to pick them off one by one. Bryce frowned and his body tensed, ready to leap into action at the first sign of violence. For a long moment they all stood frozen, waiting, until finally Fægebeorn grunted, ducked his head, and stormed off towards the barracks.

Olaf released a gusty breath, as if he, too, had been holding it in anticipation of violence.

"He's a cracked cup full of trouble, that one," Bjorn said, pulling at his fledgling beard.

Bryce, too, relaxed. "I'd watch him tonight," he warned. He

did not like the idea of Fægebeorn at the feast near Fryda and Eadith.

"That young man," Eadith said, "would very much like to hurt someone right now." She glanced at Bryce.

"It's true." Olaf gave them both a wan smile. "In truth, I would not have accepted Fægebeorn to the *gedriht*, even if he had performed perfectly. I trust him about as far as I can throw … well, you." He eyed Bryce's bulk.

Bryce laughed. "I don't know, I imagine you could toss me a fair way. Why don't you stop by the forge one afternoon and we'll find out?"

"My wife would not be happy with me if I let you pummel me into gruel and bone dust," Olaf said, "as much as I might like to let you try."

They both laughed and clasped forearms, and Olaf and Bjorn headed back into the longhouse.

"I should go, too," Eadith said. "There is so much work left to be done." She sounded tired. Bryce slipped his arm around her and planted a kiss on her temple.

"Don't work too hard," he murmured. "But I know you'll do the king proud."

Eadith smiled. "We will. And don't worry, I'll have Hild keep an eye on Theow tonight, and Olaf will watch Fægebeorn."

Five

That night in the longhouse, the *scops* stood in front of the great table with their harps and their lyres and sang epic tales from Beowulf's youth, recounting in verse his great deeds at Heorot, hall of the Danish king Hrothgar. Tonight they started with the story of Beowulf's confrontation with Unferth, King Hrothgar's envious young thane.

> "Seated at the king's   feet, Unferth spoke
> Inflammatory words.   Beowulf's arrival,
> His bravery at sea,   sickened him with jealousy."

Fryda had always felt a secret sympathy for Unferth. She was convinced everyone simply misunderstood him, especially considering the second part of the story when Beowulf went to fight Grendel's mother.

> "And an additional object...given by Unferth,
> At that time was   of paramount importance.
> The thane gave him...a hilted weapon,
> A precious and ancient   sword named Hrunting."

Why, Fryda wondered, would Unferth give Beowulf a mighty sword if he wanted the young warrior to fail? It made no sense to her.

As the night wore on, the *scops* progressed to Beowulf's battle with Grendel, which he won even though he wore no armour and used no weapons.

> "Pain invaded the   monster's entire body,
> A fearsome wound appeared   at Grendel's shoulder.
> Sinews split and his   bone-lappings broke.
> Beowulf emerged from   the fight victorious."

As the storyteller described in gruesome detail the sound Grendel's body had made when Beowulf tore the monster's arm from its shoulder, Fryda caught Theow's eye. He looked grave and worried, and she knew his concern was for her. She found herself unconsciously rubbing her own shoulder and remembered the noise it had made when the healers forced the bone back into the joint, the pain of torn muscle and tendon. She gave Theow a small, reassuring smile, though the memory left her pale and shaken.

She surveyed the room with a practised eye, alert for any problems. The first night of the feast had progressed well into the evening, and the mead-hall overflowed with laughter, music, drunken revelries, and warrior-posturing. Fryda had never seen so many men act in such a ridiculous manner. Clan rulers, warriors, and vassals alike from numerous nations across the North, Baltic, and Norwegian Seas strove to show off for the king, and the boasting competitions and contests of strength left Fryda unimpressed. Men grunted and sweated as they wrestled each other to the floor, and congratulated themselves on their supposed prowess in battle. Fryda appreciated a good, honest sparring match, but in her opinion only children, not warriors, indulged in drunken brawling. King Beowulf, on the other hand, loved every moment of it. He smacked his hand against the arm of his chair and congratulated the winners of every challenge, handing out gold coins, rings, and other trinkets as reward.

Theow had done well for his first time serving at a feast, she thought—especially one of this magnitude. She was pleased to see Eadith had taken him in hand. Theow was dressed in a dark tunic and trousers, with a simply engraved brass buckle on his belt. Fryda smiled as she recognized Bryce's work. Theow's hair was neat, though slightly damp, and his nails clean, as if he had come straight from a bath.

No. No, Fryda lectured herself. This was not the time to dream about Theow in the bath.

He moved amongst the rowdy revellers, keeping plates full and cleaning up spills of food and mead and the occasional pool of blood. He'd only dropped something once, and that was when a brawler fell unconscious on top of him. Throughout the night, Fryda would turn and find Theow's steady eyes upon her, and she was glad she had put on her best dress, a deep russet silk from Gaul, trimmed in gold and fastened with gold horse-head brooches, set with garnets, which Bryce had made for her.

Fryda herself kept busy; goblets seemed to empty themselves almost as soon as she filled them. An hour or so into the festivities, the wide, clear skies darkened and thundering clouds loured over the villagers and guests, who ran laughing into the longhouse as sheets of rain soaked everything in sight. As the mead-hall filled to bursting, Fryda dealt with problems and arguments that arose amongst the servants and the guests, and kept a sharp eye on the young women. She did not need anyone in her household finding—or seeking out—trouble at the hands of men drunk on stories, competition, and mead. Even so, more than once she had to fish a flustered serving girl out of someone's lap or away from groping hands.

Fryda weaved through the crowd with her pitcher, filling cups and bestowing smiles. For the first time, her father let her pour the mead for the head table, and she knew he bestowed upon her a great honour as well as a duty. She had heard Beowulf tell the story of how, after he defeated the monster Grendel, King

Hrothgar's young and beautiful wife, Wealhtheow, gave Beowulf a goblet of mead from her own white hands and he drank it and fell in love with her. Fryda knew Beowulf had never married and she wondered if perhaps he loved her still.

As she moved through the room, she noted with approval how the servants had dressed and decorated the longhouse. Fresh, fragrant herbs were strewn across the floor, helping to cover the scent of sweaty, drunken men. In the centre of the large room, flames crackled in the raised fire pit where spitted birds and game roasted, and a sumptuous feast was laid out on the long tables running the length of the room. Torches on the walls and flickering candles in the wrought-iron chandeliers bathed the room in soft, glowing light. The newly cleaned tapestries and banners embroidered with important clan and house sigils hung from the rafters. The kitchen women had scoured and cleaned the long benches and had moved them to flank the tables, where people feasted and drank mead.

And the mead flowed like a tumbling river, fashioning tongues into both song and sword. The boasts became more fanciful and outlandish, and the audiences more demanding as the rain kept them hostage in the longhouse. Fryda wound her way through the hall, refilling cups, and laughed when she saw her twin had been pulled into a boasting contest. It did not surprise her to see how easily he held his own. Wiglaf could convince the sun to set at midday in summer if he chose to. But her laughter tapered off and her smile fell while she watched him. His voice was a touch too loud, his gestures too loose, and he spoke in the careful, measured tones of a man trying not to slur his speech. Several young women from the outlying farmsteads draped themselves around him, hanging onto his arms and leaning against him. Their calloused hands and broad, tanned faces told the story of their humble origins. Weohstan would not be pleased.

Wiglaf's boasting opponent was none other than Olaf,

commander of the *gedriht*, who also looked a bit the worse for wear with drink. Fryda watched his temper fray as his boasts fell flat again and again, when pitted against Wiglaf's sardonic wit.

"…and then I stood at the edge of the Panta River," Olaf spoke to the hushed crowd as Fryda refilled Wiglaf's cup with watered-down mead. Olaf's wife Gudrun, a stunning beauty, stood at her husband's side with their babe on her hip, and smiled proudly while Wiglaf glanced at Fryda and winked. "The Saxon leader, Byrhtnoth, stood opposite me on the other bank, puffed up with misplaced pride and stolen glory. I gave their leader one chance. 'My Lord has sent me to you,' I shouted, 'and he bids you send gold rings in exchange for protection.'"

Wiglaf smirked. "A terrifying war-cry indeed."

"Byrhtnoth's army fought like crazed animals, but they were no match for my men," Olaf doggedly continued. "My war-brother, Cenhelm, sent a southern spear that struck the Saxon lord right through the shoulder."

Someone in the crowd gasped and Fryda stifled a laugh.

Olaf beamed at the enraptured listeners. "And so, we were victorious at the Battle of Maldon, and defeated the Saxons on their own land." He leaned back, looking triumphant.

Wiglaf took a swig from his cup. He shot an outraged look at Fryda as he swallowed more water than mead and moved to Olaf's side, throwing an arm over his shoulders. She grinned back at him, unrepentant.

"Friends!" Wiglaf proclaimed. "This is the most impressive boast I've heard this night. Olaf, your warrior poked a mad old fool in the arm with a needle and then you declare you alone won the Battle of Maldon. That's a boast worthy of the king himself. Your boldness in telling this story outshines any of my deeds in battle, so you must be the victor."

The crowd roared with laughter as Olaf blinked and scowled. His hand went to the *seax* on his belt. The Danish warrior might have challenged Wiglaf to a physical contest of arms, but the crowd of men swept him up, plying him with more mead and the choicest pieces of roasted meat. Fryda smiled to herself, relieved. Only Wiglaf could so humiliate a man and still manage to make him the toast of the contest. Her brother caught her eye and winked, and she shook her head and laughed.

From her father's chair, King Beowulf roared with laughter as several revellers staggered into the mead-hall, soaking wet from the summer showers. The king looked resplendent in a red silk tunic edged with brocade, and a huge necklace of rubies the size of her thumbnail circled his neck and shoulders. A belt of gold and garnets girded his sturdy waist, and his cloak was lined with soft fur and fastened with a ruby clasp. Weohstan, she noticed, had dressed in the muted colours of grey and black he had worn since her mother's death, and had done little more than don a rich gold ring in honour of the event.

Fryda tamped down a swell of sadness as she looked at her father. Weohstan had not once spoken to her of Ielfeta— her mother—and had never accused her, or her twin brother, of being the instrument of his wife's death. Ielfeta had birthed Wiglaf first, but with the second twin she had soon sickened and bled, and the healers had ultimately cut Fryda from her mother's lifeless body. For all twenty years of her life, Fryda knew herself to be the cause of her father's unhappiness, and her injury had only broadened the breach between them. When her promised husband broke their engagement, unwilling to bind himself to a broken wife, Weohstan made it painfully clear he had no use for a crippled daughter.

Brytan byrde, a voice whispered in her head.

But, she thought, chasing the voice away, perhaps tonight, as Weohstan allowed her to pour the mead and take over as the lady of the house, he would take a cup from her own white hand and show her something more than cold courtesies and distant affections.

Beowulf laughed, diverting her attention back to the dais, and pointed to the half-drowned guests. "Look, friends!" he shouted. "Woden himself must be envious of our celebrations, for he and his sons have sent us a fine storm to punish us for our joys!"

A loud cheer rose from the gathering, and Fryda winced at the noise. The smoke and close air oppressed her, and the mead-hall began to smell like a pack of wet wolves as guests threw their furs down near the fire to dry.

Fryda moved about the hall, filling goblets, chatting with people she knew and making the acquaintance of those she did not. Several men paid her special attention, including one petty lord from Sweden—an enormous bear of a warrior who grunted an impertinent suggestion at her—and, to her surprise, Eadgils, king of Sweden.

She noticed Eadgils watching her as she refilled his cup, his eyes cold and sharp. She smiled at him.

"Is there anything else I can bring you, my lord?" she asked, bowing her head respectfully.

"No, thank you." His voice was thin and reedy, and matched his looks perfectly. He was of medium height and rail-thin, and his hair wafted around his head like wisps of white fog. His eyes were such a pale blue they looked colourless. His skin had crumpled with age, creating deep pleats around his eyes and crevices that dragged his mouth downward. It made him look eternally petulant, as if displeased with everything he saw.

Including her. The grooves in his face deepened as he looked at her and frowned.

"So, you're the daughter," Eadgils said, fingering his silver goblet.

Fryda blinked. "Well, I am certainly *a* daughter," she retorted, and then silently scolded herself. Weohstan would not be pleased if foreign monarchs complained she was rude.

To her surprise, however, Eadgils chuckled. "No," he amended. "Not just *a* daughter. You are most definitely *her* daughter."

Fryda grew still. "You knew my mother?"

Those ice-coloured eyes regarded her steadily. "Yes. I knew her."

She wondered when and how they might have met. Weohstan had fought in Sweden, but as far as she knew, her mother had never left Geatland. Many years ago, before she was born, Eadgils and his brother Eanmund had fought against their uncle, the tyrant usurper King Onela, and prevailed with Weohstan and Beowulf's help. Eanmund had been slain but Eadgils killed Onela and became the rightful king of Sweden, and Weohstan had come back to Geatland. How, then, had the Swedish king known her mother?

"Am I like her?" Fryda clutched the pitcher of mead to her body with her good hand and was surprised to find it trembling.

Eadgils took a sip of mead. "At first I thought you merely looked like her, but now I see you are like her in spirit as well."

"Oh. Well." Fryda shifted from foot to foot. A painful longing swept through her. It was the first time anyone had spoken of her mother in years. "Thank you for telling me."

"He still never talks about her, does he?" Eadgils' eyes were shrewd.

"No, he doesn't." She did not mention that her father never spoke to her, either, if he could help it. "He loved her very much, I'm told."

A derisive sneer flashed across the king's face. Startled, Fryda stepped back and Eadgils seemed to remember himself.

"Ah. Of course," he murmured. "Of course."

Fryda blinked. Eadgils' expression of malevolence had been so real, so raw. So honest. It was as if he had torn off a mask and revealed his true face to her and she no longer understood who he was. She looked over to where her father stood, regal even in his plain clothes and with the sword he always wore at his side. He stood with his hand on the hilt, as if ready for a fight.

"Its name is Swicdóm, you know," Eadgils said, following her gaze. "The sword. It means 'betrayal.'"

Fryda looked at him in surprise. "You know my father's sword?"

Eadgils scoffed. "Swicdóm is not your father's sword, girl. It was Eanmund's, my brother's, and by rights should be mine."

She blinked. "How did my father get your brother's sword?"

"How do you think, girl?" he said, regarding her. "Weohstan killed him for it."

Her breath stilled as if all the air had left the room.

She turned to stare at her father, and then back at Eadgils. "No," she protested. "No, Eanmund was fighting against the tyrant Onela. My father couldn't have killed him."

"Weohstan was fighting *for* Onela, you stupid chit."

Fryda's jaw dropped.

"Woden's beard," Eadgils said, studying her. "You did not know. He's told you nothing." The old king shook his head. "He hasn't changed a bit."

Without another word, he turned and walked away.

Music

Fýrdraca does not hear the music, but she can feel it.

Oh, she hears the hypnotic lure of treasure-song as she nestles into her bed of gold, silver, and jewels. The Lone Survivor's curse constantly sings to her. Sings through her. She can never escape its ethereal notes, stained with blood, anger, and pain—they follow her into her dreams and lay so heavy upon her eyes that she cannot open them.

She has not looked through her own eyes in over a thousand years.

No, this music feels different. It reverberates through the rock and stone of her cave, infinitesimal but physical. Her pile of treasure vibrates in time with its lively measures and her heart seems to throb in accompaniment with its beat.

It has been a long time since a settlement of humans made enough noise to catch her attention.

Behind the music she hears far-off clangs and clashes of wood against wood, wood against metal, metal against metal. A battle? But where there should be war cries and screams of pain, she senses shouts of laughter and camaraderie. Just games, then, and friendly feats of strength amongst men.

One particularly intense shriek drags her back into the river of her memories, to the time she watched the Lone Survivor clutch a goblet on the promontory while he screamed at the destruction of his world. His pain was so vivid it was as if she lived, rather than witnessed it.

Having returned from the hunt to find his entire clan dead, his village burned to the ground, the Lone Survivor began scouring the wreckage for something or someone. He sifted through the rubble of broken ash spears and splintered lindenwood shields. He searched through piles of his neighbours' corpses, and trawled pools of their blood. He rifled through weapons and armour studded with jewels and inlaid with gold, and he searched though heaps of charred wood and blackened stone. Hidden within the burnt, broken planks and toppled rafters of the king's mead-hall, he found gold and silver plates, torques and crowns. He dug through grimy ash, uncovering chests of gold and priceless statues. The Lone Survivor flung all these riches into the hole Fýrdraca had made, searching frantically until he finally found what he was looking for.

The music fades, though the sounds of merriment continue to haunt Fýrdraca's dreams. The Lone Survivor's curse clutches at her, and the tainted gold both sustains and suffocates her. Soon, she falls back into nightmare and is lost once more to the world, but her memories of the Lone Survivor's unassailable grief break open the sky and the rain pours down like a waterfall of tears.

Six

The celebrations turned even rowdier as the night wore on. More than once the estate guards dragged away a senseless man who had thrust at another with a belligerent word or reckless weapon, and Fryda became quite adept at flowing in and out of precarious situations without coming to harm herself. At first everyone showed her due respect as the newly elevated lady of the house, but the drink had a way of altering that, too. By the time the summer sun had begun to furl in its light, she was ready to skewer the next man who pinched her bottom or tried to pull her onto his lap.

At that moment, as if one warrior had read her mind and taken her thought as a challenge, Fryda felt a man's hand press into her breast and squeeze, hard enough to hurt.

Lightning fast, she dropped her pitcher and, with her undamaged hand, peeled two large, calloused fingers from her chest and wrenched them backwards. She heard the snap of bones breaking before her pitcher shattered on the floor. The warrior, Fægebeorn—who had clearly left his good judgment in the bottom of his cup—howled in pain and outrage.

"You useless, crippled cunt!" he snarled, and swung at her. Fryda blocked his hand with her left forearm just before his fist made contact with her face. A sharp lance of pain shot from her shoulder to her fingertips as her body's old injuries roused from their shallow sleep. She gasped and clutched her arm close to her side. Her heart raced and her blood surged like the tide, drawing strength from her pain and outrage, threading it through her muscles like lightning. She grabbed Fægebeorn's wrist with her good hand and gave it a shrewd, sharp twist.

She jumped in surprise when his bones gave another snap, shattering like chalk under her hand.

The hapless warrior shrieked and made one last attempt to unseat her, hooking his foot around her ankle as if to yank her off her feet. Fryda evaded him and seized a handful of his dirty blond hair in her right hand. With all her strength she smashed his face against the tabletop. His nose broke and blood sprayed everyone in front of him. The man's body went limp and he slid gracelessly down into the pool of mead and pieces of broken pottery, his mangled hands splayed at unnatural angles.

Fryda's manic strength abruptly deserted her, leaving her feeling spent and trembling. She tucked her own throbbing hand into her sleeve. She knew the pain Fægebeorn would suffer come morning.

Useless, crippled cunt.

Other pains, however, lasted much longer.

The rest of the men at the table howled and laughed, pointing at the wounded soldier and toasting Fryda with mouthfuls of mead. She felt a tug at her elbow and she spun around, fist raised.

Wiglaf ducked and exclaimed, "Whoa! Hold off! Are you going to strike me, sister?" Fryda, relieved, dropped her arm and her brother looked at her, his face contorted with concern. "I wouldn't blame you if you did. I saw what happened. Are you all right? Did Fægebeorn hurt you?"

Fryda's breast ached, but she didn't see the need to tell her brother that. "I'm fine," she said.

Wiglaf glared at Fægebeorn's limp form. "This should not have happened," he muttered.

"What?" Fryda looked at him, confused.

Wiglaf shook his head sharply, as if to clear it. "He is a warrior," he said. "He should know better than to lose control like that. Believe me, I shall take Fægebeorn to task for his behaviour tomorrow."

"No need." Fryda opened her fist and shook a handful of the man's hair from her fingers. "I've already had a word with him myself."

Wiglaf gave a reluctant grin. His eyes sharpened as something over her shoulder caught his attention and he raised his hand and imperiously snapped his fingers.

"Bjorn!" he called. Fryda turned to see the young *gedriht* set his cup down and move to join them. He gave her a nod of respect and looked at Wiglaf, stone-faced.

"My lord?"

"Clean up this mess, would you?" Wiglaf said, and gestured to Fægebeorn's senseless body still sprawled on the ground.

"Wiglaf," Fryda protested. "I don't think that's his..."

"He doesn't mind," Wiglaf said.

"Wiglaf, no. You cannot just..."

"My lady," Bjorn murmured, his interruption gentler than her brother's. "It is an honour to serve you." Fryda noticed he did not look at Wiglaf when he spoke. Wiglaf caught the subtle insult as well, but before he could speak, Bjorn called for several more men to help him cart Fægebeorn from the mead-hall.

Fryda looked warily at her brother, confused by the anger that creased his brow. He seemed more sober than before, though his eyes looked bloodshot and tired.

"You needn't trouble father with this," she said and Wiglaf focused on her. "I would not have him worried."

Wiglaf hesitated, then nodded. "As you wish. Still. There will be some hefty consequences, and not just from the pain he will feel tomorrow." He glanced at the unconscious warrior as Bjorn and several others carried him through the jeering crowd. "Father might have a word or two to say to you about injuring his warriors, though. That one may never draw a bow again."

Fryda crossed her arms over her chest. Her breast ached where Fægebeorn's fingers had dug into her flesh and she could feel bruises blooming under her skin. "Oh. I'm so sorry."

"I'm just warning you of what our father will probably say."

Fryda considered asking Wiglaf about her conversation with Eadgils earlier that evening, but decided tonight was not the night. If her brother didn't know their father had fought for Onela and killed Eanmund, the knowledge would upset him. If he did, his knowledge of it would upset her. So, she merely shrugged and said, "He can say what he likes."

"He'll also now realize that you've been sneaking away for private lessons with someone who's been teaching you how to fight."

Fryda gulped. Her father would *not* be happy about that. "I can deny it." Then she blinked. "Wait, how did you know?"

"Every single person who just saw you beat the piss out of Fægebeorn knows, trust me. You'll have to tell me who your teacher is so I can thank him. And reward him." Wiglaf smiled and took her good hand and squeezed. "Come. Meet me outside in a few minutes while everyone's distracted. I have a surprise for you."

"Wiglaf," Fryda said. "I can't just…"

"Of course you can. You've been on your feet all night."

"It's raining out."

"No it isn't. It stopped a while ago."

"I have to pour the mead," she reminded him. "It's the first time father's let me do it, and I can't…"

"He won't even notice."

Fryda thought that if Wiglaf interrupted her one more time, he'd end up with his own goblet of mead upended over his head.

Wiglaf reached out just as Hild came by, carrying a platter of succulent roasted meat. He caught her arm. "Hey…girl. Come here."

"Woden's beard, Wiglaf. She has a name and you should know

it by now. She's lived here since she was four." Fryda shot Hild an apologetic look. Hild rolled her eyes and gave the barest shrug.

Wiglaf blinked at Hild, taking in her dark skin and long braids. "I've never seen her before in my life."

Fryda closed her eyes for a moment. "Wiglaf. We used to play together when we were children."

"Oh. You mean our Beowulf battle re-enactments?" Wiglaf grinned at Hild, his eyes skimming her hair. "She must have been the child of Grendel, then."

Fryda's jaw dropped and she felt Hild stiffen beside her.

"Or maybe she played a bear that's been hit by lightning." Wiglaf reached out and tugged on one of Hild's thick, black braids. Hild jerked her head away and Fryda's fury made her feel puffed up to twice her size, like an angry cat.

"Wiglaf!"

"Never mind. Here." Wiglaf took the platter of meat from Hild and put it on a nearby table. He then plucked up an empty pitcher and put it into Hild's hands. "You can take over for Lady Fryda for a few minutes. Go fill this from that cask." He pointed to a newly opened barrel by the trestle tables. "Make sure everyone gets some for the toasts." He grinned at Fryda while Hild stood frozen, staring at Wiglaf as if he'd instructed her to remove all her clothes and parade about the longhouse naked.

"Wiglaf, you can't just…" Fryda said, but Wiglaf had already slipped into the crowd and disappeared. "High-handed bastard," she muttered under her breath.

"He always has been."

The unexpected voice at her elbow made her start. Theow smiled at her. "Sorry," he said. "I didn't mean to scare you."

Fryda swallowed. "It's not you," she said. "I'm a little jumpy."

Theow glanced at the floor where Fægebeorn had left a small puddle of blood and she saw the muscles at his jaw clench. "I can see why." His voice was taut and hard.

Fryda swept a furtive look around the great hall. Her father was engrossed in a conversation with Beowulf, and the servants and slaves had everything well in hand. She could afford to take a short break.

She turned to Hild. "I'm so sorry about Wiglaf. I don't know what got into him. I'd better see what he wants. Will you be all right for a few minutes?"

"Yes, my lady." Hild's lips were pressed so tightly together the words could scarcely escape.

"Thank you. And please don't worry about this." She gestured to the shattered remnants of the pitcher. "I'll deal with it when I get back."

Hild's lip curled as she looked at the mess. "That Fægebeorn has been a problem for more than one of us tonight. Don't fret, my lady. We're happy to take care of it."

Fryda gave her friend a smile, though it felt strained and thin. Wiglaf's ugly words still hovered in the air between them like a noxious miasma. "Thank you. And if anyone asks for me, tell them…" She glanced at the doorway Wiglaf had walked through. "…Could you please tell them my brother needed me for something."

Hild nodded, gripped the pitcher, and glided away.

On impulse, Fryda looked up at Theow and said, "Come with me?"

He looked startled. "Where?"

Fryda paused, and then laughed. "I'm not sure, actually. Wiglaf asked me to meet him outside, and…" She shifted from foot to foot. "Well. I don't feel like going alone." She caught Theow's hesitation. "You have nothing to fear," she assured him. "No one will criticize you if you are with me. I'll tell them…oh! I'll tell them I need supplies and I brought you along to carry the heavy things."

Theow looked at her consideringly. "Yes, I'll come," he said at last. As they moved towards the door, she noticed him studying her face.

"What?" she asked. She surreptitiously rubbed her cheek, wondering if she had a smudge.

"You always ask," he said.

"What?"

"When you speak to the servants or the slaves. You always ask them. You never order or command. You're the only one who does that."

"Oh." Fryda thought about that as she stepped over a snoring, drooling body on the floor. "I didn't even realize."

Theow's face became inscrutable. "I know."

★ ★ ★

Theow and Fryda slipped through the large wooden doors of the mead-hall into the cool air of the summer night, which soothed and gentled his flushed skin. He still burned with anger at the warrior who had dared touched Fryda and hurt her. Few things in his life had given him as much pleasure as watching Fryda break the villain's bones.

He'd have to ask her what trick Bryce taught her. He'd never seen anyone break someone's wrist one-handed before.

At this time of year, the sun hovered long on the horizon, so even late at night the stronghold and its surroundings were washed in a deep, glowing blue light. It had indeed stopped raining, and the drops of water caught on blades of grass, on flowering branches, on rough thatch, sparkled, as if the world wore a cloak of gems.

Wiglaf waited for them outside the longhouse. He looked irritated and impatient at the delay, but his expression changed for the length of a breath when he saw Theow, as if an ugly thought moved from his mind to his face before he could hide it. But it disappeared with a flash of his quicksilver smile and

Theow might have imagined it—if he hadn't already known the richness and depth of Wiglaf's hatred for him.

"Ah, here you are," Wiglaf called out. "And you've brought company. Well met, Theow."

Theow stayed behind Fryda, knowing Wiglaf could make his life very difficult if he chose to.

And there were times in the past he had chosen to.

"This way," Wiglaf said. "I've hidden a little something just for us." He wobbled a bit as he entered the forge, as if the night air had ignited the alcohol in his blood.

Theow followed them, breathing in air full of the ghosts of Bryce's forge-work. It smelled of salt sea-spray, hot metal, and smoke from the hearth and the oven. Wiglaf stooped over, searched behind the enormous anvil and muttered to himself until Theow heard him say, "Ah. Here it is." Wiglaf pulled a sack from the shadows and looked around.

"You haven't had a chance to eat or drink anything tonight," he said to Fryda as he pulled bread, cheese, mead, oatcakes, and summer strawberries from the sack. He hummed appreciatively as he unstoppered a skin of mead and took a long pull. He swallowed, wiped his mouth, and passed the skin to Fryda. "You'll find none of your watered-down shite here, sister, so be careful with it. Anyway, I thought this could be like old times when we ran away from our lessons and raided the larder."

Fryda laughed and reached for an oatcake. "We did that a lot, if I recall," she said, and bit into the cake. She rolled her eyes with pleasure and passed one to Theow.

Theow took it, but did not eat. "We did do this as children," he said. "Until that one time we got caught," he said, raising his eyes to meet Wiglaf's angry gaze.

"Oh. Right," Wiglaf said. He tried to sound casual, but Theow heard the tension in his voice. "I'd forgotten about that."

"Forgotten what?" Fryda asked, looking confused. She looked from Wiglaf to Theow and back again.

Of course, Theow hadn't forgotten, and he'd made certain that Fryda never knew of her brother's cruelty. It had been a summer's evening, much like this one—cool, damp, with the sea mist wrapped around them like a delicate lace veil. They had been children, Theow a little older than the twins, though by how much they did not know. The three of them would sometimes play together in the late afternoons when the light stayed late into the night hours.

That day they played Beowulf and Grendel, and Wiglaf had said they needed food to play the celebration after Beowulf's victory. Wiglaf had snuck into the larder and taken cold roast fowl, bread and honey, fruit, and a wedge of hard cheese. Unfortunately, he had also taken a pitcher that, unbeknownst to him, contained a very costly wine meant for some celebration for Weohstan that night. Theow never learned if Wiglaf had tipped someone off, but their play was interrupted by Weohstan's guards. Fryda was immediately bundled off, but Wiglaf and Theow were hauled in front of the lord of the *burh* to account for their actions, and Wiglaf…

Wiglaf told his father that Theow had stolen the food.

For years Theow wondered why he'd done it. It seemed such a useless lie, and he doubted anything much would have happened to Wiglaf had he confessed to the theft. But he had protested his innocence and let Theow be blamed.

Theow twitched as the long, thin scars across his back tightened and itched, as they always did when he remembered the whipping he had received as punishment.

"Never mind," he reassured Fryda. "Just something from a long time ago."

Fryda shrugged and, to his relief, let it go. "So, what is the occasion, Wiglaf?" She took another oatcake. "Not that I'm complaining, but this took some advance planning. You hid food for us and everything."

"I assumed we would both need a break from our father

at some point during the festivities, considering his favourite pastime is criticizing me and ignoring you." Wiglaf swallowed another mouthful of mead. "But when I saw what Fægebeorn... well. I thought you needed a little time away." He glanced at Theow. "Alone."

"Thank you." Fryda inhaled and then slowly exhaled, as if letting the calm of the evening settle into her breath. "I did. I also did not realize how hungry I was." She bit into the oatcake with relish.

"You and your love of sweets," her brother said, laughing.

"Better than you and your love of liquor," she retorted, and licked honey from her fingers.

Wiglaf scowled, but recovered quickly. "Yes. Well. I bought you out here to discuss something important. I thought you should know there have been several offers for you."

Fryda blinked. "Offers? You mean...marriage proposals?"

Theow froze.

Wiglaf snorted. "More like negotiations for trade agreements. Several of our noble guests approached Father earlier with offers of a bride-price for you. He asked me to, as he so delicately put it, 'deal with this cursed marriage shite' for him because I, and I repeat him directly, 'know how to bilk men out of their gold and goods better than any man in Eceweall.' "

"But why are they offering for me now? I thought..." Fryda held her left hand close to her body. "I thought I was deemed unmarriageable."

Theow's jaw clenched, but he stayed silent.

"With the celebrations happening here, many of the foreign nobles are only just realizing that our father is blood-kin to the king. Marrying you would put any children they have with you into Beowulf's direct bloodline."

"Well, I hope you haven't accepted any of them!" Fryda cried.

Wiglaf chuckled. "You don't even know who they're from yet."

Fryda opened her mouth to argue, but then closed it again.

"Fine." She took a strawberry and snapped it off its stem with her teeth. "Who are they?"

Wiglaf lifted a hand and counted on his fingers. "First, Lord Iorlund offered five cows, a half-measure of gold, and fifteen bolts of silk."

Fryda choked on her strawberry. "Iorlund? The lord from Denmark? He must be eighty years old!"

"Sixty, but your point is well taken. He is far too old for you. Next," he ticked off his second finger, "Lord Ansten has offered two cows and half the proceeds from the contents of one trade ship."

"Ansten. From Sweden?" Fryda frowned. "That pasty lord who kept following me around earlier this evening? Didn't three of his ships sink last year?"

"Yes. And two cows is an insultingly low number to offer for you. Let's move on." He ticked his third finger. "Lord Rawald has offered a stud stallion, the proceeds from four fields of wheat, and twenty casks of mead."

"Rawald? The Frisian?" Fryda scratched her head. "I thought he was already married."

"He is." Wiglaf took another swig from the skin of mead. "She's apparently dying, though, and Rawald thought to put in his bid on a new wife to save himself the trouble later."

Fryda made a rude noise. "That is disgusting."

Wiglaf shrugged. "I'm just the messenger."

"Are those all the offers?"

"Yes."

"Then I can confidently say I wish you to proffer a very polite and very firm refusal to all three." She dusted her hands together. "With my thanks, of course."

Fryda glanced at Theow, and dropped her gaze into her lap.

For a while the three of them ate and drank in silence. Sounds from the feast wafted over to them, dulled by distance into a uniform gabble, though Theow thought he could make out

King Beowulf's shouted laughter over everything else. He took a strawberry and handed it to Fryda.

"The king is probably laughing at that story of how he fought Grendel's mother," Wiglaf said. "Have you heard the latest version? They have him fighting for a full day. In a cave. *Underwater*."

Theow sputtered into his mead and the three of them had to take a moment to get their mirth under control.

"It's almost as good as the Breca story," Wiglaf wheezed, wiping his watering eyes. "Fighting sea monsters after seven days swimming in the ocean is still my favourite."

"I've never liked that story," Fryda said, sneaking another strawberry. "The whole thing seems like a boast designed to ridicule Unferth. It's so ludicrous, no one could believe it. Personally, I always felt sorry for Unferth. I mean, think about it. A stranger shows up in your land, starts bossing everyone around and makes them feel inadequate because they couldn't kill Grendel on their own. Of course Unferth is going to be annoyed when this brash young warrior starts boasting. But he wanted the best for his people, so he tried to help anyway."

"Yes, by giving Beowulf a sword that failed in battle and nearly got him killed," Wiglaf reminded her.

"Oh, come now, he could not have predicted that." Fryda tossed her head. "Hrunting had never failed before and Unferth had no reason to believe it would that time. And Beowulf himself says he didn't blame Unferth. He even gave him back the sword with thanks after he'd won the battle."

"I wonder what happened to Unferth after that," Theow said, taking a swig of mead from the wineskin.

"He was exiled." Wiglaf took the skin as Theow passed it to him. "His clan was not as convinced as Fryda about the nobility of his character. They thought he tried to deliberately get Beowulf killed."

I've missed this, Theow thought as he gave Fryda the last

summer strawberry. It had been a long time since he'd been able to sit and talk and laugh with Fryda. Years. Even Wiglaf's presence could not mar his enjoyment of her company.

Wiglaf had reached that glassy-eyed, merry stage of drunkenness, and seemed disinclined to stop. He drained the skin of mead and pulled another from his hidden cache. Theow wondered, not for the first time, why Wiglaf strove for forgetfulness, when others—like himself—would give anything for the gift of memory.

A loud crash and a shriek came from the mead-hall and Wiglaf sighed. "I guess we'd better get back before they set the place on fire." His words blurred together a little. "Besides, Fryda has eaten all the strawberries, as usual."

"I like strawberries," Fryda said, standing up and dusting off her backside. "Thank you for bringing them. You were thoughtful to do this, Wiglaf."

"No. I needed an excuse to get away," he said, waving off her thanks as he staggered to his feet. He always did that, Theow thought. He almost seemed ashamed to look too generous or unselfish, so he had to make every kind thing he did about serving himself.

Fryda fell back to walk with Theow as they left the forge and headed up the path to the longhouse. "So how is everything with you tonight?" she asked him.

"Wonderful." Theow gave her a warm smile. "I was worried I'd be thrown back into the kitchens when that warrior fell on me, but otherwise it's a dream come true. I suspect it was all your idea."

"Well, yes. I told Moire I needed you in the longhouse tonight. I wanted you to have the chance to see King Beowulf."

"Thank you," he said. Without thinking, he let his fingertips brush against the back of her left hand, but she twitched away from his touch. Theow clasped his hands behind his back and drew away from her, cursing himself.

Fryda abruptly turned and stepped in front of Theow, blocking his path. He rocked back on his heels and looked at her, surprised. This time she reached for him, and as her hand settled on his arm, he tried to decipher her touch. He felt no pity for Fryda, and yet he hurt for her. Perhaps she felt this, too, for him. They'd known each other's private pains since childhood—he, whose forced abduction from his home had caused a wound in his mind erasing all memory of his previous life, and she, motherless, with an emotionally distant father, and a mangled hand she thought rendered her unmarriageable, a souvenir of her own youthful folly.

Theow knew Fryda better than anyone—better than her father or the king, or perhaps even her twin brother—but now he trembled as she touched him. He felt exposed and vulnerable in this moment, with this woman, under the weak and pale darkness of a northern summer midnight. Fryda's shaking fingers met the coarse fabric of his sleeve, outlined the hard muscle beneath it, and stroked downward. Theow tensed as she traced the outside of his bicep, the inside of his elbow, the back of his forearm. She skimmed her fingertips over his palm and twined her fingers with his. After a moment, he tightened his grip.

He stood there, lost in the grey storms of her eyes, until a rude shove brought him back to the present. Wiglaf put a protective arm around his sister and drew her away from him, forcing Theow to let go of her hand. "Come on," Wiglaf said, his voice low and serious, "before they tear down the longhouse plank by plank."

"Sounds like they've already started," Theow muttered. He missed the warmth of Fryda's skin as she pushed her brother away and hurried back into the mead-hall.

Seven

Beowulf watched as Wiglaf, scowling and clenching his fists, stormed into the mead-hall. Fryda and a tall, lanky fellow with hair the colour of a mountain sunset slipped in behind him, and Beowulf let himself relax back into his chair.

The young man, dressed in the plain clothing of a servant, melted into the crowd, as invisible as he could be in a room full of fair-haired Geats. Fryda, her cheeks suspiciously flushed, took a pitcher of mead from a dark-skinned kitchen maid with heartfelt thanks and made her way towards the dais, her dark grey eyes sparkling. Beowulf marvelled at her ability to manage everything one-handed so gracefully. He'd noticed she had a habit of hiding her left hand and he worried that the damaged arm would wither from disuse.

Beowulf passed his hand over her hair as she filled his cup and an almost unbearable love overflowed his heart. She was what he imagined a daughter would be like, had he ever had children of his own. He never regretted his lack of progeny except when he saw her. And Weohstan, the insufferable iceberg, had such a treasure and neglected her in favour of the dead.

"How is your night, sweet girl?" he asked.

"Just lovely."

He ruffled Fryda's hair again and laughed when a few gold horsehead pins sprang from the mass of curls on her head, only to be lost between the men's booted feet on the floor. Beowulf took her arm, and held her fast by his side as he stood and pounded upon the long wooden table until he gained everyone's attention.

"My friends!" he shouted, and the last trickling noises in the hall died away. Men and women settled into chairs, onto benches, and all eyes rested on him. He raised his goblet. "I thank you for this most excellent feast, and I especially thank my friend and kinsman Weohstan and his family for hosting the festivities. Weohstan has stood by my side through many battles. Many times we flew into the spear-rush together, until our ash spears and linden shields became so battered, they were more likely to wound us with splinters than save us. We took our tribute in blood and paid our warriors thanks in gold and many rings until the grim battle-play of our youth became quiet and peace descended upon our lands."

Beowulf took Fryda's hand in his own and went on. "We have heard many great boasts and stories tonight, but our gracious lady of the house, Lady Fryda, reminds me that I have one final story to tell before we all get too carried away. Like him." He gestured to a limp, unconscious figure being dragged out by two of Weohstan's guards, and scattered laughter bubbled up from the crowd. He released Fryda and she took her place at the bench by her father, who cast her a brief, cool glance.

Fool, Beowulf thought.

"I bring a mighty gift for my hosts tonight," he continued. He beckoned to one of his retainers, who stepped forward holding a finely worked leather bag trimmed with garnet beads and fur. The king took the bag and put it on the table before Weohstan. It made a solid *thunk* against the wood and a curious murmur rose from the crowd. Grinning, Beowulf untied the strings and opened the bag.

Inside was an enormous goblet, finely worked in gold and silver. He saw Fryda's mouth open in wonder as she leaned forward to examine the beauty and artistry of the cup. Lip-to-lip, the bowl was as wide as the opening of a helmet, and it would take two hands to grip the stem. Well, two normal hands. Beowulf could circle it with one, but he had hands like Woden himself. Its maker had crafted the goblet of pure gold overlaid with silver carvings and set it with the richest jewels Beowulf had ever seen. A deep silver forest cleverly provided cover for a number of bejewelled animals—deer with ruby antlers hid amongst the shrubs, a wolf with sapphire eyes peered out from behind a tree, and some sort of fat bird with a many-jewelled tail perched upon a silver branch. The workmanship of the goblet looked old—perhaps as old as the lone standing stone at the centre of the *burh*—but it still seemed in perfect condition.

"This goblet," King Beowulf continued, "was one of a pair, and it is part of a very old story." Beowulf grinned at the aged *scop*. "Rest your voice, old man, and I shall tell this particular tale." The *scop* bowed and sat, looking happy to be off his feet for the first time that night.

Beowulf had never excelled at storytelling, but he had practised this tale again and again until he could speak it clearly and well without skipping any of the important parts. He cleared his throat, centred the story in his mind, and began.

"Once, long ago, two brothers—twins—were appointed as the personal guards of a mighty king's wife. People far and wide accounted her an exceptional beauty and many evil men tried to steal her away, but the brothers were excellent guards and vanquished all who would attempt to abduct her. For this, the king gave the brothers a rich and powerful gift—a pair of goblets forged by the legendary smith, Weland."

Beowulf lifted the goblet for the entire mead-hall to see, and a rousing cheer rose to the rafters.

"Now, Weland was a friend to dragons and so they gave him a mighty gift—a drop of dragon-magic to enhance his skill. He used this magic when he created the goblets. When set together, the two goblets would fill to the brim with the finest mead, but separated, the goblets sat empty. The brothers were delighted with the gift and drank mead from the goblets every night, toasting the king and queen for their generosity.

"One day, however, an evil man, a sorcerer, sneaked into the king's hall and poured a potion into the brothers' goblets. That night they drank the mead and fell into a sleep as profound as death outside the queen's door. The sorcerer slipped in and stole the queen away. Angered at their failure, the king exiled the two brothers, banishing them from his kingdom and his protection. He allowed each brother to take one belonging with them, and both chose their goblet as a reminder of the king they had loved and the queen they had lost."

Beowulf heard gasps at the mention of exile. Few things, he knew, terrified a Geat like the threat of being cut off from their clan.

"The brothers wandered long and far, seeking any hint of the sorcerer who had destroyed their lives and stolen their king's wife. For years the brothers heard nothing, but one day they came across a village plagued with misfortune. The fields were dry and the crops dead. The warriors were neglectful and the villagers despairing. They cried, "Ever since that evil man took up residence in the tower, our village has suffered and our sheep have sickened and died.""

"The brothers realized that this must be the sorcerer they sought. They drew their weapons and stormed the tower. They kicked down the door and roared inside, where they killed the sorcerer in a ferocious battle and found the queen locked in the dungeons. They freed her and took her back home to their king, and begged to be allowed back into his service."

A few listeners leaned forward, eager for the king's answer. Beowulf almost hated to disappoint them.

"'You have done me a great favour,' the king told them, clasping his beloved wife to his chest, 'but you also failed me. I am overjoyed to have my wife back, but I cannot forget that you allowed her to be stolen in the first place. Therefore, I will allow one of you to come back, but the other must remain in exile, since I cannot trust the two of you together.' "

A collective sigh of disappointment deflated the crowd and they leaned back.

"And so they separated, and every day for the rest of their lives, the brothers drank from their goblets—which, being apart, no longer magically filled with mead—and toasted each other and their king. The brother who stayed lived to be very, very old, and on his deathbed, he gave his eldest son the goblet and told him the story. He asked that his son continue to drink mead from the goblet every night and toast his brother and his king, and the son agreed. Satisfied, the man died, never knowing the fate of his exiled twin brother.

"Well, no one knows what happened to him." Beowulf stroked his white beard. "And therefore the second goblet fell out of time and memory. But this." He fingered the goblet in front of him. "This is said to be the elder brother's goblet, passed down from son to son until my father, Ecgþeow, passed it on to me." He glanced at Wiglaf, who was seated next to Fryda, then rested his eyes on Weohstan. "And as you know, I have no son."

Beowulf traced the outline of a fox on the bowl of the cup. His heart felt hollow. Empty, like the goblet bereft of its mate. He looked at Fryda. "But you are family. You are my blood. And I am getting old." He gave her a broad grin. "Not quite on my deathbed yet, mind you, but it's been worrying me. No family. No heir." His eyes darted to Wiglaf again and his heart fell. Wiglaf's face turned pale and then flushed red. His eyes sparked with a manic fire and in that moment, Beowulf knew Wiglaf envisioned himself as king. Weohstan noticed as well, Beowulf observed, and the boy's father narrowed his eyes.

Beowulf brought his attention back to the crowd. "So, I give you this goblet as my thanks, and ask you to carry on the tradition," he continued. "Drink mead from it every night and toast your brother. And your king."

The mead-hall could hardly contain the revellers' cheers and a sudden, strong emotion gripped him. Beowulf cleared his throat. "This feast tonight celebrates the end of my fiftieth year as king of Geatland. Fifty years…" Beowulf shook his head. "They have passed so fast."

Beowulf saw a man seated near Fryda move abruptly, an involuntary jerk of the body that caught Fryda's attention and made her look at him with some concern. Eadgils, King of Sweden, glanced at Fryda and gave her a tight smile. Beowulf wondered if the old man had fallen asleep during his long story and had just now jerked awake. His eyes seemed tired and he looked drawn and pale.

"But we must also take this moment to remember the fallen and the missed," Beowulf continued. He shot a sly look at Weohstan before turning back to the Swedish king. "Eadgils, your brother, Eanmund will always be remembered as a valiant man and a true hero to my heart."

He saw Fryda go rigid and glance at her father. *Interesting.* She knew something, and he would wager his crown that she had not learned it from her father. Weohstan's face revealed nothing, as if it were carved from stone, but his hands betrayed him. One fist clenched around the hilt of the sword clasped at his waist.

Swicdóm. *Betrayal.*

"Their great deeds and the valour of our youth shall not be forgotten," Beowulf continued, his words pressing against the tension growing in the room. "We shall fill this goblet with mead and drink to all of our brothers on this night of celebration and thankfulness, and toast them and our king." He held a hand out to Fryda and she stood.

* * *

Moving swiftly, Fryda lifted a pitcher of pale golden mead from the table and poured it into the magnificent goblet. She examined the cup as the honeyed liquor splashed into its broad bowl and found herself lost in its silver trees, seeking out hidden animals and finding unexpected treasures—a cluster of ruby mushrooms on the forest floor, a raven with wings of glittering jet on a high branch, a vine of emerald ivy twining around a tree trunk. The workmanship of the piece was astonishing.

She set aside the empty pitcher and tried to lift the massive goblet by its stem. The weight dragged at her arms and a jolt of pain shot through the damaged fingers of her left hand. Fryda's faulty fingers crumpled and she gasped in pain. The full goblet tipped precariously sideways.

"Fryðegifu!" her father snapped as he launched to his feet. Only he ever used her full name. "Be careful!"

Wiglaf, who stood beside Weohstan, did not move.

However, before one drop could spill, another set of hands closed over hers and steadied the bowl, easing the weight of the goblet. Fryda looked up and found herself caught in Theow's solemn green eyes, swimming with untold stories.

Shame and confusion flooded through her—bone-deep, blood-warm, and too, too familiar. She lowered her eyes and blinked them again and again to mask the sudden rush of tears. She wanted to disappear, for the earth to once again open and swallow her whole as it had seven years before, and this time refuse to cast her broken body back out. Theow would see her now for what she was—clumsy, foolish, and broken. A damaged woman in need of saving, a ridiculous girl, an embarrassment to her brother and a constant burden to her father and the king.

Useless, crippled cunt.

She trembled, pulling her shame deep into her body as if to protect it. Her shoulders slumped forward and she curled around her pain like a hedgehog, making herself as small as she could.

Theow tilted his head at her, as if asking her a question, and when she would not meet his eyes he bent his head until he fell into her line of sight. His thumb swept against her fingers where they touched under the bowl of the goblet.

"Well caught!" King Beowulf boomed. He rescued the goblet with one hand and smacked Theow on the back with the other. Theow staggered forward with a grunt but caught himself on the edge of the table. "It's a noble man who rescues a fair damsel from taking a bath in mead."

Fryda's cheeks burned. She glanced at Wiglaf and saw him scowling—not at Beowulf, but at Theow, as if angry at him for stepping in when he did not.

Beowulf glanced at Weohstan. "What shall his reward be, my lord, for coming to the aid of your fair daughter?"

A frisson of fear tickled Fryda's spine. Her father, unlike many wealthy landowners, never gave gifts to his slaves, even for extraordinary service, but Beowulf had just trapped him into an unwanted kindness.

"A ring for Theow, valiant hero-slave of my house," Weohstan decreed, though he looked displeased.

"Excellent!" Beowulf said. He swivelled this way and that, looking for his pile of gifts and favours. It had been much depleted throughout the night, but he managed to find a rich, plain gold ring and turned back to the slave. "Theow of...wait." Beowulf squinted at Weohstan. "You have a slave named...Slave?"

Fryda saw the blood drain from Theow's face, but Beowulf did not notice. Or perhaps he did not care.

"I must hear this story," said the king, putting the goblet back on the table and seating himself. The room seemed to shift as all eyes turned to Weohstan, who took a drink from his small cup before he began to speak.

"Twenty years ago, my king, you gifted me this estate, Eceweall, for deeds done with you in the battle-storms of our youth."

"I remember it well," Beowulf chuckled.

"To run it, I needed builders and horsemen, and my wife, Ielfeta, needed an entire fleet of kitchen and serving staff. So, we took a trip to Brycg Stowe. There were plenty of Britons for sale, but it so happened a ship had just come in, and it had a whole gaggle of freckled, red-headed children on it," Weohstan continued. Theow stared at the ground and did not move.

"So, I inspected the boys and this one seemed fitter than most." He gestured to Theow. "Tall, strong, with the reddest head of hair I'd ever seen. He had a terrible wound on his face and head, however—a burn, half-healed and grotesque, so they were asking less for him than for the others. I think they worried he might die. But I knew Ielfeta could heal the wound and it would not interfere with his ability to work, so I bought him. Well. At that time, of course, he didn't speak our language but gibbered in some barbaric Celtic tongue. I told him, '*Cnap, ðu eart nu theow Geates*' but he didn't seem to understand. I bent down, looked him right in the eye, and repeated myself. 'Boy, you are a slave of the Geats now.' "

Weohstan looked down his nose at Theow. "Didn't understand a word I said, of course. I kept pointing to him and saying 'Theow! Theow!' hoping he'd understand his place as a slave. Eventually, he pointed to himself and repeated 'Theow' and I thought I'd got the point across. Well, no. It seems I hadn't."

Beowulf now leaned forward, entranced by the story. Theow had not moved. Fryda saw Hild cross her arms and scowl. Her brother stared at Theow with a smug smile.

"I brought him home and put him right to work in the kitchens. A month later Ielfeta went to check on him and she asked him his name."

Fryda saw Theow's jaw clench.

"He told her 'Theow.' 'No, no,' she tried to explain to him. 'Theow is what you are.' She wanted to know his name. He never offered her any answer but 'Theow,' so that was what we called him. He's never once given us another name."

Beowulf howled with laughter and the rest of the company followed suit. Fryda burned with anger and shame. She saw Hild look at her feet, her face carefully composed, but Fryda knew she was also furious for her friend.

"My boy, you deserve a ring for that story alone." Beowulf stood again and moved to stand in front of Theow. He put the fine gold ring in Theow's hand and closed his fingers around it. "Here you are, for valorous deeds and a steadfast heart. And as recompense for my laughing at your pain and misfortune, I hereby name you my thane for a day—my trusted retainer. For your first duty, I task you with looking after the Lady Fryda." Beowulf shot her a mischievous look. "She can't seem to stay out of trouble on her own."

Beowulf lifted the goblet and presented it to Weohstan. "My gift to you, my friend," he said. "I hope you will always have sons in your family to carry on the tradition."

Fryda huffed to herself at that, and Beowulf heard her. "And daughters!" he laughed, putting his hand on her cheek as he kissed the top of her head. "And, of course, daughters."

Weohstan took the goblet, and if he found it heavy did not show it. "I thank you, my king," he said, bowing. "It shall have a place of honour here in the hall."

The Curse

Memory still shackles Fýrdraca to a sleep that grants her no rest.

She remembers the Lone Survivor holding his treasure, turning it around and around in his hands—a goblet forged by Weland the Smith, son of giants and blacksmith of legend. The smith had fashioned the cup of gold and silver with intricate hunting scenes twining around the bowl and down the thick stem. Trees and vines, wrought in silver, camouflaged stags, pheasants, and wolves from the hunters, and garnets, emeralds and rubies glittered from every angle. The cup, large and heavy, took two hands to hold. It was beautiful, and the sight of it filled the Lone Survivor with unimaginable sorrow.

The goblet was one of a pair, his most prized possession, for his beloved brother had the keeping of its mate. He always kept his promise to drink from the goblet every day and toast his brother and his king. He had even drunk from this goblet at his own wedding two years earlier, and his thoughts strayed to how his young and beautiful wife—now burnt to cinders along with the child she had carried in her belly—had caught the mead from its rim with her full lips and kissed him, laughing and tasting of sweet golden honey.

The Lone Survivor knelt at the edge of Fýrdraca's crater and in a low, terrible voice he cursed the treasure hoard. "Now, earth, hold what earls once held and heroes can no more," he said, and the cave threw his words back to him in ghostly, mocking echoes, as if matching him curse for curse. "The gods curse you to the deepest reaches of wyrmsele *for what you have done. May no man profit from your value, no woman glory in your beauty, no warrior benefit from your protection, no king rejoice in your gift-power. May the serpents taint you with their poison and may the stink of death follow you into eternity.*" And so saying, he let the goblet fall from his fingers.

It fell soundlessly through the void until it hit the towering pile of gold that covered Fýrdraca's body like a second skin. She felt the impact. It should have been small...a trifle...but the cup had become heavy with the Lone Survivor's sorrow, with his curse, and so it nearly crushed her. The curse seeped into the mound of treasure and her body responded. Her blood flared with a fiery heat, which soon melted the precious metals against her sides. Molten rivulets of gold and silver trickled into the tiny spaces between her scales where it fused with her hide, forming brilliant, reticulated armour across her body, head, and wings. Trapped within the Lone Survivor's curse, she had plummeted into this uneasy sleep, as a strong tide will pull down the unwary swimmer, and there she stayed, unknown and unseen.

Eight

A small, far-off noise woke Theow from an uneasy slumber, plagued with dreams of blood and fire. A cry, or a whimper, worn and faded with the distance it had to travel. He stilled, cocked his head, and listened. He heard only silence broken by snorts and snores and the skittering of what might be a mouse having a feast of its own on the leavings scattered across the floor. Hearing nothing else alarming, Theow started righting benches and gathering unbroken crockery from the floor and tables, taking care not to disturb anyone.

Not that it mattered, he mused, as he accidentally stepped on a drooling warrior's wrist. The man didn't even twitch as Theow lost his balance and stumbled, accidentally kicking him in the side. How much mead had these people drunk during the feast?

He heard it again, a sound so soft and faint he could almost convince himself he'd imagined it. He could not tell who or what had made it, but something about it troubled him. It was a noise steeped in pain or fear, like an injured mouse trapped by a cat or a frightened child waking alone from a nightmare.

He wondered if he made such noises when he dreamed at night, alone on his pallet of straw and thin blankets. Theow passed through the arched doorway, which for some reason had remained open all night, and scanned the *burh* for any sign of disturbance.

He heard it again, now louder and more desperate. Pain, fear, and—this time—anger. A woman's voice, stained with panic and outrage, escaped one of the larger buildings that housed Weohstan's family.

The house where Fryda slept.

Theow broke into a run. It never occurred to him to go for help; he didn't think to alert the guards. Only one thought drove him forward as he raced through the muddy paths and grassy hillocks.

He had to get to her.

As Theow hurtled towards the wooden building, he heard her scream again. Her voice sounded muffled, as if something blocked her mouth. Theow hit the door at full speed, body cocked so his shoulder bore the brunt of the impact. The door burst apart and he stumbled through the foyer and into a large, high-timbered room.

As his eyes adjusted to the dim light, Theow saw three men. Two were strangers to him, rough and dirty and not part of Weohstan's guard. Their bodies looked weak and emaciated, and their beards spilled in twisted mats down their chests. Their teeth, now bared at him, were brown and broken, and a strong stench of sour sweat and alcohol wafted towards him. *Exiles*, Theow thought, and a thread of fear thrummed through him. It bloomed into near-panic when he saw the small, still figure the two strangers held a between them—Fryda, trapped and helpless in their grip. And the third man...

Fægebeorn.

In his bandaged hand, the archer held a long, wickedly sharp *seax* to Fryda's breast, bared through a ragged tear in her nightdress. The blade gleamed and the polished metal was inscribed with runes. The flat of the blade ran straight and true up to its centre, where it sheared off at the top and canted down to a wicked, sharp point, which pressed a dimple into Fryda's flesh. Theow could see a series of bruises, like fingerprints, vivid against her white skin where Fægebeorn had grasped her breast the night before. A gag bound Fryda's mouth, partially obscuring a small trickle of blood on her chin. Her hair hung loose, tangled and wild, and one of the filthy men held her by a handful of curls at the nape of her neck. A cut on her cheek and smears of blood on her bare chest and stomach showed where Fægebeorn's *seax* had nicked and sliced shallow ribbons into her skin as she'd struggled. Theow understood now why she stayed so still. She couldn't move her head, but her gaze shifted to meet his and she reminded him of a panicked horse, eyes rolling in fear.

Fægebeorn glanced at Theow but kept the blade on his hostage. His eyes glittered and his face shone with a greasy sheen of sweat. His nose had long since stopped bleeding, though it had not been set and still bowed at the break, and he could scarcely grip the *seax* with his two broken fingers. Lurid, ugly bruises ringed both his eyes, and his teeth were still smeared with blood. He looked mad with pain, fever, and hurt pride.

"This doesn't concern you, slave," he said, his voice low and rough. "Turn around and walk away."

"That's not going to happen," Theow said, his voice calm. Inside, however, a thousand ants crawled under his skin. He stepped forward and stopped as his foot kicked an empty cup on the floor. It skittered across the floor, clattering. "Let her go. I don't want to hurt you."

"You can't hurt me." A drop of blood, shockingly red against Fryda's pale, freckled skin, appeared at the point of the blade as Fægebeorn pushed it harder against her breast. Her eyes closed, but she didn't make a sound. "Soon I'll be rich as a king and you'll all be dead, but first I need to take care of some unfinished business right here."

"You'll not be hurting her." Theow had no weapon—had never owned so much as a knife—but he'd tear Fægebeorn apart with his bare hands if he had to. His body tensed, ready to leap.

Fægebeorn turned towards Theow and fumbled the *seax* through his fingers. As the weapon fell, the impact silenced by the rushes on the floor, Fryda took advantage of her captors' distraction. With her good hand, she jabbed her fist into one man's groin while bringing her foot down hard on the other's instep. In unison the first groaned, the second yelped, and both loosened their hold enough for her to wrench herself away and take a small step forward. She hunched her shoulder to protect her left side and drove her other fist, hard, into Fægebeorn's already broken nose. The injured archer staggered back.

Not so helpless after all. Theow raised his eyebrows, impressed, as he dodged out of Fægebeorn's path.

Fægebeorn made a terrible sound, full of animal pain and broken, gurgling moans. He cupped his hands over his battered face and fell to his knees. Fryda managed to kick the *seax* towards Theow before the other two men recovered enough to seize her, their hands violent and bruising. Fryda screamed as one yanked on her hair, drawing her head back and exposing her throat.

Theow dived for the *seax*. With one swift movement he swept it up and lunged at the man with his fist in Fryda's hair. Theow's mind went blank, his movements instinctive. He could only feel terror and rage churning through him, spurring him to act.

The blade slid into the man's gut. Theow let go of the hilt and leapt back as the exile released Fryda and looked down at himself in surprise. His back slammed up against the wall and he slid down, his breath coming in gasps, his eyes glazed over with fear and pain.

Fryda wasted no time. She twisted out of the remaining man's grip and clambered up onto his back. Wrapping one arm around his throat in a tight headlock, she gripped his waist with her legs and threw all her weight backwards with a vicious wrench of his neck. The exile seized her arms, trying to throw her off but she clung to him, pulling hard at his neck and forcing his head further back. The man gasped, choked, and scrabbled at whatever parts of her he could reach, but she did not yield. Fryda groaned at the strain on her weakened muscles and Theow saw sweat break out on her forehead, but still she refused to yield. Finally, her captor fell to one side just as she jerked his head in the opposite direction, and Theow heard a sickening *crack* as the exile's neck broke. Fryda released him as he fell, and leapt clear. She looked at the man's corpse, her entire body shaking and complexion a touch green, and clutched the ragged edges of her dress against her bleeding body.

Theow stared at her, his jaw sagging. "Did…did Bryce teach you that?" he asked, his voice feeble. It would have taken incredible strength for such a tiny woman to snap the man's neck like that.

Fryda clawed the gag out of her mouth and gasped with her first full breath. "No," she said. She gulped in great lungfuls of air. "No."

Theow drank her in, marvelling that she was not grievously hurt, not dead. She had a small cut on her cheek, which would soon form a bruise, and her lower lip was torn and bleeding, but the wounds were superficial. However, something about her was a little off, and it wasn't just the torn nightdress and shallow wounds. Her grey eyes had a glassy look, her pupils constricted to tiny pinpricks. She swayed on her feet, as if slightly dizzy, and her speech was slow.

Theow looked at the exile, noting the awkward angle of his broken neck. "I had no idea you were that strong," he said.

"I…I don't think I am." Fryda stared at him with wide eyes. "I don't know what happened. But something…*something* happened." She made a helpless gesture and put her hand to her forehead.

Fægebeorn, still on the floor, distracted them with small, pained noises. His voice overflowed his lips in groans and gurgles, drowning in the blood coursing from his nose and mouth.

Theow stalked up to the man he had impaled and, ignoring his feeble groan, pulled the *seax* from his stomach. Without hesitation, he seized Fægebeorn by the hair, yanked his chin up and slit his throat from ear to ear. The room filled with the smell of copper and urine, and Theow flung the body down. His chest worked like Bryce's bellows and his stomach turned as he stared at the first kill of his life, but one thought dominated all others.

Fryda was alive, and she was safe.

Nine

As Fryda watched Fægebeorn's lifeblood rush from the gash in his throat, her chest clenched and her stomach twisted. She clutched her torn nightdress to her body and tried to stop trembling.

After Fægebeorn rattled out his last breath, Fryda looked up at Theow and they stared at each other over the two corpses. The only noises in the room were their laboured breathing and the dying exile's groans as he tried to staunch the blood seeping from his stomach. Fryda pushed hair out of her eyes with a trembling hand.

Before either of them could speak, another man burst through the doorway, sliding on the rushes in his haste. Theow whipped around, bloodied knife at the ready, but then Fryda saw him relax. Wiglaf, still in his day-clothes, regained his balance and surveyed the scene with wild eyes.

"I heard you scream," he said to Fryda, his voice cracking. His bloodshot eyes and dark, messy hair told a story of excess and interrupted pleasure. He had what looked like fresh stains on his tunic and Fryda wondered if he was still drunk from the night before—or perhaps newly-drunk with morning mead. "What... oh." He surveyed the mess of blood and bodies. "Oh, by the gods." Wiglaf gaped at her, appalled, taking in her torn gown, her bruises, her bloody lip. "Are you well? Are you hurt?"

Fryda wiped blood from her face and shook her head, though now the moment of crisis had passed she began to feel the sharpness of her cuts and the deep aches of her bruises. Theow stepped towards her. "May I...?" he asked, gesturing to the gag still knotted around her neck. She nodded again and he used the bloody knife to cut away the rough fabric, careful not to nick her skin. He felt warm and close, so she leaned into him, just a tiny bit, and he did not move away.

"So," Wiglaf said, his voice wavering. "Tell me what happened here."

Fryda pulled her sleeve over her hand, and when she spoke her voice was rough and dry. "I got tired so I left the feast, and I came straight here. I fell asleep, I don't know for how long, but a noise woke me up. It was mostly dark, but I saw the shadows of men in my room, so I tried to sit up. I felt...dizzy and strange." She shook her head, as if to chase away the remnants of her confusion. "But then someone gagged me and put a blade to my throat." Fryda put a hand up to a tiny blood-dotted cut in the skin of her throat. Wiglaf and Theow's faces darkened in identical expressions of fury. "They wrestled me out of bed," Fryda continued, "and got rough with me...as you see." Her voice wobbled and she clutched her ruined nightdress closer.

Wiglaf's face turned ash-pale. "Did they...?"

"No." Fryda flicked her eyes towards Theow. "They didn't have the chance."

She saw Wiglaf relax. Theow, however, did not.

"It...it was Fægebeorn." She looked at his lifeless body and pressed closer to Theow. Fægebeorn's blood seeped away from the gaping slash in his throat and soaked into the rushes beneath him. "He babbled something about revenge and getting rich and how we would all be dead soon. He'd gone mad."

"I see that." Wiglaf nudged Fægebeorn's body with his toe. "I confess, I didn't expect him to be back on his feet that fast." He grimaced and shook his head. "I didn't think he'd come after you. I should have made sure, though. I am sorry."

"You...you didn't have him locked up when you removed

him from the hall?" She gaped at him. How could he have been so careless?

Wiglaf scowled. "I didn't think it necessary. I assumed you'd hurt him too much."

Fryda flinched. "I see," she said, and wrapped her arms around herself.

She saw Theow glare at Wiglaf. "Clan law clearly dictates what to do with men who touch a woman without consent," he growled.

Wiglaf's mouth tightened and his face darkened. "Listen, you miserable cur, she doesn't need..."

Just then, a feeble moan interrupted him. All three looked at the injured man, still alive but clutching his gut, trying to keep his blood inside his body. "You will all pay," he said, his voice thin and feeble. "You will all suffer. Soon. The blood-debt will be paid."

"There is no blood-debt when blood is drawn in self-defence, you *sott*." Wiglaf squinted at the dying man. "Clearly Fægebeorn attacked first."

The exile made a choking sound and blood bubbled at his lips. Laughter, Fryda realized, and her stomach turned. "You don't know," the man gasped. "You...cannot..." He fell silent then, his body going slack and his hand still pressed against his bleeding belly.

"Did you have to kill him?" Wiglaf asked, his voice hard and irritated. "We could have got some information from him, at least."

"Theow didn't have much choice," Fryda said, her voice cold, and she nestled even closer. She still shivered, so he put his arm around her, his hand at the small of her back. "Fægebeorn would have killed me."

"Well, Fryda killed that one herself." Theow pointed to the dead man with the broken neck. "She was quite brilliant." He squeezed her and her trembling eased.

Wiglaf looked at them, his expression unreadable.

"Who are they?" Wiglaf examined the two ruffians. "I don't recognize them."

"Exiles, I figured," Theow said. "There are always some hanging about, willing to do anything for some food or a bit of gold."

"On the roads, certainly." Wiglaf frowned, clearly troubled. "How did exiles get inside the *burh*, though?"

"Fægebeorn let them in?" Fryda suggested. Now the excitement was over, her head started to throb, her cuts stung, and her body felt leaden and heavy.

"They'd still have to get past the guards, and father would have been notified. He would have told me."

"Do you think maybe one of the guards...?"

"No." Wiglaf uttered the word like a proclamation, but his worried expression told a different story. "No. I...I'll have to talk to father about this. He might know them, though they are not criminals exiled from our household. I am present at every trial and would recognize them if they came from here."

Fryda averted her eyes and shuddered. Exile meant more than homelessness or vulnerability. It meant a stripping of identity. Everyone in the clan had obligations and protections, even slaves and bonded servants like Theow and Hild. Everyone knew their status and understood their roles, and the clan accepted them, offered them a home. They had a purpose and could claim the lord's protection and care. Each person was a small part of the greater body. People who committed crimes or terrible deeds were cut like tumours from the body, separated forever from their heart, their clan, their lifeblood, before they could infect it. Exiles lost their personhood and were doomed to walk the earth like wraiths, and this often made them desperate and violent.

The bleeding man stirred and Fryda jumped, clutching Theow closer. The wounded exile spoke again, his voice hardly more than a breath of air. "You will...all...die..."

Wiglaf knelt by the dying man's side. "What?" he said. "What is going to happen?"

The exile remained silent.

"I don't think we'll get much more out of him." Wiglaf scrubbed his face, looking exhausted. "We need to figure out how we're going to explain all this."

"What's to explain?" Theow asked. Fryda felt his hand rub her back. "They attacked Fryda. She defended herself, and I helped."

Wiglaf looked at him, his eyes level and cool. "And what were you doing here in the first place?" he asked. "Why are you in her room?"

Theow froze and Fryda shot her brother a look of exasperation. "The same reason you are, you daft arse." She winced at a sharp lance of pain and put her fingers up to her split lip, which had cracked open and started to bleed again. "He heard me scream and came to help."

Wiglaf's eyes narrowed as he looked at Fryda and Theow. They stood so close no light could come between them, and Fryda realized with a start that her arm had crept around Theow's waist and her good hand clutched at his tunic. Wiglaf frowned, shook his head as if to clear it, and then relaxed. "All right." He looked around the room, "But I think we're going to have to come up with a better story if we want to save Theow. We should say I got here first and dispatched these men myself."

"What?" Fryda was outraged and she tightened her arm around Theow. "That's unfair! Theow killed Fægebeorn. A man gets credit for his kills."

Wiglaf sighed. "Fryda, a *warrior* gets credit for his kills. Theow is a slave and he's in your room at a suspicious hour."

She grew rigid with rage and Theow looked at her with concern. "How *dare*...!"

"How dare I speak the truth? It doesn't matter why he's here, or that he helped you. Father will assume the worst and punish both of you. But especially Theow. You know how he is."

Fryda hesitated. "But...but you didn't *do* anything," she protested. "You know the traditions as well as I do. You cannot take credit for another man's kills."

"This was not a battle and Theow isn't a warrior," Wiglaf said.

"But..."

Wiglaf made a sound of exasperation. "All right, fine. Here. Give me the *seax*." He wiggled his fingers at Theow, who handed it over without comment. Wiglaf went to the dying man and without preamble buried the blade through his neck, just below his ears. The exile let out one soft, surprised noise and then went still forever.

"There. Now I won't be lying. I killed that one. Will that satisfy your precious principles?" Wiglaf snarled. Fryda stared at Wiglaf in surprise. She knew her brother had a temper, but she had never seen him abandon it so quickly. Wiglaf ran his fingers through his already dishevelled hair, visibly trying to regain his composure. "Look, I'm sorry, but I'm trying to save you both from certain trouble," he said. "If Father saw Theow in your room, and knew he killed one of his warriors, he could exile Theow and you would never see him again. I assume you don't want that to happen."

"But if we explained that he heard me..."

Theow gave her a squeeze. "It's probably best this way," he murmured. "I don't need credit. It's enough that you are safe."

Fryda looked up at him, troubled. "It isn't right."

Theow gave her a rueful smile and she realized she was again being naive. Theow's entire life had been a long series of much more painful injustices than this.

Fryda made a disgusted noise. "Eish, fine. You're right, I know, but I don't have to like it. Now if you both don't mind, I need to put on some clothes."

"Some of your wounds need tending," Theow said. Drawing her attention to them set them throbbing again and she clenched her teeth against the pain.

"I'll find Eadith," Fryda said. "She can patch me up. She's done it before." She reluctantly left the circle of his arms and moved away. Instantly she felt cold and unhappy. She went to her wooden chest at the foot of her bed and drew out a clean shift. "You should leave," she said to Theow. She swallowed. "I hate to admit it, but Wiglaf is right. You can't be caught in here. If Father even *thinks* you touched a woman of his house, he'll cut off your hands and exile you without question."

"Woden's beard, yes he would," Wiglaf said, moving towards the door. "I'll go get the guards. You'd best be gone by the time we get back, Theow. In fact, I'm surprised they aren't here already. Where is everyone?"

"Asleep in the longhouse," Theow said. "It was strange. Everyone just sort of fell asleep in the middle of whatever they were doing."

Fryda looked up at him and frowned. "What?"

"I didn't think that was normal." Theow shook his head. "I thought maybe it had something to do with what Hild told me this morning."

Fryda's attention sharpened. "What did she say?"

Theow told Fryda and Wiglaf about the theft of the white poppy, honey, and verbena. Fryda's heart plummeted as he spoke, but she watched Wiglaf's face closely and saw no flicker of reaction, no hint of guilt. She let out a silent sigh of relief. He hadn't stolen the drug.

"Hild said she was going to talk to you about it," Theow said. "I guess she didn't have the chance."

"No. We had a busy night and I barely saw her."

Theow picked up the small cup from the floor. "Perhaps the stolen white poppy syrup was in the mead."

Fryda inhaled sharply. "I drank that just before I went to

bed," she said. "It made me feel funny. I thought I was just tired from the celebration, but…"

Theow sniffed the few drops that remained in the cup and shrugged. "I guess there's no way to tell now if it's been drugged, but…that might explain why everyone in the mead-hall fell asleep so abruptly."

"But why would someone do that?" Fryda wondered.

Theow looked at the bodies on the floor. "I can think of one reason," he said quietly.

Fryda followed his gaze and then shivered.

"So why were you awake, Theow?" Wiglaf asked. He regarded Theow with narrowed eyes. "Why were you the *only* one who was awake?"

Theow regarded him right back, his gaze unwavering. "Probably because I didn't drink any of the mead."

"And I wonder why that is," Wiglaf said. His voice was mild, but Fryda heard the unsaid accusation.

"Probably because I was not allowed to," Theow said, "and I did not relish the thought of the beating I would get if I disobeyed."

"Right," Wiglaf said, his voice tight. "We keep this to ourselves. Do you understand me? We have no proof the mead was drugged. I'll investigate, of course, but until I find something specific, we all keep our mouths shut. And Theow was never here."

Fryda opened her mouth to protest again, but quailed under Wiglaf's fierce glare.

"I mean it, Fryda. Not a word. Promise me."

Fryda hesitated, and then nodded.

"Good. Now, I'll head up to the longhouse and try to wake someone up. If they truly are all drugged, it may take a while."

"I saw the guards at the western gate on my way here," Theow said. "If all else fails, you can get them."

Wiglaf's eyes moved back and forth between Theow and Fryda, and he strode from the room without speaking again.

Fryda had no idea what to do or say. She looked around the room, her gaze touching everything but Theow. She pretended to examine the familiar rich furnishings, the raised bed and feather mattress covered with furs, the polished wooden chest, and the fresh, sweet rushes strewn across the floor. A stout table held a pitcher and basin, as well as a beautiful vase of flowers and a bowl of fresh fruit. Tapestries hung on the walls and the last embers of yesterday's fire glowed in the fire pit. Splintered pieces of the thin wooden door hung from the damaged hinges, and a single window lay high up one wall, illuminating a strip of the room with one stark shaft of light while shrouding the rest in shadow. Dust motes danced in the light, disturbed by the violence of the morning's activity, and Fryda found it difficult to focus on anything but that hypnotic, discordant movement. The bed was rumpled, the coverlet flung to one side. She clutched her torn nightdress and imagined the unimaginable, her stomach ice-cold at the thought of what could have been.

"Are you going to be all right?" Theow asked Fryda. She wanted to say no, to ask him not to leave her alone, but she knew Wiglaf was right. He could not be found here.

"I'm fine," she said. She tried to brace her voice with iron. "It's not like I haven't seen corpses before."

"Yes, but they're the dead bodies of men who assaulted and tried to murder you."

"I...yes." Fryda twisted the fresh nightdress in her hands as she held it against her body. "I haven't thanked you," she said. She stared at the floor. How did one thank someone for saving their body? Their life? "For coming to help me. If you hadn't come when you did..." She swallowed and did not finish the thought.

"Fryda." Theow didn't move to leave, and she did not press

him to. They had a few minutes, surely, before Wiglaf could wake the guards.

They looked at each other for the space of a few breaths, both unmoving, both silent. He looked so beautiful with his sharp cheekbones and gentle eyes. He didn't seem to know what to do with his large hands, so he kept twisting them, and she found the nervous movement endearing. Her body grew tense as a bowstring while the silence stretched between them. Theow looked as if he were waging an internal war, hovering between choices but unable to make a decision. In that moment she would have given everything she owned to know his thoughts. His eyes roamed her face as if he would find the answer to an unasked question there.

She could not say who moved first, but suddenly she was in his arms, her head tucked under his chin, his cheek pressed against her hair. They gripped each other, and when Theow tried to back away to keep from pressing against her wounds, Fryda burrowed closer, not allowing him to retreat. So he held her and she relished the feeling of his body against hers. His heartbeat, quick and determined, fluttered against her cheek. Almost immediately, however, she pushed him away.

"Go," she said, averting her face. "Go now, Theow. You need to leave before Wiglaf comes back with the guards." She picked up the gown she had dropped and backed away.

"All right." He closed his hands into fists as if to prevent himself from reaching for her again. "If you're sure…"

"Go!" she insisted and turned her back to him. If she had to watch him leave, she would not bear it.

She heard Theow move towards the door and then stop, as if hoping she'd turn to look at him again.

But she did not, and so he slid through the broken doorway and slowly made his way back to the kitchens, unseen and unheard as the household stirred and wakened with the new morning.

Ten

Fryda headed towards the smithy. Not even the early morning sunrise, saturated with pinks and oranges and rose-tinted clouds could lift her spirits. Bryce would be working the forge and she felt the need to learn a few new fighting moves. She wanted to hit something.

Fryda saw billows of smoke rising from the forge and crept in so as not to interrupt the blacksmith. The forge was her favourite place in the *burh*. The open-built room let in the light, and airy breezes swept away the smoke and fumes of molten iron. Here Bryce designed his masterpieces, from the heaviest armour to the most delicate jewelled ornaments. The smooth, polished surface of the petrified tree stump that served as his anvil had for decades stood strong beneath the fall of his hammers and had witnessed the birth of Bryce's most beautiful creations. Fryda's eyes went to the sword hanging above the hearth, as they always did, and she wondered again about its story. It was far too old for Bryce to have crafted it himself.

Bryce stood at the fire, concentrating on some bit of iron. He freed what looked like the hilt of a sword from a clay mould, and Fryda watched, entranced, as he placed it back into the hearth where the heat of glowing coals softened the metal. He waited a few moments, and then withdrew it with a pair of sturdy tongs. With a sharp tool, he pressed patterns into the heated iron all the way around the edge of the crossguard, and she noticed that he'd already decorated the pommel with silver-gilt plating in a lovely cross-knot pattern.

When the hilt had dimmed from bright red to dark, Bryce plunged it into a barrel of water, which hissed as the hot iron brought it to an instant boil. The steam pearled in Bryce's hair, making it damp and curly, and his beard dripped with condensation and sweat. He looked up, saw Fryda watching him, and grinned at her.

"Well met, Sunbeam," he said.

"Greetings, Weland," she responded, and he laughed at the nickname she had given him as a child. Weland the Smith was the heroic blacksmith of legend—sired by giants, friend of dragons, and a genius at the forge who crafted masterworks in iron for kings, as well as beautiful rings set with gems in gold and silver. *And, according to Uncle Beowulf, magical gold and silver goblets*, she thought. Bryce had once been a great warrior for another clan, she knew, but had been welcomed by her father into the Waegmunding clan around the time of Fryda's birth. He had never once lifted a sword in service for her father.

"I've seen enough of battle and death," he'd once told her. "Now I can make shoes for the horses, dress fastenings for the women, belt buckles for the men, arms and armour for the warriors, and tools for the lord. I can be useful without having to kill." A shadow passed over his face then, and Fryda had never again asked him about his days as a warrior.

She glanced at the hilt Bryce had just made. "That's lovely. Who is it for?"

"The king wants it as a gift for one of the clan leaders," Bryce said, removing it from the water and placing it on the petrified stump. "Apparently he won some great battle or something."

Fryda chuckled. "That could be any of them." She paused for a moment before she added, "I think I saw your work last night. A *seax*, inscribed with runes."

"Did it look like a small dagger?" he asked. "Or was it bigger, like a short-sword?"

"Dagger," she said. "Gorgeous piece, looked almost new."

"Must have been the blade I made for Olaf. His reward for the victory at the Battle of Maldon. That's the only *seax* I've made in a good while. Where did you see it?"

Fryda wondered how Fægebeorn had got his hands on the *seax*, and then remembered Olaf, long after the boasting contest with her brother, had passed out on the floor. Anyone could have stolen his trousers, let alone his weapon without him noticing. She did not want to admit that a blade Bryce forged had hurt her, so she said, "At the feast, though I think it's possible someone nicked it from him."

Bryce laughed. "Well, I inscribed his name on it, so he shouldn't have too much trouble getting it back, if he finds out who took it."

Fryda paused. What *had* happened to the *seax*? She hadn't thought to ask in the general chaos and fuss. She'd last seen it in Wiglaf's hand, when he killed the second exile.

Bryce stepped closer and peered at her face, frowning. "What happened to you, Sunbeam?" He gestured to her lower lip, still red and swollen, though it had begun to heal over. "Did someone lay hands on you?"

Fryda's anxiety and restlessness returned. She had forgotten for a moment, while she watched Bryce work, that there were such things as fear and pain and problems to solve.

"Yes," she admitted, "though I have you to thank that nothing worse happened. I used some of the knowledge you taught me."

Bryce's face hardened as he studied her wounded face. "Is he dead?"

"Yes."

"Shame. I would have welcomed the opportunity to usher him out of this life myself. Did Wiglaf do the deed?"

"No. Theow," Fryda said. Bryce's eyebrows shot up to his hairline.

"Did he now?" The blacksmith smiled. "I think I'll be making him something special as thanks for that. So what happened?"

She told him everything. She described how she had defended herself against Fægebeorn in the mead-hall and the attack on her that had left her room littered with dead bodies. She told him of the drugged wine, her anger at Wiglaf for taking credit for Theow's kills, and about the exiles' cryptic warnings.

Bryce's expression turned sober. "Fægebeorn. I knew he would be trouble. I should have taken care of him yesterday when I had the chance." Fryda looked at him questioningly, and he shook his head. "Eadith and I happened upon him bothering Olaf and Bjorn. It's nothing. Did you tell your father about this?"

"Wiglaf said he'll tell him later today. Father wants to see him." Fryda balled her hand into a fist. "Of course, he won't be telling Father the truth," she said bitterly. "This was a perfect way to show him I'm not as weak as he thinks I am, but I can't even let him know."

"Sunbeam." Bryce rested one enormous hand against her cheek. "You must understand something about your father. No, listen," he said as Fryda attempted to pull away. She did not want to hear excuses for him. Bryce reached down and touched the sleeve of her dress where it covered her twisted hand. "When you were hurt, your father nearly went out of his mind with worry."

Fryda blinked. "What? No. After that first night, he never even came to see me."

Bryce shook his head. "You don't remember because you were fighting for your life, oblivious to everything around you. I visited you every day, but Weohstan never once left your side. For three days and nights he sat by your bed and watched you suffer. Eadith had to bring his meals to him, and he ordered a chamber pot brought to the room because he would not even leave to use the necessary."

"I...I didn't know that." An aching, bewildered flare of hope sprang to life in her chest. "Why didn't you tell me before?"

"Because Weohstan told me not to."

The hope died as quickly as it had appeared.

"Believe me, I wanted to tell you, but if he found out, he would have sent me away and I couldn't let that happen." Bryce hooked his hand behind her neck and drew her in for a fatherly kiss on her forehead. "I had too much to lose here."

"Why wouldn't he want me to know?" Fryda asked. Perhaps if she had known he cared for her, she could have been more patient with him, more understanding.

Bryce let her go and crossed his arms across his massive chest. "Weohstan considers his emotions a weakness and he didn't want you to see them. I think when your mother died...I think he became afraid to love anyone the way he loved her. If he distanced himself, he thought it would not hurt as much." Bryce chuckled. "Clearly that didn't work. As soon as he thought he might lose you, he went almost mad with fear and grief. But he still could not let you see it, or even let himself feel it for too long." He cocked at eyebrow at her. "I assure you, though, that despite his coldness, the thought of losing you is unbearable to him."

"Huh." A lifetime of neglect still made Fryda sceptical, but this was a side of her father she had never known.

"As for Fægebeorn," he said, "you did well, as did young Theow. That young man has a good head on his shoulders, and he knows how to use it. In a different life he would have made a fine warrior."

He saw Fryda's expression and put a hand on her shoulder. "I know. It is not fair, and you feel he has been robbed of his honour as well as his kills. However, I would wager that this matters not at all to him. Am I right?"

Fryda nodded. Her body started to tremble again.

"He only wanted to keep you safe, and he did that." Bryce gave her a piercing look. "I've always thought our Theow was a bit sweet on you." He sobered. "But Fryda, I am troubled by these events. You need to be careful. If those men meant to ransom you, you may still be in danger."

Images of the *seax* slicing through her skin and blood welling from her body flashed through her mind, and her breath grew thick and difficult. After the guards had disposed of the bodies and servants had cleaned up the blood, Fryda, her body aching and exhausted, had tried to get some sleep. But she lay awake, jumping at every sound and fancying she could still smell blood, despite the thorough cleaning of her bedchamber. When she did sleep, she dreamed of knives and pain and hard, cruel hands, and she woke again and again to aching wounds and bruises. Towards daybreak her dreams shifted, and the hurtful hands gentled, gathering her close against a strong, wiry body. Theow. She clung to him and then it was his hands in her hair, gentle against her stinging scalp, and his mouth on her lip, torn and bloody from Fægebeorn's teeth. Her body ached in different ways now, straining with want and need. But then Wiglaf appeared next to them, *seax* in hand, and before she could speak, he had thrust the blade sideways through Theow's throat, spraying her with hot blood. She'd woken with a strangled gasp and it took her several moments to remember it had only been a dream and Theow was very much alive.

She shook herself, and the memory dissipated like smoke. She could hardly tell Bryce such things, but he could help her in other ways. "This is why I need you to teach me how to defend myself when someone has a grip on my hair," she said, and rubbed her sore scalp. "I almost lost a chunk of it when one of the men seized me by the back of my head."

"All right, then. Come." Bryce banked the hearth-fire and then they walked into the expansive field of green and yellow grass behind the longhouse. He led Fryda to the centre of the field and grasped her shoulders, turning her until she faced away from him.

"Careful," she warned him, fidgeting. "My head is a bit sore from the last man who gripped my hair."

"Don't worry. I won't hurt you." He pressed his fist to the back of her head and she relaxed when his grip stayed loose and painless. "All right. Now. Any blows you deliver to a man behind you will be weak and ineffective, so you need to change your position. Reach up and grab my wrist with your good hand. Then, hook your opposite leg behind you around my body to upset my balance, and fall backwards. The force of the fall, with your weight on me, should be enough to get you free."

Fryda shoved her sleeves up and set herself to working her way out of Bryce's grip, for once not worrying about hiding her weak hand.

★★

"Plant your feet." Bryce tapped his boot against Fryda's bare heel. "And put this foot forward a little. You'll be too easily overbalanced otherwise, like last time. Remember?"

Fryda adjusted her feet and he nodded his approval. She had removed her slippers and stripped down to her shift as the morning warmed, and they were both slicked with sweat, dirt, and stray bits of grass. Bryce felt a swell of pride as he cast a critical eye over her. The lass worked hard and improved day by day. Such a shame, he thought, that she'd been born daughter to a lord. At least, daughter to this particular lord, he silently amended. She would have made an exceptional shield maiden.

"All right. Try again," he said, and slid his hand into her hair. She flinched at his touch, despite his determination to be gentle, and he again wished Theow had not been so quick to kill Fægebeorn. He burned with the desire to tear the man's head clean off.

However, Fryda minded his instruction and pulled the new move off perfectly. One moment he stood behind her with a loose grip on her hair, and the next he was on the ground, her slight weight forcing his arm nearly out of its socket.

"Excellent!" he said with a grin. "Now unhand me, unless you mean to make a Grendel out of me."

She released him and clambered to her feet. "It was easier that time," Fryda said, beaming.

Bryce couldn't help but smile at her enthusiasm as he stood and shook out his arm. "That's because you've practised it about fifty times on me today." He flexed his shoulder and rubbed the joint. "How about we try something else?"

"Yes, please, Weland," she said.

"All right," he said. "Let's see what you can do with this."

Fryda watched him expectantly. Bryce opened his mouth as if to say something, but then looked over her shoulder, as if arrested by something he saw there. Fryda caught the glance and turned to see what had grabbed his attention. Bryce leapt. Despite his bulk, the blacksmith could move with extraordinary speed, and so before Fryda had even focused her eyes on the void behind her, he had locked his arms around her at the chest and pinned her limbs to her sides.

WHUMP

Bryce's body buckled under a monumental blow—not in his arm or his chest or his legs, but along his entire person. His eyes slammed shut against the impact, and the next moment he felt the wind streak past him, as if he fell from a great height—only he fell *upwards* and sideways rather than down. He opened his eyes and realized he was hurtling backwards through the air, his braids streaming across his face and his arms dangling, weightless, in front of him. He blinked. Then inhaled. And still he flew, his body making a graceful arc above the ground.

He eventually landed in a great heap on the grass. The impact knocked the air out of him, and for one panicked moment, Bryce could not breathe. He struggled to draw a breath, but his body refused to obey him. He rolled over to his side, arms clutched around his chest, and he tried not to black out.

"Bryce!" He heard Fryda's voice, frantic and thin as if from a very great distance. *Lovely*, he thought. He would first go deaf before he died from lack of air. He managed to raise his head, his eyes streaming as he fought to open his lungs, and realized that Fryda was, in fact, running to him from some distance away. He must have been knocked back thirty feet or more.

He lost his fear amongst his wonder, and in that moment the air rushed into his body and he gasped for breath after breath, his chest heaving like the bellows at his forge. His head stopped spinning and the world straightened, becoming solid once more.

He sat up and gingerly tested his limbs to make sure nothing had broken. Fryda flung herself down beside him, her face full of concern and her windblown hair flying around her head.

"Weland," she gasped. "Are you all right?"

Bryce ran a hand down his legs, testing for fractures. "I think so," he said. His voice sounded rough and gravelly. "Woden's beard. What happened?"

Fryda clutched at his arms with shaking hands, and Bryce forgot his own hurts and took a good look at her. Her face was snow-white and she trembled all over.

"I don't know," she said. She forced the words past chattering teeth. "I don't know."

"Did you hit me?" he asked. He covered her cold hands with his warm ones.

"I don't know." She shook her head, as if trying to deny what had happened.

"All right, Sunbeam." He squeezed her hands. "Calm down now. Calm yourself, and tell me what happened."

Fryda's whole body shook as if in the grip of a furious fever, and she clutched her damaged hand as if it pained her. The girl was in shock, Bryce realized. He reached for her and pulled her close, dragging her into his lap so he could wrap his arms around her. She burrowed against his chest, hiding her face from him and gripping his tunic with her good hand.

"Shhh, shhh," he whispered, passing his hand over her mussed hair. "You're all right."

She gave a sob against his chest. "But you're not," she said, her voice muffled and squeaky. "I hurt you."

"I am all right, lass. I am." He took her by the arms and drew her away from him, forcing her to look him in the face. "Look. I'm all right. Got the wind knocked out of me good and proper, but I swear to you, I am not hurt."

Tears ran down her face as she passed her hands over his arms. "You're sure?" she asked, her voice tremulous. "I saw…it looked like you…" Her mouth twisted as if she could not bear to speak of what she saw.

"I'm sure. Now. Tell me what happened."

Fryda took a few deep breaths and managed to stop her tears. "I thought there was something or someone behind me, but when I turned nothing was there." She looked at him accusingly. "You tricked me."

"I did," he admitted. "But I wanted to see how you would react when taken by surprise." He rubbed his chest. "I confess, I did not expect you to fling me halfway across the meadow."

"I just…it felt like when Fægebeorn attacked me. He dragged me out of bed and someone grabbed me from behind." She wiped her damp cheeks with a grubby fist and left smears of mud across her face. "It scared me."

"I'm sorry." Bryce tamped down the flush of shame that came with the apology. "But I had to see how you would react."

"Yes. Well." Fryda plucked at a blade of grass. "As soon as I felt you behind me, I panicked. I couldn't remember any of the things you taught me. It was as if my mind just…froze."

Bryce nodded and plucked a piece of straw from her hair. "And then?"

"I don't know," Fryda repeated. She shook her head in obvious bewilderment and yanked the sleeve of her dress over her twisted left hand, as Bryce knew she always did when upset or insecure. "I lashed out, and then I was free."

Bryce pressed a hand to his breastbone, remembering the enormity of the walloping he had received there. "Lashed out how?" he asked. "With what? I had your arms pinned."

He did not add that while he did not doubt her strength or skill, he rather did doubt that she could throw him thirty feet, whether her arms were pinned or not.

"I...I don't know," she said. She looked at him, and her face was bleak. "I suddenly felt...something. Like a powerful strength that entered my body." She rubbed her wet cheeks. "It's happened a couple times before, and it happened last night when I...I was trying to escape from one of the exiles when suddenly I felt a rush of strength. It was like when your heart speeds up and gives you a charge, only infinitely stronger than that. I mean...I broke a man's neck with one arm. I shouldn't be able to do that!"

Bryce pondered that for a moment. "All right," he said. He reached out and tweaked one of her bouncy yellow curls. "Don't fret about it. You're safe and I'm unhurt, so let's just leave it there, yes?"

"Should...should we try it again?" Fryda asked, and Bryce could see that she wanted to.

He clambered to his feet and reached down to help her up. "Yes," he said. "We can try it again." He grinned at her. "But please, this time try to not throw me across the field."

"Hah," Fryda scoffed as she brushed off her thin shift. "As if you could take me by surprise like that again."

Bryce laughed and reached for her. She skittered away and the dance of battle began once more.

★ ★ ★

Theow rubbed his stinging ear as he made his way up the small hill towards the forge. With all the extra work and pressure of the King's second celebration happening that night, Moire had been freer with her fists than usual and he predicted his ear would be the size of an apple by the day's end, and just as red.

It hadn't been his fault the ancient iron cauldron had fallen and cracked on the stone hearth. He hadn't been anywhere near it. He had just been the most convenient target, and so he had borne the brunt of Moire's wrath. Now he trudged up a hill to ask the blacksmith to forge a new cooking pot for the kitchen. At least the errand got him outside in the fresh air.

As he walked, his mind drifted back to the scene in Fryda's room, as it had done ever since he left her there, alone, wounded, and surrounded by the dead. His gut twisted as he remembered the feel of her in his arms, trembling in her torn gown but willing to let him touch her as she turned to him for comfort. She trusted him…and he wanted her. He wanted her safe and happy. He wanted her to be his. And she had held him as if she wanted that, too.

But the chasm between them stretched broad and deep, and he had no business dreaming about her freckled skin and wild, unruly hair. He had nothing to offer her—not even his name. He had lost that in a past he could not remember while dreaming of a future he could not achieve.

His gloomy thoughts kept him company as he crested the hill. A strange silence hung about the smithy as he approached. Usually the resounding ring of hammer against iron could be heard across the *burh* throughout the day, but all was still this morning. Theow wandered into the forge, searching for signs of life. The glowing embers in the hearth were banked and the hilt of a newly forged sword lay on the anvil. He could not see Bryce anywhere, but he could hear people talking in the meadow out back, so he skirted the building and headed towards the field.

Theow walked out into the lush green and yellow grasses, knee-high and smelling of the sweet summer sun. He surveyed the field and stopped in his tracks. Two people, an enormous man and one small woman wearing nothing but a thin shift, grappled perhaps twenty paces away. His stomach lurched as he saw Fryda twisting in the man's grip, but relaxed when he realized it was the blacksmith.

Surely it was too soon after her assault to be so rough with her…

"Bryce?" he called, trotting up to the pair. "Why are you attacking Fryda?"

Bryce looked over at him and gently disengaged. Fryda bent over with her hands on her knees and gasped for breath, but to Theow's relief she looked unharmed. "Because she asked me to," Bryce said. He caught Theow's expression and understanding dawned. The blacksmith's eyes were sympathetic, though his mouth twitched with amusement. "We were just sparring, Theow. She wanted me to teach her how to defend herself when caught from behind."

Fryda said nothing. She stood away from the two men, arms folded around her middle. Theow suddenly felt foolish for talking about her as if she weren't there.

"Are you all right?" he asked.

She nodded, but still did not speak.

"Did you need me for something?" Bryce asked, wiping his sweaty face on his sleeve.

It took Theow a moment to remember why he had come. "Oh. Yes. Sorry. Moire sent me. The large iron cauldron cracked today and she's asking for a new one."

"Eish. I'd better get to work on it, then. She'll be wanting it done by tonight, if possible." Apparently even the large blacksmith did not want to get on Moire's bad side. Bryce glanced at Fryda. "Sure you're all right?"

She nodded.

Bryce huffed a small laugh and said, "Right then." He turned away, and Theow heard him muttering to himself about unreasonable kitchen mistresses as he made his way back to the forge.

Theow steeled himself and looked at Fryda. She still stood and stared at the ground, unmoving, as if frozen to it. She wrapped her arms around herself as if she would fly to pieces if she let go.

She looked a glorious mess, this fierce and determined woman who loved strawberries, fought like a warrior, and hid her left hand from the world. The freckles across her nose stood out against the unusual pallor of her skin, which glowed with sweat from her exertions. Her hair tumbled in wild, loose curls to her waist. She had a tiny mole at the corner of her right eye, and a beautiful dark mark on her neck under her ear. She had a luscious mouth, pink and full, and he wished he could brush a gentle kiss across her bruised and split lower lip, erasing the evidence of violence with his tenderness. She wore no shoes and her thin shift was stained with dirt and grass. She had straw in her hair and a smudge on her cheek, and Theow had never seen anything more beautiful in his life.

But he also loved the determined tilt of her jaw, the defiant glitter in her eyes, the strength he saw in her refusal to fall apart. He loved her passion for justice and her unbending sense of right and wrong, even when her idealism skirted the boundaries of the logical. He loved her fire and her spirit and her love of sweet things.

He loved her.

"Um," he said. "Fryda, are you…do you need…?" He stumbled to a halt, not knowing what he could offer that she could possibly want or need.

She stared at him with haunted eyes, as if waiting for him to do or say something, but he could not tell what she was thinking. He wanted to ask what he could do to sweep away the stormclouds in her eyes, but the words remained locked behind his lips.

"Well," Theow said when she did not respond. He looked over his shoulder to the longhouse. "I'm going to go...I suppose."

Fryda's mouth twisted in a wry smile and she finally spoke. "I...yes." Theow thought she looked disappointed. She picked up her dress, which lay in a heap in the grass, slipped it on, and started to fasten the brooch clasps up the front. "I have to get back to the longhouse. Father is hosting a huge breakfast for all the important guests this morning, and I need to be there. When you get back to the kitchens could you please tell Moire that Bryce is working on her cooking pot?"

Theow couldn't help himself. He closed his fingers over hers as they fumbled with the last clasp. "Always asking," he murmured. "Never an order."

Fryda flushed. "If I ever do give you an order, I hope you won't let it go unchallenged," she said. "I am not your superior, and you are not a slave to me."

Theow let that pass, though he knew this was a talk they would need to have, eventually.

"I'll come to the kitchens later and we can go to the feast together," she said. "I liked having you there last night, so Moire will have to put up with you being in the longhouse again." She hesitated, looking at him with those hopeful, stormy grey eyes, and Theow nearly wrapped her in his arms and kissed her. But as he glanced down at her lips, he saw the ragged tear left by Fægebeorn's teeth and knew his kiss, no matter how gentle, would break open the tender scab and hurt her.

He could not bear the thought of it.

But neither could he leave her looking so bereft. He heard her breath catch as he reached for her, his hand sliding into her wild hair. He leaned down and pressed his lips to her forehead, holding his breath for a long moment as she stilled against him.

He stepped back and Fryda gave him a tremulous smile.

"Later in the kitchens, then," she said, and her cheeks flushed pink. Theow nodded, pleased to see her unnatural paleness banished by the hectic colour.

Fryda picked up her shoes, threw him one last glance, and walked towards the forge. Theow stood there, feeling like a star thrown from its seat in the sky, having stepped over the edge of a moment that would change his life forever.

Eleven

Wiglaf paused outside the entrance to the mead-hall and willed his mind to settle.

He wished he had brought a flask of mead with him. A fortifying draught would give him the...not courage, he thought. He had plenty of that. The *endurance* to survive this meeting with his father. No doubt it would be a painful one.

He had been summoned. Never a good sign.

At least he had something to offer this time—a tale of his bravery, having saved his sister from the vile clutches of Fægebeorn and his exile friends. It mattered not that the story was untrue. It didn't need to be true—it only needed to convince Weohstan that Wiglaf was more than a drunken layabout, unfit for leadership.

Perhaps it was best he hadn't brought the mead after all.

Wiglaf straightened his tunic and adjusted his belt. He'd come to realize over the last two days the degree of contempt in which everyone held him, and it bothered him more than he liked. Weohstan...well, his father had always scorned Wiglaf and his choices, so that wasn't surprising. But King Beowulf? Wiglaf paced up and down the stone path that led to the longhouse doors. *That* he had not expected. Why, since his arrival the king had shown more attention and favour to a *kitchen slave* than he had to Wiglaf. His face burned and he clenched his teeth as he again remembered Beowulf handing Theow a gold ring. And for what? For helping Fryda hold a bloody cup?

Fryda. She hurt him most of all. His own sister, his twin, the woman he had watched and protected their entire lives, disrespected him in front of the *burh* and their honoured guests. First, she had given him watered-down mead, as if he were a beardless boy. And as if that hadn't been insult enough, she had taken Fægebeorn down on her own rather than waiting for him to take care of her. Wiglaf had seen the archer grab Fryda's breast and a murderous rage had taken him. He wanted to gut him like a fish and make him eat his own entrails. But before he could get to her, she had already snapped the man's fingers and wrist as if they were kindling.

Impressive for a cripple, he grudgingly thought. He never would have believed it if he hadn't seen it with his own eyes.

And *then* she had the audacity to invite Theow to the picnic he had planned for the two of them alone. As if she enjoyed spending time with a kitchen slave more than with her own brother.

So. He had decided he must do something to repair his reputation. To show them all he was more worthy of respect than Beowulf's bloody "thane-for-a-day" slave. In the privacy of his own thoughts, he could admit he had perhaps earned his poor reputation, but that just drove him on more.

Wiglaf took a deep breath and resisted the urge to run back to his rooms for a quick, bracing drink. He grasped the handle of the great arched door and pulled.

Weohstan spent every morning in the longhouse, sitting in his carved chair as he read through reports—*fuþorc* runes scraped onto skins by learned scribes—and heard the messengers who came with news and information. The business of being lord did not stop because the king came to visit, Wiglaf supposed. As he strode into the hall, he saw Fryda sitting near their father on a long bench against the wall, mending a bit of lace. She looked up and their eyes locked for a moment, before she looked away.

Wiglaf hoped she would hold her tongue. One look at their

father's hard, uncompromising face convinced him that he'd been right. They could not tell him the truth. Weohstan had no room for such truths in his well-ordered world.

"My lord," Wiglaf said, coming to a halt in front of his father. He gave a brief bow. "I am here as you requested. However, before you deliver the news you summoned me to hear, I ask an indulgence, for I have a report of utmost urgency to give you."

Weohstan did not move or speak. He merely scanned his eyes over the report he was reading and forced Wiglaf to wait.

Wiglaf's guts seethed and writhed, as if filled with angry snakes, but he stood quietly and waited until his father put the skin aside and looked up at him.

Wiglaf blinked. It had been some time since he'd looked at his father's face—really *looked* at him—and was surprised to find him so...old. His dark hair was thinner than he remembered and streaked with silver. Deep lines framed his mouth and eyes, and his knuckles were gnarled and swollen. He had never seen his father so tired.

"Utmost urgency, is it?" Weohstan asked, his voice wry. "Are you here to tell me the casks of mead have all run dry? Or that all the village girls have suddenly lost interest in you?"

Wiglaf stiffened.

"No, Father," he said. "This concerns the safety of your daughter, the king, and, indeed, the *burh*."

Weohstan raised his eyebrows and gestured for him to proceed.

Wiglaf related to Weohstan the carefully expurgated version of the story they had concocted the previous night. His father listened without speaking and, to Wiglaf's relief, Fryda also remained silent.

"Well," Weohstan said when Wiglaf had finished. "It seems thanks and congratulations are in order." He glanced at Fryda. "I hope, Fryðegifu, you are suitably grateful to your brother."

She glanced up from her lace. "I am, Father, and I have said as much to him," she said, her voice calm and low. However, Wiglaf saw the two patches of red flare high on her cheeks.

His annoyance flared once more. Was it so difficult for her to be grateful to him? If it weren't for him, she'd be married off to some undeserving lord and halfway to Sweden or Norway by now. He did everything he could to keep her safe and then she had the audacity to get angry about it.

She had no idea what her life would be like without his protection. *Perhaps*, a voice whispered in the back of his mind, *it would do her some good to find out.*

Weohstan brought his gaze back to Wiglaf, who shivered under the coldness of those eyes.

"I shall declare tonight's feast a celebration of your courageous deeds," Weohstan said. He sounded approving...even impressed. "The king will be very well pleased."

"Thank you, Father," Wiglaf said, and relaxed. *Perfect.* "Can I help you with your work today?" he asked, craning his neck for a look at the scrolls on Weohstan's table. Fryda looked up at him in surprise. "Perhaps I could ease your burden a little, and you could spend some time with your guests. Where is King Beowulf, anyway?"

Weohstan sat back and crossed his arms. "The king enjoyed himself rather...thoroughly...last night," he said, "so he decided to have a rest before tonight's celebration."

"Well. Let me help you anyway. I'm certain I have much to learn from you."

"No." Weohstan flicked his fingers in a dismissive gesture. "I have no time to teach you now. You needn't concern yourself with any of this."

Wiglaf stared at him, stunned. "Father, you're always telling me I need to live up to my responsibilities. And here I am, offering to do just that."

"That time has passed."

Wiglaf saw Fryda flinch at the sharpness in their father's voice. He frowned and took a step forward.

"What do you mean by that?" he asked. His fists clenched and he tried to relax.

Weohstan looked up at him, his dark gaze unblinking. "It means you no longer have any responsibilities concerning the *burh* to worry about."

Wiglaf barked out a humourless laugh. "Father, you've been telling me for years that I must prepare to take your place as lord of Ećeweall. I'm telling you now that I'm ready to…"

"You will not take my place as lord of Ećeweall."

Fryda jumped and dropped her lace. Wiglaf stared at his father.

"What?"

Weohstan sighed and sat back in his chair. "This is not the way I'd planned to tell you, son."

"Tell me what?" He could hear the high-pitched panic in his own voice.

"I have decided to make Olaf my heir." Weohstan rubbed his forehead. "He shall become the next lord of Ećeweall."

Fryda inhaled sharply.

A lump of cold anger formed in Wiglaf's stomach. "Olaf."

"Yes. He knows all the workings of the *burh* already. He has good relationships with the other clan leaders, as well as the warriors. He has the loyalty of the *gedriht*." Weohstan pinned Wiglaf with a sharp look. "And more to the point, he knows how to keep the mead in the cask and his *pintel* in his pants."

Fryda had abandoned her lace entirely and looked from Wiglaf to their father, an expression of horror on her face.

"Olaf…but Olaf isn't even from here. He's a Dane."

"He may not have been born here, but he's been a member of this clan longer than you have been alive," Weohstan said, a hint of warning in his tone. "He has proven his loyalties countless times since we accepted him as one of our own. More so than you ever have."

Wiglaf saw Fryda wince and his expression grew thunderous. What was Weohstan thinking, humiliating him in front of her like this? "You cannot do this."

"It is already done." Weohstan sighed and rubbed his eyes. "Wiglaf, you could not have made it clearer to me that you have no interest in your obligations. Now you are free to…" His face contorted in disgust as he waved a hand towards Wiglaf, "…live as you please."

Wiglaf realized his pulse was racing and he tried to control his breathing. His fingers curled and uncurled, making fists over and over. He gave a laugh, unconvincing even to himself, and said, "And here I thought I'd just proved to you I was a worthy son."

"I am grateful for your assistance to your sister," Weohstan said. He spared a glance for Fryda, but it was cold and sharp, and she shifted under his gaze. "But that was one incident out of a lifetime of negligence. You cannot imagine one act in the service of another would erase your selfish nature. Make no mistake, Wiglaf. You proved to me long ago what manner of man you are."

Wiglaf froze. His jaw clenched and his facial muscles worked, chewing on the words he wanted to say but would not.

So what manner of man am I? he wanted to shout. But he did not. He didn't want to hear the answer. Did his father know what he'd done to Theow? What he'd done to…

No. If he knew about *that* Wiglaf would be an exile now.

After several wordless moments, Wiglaf spun on his heel and walked out of the mead-hall and Weohstan watched him go, his face like stone.

★ ★ ★

Fryda stared after her brother as he stormed out of the mead-hall. She could not believe what she'd just heard and seen. Wiglaf's expression at her father's words had bordered on murderous. The way his mouth twisted into an ugly snarl, like a feral dog, would haunt her dreams for some time.

"Father?"

Weohstan turned his dark eyes on Fryda. "It is not for you to question me or my decisions, girl."

She picked up her lace with trembling hands. She could hold the lace with her left and work the needle with her right, though it was difficult. "Of course, Father. I just meant to ask...Wiglaf told you what happened in my rooms last night. Aren't you concerned about how the exiles got into Eceweall? Or why they were here? What if there are others?"

"I'm certain you have no reason to worry. There will always be exiles and vagrants hanging about, taking advantage of honest folk." Weohstan picked up another piece of vellum and started to peruse it. "If there are others, they will have heard what Wiglaf did, or they soon will, and make themselves scarce. Fortunately, they didn't have a chance to hurt anyone."

Fryda gaped at her father. "Didn't hurt anyone?" She touched her chest and belly where a half-dozen shallow knife wounds itched under newly forming scabs. Hot blood throbbed in her split lip. The concoction Eadith had spread over her cuts—medicinal herbs pounded into pig fat—burned. "Did you not understand what Wiglaf told you? They attacked me. They nearly killed me!"

"Fægebeorn nearly killed you," Weohstan corrected her, and she found his calm, pedantic manner infuriating. "And he's dead as well, so we don't have to worry about him either. Unless you've injured any more of my warriors who might be looking for revenge?" He lifted an eyebrow at her.

"I knew it." Fryda grew hot with fury as she leapt to her feet, her lace forgotten. "I knew you would blame me for that. I defended myself, Father. He assaulted me and..."

Weohstan made a rude noise. "Assaulted you. Don't be

dramatic. He was drunk and he touched you…familiarly. That's not…"

"You just said he nearly killed me!" Fryda crossed her arms over her chest and tears prickled behind her eyes. "He didn't only touch me at the feast, Father. He left bruises. He hurt me."

Weohstan blinked and seemed at a loss for words. Fryda pressed on, taking full advantage. "Fægebeorn was mad with pain and fever, but he said something about how he would be very rich soon, and we would all be dead. The exiles also talked about something big that will happen soon, something we are not prepared for and don't know about. One of them mentioned a blood-debt."

"They wanted to ransom you, most likely." Weohstan flicked his fingers as if to brush away her words.

"Well you don't seem very concerned about that!"

"Because they failed." Weohstan's stony demeanour cracked for a moment and the constant anger that lived beneath the calm surface leaked through. "Why should I concern myself with the actions of three dead men who no longer pose a threat to anyone?"

A familiar pain spread through her, like ripples in her blood as her father cast a hard, sharp stone into the wide-open ocean of her heart.

"Because perhaps there are others involved in the plan and they might try again?" she asked. She tugged at her sleeve, making sure it covered her hand.

"Considering the outcome of last night's adventures, they would be fools to try it," Weohstan said.

"Well, we know they are fools," Fryda snapped. "They clearly didn't think their plan through if they thought you would pay enough for my life to make them rich."

She regretted the words as soon as she uttered them. Her father's face went white, then red, and he pressed his lips thin. He stood and stalked away without another word.

Too angry to return to her work, Fryda stormed out of the longhouse and went to find Bryce. The forge, however, was empty, so she found herself heading to the kitchens instead. Inside, everyone scurried to prepare for the second feast and Moire's voice was hoarse as she shouted out instructions and imprecations with equal fervour. Toland, his hand wrapped in a dirty bandage, turned a goose on a spit and she spied Lyset chopping vegetables into a large pot. Fryda searched for Theow but could not see him in the chaos. She spotted Hild putting freshly made barley dough into the ovens, so she made her way over to her.

"My lady," Hild said in surprise. She peered at Fryda's face, at the hollow shadows under her eyes. "Are you all right? Do you need more medicine for your wounds?"

Pressure welled up in Fryda's chest and she swallowed, and swallowed again. "No," she said. Her voice shook. "Can you come with me for a moment? I need to talk with you."

Hild shot a look towards the ovens. "Yes, I think so. These won't be done for a while."

That was all the encouragement Fryda needed. She grabbed Hild's arm and pulled her from the kitchens into the back meadow. She felt a little better after taking a few deep breaths of fresh air, but that did not stop the anger from twisting her insides into knots.

They sat in the tall grass and Fryda told Hild everything —the attack in her rooms, her dreams, the lies Wiglaf had told Weohstan, his decision to make Olaf his heir, and her father's response to her fears. By the end, her words fell from her mouth on the back of great gasps, torn violently from her throat. Hild sat and held her hand, unspeaking, until she was finished.

"My lady," Hild said. Her eyes were round and horrified. "That is…I'm amazed you haven't taken to your bed! You must let me mix you a tincture to calm you."

Fryda took a few deep breaths. She felt lighter, calmer after sharing her burdens, and she shook her head.

"I was fine until I tried to speak with Father," she said, and her anger rekindled. "I know Bryce said that he loves me, but... it's very difficult to believe when he does nothing about a threat on my life."

Hild squeezed her hand. "My lady, I guarantee that as soon as you left, Lord Weohstan assigned some guards to watch you, and there will be someone posted at your door tonight after you retire for bed."

Fryda looked at their joined hands. Her skin looked very pale in Hild's warm, brown one. "You think so?"

"Yes, I do. Your father may not tell you, but he does love you and will take care of you." Hild's gentle smile fell. "My lady, I hate to add to your burdens, but...did Theow tell you about the theft in the stillroom yesterday?"

"Yes, he did, and we think the incidents are connected. I think that's why I felt so fuzzy when the men in my room woke me up. I took a small cup of mead from the feast and drank it last night before bed, so we think someone put the white poppy syrup in a cask of mead." Fryda shook her head. "I'm convinced the attack on me was part of some bigger plot. The exiles practically said as much."

Hild frowned, clearly troubled. "Best not to eat or drink anything at the feast tonight, my lady," she warned. "I'll put some food aside for you, but please, don't take anything that doesn't come from my own hands. Promise me?"

Fryda hastened to reassure her friend. "You keep your eyes open in the kitchens as well," she said. "Perhaps we should tell Eadith what's going on."

"That's a good idea. And, my lady, if I may suggest...?"

Fryda raised her eyebrows.

"Have Theow in the mead-hall again tonight," Hild said. She

gave an unrepentantly cheeky smile. "I'd feel better, knowing he's there looking out for you."

Fryda's cheeks warmed. "I...um...I already told him he would be with me in the longhouse tonight." She hadn't told Hild about her talk with Theow earlier, or how he had kissed her. It still felt too new, too private to share, even with her dear friend. "I'll run and tell Eadith to keep her eyes on the casks tonight. I'll meet you back in the kitchens when I'm done."

Twelve

Theow sat on the floor and wrapped a scrap of clean cloth around his cracked and bleeding hand, silently cursing Moire. He'd washed so many pots, cups, dishes, and plates, he'd worn the skin from his fingers. His mind kept drifting back to the field behind the forge, lingering over the memory of Fryda's hand in his, the feel of her soft skin against his lips. Hers was the only touch of gentleness he'd known in a long time.

Hild suddenly popped up beside him and he jumped.

"Theow! I hear Lady Fryda wants you in the mead-hall again tonight." Theow's thoughts filled with music and he smiled. "But first I have another riddle for you," she continued. "Are you ready for this one?"

Theow groaned.

"Listen carefully, Theow. Here it goes. 'I'm a wonderful thing, a joy to women, to neighbours useful. I stand up high and steep over the bed, and underneath I'm shaggy. What am I?'" Hild looked at him with twinkling eyes.

Woden's ghost, he thought. How many dirty riddles did she know about a man's *pintel*?

"Ummm. Are you a broom?"

"Not a broom," Hild said. "Brooms don't have beds."

"Then I have no idea."

"Really? You have no idea what women love that stands up straight in bed and is shaggy underneath?"

"Hild..." His face flamed.

"It's an onion, you dirty-minded thing!" she crowed, and laughed at his expression.

"Onions don't have beds, either," he protested.

"Garden beds, silly," she said.

Moire stormed into the kitchen, glaring at everyone. The laughter stopped and everyone grew still. Something at the back of the room drew Moire's attention, and Hild's eyes suddenly widened and dismay flooded her face.

"Oh no," she whispered. "I forgot about the..."

The smell of something burnt filled Theow's nose and a waft of smoke stung his eyes. Moire whirled and focused on her new target. "HILD! I told you to keep an eye on the fire and not let it get too hot!" Hild scuttled towards the ovens and her burning loaves of barley bread.

Theow sat, unable to move.

The room grew hazy with smoke and his body tried to remember how to breathe, how to unclench his hands and tamp down the rising terror coursing through his body and blood. He became aware of the marred, stretched flesh on his face and his scar throbbed in time to the pounding of his pulse. He could not remember his name, his family, his home, or his language, but his body never forgot the fire that had marked him as its own. Fire, and pain, and overwhelming fear. He sat motionless, caught in the grip of an unshakeable, yet all too familiar terror.

Grey smoke, roiling through the air.

Flickering tongues of vivid orange and red, licking at the thatched roof of the ráth, the roundhouse where he lived.

A man writhing in agony, pinned to the floor on the end of a sword.

A rain of burning straw, and embers like a swarm of fireflies swirling around his head.

Sickening pain and blurred vision. The smell of blood creeping in under the smoke.

A giant with yellow braided hair dragging him to a longship.

Theow's scar twitched violently as the room spun and his chest clenched. His lungs rebelled against the smoke; refused to draw it into his body. In his mind he knew that smoke from some scorched bread would not hurt him, but his body refused to listen or believe. He forced air through his throat in harsh little gasps and struggled in vain to draw a full breath. His eyes watered and the world tilted beneath him.

A commotion at the doorway drew his attention. Servants and slaves scurried around someone, but his vision blurred from smoke and tears and he could not see. The visitor pushed through the crowd, eyes scanning the room until they came to rest on him. He blinked his eyes to clear them.

Fryda.

She rushed forward and grasped his arm, trying to help him stand. His knees buckled and refused to support him, and he discovered that her presence made breathing even more challenging. Fryda, however, took in the situation—the burned bread, the smoke, Moire's shrieks, and Theow's panic—and threw one of his arms over her neck.

"You have to get up," she murmured. "Theow. I can't lift you. You have to help me."

She put her weak arm around his waist and he felt her clawed, twisted fingers try to grip his tunic. Gasping, he hauled himself to his feet and Fryda steadied him as the room spun and he wavered.

"Moire, I'll be needing Theow in the longhouse tonight." She nudged him towards the doorway. He stumbled but she gripped him and did not let him fall. "He won't be coming back here until tomorrow."

Moire, caught unawares, gaped at Fryda while Hild took advantage of her distraction to scoot discreetly out the back with the burned bread. Fryda scowled as she caught sight of Theow's bandaged hands and the new bruises on his face. "In fact," she told Moire with a fierce glare, "I don't think he'll be coming back here at all. And you and I are going to have a talk tomorrow about the way you treat my kitchen workers."

For the first time, Theow saw Moire flinch. He would have grinned at her, but he still could not breathe.

Fryda guided Theow outside, staggering a little under his weight. "Don't you fall on me," she whispered as they emerged into the sweet summer air. "I'll never get you back up again." The smell of smoke dissipated, yet still Theow struggled for breath.

"Theow, look at me." Fryda took his face in her hands and gazed into his eyes. "You're all right. There is no fire. You're safe. You're safe and I'm here. I'm with you. Breathe, Theow." She placed a palm flat on his chest. "You need to breathe."

And as if his body would willingly grant her every wish, his chest loosened and a great rush of air flowed into his lungs. Theow gasped, eyes streaming, and he sucked in breath after breath, feeling the strength return to his limbs. Fear and memory receded like the ebbing tide. He gripped Fryda, his fingers clutching the fine red linen of her dress, not caring that they stood outside where anyone could see them. He looked into her eyes and marveled at what he saw there. Concern. Understanding. Tenderness.

He slid a hand up and rested it against the side of her neck, fingering a stray curl that had escaped from its pins. "How did you know?" he asked, his voice rusty and creaking.

"I saw you this way once before," Fryda said. She swept a teardrop from his cheek with her thumb as he blinked remembered smoke from his eyes. "When we were children and a torch tipped over and set some straw on fire in the horse yard. As soon as you smelled the smoke you went dead white and couldn't breathe. You looked exactly like that just now." She studied him. "Put that together with this," she stroked a fingertip over his scar, "and it doesn't take a *hægtesse* to figure out the connection."

Theow chuckled. "You have your own sort of sorcery." Slowly, his breathing calmed, and his body settled back to normal. He became aware of how ridiculous he must seem, shaking and crying over a bit of burnt bread. He averted his eyes and stepped away.

"I..." he started, but Fryda rolled her eyes.

"Oh please," she said. "Do not turn all timid on me because fire frightens you." She seemed to realize they still stood out in the open and flushed pink. "Come with me." She tilted her head towards the western gate. "I want to show you something. It's not that far."

They walked through the *burh*, keeping to the path that separated the outer buildings from the residences. Fryda nodded to the people they passed but did not stop to speak to anyone, not even the ones who called her name or tried to wave her down. They moved through the farmsteads towards the protective wall. Once she and Theow passed through the gate and were out of sight of the guards, he took her hand in his and they walked across the grass towards the Baltic Sea. The afternoon had a crystalline quality as the sunlight reflected off the facets of the world. Every stone surface, every blade of grass, seemed to stand out in sharp relief against the clear, crisp light. The sky had turned an impossible shade of blue and the wind carried the scents of wildflowers and field grasses. Theow drank it in like fine mead, clearing the last of the smoke from his lungs and releasing any lingering fears with every exhalation of breath.

The land levelled out after they had walked a few hundred feet, ending in a sharp cliff edge to the north. At the bottom of the cliff, a rocky shore stretched a short distance before it touched the ocean, and the water splashed and played over the rough boulders. Walking along the top of the cliff felt like balancing on the edge of the world. Beyond lay danger and chaos. Sea monsters and strange gods lurked in the waters to waylay unwary travellers, and somewhere far past the horizon would be other lands, other tribes, warlike clans and fantastic creatures Theow couldn't even imagine.

And out there, somewhere, was his home.

He glanced at Fryda. For the first time in his broken memory, he thought it possible for this place to feel like home.

"I'm sorry I did not ask before, but...how are you today?" Theow brushed his fingers against her belly where he knew her healing wounds lay under the fine linen of her dress. "How do these feel?"

"They're itchy," Fryda said, "but healing well. I'll be fine."

"Your lip?" It still looked a little swollen, but the redness had gone down and the cut had thoroughly scabbed over.

"Much better. I just have to be careful not to smile too wide."

Worry gnawed at him. "Maybe you shouldn't spar with Bryce until you're healed up a bit more."

Fryda shot him a smiling look. "They are very shallow cuts. Scratches, really, and none of them needed stitches. You don't have to worry."

"I always worry," Theow told her. "I've just never been able to tell you before."

To his delight, Fryda turned pink from the tips of her ears to the freckles that dipped below the neckline of her dress. She stared at him, lips parted and eyes luminous.

He opened his mouth to say...something...but everything fell out of his head as Fryda surged up onto her toes, clutched his tunic in her good hand, and touched her lips to his.

Theow's entire body jolted, charged as if he'd been struck by lightning. After one stunned and bewildered moment, he gathered her close and held her, tilting his head so he could capture her mouth more firmly with his. She made a surprised little noise deep in her throat and gripped him harder. Theow's entire body trembled and he knew she could feel it, a staccato message only she could decipher through flesh and skin, wool and silk. Her lips turned soft and yielding under his as he returned her kiss again and again. And yet again. He ran one hand up her back into her hair, and touched his fingertips to her cheek with the other, angling her face up to his as he gently brushed his mouth against her bruised, full lower lip.

By the time he realized he ought to have pushed her away, he had settled too deep into the kiss, and Fryda gave no signs she wanted him to stop. His mind and heart raced each other as she clung to him, and her mouth opened under the pressure of his. He gripped her, anchoring himself, and let himself fall into her.

As each kiss changed from *now* to *then*, he sealed his mouth against hers again, not yet willing to shift from *we are* to *we did* and write this moment into memory.

The need for breath eventually forced them to part and they gazed at each other in mutual astonishment. Fryda's chest heaved and she smiled shyly at him.

Theow closed his eyes and touched his forehead to hers, and they stood like that for one perfect moment. As he ran his fingers through her hair, something in his chest unclenched and he realized she had handed him the answer to the only question that had ever mattered to him.

"We should move," he said at last. "We can't stay here all day."

Fryda made a frustrated noise. "I know." She tightened her grip on him instead. "I'm just having a little trouble letting you go."

He huffed out a laugh and kissed her hair. Fryda stepped back and ran a hand over her curls. The dreamy smile fell from her face and a line appeared between her golden brows.

"Things are going to get complicated for us now. Aren't they?" She looked up at him, and he could see the birth of storms in her grey eyes. "For you, really. You're the one in danger if my father finds out about...about us." She blushed and Theow reached out and tucked a wayward curl behind her ear, marvelling at how natural the gesture felt.

"I know." He could not deny it, and he would not pretend it did not happen, had no thoughts of *we can never do this again.* Not unless she told him she wanted that. "But you're worth the risk."

Fryda twitched, as if startled or knocked off balance. "Theow, I would never forgive myself if something happened to you because of me."

Theow pressed a brief kiss to her forehead. "Stop worrying," he told her with a smile. "There is no one here but us, and that's enough for me right now. As for the future…we'll work it out. Together." He tried to sound more confident than he felt, for in truth he could not see a path that ended with a slave and a lord's daughter being allowed to marry.

If she even wanted that. One kiss did not seal their fate for life, he reminded himself, and it would more likely result in Weohstan feeding him to the sea monsters as Bryce had predicted.

Fryda sighed and nodded. "Come on," she said. She twined her fingers with his and gave a gentle tug. "I still want to show you something."

They walked for what seemed like ages in the quiet afternoon, their only companions the butterflies, the soft breezes, the distant mountains, and the tall, green grass—but in truth the sun had crept only a short distance across the sky when Fryda gripped his hand and pointed towards a small outcropping of rocks. "There."

They stood near a massive chasm that plunged down two hundred feet or so. The earth had split at the cliff's edge and cracked inland, like an enormous, open wound. Its jagged edges and dark depths reminded him of torn, unhealed flesh. The fissure stretched so far across that no man could leap from one side to the other. It reached so deep inland that it would take less time to build a bridge over the gap than to find a way around it. Theow, who had only ever seen it from the beach far below, stared at it in wonder.

"Is this where...?" He hesitated.

"Where I was when the earthquake happened," Fryda finished for him. "Seven years ago, this was all plain, smooth grassland. Father had been making plans to expand the farms into this area, but now, well...that's not possible anymore."

"And you fell into *that*?" Theow stared at the fracture, trying to picture a force so great it could crack the earth open to the core. "You're lucky you survived."

"I almost didn't. I fell in right over there." Fryda pointed to an indentation in the near lip of the chasm. "I had tracked a wolf to this place when the ground jerked under my feet. I fell over, and I remember just...just gripping the grass, trying to keep from getting tossed around. I heard a loud *crack* and a rumble, like thunder, and the ground vanished out from under me."

Fryda's face looked pale, but her voice remained steady. Theow noticed she stayed well back from the edge.

"I fell in. I'm not sure how I managed it, but somehow I snagged a rock jutting from the chasm wall. It cut my hand and the blood made it too slippery for me to hang on, but it slowed my fall enough for me to save myself."

Fryda lifted her left hand, inviting him to look at it. She trembled, as if displaying her deformity frightened her. As if she thought he would look at her with disgust and push her away. Carefully, Theow took her small, twisted hand in his. She kept her eyes on his face and looked more vulnerable than he had ever seen her. He traced a faded, white scar across her palm.

"Here?" he asked.

Fryda nodded. She clearly wanted to pull her hand away, tuck it up into her sleeve, but she seemed to steel herself and let him hold it. "I fell again after my grip failed, but I managed to wedge my hand into a crack in the rock. It stopped my fall, but the force of it broke nearly all the bones in my hand and tore my shoulder out of place." She gave a shaky laugh. "If we'd still been children, I would have been able to play Grendel after that, instead of you."

Theow chuckled, but only to put her at ease. He did not feel like laughing. Fryda hid her damaged hand so often he almost never saw it, and seeing it now, lying in his palm so pale and so fragile, caused him profound pain. Pale scars lined and dotted her skin where her flesh had torn and broken bones had pierced through. The hand itself tilted to the left from a break at the wrist that had healed aslant, and her index and fourth fingers angled too much to the right. Her middle finger curled under against her palm and she could not fully straighten it, and the smallest finger on the end, which had borne the worst of the injuries, jutted in all different directions from multiple breaks. He knew she had limited use of the hand, and had difficulty picking up very small objects or lifting heavy ones, like Beowulf's gift of the golden goblet. He also knew the man her father had contracted her to marry, a young warrior named Dysg, called off their wedding because he could not bear the touch or sight of that hand. He closed his fingers around hers, hoping the warmth from his skin would reassure her

"I just...hung there. For hours," Fryda said. "I was stuck. I couldn't get the leverage to pull my hand out. It hurt so much, I could not even try."

"But if you'd freed your hand, you would have fallen." Theow stroked her fingers, caressing the thin white lines, the bulges of bone, with the pad of his thumb.

Fryda shuddered. "After a while I wanted to. Every time I moved, I felt such pain. So, I screamed as loudly as I could. I screamed and screamed until my voice broke. After a while everything went dark. I don't know if I slept, but I think I started seeing things, hearing things, even smelling things that weren't there. Maybe they were dreams, I don't know. I thought I heard music once, coming from the bottom of the chasm. When I came back to myself, night had fallen and I started crying again, begging for help, screaming for someone to come."

Her whole body now trembled and Theow rubbed her arm, his fingers making soothing circles to calm her. She gripped his other hand. "I didn't know there could be so much pain in all the world." She wiped tears from her face. "I'm told I hung out there for an afternoon and a full night, but I don't remember most of it. I remember being thirsty—so thirsty—but I had no water. I remember that when it grew dark, I thought I was going to freeze to death. I remember wanting to die so the pain would stop, and I remember thinking that if I wrapped my belt around my arm, I could use my hunting knife to cut off my hand and free myself. I was about to do it, too, but just then I heard voices and Father's men found me.

"Somehow I was still alive when they found me. They got me out—I don't even remember how—and you know the rest."

He did know. They had brought her back and she had nearly died from fever over the next few days. He pulled her into his arms and pressed his lips to the top of her head.

A jewelled pin sprang from her braids and flipped end over end to be lost in the deep grass. Theow jerked back in surprise and Fryda gave him an amused look.

"My hair," she said, blowing an errant curl from her face. "I lose pins all the time. It refuses to be tamed."

"I love that about your hair," he said, and kissed her again. "And about you."

He didn't dare say it plainer than that. This new understanding between them felt too new, too fragile for those words just yet.

Fryda squeezed his hand. "I wanted to show you this place and tell you the story, so you know you aren't alone in your nightmares. I know you dream of fire and smoke and how you got this scar." She reached up and ran one crooked finger across it. "My dreams are full of falling and hanging and pain and thirst, and I sometimes wake up crying or shaking all over."

Theow turned his face into her hand and kissed the scarred palm.

Her breath hitched, and she swallowed. "For years I thought my hand made me…I don't know. Less. I was broken. It made sense, all of a sudden, why my father couldn't love me, and why Dysg refused to marry me. After the accident, I convinced myself I didn't deserve to be loved. I believed that for years."

She glanced at Theow and hastily added, "I don't think that any longer," and he tried to erase the stricken look from his face. "Well, not as much, anyway. I know people still sometimes call me the *brytan byrde*…"

The lord's burden. Anger kindled in Theow's gut. "No. You are *not* your father's burden." If he ever heard someone talk about her that way, he'd ask Bryce to take his blacksmith's hammer and his blacksmith's muscles to them. And he knew the man would gladly do it.

"I know that." Fryda played with a lock of his hair between her fingers. "Even if my father doesn't. Other people don't always understand what it's like."

"Is that why you brought me here?" Theow brushed away the curl that fell into her eyes. "Because you understand what it's like?"

"Yes."

They stood silently for a moment, just breathing together. Theow traced her fingers with his and considered his own affliction. "It doesn't happen all the time, you know," he said. "The fear when I smell smoke or see fire, I mean. I work in a kitchen—there's always fire and smoke."

Fryda pulled back so she could look at him. "I wondered about that."

"It happens when I can't see it. When I don't know it's coming." Theow took a deep breath. "It's strange…it's not the fire that causes the reaction. It's when I smell smoke, and when I don't expect it to be there. If a piece of meat is roasting on the fire, that smoke does not affect me. But I had no idea that the bread had burned, and so…" He shrugged. "It doesn't happen very often."

"I'm glad," Fryda said. "I would worry otherwise."

He pulled her close. "I thought you were going to die that night." Theow shuddered, remembering the alarming amount of blood she had lost and the ice-white pallor of her face. "But somehow you were strong enough, even then. Your father and brother wouldn't let me in your room while you were recovering, but sometimes at night I'd sneak in through the hole in the roof, just to see how you were doing."

"I remember." Fryda smiled up at him. "I woke once when you climbed into my room. I thought you were a thief or a murderer at first. We talked all the rest of that night, whispering so no one would hear us." She turned pink. "I remember being awful to you at first because I didn't want you to see my hand. I was so feverish and…and afraid and ashamed."

Theow frowned. "I know. I realize that now." He captured her lips with his in a brief kiss. "Though back then I never knew you felt that way. I didn't think you needed to feel ashamed. I never told you this but…" Theow's chest tightened with remembered emotion. "I felt guilty for what happened to you."

Fryda stared at him. "What? Why?"

"I knew where you were going that morning," he confessed. "I knew you went to hunt that wolf. I should have stopped you, but…I wanted you to show your father you could be a true shield maiden."

"Oh, Theow." Fryda leaned in and slid her arms around his waist. "None of that was your fault. It was my foolish pride alone that took me there."

A distant clatter startled them, and they sprang apart. It came from the depths of the chasm and sounded almost musical, a clink and chime that echoed as it found its way up to the open air.

"What was that?" Fryda asked, her eyes wide. "That…that sounded exactly like the music I heard seven years ago. I thought I'd imagined or dreamed it while I was hanging there."

"Probably just falling stones," Theow reassured her. "The echoes distort the sound."

"Right. Of course, that makes sense." Fryda frowned and looked at her damaged hand. "So this…this doesn't bother you?"

The anxious quaver in her voice made Theow's chest clench. He took the little hand and brought it to his lips as he considered his answer. Fryda would see through any pandering to her pride and reject any soothing lies as insults. He owed her the truth.

"It bothers me when I think about how much pain it has caused you," he said, "and it bothers me that you still feel ashamed or embarrassed about it sometimes. But this little hand?" He kissed it again. "Nothing about this hand bothers me, and I do not think you are less, or broken, or ridiculous because of it."

She smiled and snuggled back against him, soft and warm. "Thank you, Theow."

"And my scar?" He already knew the answer, but he wanted to hear her say it. "Does that bother you?"

"No. I feel the same," she said. "I hate that it caused you pain, but your scar has always been a part of you, as long as I've known you. And there isn't anything about you I don't like."

Theow stilled. He gathered his courage and then asked in a rush, "What about the fact that I'm a slave?"

Fryda pulled back and stared at him, frowning. Startled, he caught a spark of anger in her stormy eyes. "I don't think of you that way," she said.

"And yet, that is what I am." He stroked her cheek with gentle fingertips. "There's no point in pretending otherwise."

Fryda made a noise like a growl. "It isn't your fault," she said. "You were stolen as a child, and that is not your fault. Slavery isn't what you are, it's something awful that happened to you. So no, that doesn't bother me in the slightest."

They stood there, leaning into each other, and enjoyed a moment of closeness. "We should get back soon," she said after a while, her voice muffled against his chest.

Theow groaned and Fryda laughed. "I know," she said. "But I have to make certain the longhouse is ready for the feast tonight, and you need to pick up the new cooking pot from Bryce and take it to the kitchens." She eyed him sharply. "Come find me right after that, though. Don't let Moire strongarm you into doing any more work for her."

Theow laughed. "Is that an order, my lady?"

Fryda scowled. "Let's call it a strongly worded suggestion."

"All right." He swept her up until her feet dangled above the ground, laughing as she squealed and clutched his shoulders. "Let's go."

"Put me down!" she cried, laughing and struggling against the strength of his arms. Theow started walking back towards the *burh*.

"Another strongly worded suggestion, I see," he teased. "I don't think I'll take this one, though. After all, the king tasked me with taking care of you. What if you were to fall and twist your ankle? Or what if a snake bit you?"

Fryda looked at him in exasperation. "There are no snakes in Geatland."

"Not true. There are adders."

"No one has *ever* seen an adder anywhere in this area."

"Well, obviously, that's how they get you." Theow hitched her up higher into his arms and strode forward. "They hide in holes until young women with tempting ankles wander by."

Her laughter sounded like music.

She looked down at him and brought her hand to his cheek, running her fingertips over the stubbly afternoon growth of his beard.

"You can't carry me the whole way home," she murmured.

"I would spend my last breath making sure you never had to suffer again," he said. "Carrying you home hardly seems like an effort in comparison."

She laughed again and pretended to struggle as he made his way back to the *burh*, holding her secure in his arms the entire way.

The Saviour

A *familiar noise, yet strange after so many years of absence,
rouses Fýrdraca. In sleep, she might hear the wind and the rain,
the call of birds, the crash of waves on the shore. The creak of
the birch and the ash. These sounds visit her in dreams and have
become old, familiar friends. She knows the voice of Winter and
the song of Spring, and has been intimate with the seductive
whispers of brief Summer's caress that warms the earth and the
gold against her back.*

*But these new noises are interlopers, uninvited and unwelcome,
that grate against her bones.*

A familiar voice speaks. Where has she heard it?

*She burrows deeper into her pile of gold, trying to lose herself
in treasure-song. She has long given up resisting the heat of the
Lone Survivor's curse.*

*But even the sweetness of gold cannot drown out those voices.
They go on and on.*

*She shifts, irritable, and a cascade of glittering treasure falls
away from her body. It flows around her to the floor of the
cavern, composing music of its own.*

*She hears the voice again. It sounds different to the way she
remembers it. Not so shrill. More steeped in knowledge and
experience. Stronger.*

Magical.

Ah. She remembers now. The little wasp. The captive of the rock and earth. Her saviour...the one who would break the Lone Survivor's curse.

Fýrdraca becomes restless. No one knows what became of the Lone Survivor after he cursed the treasure hoard, and the dragon beneath it. Perhaps he wandered the earth like a wraith, alone in his bitter exile until his death granted him peace. Or maybe he took his own life, thereby exiling himself from all remembrance, falling out of time and memory into obscurity. But there are those who tell of a man who, bereft of all his kin, travelled across the ocean to haunt the land of his enemies, where he withered and shrivelled into a monstrous form. Stories surface now and again of a creature so foul and twisted, people said the sun would not suffer to shine upon his face. A she-demon, the scops would tell, adopted this creature and they lived together in darkness, far beneath the surface of a rank and polluted mere. He could not endure the life-love of people, for he had locked his heart fast away in a cave, and a man is no man without his heart. And one day, after many long and cold centuries—so many the Lone Survivor had lost the memory of his true name—a strong king planted his own heart too close to the creature's mere. There the monster wreaked his revenge upon the blood and bones of his enemy's descendants, until a great hero crossed the ocean to put an end to his misery and pain.

Or so it seemed...

Thirteen

"I cannot wait for life in the *burh* to get back to normal," Bryce said as Theow entered the forge.

Theow looked around. "Things look pretty normal to me," he said. The forge-fires blazed, and tools and scraps of metal littered every surface. Bryce, stripped to the waist, looked like Thor himself, his muscles flexing under a sheen of sweat and his hammer, like Mjolnir, gripped in his enormous fist. A brisk breeze wafted through the open walls of the forge, carrying the perfume of the salt sea to mix with the scent of hot iron. Best scent in the world, Bryce always told him.

Nothing *felt* normal, though, and Theow could still feel Fryda's kiss burn against his lips, as if it had branded him for all to see.

Bryce shot Theow an exasperated look as he threw down his hammer. He leaned down and lifted Moire's new cauldron as if it weighed no more than a water-cup and set it down in front of him. How, Theow wondered, was he supposed to get it back to the kitchens?

"You should tell the king what you did. Or at least tell Weohstan," Bryce told him, rubbing the back of his neck as he bent to bank the fire in the enormous hearth.

Theow, still thinking about the kiss, blinked and felt the blood drain from his face. "Wh...what?"

Bryce levelled a look at him. "Tell them that you are the one who killed Fægebeorn and the exile in Fryda's room."

Theow stared at him. "How did you...oh. Fryda must have told you."

"She did, and she was mightily upset that Wiglaf claimed your kills and reaped the glory."

Theow rubbed the scar above his ear, as it suddenly itched and burned. "Bryce, they have no reason to believe me, and even if they did there would be no glory in it for a slave. You know that."

"They would believe it if Fryda and Wiglaf backed you up."

Theow knew Wiglaf would never willingly do such a thing for a slave—especially him. "Well, it's a bit too late for that now, isn't it? We've already put the story in place, and I refuse to reveal Fryda as a liar. Besides, you're the one who warned me about getting too close to Fryda. Weohstan would not be pleased to learn I was in her room and I don't fancy becoming dinner for sea monsters."

Bryce threw a shrewd glance at Theow. "You often have to let others take credit for what you have done, don't you?"

"I don't care about that." Theow smoothed his fingers over his scar again. "Fryda is safe. That's all that matters."

Bryce rolled his eyes. "Woden's beard, was I ever this obstinate as a lad? Of course it matters, lad. You may be a slave, but you're still a man, and you have a man's pride." Bryce clapped him on the shoulder and Theow staggered. "It would be strange indeed if you did not feel it when others claim your deeds as their own."

Theow made a helpless gesture. "All right, it bothers me, but that won't change the fact I'm a slave. If I went to the king or Weohstan with this story, I'd be laughed out of the *burh*. To them, I have no more credibility than a child."

"I suppose that's true enough." Bryce gripped his shoulder and gave him a shake. "But I think there's maybe something we can do about that."

Theow shook his head, his stomach in knots. What happened that day with Fryda had changed everything...on the inside.

Outside, unfortunately, they still faced the same obstacles and prejudices. "No. I'm used to it, Bryce. There's nothing to be done. Thank you for the cooking pot. I'll take it to Moire."

"Hold on a moment." Bryce shifted, as if suddenly nervous. "This is actually something I've wanted to discuss with you for a while now and I think the way things are going..." He stopped and rubbed his neck.

"The way what things are going?" Theow asked.

"Look, sit down." Bryce gestured to a low bench. Theow lowered himself onto it and Bryce sat on another opposite him.

"I've been mulling something over for a while now, and I'd like to hear what you think," Bryce said. He rubbed the back of his neck again. "This...this is difficult for me to say to you. I value your friendship and I don't want to lose that."

Theow rocked back on the bench and stared at the blacksmith. What could Bryce possibly say or do that would end their friendship?

Bryce plunged on. "When I was a warrior, I earned many gold coins and rings for my deeds, and I took my share of plunder from raids for many years. This, with what I've earned through my craft, has made me a very rich man."

Theow raised his eyebrows. Bryce did not live like a rich man, but even if he were, Theow would have no use for Bryce's hoarded gold. Even if the blacksmith wanted to offer it to him, slaves in Weohstan's house could not own or use coins or currency. Weohstan provided Theow with everything he had.

"Well, I finally decided what to do with the gold. Or at least part of it." Bryce took a deep breath. "I'm going to sit down with Weohstan and negotiate to buy your freedom."

Theow's jaw dropped. He blinked, and then blinked again. "What?" he asked. "I...what?"

Bryce smiled. "Close your mouth, lad, you look like a sturgeon."

Theow snapped his jaws shut.

"It can be done, you know," Bryce said. "Weohstan discourages it, but many freed slaves live amongst the clans. They own land and farm. And marry." He gave Theow a shrewd look. "I'm not sure any freed slave has reached so high as to pluck a lord's daughter for a wife, but I reckon you're halfway there already."

Theow shook his head. "But...what would that cost? What would *I* cost?" He dropped his head into his hands. "I have no idea how much Weohstan paid for me in the first place. I've never asked, never wanted to know my own *wergild*."

"Theow," Bryce said, his voice gentle. "Slaves don't have a life-price."

"I know. I just always thought..." Theow shook his head.

"It doesn't matter, lad," Bryce said. He reached out and clasped the boy's arm. "I have the gold. Enough for two lifetimes. I may as well spend one of them on a good man who deserves a chance."

"But how would that be different from purchasing a slave?" Theow leaned away and Bryce released his arm. "I mean, I understand the laws of the land allow such transactions, but I would still feel bought and paid for...owned."

"No." Theow started at the vehemence in his voice. "I do not purchase *you*. I purchase your freedom, which would then belong to you. You would belong to no one but yourself, Theow. You would be free."

Theow had never realized hope could feel so much like panic. Sweat sprang out on his forehead, his upper lip, under his arms, behind his knees. He had no words to express the joy and hope that stuttered on his tongue, so he clutched his hands together to keep them from shaking. Freedom. Was it possible? "But I could never repay..."

Bryce leaned forward and prodded Theow in the chest with one thick, meaty finger. "You listen to me, Theow. You are a good man, and I suspect Fryda loves you. And I love that girl.

Love her like she is my own daughter." A spasm of pain crossed his face, and he rubbed sooty fingers against his eyes.

"Bryce." Theow reached out in concern.

"I had a family once." The abrupt confession stopped Theow cold. How in all these years had he not known this? The blacksmith lifted his head and Theow saw his eyes were wet. "I had a wife and a daughter many years ago. Long before I came here. I would leave them for long stretches of time when I went on raids for my lord or the king. I never questioned that. It was my duty. I was loyal. So I left them, again and again, and they were always there when I returned. My beautiful wife Arleigh, each time a little bit older. My darling Ælfgifu, always a little bit taller and on her way to becoming a beautiful young woman. And then one day I came home from a raid and they were not there."

Theow closed his eyes. He had wondered before what had made Bryce renounce his favoured warrior status and become a humble blacksmith.

"Our mead-hall was...was attacked while I was gone." Bryce seemed to choose his words carefully. "Most of my people survived, but about thirty or so were butchered and..." He closed his eyes. "My Arleigh was amongst them, as was our daughter, Ælfgifu."

Bryce looked at Theow, and the tortured, naked grief in his eyes made Theow grateful for the first time in his life that he remembered nothing from the time before Weohstan bought him at the slavers' block.

"Fryda is what I always imagined Ælfgifu would be like if she'd..." Bryce stopped, and then swallowed. "Strong and determined. Smart. Beautiful. Both precious gifts, as their names proclaim. And I know Fryda never received a father's love from the one man who should have given it to her." He gave a helpless little shrug. "So, I loved her. And now she's as much a daughter to me as my own blood. I want to know she is safe and protected in case trouble comes...and lad, trouble always comes. When

Fryda told me how you killed Fægebeorn, I knew then you would do anything to keep her safe. So, the least I can do is buy your freedom."

Theow swallowed. "I...that..."

A thought, then, stopped his tongue, and he looked at Bryce.

"I know you love Fryda," Theow said. "I've known for years. But it's more than that, isn't it?"

Bryce raised his eyes, and Theow was startled by the depth of anguish he saw in them.

"You told me yourself that Weohstan would never consent to his daughter carrying on with a slave, let alone marrying one. Even if he agrees to your request, he wouldn't want me near her." Bryce looked down again. "My freedom might make Fryda happy, but it would do nothing to change our situation. Not while her father and her brother live. And I'm pretty certain if you paid off Hild's debt, Fryda would be just as happy with that. So why me?"

Bryce's face twisted with some powerful emotion, but he did not speak.

"Why are you so intent on helping me?" Theow asked. His breathing quickened as some nameless fear gripped him. "What don't you want to tell me?"

Bryce swallowed, his throat working as if he had to force the words past his teeth.

"You have to understand," he said thickly, "I was a different man then. A completely different man."

The blacksmith's eyes pleaded with Theow, begging him to understand something so secret, so monumental, that Theow knew he was going to change his life forever.

"I was a warrior, one of the *gedriht*, my lord's favoured fighters. I went on every raid and never questioned whether what I did was right or wrong. I never thought of the people I killed, or the innocent victims we put to our swords, or stole to sell into slavery. I was trained to obey my lord, and so I did."

Theow clutched the edge of the bench and remained silent.

Bryce rubbed his face with rough hands and hung his head, but his voice was clear as he continued his story.

"The raid...the one I came back from to discover my wife and daughter gone." He paused and remained silent for so long Theow thought he would not speak again. But then Bryce raised his head and he saw that the guilt in his eyes had been taken over by a self-loathing so profound it made Theow's chest ache.

"For that raid, my lord sent us to the island of the Celts, to Ériu. We landed at the mouth of a long inlet and worked our way inland. Our instructions were clear, and we followed them without question." Bryce pressed his lips together, but he could not stop the words as they tumbled forth. "We were to take whatever spoils we could, but most importantly, we were to take the children."

Theow's body felt hollow. Bryce held his gaze, however, refusing to look away again.

"So we sailed up the inlet and landed at every settlement. We raided the *ráths*, the Irish ringfort villages, and put them to the torch. We took the children from their homes and piled them in our ships, and when we were done, we sailed to the Saxon village of Brycg Stowe to sell them to the slavers."

Theow opened his mouth to say something...he did not know what...but no sound came out.

"I was part of the raid that stole you from your family, lad." It seemed odd that Bryce's face could hold such anguish while Theow himself felt nothing. "I may not have taken you myself, but all these years I've felt responsible for what happened to you. And I have always imagined that losing my own family was the gods' way of punishing me, of putting right the wrong I did."

"So..." Theow managed to find his voice, but it sounded unfamiliar to him. "So all this time, you knew. You knew where I came from."

"Yes."

"And you didn't tell me."

"No."

"Why?" With that one, plaintive word, all the hurt and anger and bewildered sense of betrayal filled and overflowed the hollow cavern in his breast.

"I came to Eceweall about two years after I lost my family, and I didn't say anything at first because I did not realize you had been stolen during that particular raid," Bryce said. He ran his fingers through his hair. "It wasn't until I first heard Weohstan tell the story of how he found you at Brycg Stowe that I realized you must have come on the ships from Ériu."

Theow clenched his fists. "And still you said nothing?" he demanded. "You knew I had lost my memory. You knew I was desperate for some knowledge of my home, my family. I have spent my *life* wondering who I am, and it turns out you knew all along?"

"Yes." Bryce's honesty was unflinching in the face of Theow's anger. "I have no excuses, though perhaps one day you will understand my reasons. Losing my family broke me. As I told you, I was a different man then. And then, once I came here and discovered you, I thought the gods continued to punish me by putting you, a reminder of my shame, before my eyes nearly every day." Bryce launched to his feet and began pacing around the forge. "But as I watched you grow into a man, and I saw you become good and strong, watched you fall in love with Fryda, and she with you...I knew I'd eventually have to tell you my secret. Even if it meant sacrificing the friendship I felt between us. But I knew Weohstan would never agree to free a slave child, so I had to wait until you grew to manhood, until you'd proven you could contribute to the clan. So, I waited. And waited. And I guess I just never had the heart to tell you before now."

Theow also stood. His whole body trembled and his mind spun so wildly he could not seem to catch any of his thoughts.

"So...so you don't know who my family was?" he asked eventually. "Or which village I came from?"

"No, lad. I'm sorry." Bryce leaned against his worktable, looking defeated. "I know you're Irish, and you came from somewhere along that inlet."

It wasn't much, but it was more than he'd had. Vague memories surfaced, half remembered dreams of yellow-haired giants gripping enormous swords and carrying all the children into ships waiting offshore...somewhere. In Ériu.

And Bryce had known all this time.

Theow spun and walked to the doorway. He could not bear to look at the blacksmith. He needed to find Fryda, to tell her everything so she could untangle this knot that kept tightening and strangling him from the inside.

"Lad, wait."

Theow stopped.

"You see now, don't you?" Bryce voice was heavy and resigned. "If I can convince Weohstan to free you, I can help you find where you came from. I can help you find the answers you seek. And perhaps I can begin to pay back the harm I've done to you."

Theow turned his head, but did not meet his eyes. "You would do that?"

Bryce let out a puff of air that, under different circumstances, might have been a laugh. "It's the least I can do, lad," he said. "We can talk again after I've spoken with Weohstan, come up with a plan..."

Theow stood in the doorway, uncertain and undecided. He wanted to say *yes*, of course he did, but...he felt raw and hurt and angry. He wished Fryda had come to the forge with him. She would know what questions to ask.

Fourteen

Fryda hurried towards the longhouse, having stopped in her rooms to change into her favourite blue dress for the second night of the feast. Her feet danced and heart sang as she climbed the path up the hill. She felt as if she floated off the ground, as if Theow still carried her in his arms. The clean scent of freshly cut grasses transported her back to the chasm, and Fryda traced her lips with a fingertip. She could still feel the pressure of Theow's mouth on hers, and she smiled.

She'd finally done it. She'd kissed him. She had realized that afternoon, while she waited on the windy bluff for him to come to her, that he never would—no matter how much he might want to. She also realized he would always think of himself as a slave and of her as the lord's daughter, and he would never let himself cross that boundary. In fact, she anticipated quite a struggle with Theow to allow *her* to cross it as well. She would have to be careful. She didn't want him to think their relative positions meant she held all the power between them.

But even such dour thoughts could not dampen her spirits. She wrapped her arms around herself and indulged in a soft, girlish giggle. Theow had kissed her back. He wanted her, and today nothing could flatten the happiness that coiled within her. She would worry about all the new problems she had created for herself later.

Duties, she thought, taking a firm grip on herself. She had duties and responsibilities, and daydreaming of happiness and kisses would not see them accomplished. Fryda especially needed to tell Eadith to keep a sharp eye on the casks of mead for the feast that night. They still had no real proof of what happened to the stolen white poppy syrup.

Fryda stopped in her tracks. Despite the day's distractions, the theft from Hild's stillroom continued to trouble her, especially when brought together with other oddities from the past few days. The drugged mead. Fægebeorn's assault during the first feast, and the attack in her rooms later that night. Even the contradictory reports regarding King Eadgils' whereabouts and his extraordinary conversation with her the night before seemed ominous.

King Eadgils. Fryda frowned. She had not seen him or his men since he left the feast shortly after Beowulf told the story of the goblet, and that, too, was strange. He'd been absent from the massive breakfast Weohstan had hosted that morning for the foreign leaders and ambassadors, and she'd heard nothing of any orders from him to the kitchens or household servants.

It was as if he'd disappeared from the *burh* entirely.

Her mind strayed again to the stolen poppy. Her father had wondered why Eadgils had accepted Beowulf's invitation to attend the celebration feasts in the first place, and Eadgils himself had made it clear he was not there for love of either Weohstan or the king. *What if,* Fryda thought, *he was here for revenge?* If her father truly had killed Eanmund and taken his sword—her mind still boggled at that—Eadgils might think Weohstan owed him a blood-debt.

But if so, then why wait forty years to demand fulfilment of his brother's *wergild*? What would be the point of drugging the mead and putting everyone to sleep?

She could make no sense of it.

Fryda turned from the longhouse and headed towards the kitchens. She would have Hild make her a draught for stomach sickness and then she'd bring it herself to King Eadgils' room with a story of concern for his health. Her motives were not entirely false, she assured herself as she felt a pang of guilt. She should check he was all right, and that nothing was amiss.

She also needed to let Moire and Eadith know Theow would not be returning to the kitchens. Ever. Her father would not thank her for interfering with his household arrangements, but she was lady of the house now and she should have taken over those duties herself long ago. She would find a better situation for Theow—perhaps one that allowed her to stay closer to him.

Fryda squashed that thought. Staying close to Theow would be dangerous, especially for him. She would not be able to resist touching him, and eventually they would get caught. Her father would exile or kill Theow if he thought a slave had meddled with his daughter.

The kitchens were in a panic of preparation for the second feast. Fryda did manage to make it clear to Moire that Theow was no longer under her authority, and if she ever saw even the ghost of abuse on another slave or servant's person, Fryda would personally see to it that Moire left the *burh* in disgrace. Pale and silent, Moire nodded and Fryda saw more than one smile on the workers' faces as they bent industriously over their work. Next, she hunted down Eadith, who was overseeing the cleaning in the longhouse, and told her about the drugged mead.

Eadith looked at Fryda, aghast. "Are you sure?" she asked.

"No," Fryda admitted as she watched the servants bustle and scrub. "But I thought we should be careful nonetheless."

"Yes." Eadith's forehead puckered with concern. "I'll personally inspect every cask of mead that goes out tonight. You have my word."

"It wasn't your fault," Fryda said. She took one of Eadith's gnarled hands into her own sound one and gave it a gentle squeeze. "If someone did drug the mead, there's no way we could have known about it beforehand."

Her errands complete, Fryda gripped the little pot of medicine and made her way down the hill and across the green to the guest house appointed for King Eadgils' use.

"My lord?" she called and rapped on the door. "My lord, are you at home? It's Lady Fryda. I've come to see if you need anything."

She was met with silence. Cautiously, Fryda pushed open the door and stepped inside. She padded through the spacious foyer into the large main living area. Fryda saw no one, though a fire crackled in the firepit and she noticed signs of recent activity—a linen wrap lay draped over a chair, a half-eaten oatcake and cup of mead sat on the table. She saw a sword and shield propped up against the wall, and the rushes on the floor were disturbed, as if moved and scuffed by numerous feet—or one pair of feet pacing restlessly back and forth.

"My lord?" Clutching the medicine, Fryda crept to the open doorway that led into the king's expansive bedchamber. Embroidered hangings covered the walls and the room's wooden furniture was polished to a deep shine. The enormous bed was rumpled but empty, and the washbowl had been used but not yet cleaned or refilled.

Eadgils had not left the *burh*, but he was not in his rooms. Where had he gone?

Feeling like a traitor to every tenet of hospitality and basic good manners, Fryda crept into the bedchamber and set the pot of medicine on the table. On the surface, everything looked normal and nothing in the rooms hinted at what Eadgils had been doing since he left the feast. She peeked into the large, elaborately carved wooden chest at the foot of the bed and poked through the folded clothes. Nothing. Another carved box she didn't recognize stood in one corner and she thought Eadgils must have brought it with him. Fryda's heart raced as she lifted the lid, but was disappointed to find only furs, jewellery, and clasps. Combs, razors, and other personal items rested on the table with the washbowl, and a set of shelves held a few pieces of pottery, an exquisite little stone horse, and a casket carved from pieces of ivory held together with bands of silver.

She examined the box. It was about the size of a small soup pot and carved all over with knights, horses, and the various trappings of war. A lock held the silver bindings fast and *of course*, Fryda thought as she scanned the room with frustration, there was no key in sight.

Fryda examined the lock. The small keyhole was shaped like an hourglass with a tiny latch inlaid beneath it. She had seen these locks before. Bryce had explained to her how he made them and how they worked. A small metal hook was attached to the inside of the lid. Sliding the latch moved the hook to one side, where it dropped and caught on a stud or metal bar. The hook made it impossible to open the lid without breaking the box itself. The key lifted the hook and allowed the latch to move to the other side, freeing the lid and unlocking the box. Fryda could not break the box—Eadgils would immediately know someone had been snooping in his rooms. Fortunately, Bryce had also taught her a trick or two about opening locks without a key.

Fryda reached up and put a hand in her unruly hair. She wiggled her fingers back and forth, and a lone hairpin sprang from the mess of braids and curls. She retrieved it and pressed the slim metal prong against the floor until it had a single, clean bend. She fed the pin into the keyhole and wiggled it about, searching by feel to displace the hook inside.

It took several tries, but eventually she felt the hook give and the lid of the box come loose. She slid the latch to the left and opened the box.

She leaned against the shelf, her breath trapped behind her ribs as she looked down at the little flasks of white poppy syrup. About half of them were empty.

Oh bollocks.

Before she could think or do anything else, she heard voices coming from the big main room. Fear flamed through her blood and she looked frantically around. There was only one way out. She was trapped.

She moved towards the doorway, her soft slippers making no noise against the straw-strewn floor, and flattened herself against the wall. She cocked her head, trying to hear the low, muttered words over the pounding of her heart.

"...need to make sure she drinks more of it this time." Fryda recognized Eadgils' voice. "She wakened too easily the other night and managed to rouse the household."

Fryda froze.

"And this time you are not to interfere with her body in any way," Eadgils continued. "That was Fægebeorn's mistake and it got him killed. Do not repeat it."

Someone grumbled something she could not hear, the voice low and masculine, but Eadgils' voice, rich with anger and contempt, carried clearly.

"She and that halfwit Celt of a slave killed three of my men, you *sott*," he snarled. "I need the strength of all my men to overcome Weohstan's guards. Just make sure she drinks the poppy and then bring her to me."

Fryda grew lightheaded as the blood drained from her face. For a moment her mind blanked, as if unable to grasp the enormity of what she had heard.

She missed what Eadgils said next. Her thoughts scattered every which way, each one so dreadful she could scarcely face it. She tried to piece together one fact at a time. Eadgils planned to kidnap her and murder her father. He had staged the attack on her, so the exiles she and Wiglaf had killed were his men. Eadgils knew Theow had killed Fægebeorn in her room last night. Only three people in the world, including herself, knew the truth about that. Four, she corrected herself. She had told Bryce. So how had Eadgils known Wiglaf had not killed the three attackers as they had said?

Only one person would have told him.

Her mind dodged around the knowledge, his name too painful to contemplate. Panic clawed at her insides. She had to get out of there, but she knew the instant she left the room the men would see her.

"…will see to the other arrangements," Eadgils was saying as she refocused her attention. "Remember, you must retrieve my sword. I cannot leave without it." His voice grew louder and Fryda realized he was walking towards the bedchamber.

She had one instant to decide what to do.

Best to brazen it out, she thought. She snatched up Hild's stomach remedy and plastered a smile on her face just as Eadgils entered the room.

"King Eadgils." Fryda tried to sound unconcerned and natural. "Here you are. I was worried when I didn't see you at the breakfast banquet this morning."

Eadgils' eyes widened and the thin, gossamer skin of his face grew pale. He had deep shadows under his eyes, as if he had not slept, and his gaze instantly darted to the casket.

The casket she had neglected to close.

"What are you doing here?" he asked, his voice low and calm.

"I was worried for your health, my lord." She bundled up her courage and sailed past Eadgils into the living room. Four men dressed in Swedish colours, blue and gold, stood by the firepit, hands on the hilts of their swords. The king followed her into the room and snapped out an order in Swedish. The men reacted instantly. Two of them moved into the doorway behind the king, as if to ensure she could not retreat back into the bedchamber. The other two took up position near the outside exit.

Eadgils stopped in front of her, standing a little too close for comfort. He took her hand and she had to crane her neck to meet his eyes, for though he was not a tall man, the top of her head only came up to his chin.

Eadgils frowned at her. "Worried for my health." It was not a question, and his ice-blue eyes pierced hers. He released her hand and she stepped back a little too hastily.

"Yes." Fryda swallowed. "When I didn't see you today, I thought perhaps too much feasting last night upset your stomach." She held up the little pot of medicine. "I stopped by with a remedy for you."

"No." Eadgils' eyes focused on her torn lip. "I am not ill."

"I am glad." She took another small step back towards the door. "I apologize for the intrusion, my lord, but I saw the servants had not been here yet, so I thought to straighten things up for you."

"You. The lady of the house? Cleaning my room?"

He did not believe her, and Fryda couldn't blame him. It was a weak excuse. She edged closer to the door.

"Did I hear you say something about your sword?" Another step. She could not pretend she had heard nothing of their conversation. "Did you take it to Bryce, the blacksmith, for sharpening? If you did, you shall not be disappointed in his work. He is the best blacksmith in Geatland."

The Swedish king's expression did not change at the mention of Bryce's name.

He stared not at her but through her. Fryda could not hide her trembling.

"I see." Eadgils stepped towards her now. "Yes, I see everything."

Fryda stepped back once more, maintaining the distance between them. "Well. I'll take my leave, then. I'm happy to hear you are well and I hope to see you at the feast tonight, my lord."

Eadgils sighed as he regarded her. "Of course." He brought one wrinkled, spotted hand up to rub his forehead. "Of course you would make this difficult for me. You are his daughter, after all."

"I don't know what you mean, my lord." As she continued to

back towards the door leading back to the *burh*, Fryda bumped up against a hard surface and found herself gripped by the two guards behind her. She twisted, struggled, and for the first time got a good look at their faces. Matted beards and brown, broken teeth. Hollow cheeks and hollow eyes. Wasted bodies dressed in Eadgils' colours.

Exiles.

Fryda looked back at Eadgils. "What...why...?"

"Oh, come now," he said, his reedy voice contemptuous. "Do you think I could persuade my true and noble soldiers to break trust and treaty with King Beowulf and all of Geatland? Use your head, girl. I sent my army north to distract them and keep them out of my way."

Fryda's heart pounded in her ears. "Wh...what?" Her voice sounded high and frightened.

Eadgils smiled, and he looked like a feral animal, all bared teeth and malevolence. "You're stronger than I thought you'd be." He moved towards her. "And even more clever. I had only heard you were Weohstan's crippled daughter, so I assumed you would be easy to handle. Foolish of me, I suppose."

He looked at her hand, for once uncovered, and an expression of disgust crossed his features. His gaze travelled with almost prurient fascination over her malformed fingers and strangely angled wrist. Fryda gritted her teeth and longed to tuck her hand inside her sleeve, but she could not move her arms with the guards holding her. "Why are you doing this?" she demanded, dropping all pretence. "What do you want with me?"

Eadgils said nothing. He stopped in front of her and smiled as she struggled. He reached out and ran a gnarled finger across her cheekbone. She jerked away and the back of her skull collided with her captors' armour. A single hairpin dislodged from her mass of curls and fell to the floor, its musical *clink-clink* lost amidst her struggles.

"I need you to help me prove a point to your father." Eadgils stroked her jaw. Fryda strained her neck trying to escape his touch. "As well as to the traitorous King Beowulf who helped me defeat Onela with one hand while he saved and sheltered my brother's murderer with the other."

"But…that happened years ago," Fryda protested. "Decades. Why did you wait until now?"

Eadgils caught a curl of her hair between his fingers and caressed it. Fryda's stomach heaved.

"Your father will watch as I kill you and your useless drunk of a brother," he said, ignoring her question, "and he will know the pain I have felt all these years. Then I will cut out his heart and call his blood-debt satisfied. Your family owes me that debt." Eadgils leaned in, sliding her hair between his fingers.

Fryda shrank back until her body pressed fully against the exiles behind her. "The *wergild*, your brother's life-price, was forgiven."

Eadgils' eyes glittered. "Not by me."

"Why are you telling me all this?"

"Do not insult me." Eadgils scowled and looked through the doorway into his bedchamber. She hadn't time to close the unlocked box and its contents were displayed for all to see. "You searched my room. You found the poppy. You overheard the directions I gave to my men." He moved uncomfortably close and looked down at her. "There is little point in pretence now."

Enough of this, Fryda thought, and kneed Eadgils in the groin.

The king doubled over, groaning, and the two exiles behind him ran forward to help. Taking advantage of their distraction, she tried one of the defensive strategies Bryce had taught her that morning. She sagged, letting all her weight hang from the hands of the two men who gripped her arms. Taken unawares, they dropped her and she fell to the ground. They reached for her, but she slithered between their legs. She had never been so grateful for her diminutive size as she was right then. While the exiles twisted and turned to look for her, she scrambled to her feet and ran without looking back. She fled out the door, across the green, and up the hill towards the forge, her yellow hair streaming behind her like a frayed war banner.

Fifteen

Fryda had never run so fast, and had never felt such relief as when she saw Theow standing in the blacksmith's doorway.

"Fryda." Theow ran to meet her and caught her by the arms as she skidded to a stop in front of him. She could feel herself shaking as she bent over and clutched at Theow's tunic with a desperate hand. "What's wrong?"

"It's King Eadgils." She panted, her breath spent from running and fear. Bryce appeared beside them, watching her with concern as her words tumbled over each other in her haste. "He brought the exiles into Eceweall. He planned the attack on me. He's going to kill my father, and I think that Wiglaf...Wiglaf..."

Theow supported her while she struggled to compose herself and Bryce said, "Slow down. Tell us what happened."

Theow's hands tightened and drew her closer as Fryda told them about her confrontation with Eadgils in the longhouse, his anger at the king and plans to assassinate her father, and the exiles disguised as Swedish guards. By the time she was finished, he had her in a full embrace, his arms locked tightly around her. She glanced at Bryce, worried about his reaction, but the blacksmith hardly seemed to notice.

"How did you get away?" Theow asked.

Bryce grunted in approval when she described her escape, but Fryda growled, "I'm getting tired of men accosting me and having to hit them in the nethers for it." Theow's eyebrows shot up and he let her go. Fryda stifled a wholly inappropriate laugh. "Not you, silly."

Before he could respond, a great shout went up near the longhouse. On its heels the blast of a horn sounded in the stronghold, a long and mournful cry that seemed like a lament for deaths soon to come.

"What is that?" Theow asked. Bryce did not answer, but ran into the forge. Fryda looked at Theow and saw such concern and tenderness in his eyes her own fear nearly melted.

Nearly.

"It's Eadgils," she said. "He's called his men to attack."

As she spoke, a great roar rose from the guest houses and the barracks that sheltered the guards. Doors burst open throughout the *burh*. She and Theow watched in horror from their position atop the hill as men swarmed from the buildings wearing the blue and yellow colours of Eadgils' house, brandishing spears, swords, bows, and *seaxes*. Bryce came running back from the forge, his arms full of iron.

"Can you swing a sword?" he asked Theow.

Fryda immediately sensed that something had happened between the two men—something that caused them to be strange and awkward with each other. The blacksmith met Theow's eyes as he held out a short-sword, and Fryda saw a miscellany of complicated emotions written upon both their faces.

Theow appeared to wrestle with himself and finally took a deep breath, his tense shoulders relaxing. "I...yes, well enough," he said. "I've never been allowed a weapon of my own, but Wiglaf and I used to play at sword-fighting with sticks when we were children. I learned a few tricks from him."

Bryce thrust the sword at him, all business now as the roar of fighting men escalated. "Don't stab yourself with it. The pointy end goes into the enemy." Theow rolled his eyes as the blacksmith turned to Fryda. "Dagger or iron poker?"

Fryda's blood sang. *Finally!* A chance to prove her mettle in real battle!

"Why don't I get a sword?" she demanded.

"Too heavy." Bryce held up the poker and the dagger. "Which one?"

She huffed. "Poker, please. If I'm close enough to use a knife, I'm probably already dead."

"Good. Try to stay as far away as possible from the people trying to kill you, and stab or smash in their heads with this if they get too close. Remember how I taught you to use your left hand. Brace and balance." Bryce handed her the long, sturdy shaft of metal he used to turn the heavy logs in his largest hearth, and he tucked the dagger into his belt. In his own hand, Fryda noted, Bryce held the sword that usually hung above the hearth, its long and elegant blade gleaming in the sunlight and covered with dark, secret runes.

The noise of the attacking exiles swelled until it sounded like a thundering waterfall, and Fryda could now hear the clash of iron as the unintelligible shouts of men grew closer.

"We have to find Wiglaf and my father!" An unexpected stab of sorrow lanced through Fryda at the thought of her brother, who had betrayed her—and all Eceweall—to Eadgils.

"And King Beowulf," Theow added.

"They were not in the longhouse," she said, "so they're probably still in our private rooms. If we get separated, make your way there."

Theow looked at her and Fryda saw the exact moment he decided to protect her. She scowled at him and lifted her chin to a defiant angle.

"No," she said.

"But I haven't..."

"I am not staying behind, so don't even suggest it." She made her voice calm but her tone unbending.

"I said I would spend my last breath to keep you safe," Theow reminded her, looking troubled.

Fryda glared at him. "Don't you dare breathe your last on my account, Theow of Eċeweall, or I will never forgive you."

Theow caught her around the waist and pressed his mouth hard, demanding, against hers. She momentarily forgot that Bryce was *right there* watching them, that Eadgils had brought an exile army into her home to destroy her father. Theow pulled away and looked at her. "That, I believe, was an order," he told her, smiling. "You told me to challenge you if you..."

Fryda grasped him by the hair and ravaged his mouth with hers, as desperate and demanding as he had been. She let him go and glared at him. "*Please* try not to get yourself killed. Better?" She stepped back, feeling less like a fierce shield maiden and more like a slightly mad scullery maid with her rumpled hair straggling from its pins and braids, and her small hand clutching the iron poker.

Theow gripped his own weapon, muttered an invocation to whatever gods might be listening, and ran into the storm of spears. Fryda and Bryce followed close behind.

Fryda quickly realized that a lifetime of stories about great battles could not prepare her for the experience of actually being in one.

She ran after Theow but almost immediately lost him in the maelstrom of men flooding the grounds of the *burh*. When the *scops* sang about the clanging of arms and the shouts of men, of the clatter of iron as warriors made a shield-wall and the rattle of fire-hardened ashwood spears, they neglected to mention the resulting cacophony was so disorienting that commonplace skills —such as walking and navigation—would desert her completely.

Exiles clad in Eadgils' colours clashed with her father's warriors, who streamed from the barracks as they tugged on their mail shirts and stiff leather greaves. Members of the *gedriht* shouted orders and shield maidens unleashed their war-cries. Older children, not yet grown enough to do battle, gathered up the small ones and herded them towards the farmsteads near the western gate, far from the worst of the fighting. Fryda tried to keep her bearings as she ducked and dodged her way through the mayhem, searching for a glimpse of Theow's fire-coloured hair. Her lack of height meant she could not see over the heads of the men, and their bodies obscured her view of the buildings. She stopped in the middle of the clash of arms, dizzy and disoriented.

An exile thrust his sword at the back of one of Weohstan's warriors, who was engaged in battle with another man. Without stopping to think, Fryda darted forward and swung her poker at the exile's helmet, which made a resonant ringing noise, and the man crumpled to the ground.

Fryda crouched down and made herself as small as possible while she moved through the pulsing throng, searching for anything to pinpoint her location. She tucked her damaged hand under her other arm, trying to protect it from the frenzied violence of the battle. One of her father's own men, giving chase to an exile fleeing his spear, saw the blue of her dress and the yellow of her hair and, obviously thinking her an exile, kicked her in the ribs as he passed her.

Fryda dropped like a stone. Lightning and fire seemed to shoot through her side, and she groaned as every breath tore new definitions of pain through her body. She clutched to her ribs with her good hand. *They must be broken*, she thought. In her experience, only cracked bones could hurt this much. A man in blue and yellow, a spearhead sticking out from the centre of his chest, tripped over her and he fell atop her body. She managed to twist her torso at the last minute to avoid the spear protruding from his ribcage, but the impact jarred loose every ache in her body and lancing pain from her ribs, shoulder, and hand. The exile's face, covered in sweat, hovered only inches from hers and his blood made dark, wet patches on her blue silk dress. His mouth twisted into a snarl, but Fryda could not tear her gaze from his eyes. They pleaded with her, full of fear, as if begging for reassurance that death had not at that moment conquered him. But she saw the life leave his body and he slumped against her, heavy and immovable.

It took some doing, but she eventually managed to wriggle out from under his corpse. Gasping, she staggered to her feet. She had to find her father, but there were so many men. At first the exiles seemed to swarm the *burh* like ants on honey, their numbers greater than her father's fighters. However, as warriors belonging to the other kings and clan leaders answered the call of the horn and gathered from every corner of the *burh*—soldiers from Denmark, Norway, Frisia, and Skåne—the number of blue and yellow-clad fighters began to diminish. In their armour, the warriors seemed twice their usual size. Booted feet kicked up dirt and dust that stung Fryda's eyes and made her cough. Thick, black smoke rolled over the battlefield like dragon's breath. The exiles must have put the *burh*'s outer buildings to the torch, and Fryda chilled to think of Theow there. Her mind conjured grotesque images of her family trapped inside a burning building, unable to escape. Beneath the acrid stench of flame and fire lay the uglier odours of blood and death, of fear and desperation.

The warrior's shouts heaved up to the sky, songs of triumph mingled with the music of suffering, offerings of carrion to the eager ravens and eagles circling the battle high above. From their hands they let fly fire-hardened spears, and their bows were busy with the business of death. Slaughter fell upon the earth, and Weohstan's men stood steadfast against it. They engaged their enemy with courage, dancing face-to-face with doom and deep wounds. The smell of blood and disembowelled offal made Fryda's stomach churn. She clutched her side and set off again.

She saw a warrior in Eadgils' colours raise a two-bladed axe and cleave one of her father's warriors in half. The trunk of his body slid, then split. She saw Olaf bring his enormous two-handed sword down on an exile's head, which burst open. Fryda panted in short, shallow breaths, clinging to her poker and holding it at the ready as she made her way through the carnage.

She yelped as one of her father's men leapt in front of her and thrust his sword through an exile's belly. As the victor wrestled his weapon from the corpse, another exile seized him from behind and slashed his throat with a sharp *seax*.

She heard the blast of the horn calling the rest of her father's troops, those out for the hunt or down by the ships, back to the *burh* to join the fight. Soon after, the notes sounded, clear above the din, marshalling King Beowulf's men to him, though she could not see him anywhere. All around her, warriors grunted and perspired, snarled and screamed as they fought and died. The ground ran red.

Fryda fled, heading for higher ground. An exile rushed at her and she readied her poker, but he choked and fell after a few steps, an arrow protruding from his back. She clambered over his body and then skidded to a halt as she saw a group of servants and slaves armed with heavy pans and sharp knives rush into the fight. She must be near the kitchens, she thought. That meant she was close to the longhouse.

Fryda watched in astonishment as Hild, armed with nothing more than a long-handled kitchen knife, charged a cluster of exiles. Hild and her thin knife brought down three men in quick succession. The rest of the kitchen staff followed her, like a well-trained regiment. If they lived through this, Fryda would definitely talk to Olaf about adding Hild to the shield maidens. He could work her debt and years of service out with her father.

If her father still lived.

Fryda lost sight of Hild as she darted through the clash of men once more, and the ever-shifting battle pulled at her like the ebb and flow of a relentless tide. She struggled against the current, trying to maintain her feet and not get dragged down by the undertow. The smoke billowed thicker now and clogged in her throat as she tried to control her sharp, rapid breaths. Her side throbbed. Two of the smaller outbuildings were on fire, but the rest of the *burh* looked intact so far.

An exile lunged at her, his blade nearly impaling her. She leapt back, wincing at the pain from her wounds and bruises. He lunged again, snarling, his broken teeth brown and jagged and his filthy, matted hair falling to his waist.

Fryda scrambled backwards, but the exile would not let her go so easily. He grinned an evil grin, reversed the sword in his hand and came at her, ready to strike her with the pommel. Not to kill her, she understood, but to render her insensible. Dread clenched in the bottom of her belly.

Something deep within her woke. She did not know its name... courage, anger, or perhaps a long-sleeping gift bestowed by her berserker ancestors...but a relentless pressure burst through the seams and edges of her. She'd felt something like this several times before—when Hild attacked her during practice, when Bryce had surprised her in the meadow, and when Fægebeorn came to her bedchamber. Her pain dissolved and her fear drowned as a surge of intense energy flooded her limbs. A glorious heat, like liquid gold, flowed through her body. It seemed to harden her muscles to stone and run through her blood like living iron, giving her unnatural strength. It flooded from her mouth in a bloodcurdling war-cry, high-pitched and clear above the guttural sounds of fighting men.

Startled by the wild sound, the exile stuttered to a halt, his weapon still raised. Fryda leapt at him and swung the iron poker in a perfect arc. It connected and smashed through the side of his head, and the man crumpled to the ground.

She stared at the body, half in horror and half in frenzied exhilaration. Blood and brains leaked from the man's shattered skull onto the torn ground. His jaw hung at an awkward angle from his face, and his eyes bulged from their sockets. Her strength deserted her and the pain in her side rushed back, doubling her over.

Someone seized her arm, and she swung the poker again as hard as she could. Iron clashed with iron as Bryce brought his ancient sword up to block her blow, and she cried out as the reverberation set her ribs on fire.

"Oh gods, I'm sorry," she gasped over the din, mortified. "I didn't see you."

"As if you could hurt me with that hairpin." Bryce glanced at the corpse. "Well done, Sunbeam," he said. "Now come. We need to catch up with Theow."

"My father?" Fryda's voice shook as she pulled her sleeve over her hand.

Bryce shook his head. "Haven't found him yet. He'll be in his rooms, most likely." He grabbed her arm and dragged her away.

Together they weaved in and out through the chaos, dodging sparring warriors and leaping over bodies strewn across the ground. Booted feet had churned the fresh green grass into mud. The standing stone that had graced the centre of the green for untold years now lay on its side. The fighting thinned as men dropped, wounded or lifeless. She breathed with relief to see that most of the bodies wore blue and yellow and those left standing were her father's warriors and their guests. They had done well, despite having been taken unawares.

Bryce slid his arm around Fryda and jogged her along. The sky had darkened as the sun began its journey to the horizon. Soon she saw the raised wooden building where her father and brother often slept, and she nearly wept to see it unharmed. She stumbled as Bryce carried her towards the door.

They ran up the steps. Two of her father's guards lay dead in front of the open door, one with a slashed throat and the other with an axe embedded in his chest. Fryda stepped over their bodies and ran into the house.

"Father!" she called, gasping. "Wiglaf!"

She ran through the foyer and turned into the main area of the house, Bryce on her heels. She emerged into a familiar airy room. A throne-like chair stood by a huge fireplace. Wiglaf—clearly dosed with mead, or white poppy, or both—sprawled sideways across the seat, his face slack and his eyes half-closed. Eadgils, King of Sweden, stood with hands clasped behind his back in front of two men who held her father between them. She could not see Theow.

Fryda stumbled to a halt. Weohstan's face was smeared with blood, his clothes torn, and his silver-streaked dark hair pulled from its braids. Eadgils stood calmly, but his eyes shone with unholy fire as he raised his hand. One of the exiles smashed his fist into Weohstan's face.

Fryda screamed, unable to stop herself while Bryce gripped her, preventing her from running to her father. Every head but Weohstan's turned to look at her.

Wiglaf peered at her through bloodshot eyes. "Fryda!" he cried, his voice blurred and uneven. "Come to the party, have you, love?"

"Ah." Eadgils gave her a thin smile. "How kind of you to join us, my lady. After your histrionics this afternoon, I would have thought you would be far, far away by now. Yet here you are, and you brought some strength with you." Bryce's grip around her waist tightened, his arm.

"Let them go." Fryda winced. The demand sounded feeble and foolish even to her ears. Bryce swung her behind him, putting his body between her and the mad Swedish king. Irritated, she elbowed Bryce in the ribs and moved to stand beside him.

"No," Eadgils said, his voice calm. "No, as I told you, your father is going to feel my pain before he dies." He turned back to Weohstan, who managed to lift his head and glare at Eadgils. Eadgils brought his hands up in front of him and Fryda saw he held her father's sword, Swicdóm.

Not her father's sword, she remembered. Eanmund's sword.

Eadgils ran a hand along the flat of the blade. "My brother was the best of men," he said. "Eanmund was strong and kind and brilliant, and he would have made a much better king than I have been." He glanced at Weohstan. "And you killed him. With his own sword, no less, which you then stole and kept, as though it were a war-trophy. As though you were worthy of it."

Bryce looked at the king with narrowed eyes. "Onela gave him the sword."

"It was not his to give!" Eadgils shouted. "This was *my* brother's sword, and it should not have gone to the man who murdered him!"

Fryda glanced at her brother. "Wiglaf." She heard her voice crack. "Are you able to move at all? Can you do nothing?"

Wiglaf settled himself more comfortably on the throne. "Oh, I'm about to do something," he said. He looked at their father, his face unreadable. "I'm about to become lord of Eċeweall." And then, shockingly, he laughed.

Fryda stared disbelievingly at her brother.

Eadgils shook his head. "I made a mistake. I thought I could use Wiglaf to hurt his father," he said. "I underestimated the animosity between them." He eyed Fryda. "You, however…"

"No." Bryce raised his sword. "You will not touch her."

"You look so like her," Eadgils said, as if Bryce had not spoken. "Your mother. Ielfeta. She had the same colouring, the same wild, curly hair. The same eyes." He tossed a contemptuous look at Weohstan. "He took her from me, you know. Your mother. That alone is reason enough to kill him. He took her, brought her to this barbaric land, and then he killed her."

"No." Fryda looked at her father, who still hung limply between the two exiles. Her chest grew tight and tears pricked behind her eyes. "I killed her."

"He should have known she would never survive birthing his brutish babes. But as soon as I saw you, I knew you for her daughter. It is why he cannot bear to look at you. You are a reminder of the woman he loved, a constant source of pain. But make no mistake…to watch me kill you will hurt him. Oh yes." The ice in his eyes glowed, and Fryda shrank back against Bryce, shivering. "Yes, it will hurt him very much indeed."

Bryce didn't speak. He lifted Fryda off her feet and backed towards the door, holding the rune-inscribed sword out in front of him. Fryda did not protest, though the blacksmith's solid grip caused pain to lash her ribs.

"What goes here?" a voice bellowed from behind. Bryce turned, still holding Fryda off the ground, and she saw the silhouette of King Beowulf framed in the doorway.

Sixteen

The king strode into the room brandishing a mighty sword, a gold-chased heirloom studded with gems, and Fryda felt a spark of hope. The ancient sword, Nægling, had never failed the king in battle. Oddly, she felt Bryce stiffen, and he made a movement as if to run, but then thought better of it. He stilled and sighed.

Beowulf stopped and stared at Bryce. He glanced down at the runed sword in Bryce's hand and his eyes widened.

"Unferth?" Beowulf's voice cracked. "Is that you, Unferth?"

Bryce did not move or speak.

Fryda blinked. *Unferth?* She turned to the blacksmith.

His face spoke the truth before she could even ask it of him. He looked guilty...stricken.

"Bryce?" she said, and her voice wavered. "What..."

She heard a soft step behind her. A crack, a grunt, and a clatter broke the silence and Bryce abruptly let her go. Unprepared, Fryda stumbled. She turned and put a fist to her mouth to stifle her wordless cry.

Bryce stared down at the exile's sword that had pierced his body from back to belly. There had been no time to don any armour and so the blade slid in smoothly, easily. His magnificent sword lay on the floor where he had dropped it, and his face turned ash-grey. He looked at Fryda, his expression one of surprise and wonder, and fell to his knees, gripping the blade.

"No!" Fryda dropped to her knees and scrambled towards

Bryce. His murderer stepped up behind him, propped a booted foot against Bryce's back, and wrenched the sword free. "Weland, no, no, no..." Men started shouting, but she did not hear their words. She heard Beowulf's bellow and Eadgils' sinuous response as she gripped Bryce by the shoulders. His dark gaze boring into hers as if to memorize her face. With a grimace, he reached down and swept his sword up from the floor. In one fluid movement, he turned on his knees and shoved the blade upward into the belly of his murderer.

His assailant toppled over, and Fryda eased Bryce down to her lap, cradling his head in her arms.

"Sunbeam."

"No, no..." Her hand hovered over his belly, over his face, afraid to touch him but desperate to staunch the rivers of blood. Her blue silk dress became soaked. "What do I do?" she whispered to him. "Bryce, what can I do?"

Bryce opened his mouth and a flood of red gushed forth. He coughed, and tremors seized his entire body. She clutched him closer.

"I'm sorry." His voice was weak, thready.

"No." She leaned over him. "You don't have to be sorry. Just don't die..."

"Lied." Bryce reached a shaking hand to her hair. "Don't... hate..."

"Don't leave me," she begged, and lowered her forehead to touch his. "Please, don't leave me. I could never hate you. I need you. I can't..."

A loud crash drew her attention, and she raised her head. Beowulf was wielding Nægling in battle with one of the exiles, his strength and speed undiminished, despite his years. Fryda looked back at the dying blacksmith.

"Everything I own," he gasped, and tears leaked from his eyes at the effort. "For you, Fryda. For Theow."

"No." Fryda rocked him back and forth as if soothing a

frightened child. "No, we don't want that. We want you. Please stay with me. Please stay." She stroked his cheek as her tears fell and mingled with his blood.

"Can't. Important." Bryce's voice was a mere shadow of itself now. "Freedom. Free. Love...you..."

Rough hands grasped her and yanked her to her feet. Bryce's head thudded against the wooden floor and she struggled in the exile's hands. "Bryce...no! No, let me go!" She twisted and turned in an iron grip, writhing like an angry cat, heedless of her cracked ribs. She stilled as cold metal pushed against the delicate skin under her chin.

This felt far too familiar, and she knew no one could save her this time...not even herself.

Beowulf stood over the corpse of an exile, with blood on his sword and spattered across his face and tunic. He glanced at Bryce's body and his jaw clenched. His chest heaved and he looked at Fryda—and at the knife held to her throat.

"Eadgils. My friend." The king's eyes never left Fryda's. "Tell him to let her go."

"Friend. Pah." Eadgils spat onto the floor. "If you move, Beowulf, if you so much as twitch a finger towards her, Aegan will cut her from ear to ear. Bring her here."

The exile nudged Fryda forward until she faced the mad Swedish king and her father. Weohstan had fallen to his knees and blood was pouring in thin streams from his mouth and nose. Eadgils grasped Weohstan by the hair and yanked his head up. Fryda gasped when she saw her father's battered face. The skin on his forehead, nose, and cheeks had been slashed open and one eye was swollen shut. Black holes gaped in his mouth where several teeth had been knocked out and he panted for air in short, pained gasps.

A small, wordless mewl of distress slipped from Fryda's mouth. She looked at Wiglaf, still in thrall to the drugs he had drunk. He had a slight smile on his face, as if enjoying a festive spectacle or hearing a lovely poem, and his eyes were half-closed. Bryce, slumped on the floor where he had fallen, did not move.

Fryda blinked tears from her eyes. "Wiglaf," she said, her voice pleading. "Help me."

Her brother did not stir.

Eadgils shook Weohstan's head, hard, and her father's visible eye rolled back. "Watch," he barked. "Watch as I take Eanmund's *wergild* out of your daughter's flesh."

Her father, however, looked not at her, but at Beowulf. He spat blood once...twice...and then spoke as if feeding all his remaining strength into his words. "Don't." His voice rasped like ground glass. "Not Wiglaf. You cannot..." He coughed. "You cannot name Wiglaf your heir."

Fryda heard a manic giggle from the direction of the throne, but did not turn her head to look.

"Not now, Weohstan," Beowulf said, eyeing Eadgils.

"You mustn't...Fryðegifu. Danger. You cannot let Wiglaf..."

"Uncle Beowulf?" Fryda's voice quavered. The exile shifted his grip and the edge of the blade bit against her skin.

Beowulf's glance darted everywhere and at everyone, evaluating time, distance, risk. She watched him create and discard half a dozen plans in seconds, searching for the one that would save her and spare himself. She heard the stretched song of a drawn bowstring and Eadgils chuckled.

"I wouldn't, my king." He spat the last two words. "Even if you could get to her before the knife digs in, Aesc is a rather good shot." He gestured to the man with an arrow trained on Beowulf.

Eadgils held out the sword, Swicdóm, to one of his men, who took it from him.

"You can't even do your own filthy work, can you?" Fryda said. "King or no king, you disgust me. Bryce was a blacksmith, but he was ten times the man you are." Had she been able to move her head, she would have spat at him.

Eadgils smiled at her. "I prefer to watch."

"Father!" she cried, and Weohstan finally focused on her, blinking blood and tears out of his single working eye.

"Ielfeta," he murmured, and she sobbed in despair. Her mother's name on his lips brought only one comfort—at least she would die knowing her father loved her, even if he had mistaken her for someone else.

The thought turned her to ice. She was going to die, and her senses awakened with sharp clarity in that moment. It was as if her body knew that every sound was precious because she would soon never hear another. The taste of her own tears on her tongue, the feel of the blood-soaked silk against her skin, every colour, every scent on the air would be her last. Fryda could still hear intermittent fighting outside as she watched the exile walk towards her with the evil sword, Betrayal, in his hand. Dread pooled in her belly. She would die, afraid and in pain while her brother watched, uncaring. While King Beowulf stood by, unable to avoid his own death in preventing hers. Only one person would have risked everything for her, and he was not there.

"Theow," she whispered. The exile grinned. He looked little more than a youth, but hardship had written deep stories upon his face and she knew he would have no pity for her. He ran Swicdóm up and down her torso, caressing her breasts and stomach. She closed her eyes and thought of hair as red as a summer sunset and green eyes flecked with gold, like sunlight peeking through a canopy of leaves. "Theow..."

She heard a sharp *twang* as an arrow left a bow. "No!" She opened her eyes to see if the arrow had found its target in Beowulf's chest. But the king still stood, unharmed—and he, too, searched the room for the source of the arrow's flight. The exile tasked with ending her life lurched forward and fell against her, knocking her and her captor off balance. In his effort to save himself from falling, the man dropped the knife from her throat and released her. She scurried as fast as she could towards

Beowulf, who wrapped her in his brawny arms. Swicdóm fell from her would-be executioner's hand, and Fryda saw that an arrow was buried at a steep downward angle in his neck.

She looked around, wondering who had shot it, where it had come from. Then she realized...the angle of the arrow told her everything. She looked up and saw Theow crouched atop an arched rafter, bow in hand, another arrow already nocked onto the string.

Seventeen

Fryda experienced a bright, almost painful jolt of happiness when she saw Theow, crouched up in the rafters like a raptor. He was alive, he looked unhurt...and he was *here*.

Another exile cried out and fell to the floor, Theow's arrow protruding from his ribcage. Eadgils gave a wordless, impotent shout of rage and snatched Swicdóm from where the dead man had dropped it. Beowulf shoved Fryda behind him and, raising Nægling, launched himself at the Swedish king with an answering cry.

She saw Theow slide to the lowest point of the beam and swing himself down. He let go and dropped to the floor, and she hurried across the room to meet him. She skirted Beowulf and Eadgils as they locked together in combat, and she saw that Eadgils' manic frenzy made him a formidable match for Beowulf's towering strength. Theow also avoided the pair and ran instead towards her. They both skidded to a halt, still separated by half the room, as two exiles appeared in front of Theow, swords pointed at his chest. Fryda caught a glimpse of Eadgils' archer, the man named Aesc, behind them. Aesc steadied his bow and aimed an arrow right for Theow's heart. Theow kicked the sword from one exile's hand and pulled him close to his body, using him as a shield just as Aesc loosed his bow. The arrow thudded into the exile's back. Theow leapt back as the second swordsman came at him with a snarl, blade raised high. Theow dropped to the ground, rolled, and came back to his feet holding the dead man's sword. He brought it up just in time.

Fryda darted towards Bryce's body. His unnatural stillness and sightless, glassy eyes tore open the reservoir of grief within her and it washed through her like a tidal wave. She dropped to her knees next to him, careless of the oozing blood soaking into her skirt, and with a tearful apology she took the *seax* from his belt.

Blinking away hot tears, she gripped the dagger, and stood. She spared a glance for Wiglaf, now comatose on the throne, and turned back to the fight. Beowulf had turned the tide against Eadgils, who still seemed powered by his mad strength. Eadgils held Swicdóm in both hands as if he lacked the strength to lift it with only one, and had shifted from violent assault to defence. Beowulf, on the other hand, fought with all the vigour of a much younger man. He wielded his mighty sword with authority, determination, and a single-minded focus that made Fryda understand how the legends of him had been born.

Theow was locked in combat with the last remaining exile swordsman. Theow's unpractised moves would not have impressed a truly skilled fighter, but they were enough to keep a weakened exile at bay. Theow would not come away unscathed —she winced as his enemy's weapon scored a few painful hits on his body and blood seeped through his torn clothing from several shallow cuts. But, malnourished and worn down by the hardships of life, his opponent tired quickly and made sloppy mistakes. He focused on Theow's weapon and so did not see the blow coming from his fist. One lunge with the sword and Theow put him down for good.

A flicker of movement over his shoulder caught Fryda's attention. Just behind him, she saw Aesc, the only surviving exile, raise his bow and draw it. She screamed. Theow dropped onto his stomach just as the arrow flew over his head and hit Beowulf in the arm.

Beowulf bellowed and dropped Nægling. Fryda stared in horror at him, at Bryce dead on the floor, at Weohstan broken and crumpled. At Theow, still crouched close to the ground, and her flood of grief turned to rage. The now-familiar surge of power invaded her once more, making her stronger, sharper. A deadly weapon. The pain in her side vanished, and the ache in her shoulder and hand dimmed. She flung Bryce's *seax* at Aesc and buried the blade deep in his inner thigh. Aesc bellowed, dropped his bow, and yanked the blade from the wound. A startling gush of red sprayed across the room.

Fryda heard Beowulf curse. The arrow was lodged in the fleshy part of his upper arm, and without his sword, he was hard-pressed to fend off Eadgils.

Fryda felt power flood through her, like a welcome gift. Before Eadgils could complete his swing, she hit him with a force far greater than her small frame should allow. Swicdóm clattered to the floor as he struck the wall with a bone-shattering crash, and Fryda ran to where Beowulf had dropped Nægling. She swept the sword up as Eadgils staggered to his feet.

She bore down on Eadgils like his own avenging fate. Blood stained his tunic and sweat poured down his face, seeping through his clothes, creating dark patches on the rich blue cloth. He raised one hand, as if to fend her off. She heard urgent voices behind her, but did not heed them. She swung Nægling at Eadgils, but he managed to retrieve Swicdóm and blocked her blow.

She hauled back, prepared to swing again, and Eadgils scrambled to his feet. He lifted his sword as she came at him, and Nægling and Swicdóm shrieked as metal scraped against metal. She was dimly aware of Beowulf's bellow, of Theow's pleading, but in her red rage she knew only loss and anger and betrayal.

King Eadgils would pay *her* a blood-debt, for torturing her father and murdering the man she had loved as one.

The ornate sword dragged heavily at her hand and it seemed to drain her strength moment by moment. Even so, she attacked again. Eadgils fended off her blows with contemptuous ease, though his movements grew weaker as the fight went on. All other sounds faded until there was nothing but harsh breath and the song of swords in the room.

Nægling's heaviness grew quickly, and Fryda's movements slowed. She could no longer hold the sword with only one hand, but when she tried to alleviate the weight with her left hand, pain shot up to her shoulder. Her ribs throbbed and her strength ebbed and she began to rethink the wisdom of her choices.

Eadgils, aged and unused to battle, tired as quickly as she did. Shaking with fatigue, he attempted an underhanded lunge with Swicdóm, a desperate move to bite deep into the muscles of her legs. Fryda leapt back and lost her balance. With her last push of strength, she tossed Nægling to Theow and fell to the floor. Theow caught Beowulf's legendary weapon, swung it in a deadly arc, and took Eadgils' head off at the neck.

Fryda tried to catch her breath and surveyed the room. The carnage was impressive—six exiles lay dead next to their murderous king. Bryce lay where had had fallen, Wiglaf sprawled senseless on their father's chair, and Weohstan himself…

Fryda pulled her sleeve over her left hand and ran to where her father lay on the floor. She knelt beside him but did not embrace or even touch him. She looked at him, her eyes dry, and knew the name of the shadow that settled over him.

She heard footsteps as Theow came to stand beside her. He said nothing, but she took comfort from his presence.

"He's dead." Her voice cracked on the words.

Theow brushed a hand over her hair and knelt next to her. Weohstan's grey-black hair was loose and tangled and his mouth hung open, filled with blood. Theow gently lowered both his eyelids. He looked at Fryda.

"What do you need?" he asked. "What can I do?"

Fryda shook her head and stood up without speaking. She didn't know what she felt, let alone what she needed. The loss of that invasive power seemed to dull her senses as much as its presence had sharpened them, and she felt…numb.

Beowulf moved to stand over Bryce, his back rigid. An arrow still jutted from his arm, though he seemed not to notice. Fryda took one last look at her father and then moved to stand next to the king. Theow followed and they stood for a moment, silent, over the body of their friend.

"Uncle Beowulf…" Fryda began, but the king held up his hand to stop her.

"Not now," he said. Beowulf sighed and looked around the room, his face tight. "And not here. We need to get Wiglaf out of here and take care of your father and Unf…Bryce. Get this mess cleaned up, somehow." The king gripped the arrow in his arm and yanked it out, wincing as the head tore through more of his flesh. "I need to see how your father's soldiers fared and rout out any remaining exiles." He caressed Fryda's hair. "I promise, sweet girl, I'll tell you everything, but there's too much to do right now. We will postpone the feast tonight and have proper honours for your father."

Fryda took Beowulf's hand. "For my fathers," she whispered. She looked at Bryce and her tears finally began to flow. "Both of them."

Rescue

This music...this remembered music has the perfect pitch of true violence. These are not children's games meant to distract and entertain, but are the tunes that pierce and flay, the notes that draw out the blood. Men and women sing in screams and take their bows, never to rise again.

The curse in Fýrdraca's blood rears to meet the song and she stirs, fighting to throw off a thousand years of slumber. She longs to join the fight, to let loose her flame and hear the sweetest music of all.

But the gold. She cannot leave the gold. It anchors her to this place as it destroys her, minute by minute, century by century, as if she's drowning in cream, in the finest wine, as if she's being suffocated in silk and velvet and love.

Yet still she struggles.

But then she feels the magic again, that burst of warrior-power she'd first encountered in the woman-child seven years ago, and then again earlier this very day. This spark of magic sings to the one part of her, deeply buried, that the Lone Survivor's curse cannot touch. The bit of magic that makes her a true dragon. For a brief moment the girl's magic brings Fýrdraca to life, whole and unblemished, and in that moment she sees the end of all things.

The girl, Fýrdraca realizes, is about to die.

Time shifts out of phase with the world and the trapped dragon can see the past, the present, and the future together. She sees the Lone Survivor standing in the ashes of his home and family. She sees him as a monster tearing into Heorot's men, consuming them in his desperate desire to gain their strength and fellowship. He sprawls across a throne, insensible and treacherous, while his father, sister, and king are killed. He is the future lord and king, constantly drunk on mead and power. The dragon-magic thrums its rhythm in time with her heartbeat, from the girl, from the aged hero whose lives are about to end.

She sees the death of all magic, and her entire body revolts against it.

With a mighty effort, Fýrdraca projects her power through those thin filaments connecting her magic to theirs. She must divert the river of their future and her memory to save the magic, the only uncorrupted part of her left in the world.

She hopes it is enough. It must be enough. But before she can test the waters of time, the Lone Survivor's curse drags her back down into the deep and muddy depths, where memory and knowledge fade into nightmare once more.

PART II

Eighteen

Beowulf could not think of a more fitting tribute to his fifty years as king than a glorious battle, hard fought and well won.

All in all, Weohstan's people had fared well. The fighting had lasted little over an hour, but Eceweall's warriors emerged the clear victors. The exiles had the advantage of surprise and strength in numbers, but that could not make up for their lack of training. Weohstan's people had fought with discipline, well practised and effective. Their losses were minimal while Eadgils' exiles had been cut down to the last man.

Fryda, Beowulf noted with relief, seemed unhurt, despite all the blood on her dress. If only he'd been so lucky, he thought, wincing as his newly bandaged arm gave a wicked twinge. He knew, however, that Fryda bore a deep wound inside from the loss of the blacksmith and her father. Wiglaf had taken to his bed to recover from the white poppy, and Beowulf, with his own hands, had spent the rest of the afternoon helping to build the funeral pyres for Weohstan and Unferth. He personally dressed and prepared their bodies, laying them out with rich clothing and treasure.

Unferth. As he stacked the wood and anointed it with oil, he wondered how fate had managed to bring them together one last time, only to separate them for eternity. He had spent more than one sleepless night in his youth worrying about Unferth's fate, though time and distance had eventually acted as a salve for that wound. And it turned out he'd been here, on his own kinsman's land, for the last twenty years. How had he never seen him? he wondered. And then he remembered the way Unferth had flinched when Beowulf had arrived at the house, as if instinct urged him to run and hide.

Beowulf had never found Unferth because Unferth had not wanted to be found.

Beowulf ran a hand over his face. His body suddenly felt heavy, sluggish, and he wished he could fall into bed and sleep through the funeral tonight, as well as the third celebration tomorrow.

That night the entire clan gathered in the field behind the forge to pay their respects to the dead. Even Wiglaf, still hollow-eyed and unsteady, joined them. Beowulf eyed Weohstan's son, remembering his disgraceful behaviour during the battle. He did not know if Wiglaf had been incapacitated by Eadgils and his men, or if he had followed his own natural proclivities, but Beowulf felt a profound sense of disappointment in the boy. And he was not the only one, he noticed. Weohstan's *gedriht*, knotted together in a tight, closed group, regarded their new lord with narrow suspicion. Beowulf had, indeed, briefly considered making Wiglaf his heir, but after Weohstan's deathbed warning and his own observations, this was no longer possible. Wiglaf had a weak, untrustworthy character, and Beowulf knew it would break Fryda's heart as soon as she found that out.

But...if not Wiglaf, then who? This question more than any other kept him awake at night. Had he died in battle that day, what would have become of his kingdom, his legacy? As he had not yet named an heir, who would have stepped into his place and taken over the throne?

All the inhabitants of Eċeweall stood on the headland, the two wooden pyres built high against the backdrop of the ocean. The twilit sky hung like draped velvet, and the air smelled sweet with the scent of summer flowers and sea-spray. Beowulf spoke first, as was his kingly right.

"Now your leader's laugh⠀⠀is silenced and your friend's
High spirits quenched.⠀⠀Many a spear, dawn-cold to the
⠀⠀touch,
Will be taken down⠀⠀and waved on high.
The swept harp will not waken⠀⠀these warriors, but the
⠀⠀raven,
Winging darkly over the doomed,⠀⠀will see their spirits
⠀⠀lifted on his wing."

For once, Beowulf felt as old as his years as he took Hrunting, Unferth's darkly-runed sword, from one of his warriors. He held it reverently. In his hands, the mighty blade looked almost dainty, its wooden two-handed grip covered by his single fist. The sweeping curves of iron above and below glimmered in the setting sun and the wide blade hoarded its secrets within the unintelligible runes.

"Uncle Beowulf." Fryda broke the stillness, her voice thick and halting. "Why did you call Bryce 'Unferth' when you saw him?"

For a long time, Beowulf did not answer. He looked at the sword, remembering their youth and Unferth's angry words, his regret, apology, and this gift to commemorate their brief, doomed friendship. But then Beowulf closed his eyes and rubbed his face with one enormous hand.

"Because he *is* Unferth." Beowulf's face contorted. "Was. He *was* Unferth."

Theow stepped forward and stood near Fryda. Not near enough to raise eyebrows, Beowulf noted with a flicker of amusement, but close enough to give and take comfort with her. "He's the…the man from the stories?" Theow's voice was subdued. "The one who challenged you in Heorot in front of King Hrothgar when you went to fight Grendel. That Unferth?"

"Yes," Beowulf said, "but as with many things, the stories don't necessarily reflect what really happened."

A few tears spilled down Fryda's cheeks. "Will you tell me?" she asked, wiping them away.

Beowulf walked over to her and brushed the tears from her face with his huge, gnarled fingers. He sighed. "Unferth, or Bryce as you called him, was my friend, long lost. When we were young men in Hrothgar's hall, he spoke brashly to me, said unkind words of envy and spite. Many witnesses heard him, and this proved his undoing. But I will have it known, here and now, that he was a good man, and my friend. He regretted those words that sprung from both terrible grief and drink, and before I matched my strength with the monster Grendel's mother, he brought me this."

Beowulf held up the sword, the etchings on its blade seeming to writhe and twist in the flickering firelight of a dozen torches. "Hrunting, the marvellous sword of legend, never defeated in battle until that day. Unferth knew I faced grave danger, and he brought this relic from the old gods to aid me."

Beowulf looked at Fryda and spoke the next words to her alone. "He did not know the sword would fail. No one could have predicted the enchantment would be ineffective against the she-fiend. As the stories say, I tested Hrunting's mettle and it would not pierce the monster's thick hide, nor could all my strength make a slice against her flesh. In the end, I found a sword in her den that could do the job, but I gave Hrunting back to Unferth with my sincere thanks and a vow of friendship."

Beowulf paused, remembering that fraught battle. It had been the first time in his cocky, arrogant youth that he had genuinely feared for his life. If fate had not placed the ice-giant's sword in the monster's cave, his bones would probably be down there still.

He shook his head and came back to the present. "Several years later I learned of Unferth's fate, but by then I could do nothing to reverse it. His own clan, it seems, remembered Unferth's ungenerous words to me and decided he had given me the defective blade to undermine my purpose. And I, full of pride and boasting and celebration of my feats, was not there to defend him."

Beowulf looked at the sword in his hands, and then passed it to Fryda. He saw her wince as she reached out to take it and remembered she'd been wounded in the battle earlier that day. He would have someone check on her injury later.

"His clan exiled him," Beowulf continued. A familiar pang in his chest made him shift and fidget. "When I discovered it, I sent men out to search for him, but they found nothing. I never knew his fate until this day." He shook his head. "And to think, all this time he lived right here under my nose."

Beowulf took a torch from a nearby servant and held it out to Fryda. She handed the sword back to him, keeping her left hand tucked away in her sleeve, and grasped the torch. "Tonight, we honour him," he said to her. "We honour Unferth, Hrothgar's loyal thane and a good man to Weohstan's clan. We honour Bryce, skilled blacksmith, friend, and protector. Do not hold his youthful tongue against him, for which of us has not spoken harsh, hasty words in this life? Instead, remember that he helped me and was punished for his kindness. He loved his family and lost them to great evil. He loved you like a daughter and died defending your life. No warrior could earn a better death."

Beowulf stepped back and Fryda moved forward with the torch. Bryce had been laid on his pyre and dressed in his old warrior's armour. Fryda had insisted he be surrounded with his beloved blacksmith's tools. Tears shone on her face as she held the flame to the seasoned wood. The oiled pyre caught and held fast the flame, and soon Bryce's body illuminated the night sky. Fryda tossed the torch onto the pyre and stepped back.

Beowulf heard a soft sob and looked towards the sound. A woman of perhaps sixty years, her face lined and hands gnarled with work, stood off to one side of the crowd. Eadith, Beowulf remembered. Her name was Eadith and she took care of the house. But now her face was a mask of sorrow, tears running unchecked down her weathered cheeks. Her lips trembled as she watched the fire burn, her grief immense. Her thin, frail body bent under its weight and he thought for a moment it would crush her entirely. She must have felt strongly for the blacksmith, Beowulf thought. Unferth, it seemed, had touched many lives.

Beowulf saw Theow look back at Fryda and edge closer to her. Beowulf was beginning to suspect that something more than friendship had blossomed between his sweet girl and the red-haired slave—a suspicion that was immediately confirmed when she turned and buried her face in the boy's chest.

Theow automatically wrapped his arms around her and then, as shocked murmurs and whispers flew around the crowd, he froze. Beowulf saw Wiglaf's eyes upon his sister and the slave. The young lord's expression was a portent of malevolence. Cold, angry...hateful. Murderous.

Theow turned with Fryda in his arms and gently pushed her towards Beowulf. Theow backed away and rubbed the scar on his face.

Beowulf held Fryda for a moment while she cried, wishing he could soothe her pain. But he knew he could not, and so he released her and once again handed her Unferth's sword. She stepped to the side and wiped the tears from her face.

Beowulf took a second torch. He faltered, then. He blinked back tears and cleared his throat.

"Weohstan has been my friend from our boyhood," he said, his voice tight, "and I meant every word I spoke of him at the feast. He made his own mistakes, and had to live with them, but he was a good man and a good leader. A bright torch extinguished too soon." He handed the second torch to Wiglaf, who thrust the fire into the wood. Together, the people of the *burh* watched the pyres burn, standing vigil for the two great men who fell to Eadgils' treachery until the fires flickered and went out, leaving nothing but ash.

★ ★ ★

Fryda clutched Hrunting and watched the embers of the funeral pyres crackle and glow, taking some small comfort in the presence of the clan around her.

Her father was dead. And Bryce had lied to her.

Now he was dead, too.

She looked at the sword, remembering how many times she'd seen it in Bryce's forge, hanging above the fireplace. She thought of how often she'd wondered about its story, its history, the meaning of the runes on its blade. She had never imagined it was Hrunting, the famed sword of legend, the sword given to Beowulf by Unferth in Heorot, Hrothgar's hall.

Unferth. Bryce was *Unferth*. She still could not believe it.

Fryda hugged the sword to her body. Somehow the knowledge of Bryce's lies hurt more than the reality of her father's violent death. For so long he had seemed the only person in her life she could trust unconditionally. Now she didn't know what to think.

Wiglaf appeared at her side. His face was pale and his eyes looked bruised and rimmed with red, though she knew he had not wept. He stood with her a moment in silence, watching the fading embers with her.

"Did you know?" she asked.

He did not look at her. "No."

"Do you think Father knew?"

Pause. Then, "No. He would have told me. Or…he would have told someone who would have told me."

It did not surprise Fryda that Wiglaf had spies in their father's house. There was more she wanted to ask, but she would not voice the question that haunted her.

Why did he not tell me?

"So, what was all that with Theow?" Wiglaf asked. His tone was even and his voice mild, but Fryda heard the tension beneath it.

"What was what?"

Wiglaf jerked his shoulders in a sharp, angry movement. "Don't play stupid with me, Fryda. I saw you fling yourself at him."

His voice rose angrily and people looked towards them. Fryda saw Hild frown at Wiglaf, clearly troubled by his tone.

"I did not *fling* myself at him," she huffed. "I was distraught. And besides, I thought Uncle Beowulf stood beside me."

That was close enough to the truth.

They remained silent, watching as Eċeweall's warriors gathered up the bodies of the dead exiles and threw them unceremoniously into piles near the cliff. Their own fallen warriors had received respectful send-offs in wooden boats after the battle.

Beowulf joined them. His shoulders were hunched and he still wore his clothes from the battle, torn and spattered with blood.

"What will happen to them?" she asked, gesturing to the growing pile of bodies.

"Fish food," Wiglaf said, his voice curt.

"More like shark food," Beowulf said grimly. "And here comes the bait."

Fryda looked up and saw Olaf dragging a naked, headless corpse by the foot towards the pile of bodies. Bjorn, the young, dark-haired *gedriht* warrior, followed behind, carrying the bloody head by its wispy, white hair. It took her a moment to recognize Eadgils, and then another to remember it had been Theow who separated the mad Swedish king's head from his body.

"Come!" Beowulf boomed, and the denizens of Eċeweall gathered near the cliff. The dim light of evening cast a pall over the landscape, painting shadows over the faded greens and browns of grass, leaf, and tree. The people's movement through the tall grass called out tiny lights, yellow-green flickering fireflies that hovered over the meadow like unearthly sparks of flame.

The *burh* thrummed with a strange mixture of excitement for their victory in battle and deep sorrow for their losses. Beowulf gestured for everyone to come together in a group and held out his arms as if to embrace them all. Fryda saw Theow watching her with concern. She saw Hild surreptitiously eye the wild growth of the meadow, no doubt thinking of her potions and salves. She saw Eadith, her face still stained with grief. Olaf and Bjorn stood at respectful attention before King Beowulf. Moire, Lyset, Toland, and all the others gazed at him, hoping he could tell them something that would put their fears and sorrow to rest.

"My fine people," Beowulf began, "your lord and leader is dead."

The people shifted and murmured in distress, and Fryda closed her eyes. That was not how she would have chosen to begin.

"But fear not," Beowulf bellowed and gestured to the large pile of bodies, "we have avenged him!"

A great cheer rose from the crowd.

"Tomorrow we shall have a ceremony, and I will announce the new lord of Eceweall. But tonight, we deal with what's left of the scoundrel who killed him." He kicked Eadgils' headless corpse with a sickening thud. "Shall we give them what they deserve, my friends?"

The cheer turned wild and ugly, laced with hostility and a greedy desire for revenge. Fryda shifted, uneasy.

"Then have at them, my friends," Beowulf shouted. "Rip them asunder and feed them to the sea, and then we shall repair to the mead-hall for the second night of my feast and celebrate our mighty victory!"

The crowd needed no second urging. They surged forward, drunk on victory and bloodlust, and fell upon Eadgils' body. Knives, swords, and axes bit into cold, stiffening sinew. Grasping hands tore chunks from the body and wrenched bones from their joints. Men and women shoved at each other to get close enough for their portion of enemy flesh, teeth bared and bestial snarls rattling in their throats.

Fryda started as she recognized a head of dark braids. *Wiglaf.* He had slipped from her side while she was distracted and joined the mob tearing Eadgils limb from limb. He held a *seax* in one bloodstained hand and with a guttural shout he raised the other.

Beowulf strode back to her and it took her a moment to realize he held Aesc the archer's head in his hands.

"And here is another hero of the day," he said, pitching his voice low for her ears only. Her face grew warm and she looked down, adjusting her sleeve.

Beowulf put his fingers under her chin and tilted her head up to look at him. "No, sweet girl," he said. "Don't shy away from this. If you had not been there, these traitorous bastards would have killed me. Killed us all." He looked ruefully at the bloodstained bandage on his arm. "This honour is for you, shield maiden. A warrior takes credit for her kills." He held the head out to her.

Shield maiden.

The words felt like a slap, it startled her so much. It had not occurred to her until now that with her father gone, her lifelong dream might finally be possible.

Something flared within her, a tiny echo of the power she experienced in battle. It felt like…purpose. She reached out and took Aesc's head from Beowulf, no longer flinching from the grim reminders of death. She had not been able to save Bryce or her father, but she had protected the king. She had saved Theow.

She looked at the head. The bloodless flesh was unnaturally white and the eyes clouded over. The mouth gaped open, filled with stained teeth smeared black with blood. The exiles had tried to destroy her home, but she had stopped them…she and Theow, Hild, and all the others who had risked their lives to bring down the threat.

A chant grew from the crowd, weak and lacking rhythm at first, until taken up by more and more people.

"Fryda...Fryda...FRYDA...FRYDA...*FRYDA*...*FRYDA*..."

She looked around in wonder. She saw Theow, beaming at her with pride and something else...something that looked like love. She saw Hild with the biggest grin on her face. And she saw Wiglaf, who looked thunderously angry, and remembered tonight was supposed to be about celebrating the lie that he had saved her from Fægebeorn and the exiles the previous night.

A warrior takes credit for her kills.

Raising her head high and surrendering to that little pulse of power within her, Fryda did not move to the edge of the cliff, but instead allowed the surge of power to overtake her. She drew her arm back and flung the head as hard as she could towards the water. The chanting died and people gaped as it flew out...out... and even further out, until it became little more than a speck on the horizon. Finally, after many interminable moments, it landed with a miniscule splash far out to sea.

In absolute silence, the village turned and stared at her.

Fryda, if she were being honest, was as shocked as anyone, and more than a little afraid. She was beginning to think all those ridiculous stories of great heroes and their superhuman feats of strength might have some kernel of truth in them. If she surrendered to that strange, alien power, would she, too, be able to fight a monster like Grendel and tear its arm off at the shoulder? Could she hold her breath for hours underwater? She did not know. During the battle she'd felt as if she could fight a dragon and win.

"To the feast!" roared Beowulf, and the crowd roared back, happy to drown their grief, pain, and sorrow in a mug of mead. As they headed back to the longhouse, Fryda noticed people staring at her. A few offered her looks of approval, but most ranged from suspicion to outright hostility. She didn't know if her unthinking show of strength or her foolhardy show of affection towards Theow at the funeral was the cause. She hoped both might be forgotten amongst the feasting, and that the ugly look on Wiglaf's face would turn to just a memory.

Nineteen

The next morning, all of Eċeweall's guests gathered in front of the longhouse. Inside, the *burh's* warriors and *gedriht* sat on wooden benches, while Beowulf sat in Weohstan's chair. Wiglaf could not yet think of it as his own. He watched as Fryda took her seat at the king's left hand, while he took his own place at his right.

His insides were still all tied up in knots about Fryda, and he couldn't decide if he should stay furious at her, rejoice in her achievements, or simply be relieved she had survived the last two days. More and more, however, fury seemed to win out. He could not believe his twin had been so reckless as to *join in the battle*. His guts twisted and hands clenched at the thought. She could have been hurt. She could have been *killed*. The *scops*, however, had quickly written verses to celebrate Fryda's glorious victory over Eadgils. They included Beowulf, Bryce, and even a verse about *the kitchen staff* and their bloody fry pans.

A ragtag band of servants and slaves merited more notice than he did, and Wiglaf knew Fryda was to blame for that. She had mentioned Hild and the other menials when she'd told her story at the feast. And she'd said not a word about him.

To be fair, he privately admitted, it was probably best she hadn't revealed his deeds in the battle. He had little memory of the day, having spent most of it under the influence of opium. Well, at least she hadn't said anything about Theow, either.

Unthinking wrath lashed through him at the memory of

Fryda in the arms of that squalid red-haired slave. Wiglaf did not understand how she could bear to touch him, nor how he dared touch her in return. He defiled her every time he laid his grubby hands on her, and she *allowed* it.

Wiglaf had encouraged her to reject those marriage proposals during the first feast, thinking to keep her under his own protection a while longer. He had thought she was the only one who truly understood and valued him, but…now he wondered if she wouldn't be safer away from Eċeweall and the corrupting influences within it.

And he would be safe from her knowing eyes and blade-sharp intellect. Wiglaf knew it would not take her long to figure out his role in yesterday's affairs. She was transforming from his only solace into his greatest threat.

Beowulf stood and raised his hands. The chatter subsided and Wiglaf's jaw clenched as the king began to speak. Here would be his moment of truth.

"While the death of your lord and my kinsman is a terrible loss to us all, we do have two things to celebrate this morning. Today, we welcome your new lord of Eċeweall to this seat." Beowulf ran a hand over the carved throne as cheers erupted from the crowd.

Wiglaf, with an effort, managed not to look at Olaf. He had no way of knowing if Weohstan had spoken to Beowulf about his decision to cut Wiglaf from the succession.

"But first," Beowulf continued, "I have another happy announcement. Olaf, if you would come up here for a moment?"

Wiglaf gaped as the chief of the *gedriht* stood and made his way to the dais. It was over. He would be reduced to uselessness in his own *burh*.

Olaf held something under his arm. Swords, two of them, and some strips of leather. A flutter of panic licked at Wiglaf and he leaned forward, poised to flee. Did they know everything? Were they here to bind him, to cut him down?

Beowulf clapped Olaf on the shoulder, beaming with pleasure. "Last night, my old friend Olaf and I decided some rewards were due for bravery and great deeds during the battle with the exiles."

Wiglaf relaxed and leaned back in his seat.

Olaf grinned at the king, who said, "First, I'd like to recognize Eawynn." His strong voice projected all the way to the people outside. A young woman leapt to her feet and pumped her fist in the air. A host of cheers filled the mead-hall and Beowulf waited until they settled down again before he continued. "In the heat of battle, she saved three of her fellow fighters from death through heroic acts of bravery. Olaf has thereby nominated Eawynn to the ranks of the *gedriht*."

Eawynn sobered and her eyes grew enormous. She approached the dais and stood before Olaf. He gave her an elaborate brown leather belt—the hallmark of the *gedriht*—and King Beowulf put a handful of gold coins and rings in her hands.

"Next," Beowulf boomed, "we honour a young man who has already proved his mettle in battle many times. Bjorn, step forward!"

The young *gedriht* detached himself from the crowd and came to stand before the king. His brown hair and beard were neatly braided, and his body was trim and well-muscled. Wiglaf, aware of the softness of his own body, felt his resentment grow.

"Yesterday," Beowulf said, "this man singlehandedly protected a group of children from a horde of exiles bent on their deaths. He fought ten men all on his own and thanks to him, not a single child died in the fight. Therefore, it is my honour to raise Bjorn of the *gedriht* to the position of thane, and appoint him second to Olaf, chief of the *gedriht*."

Thunderous applause nearly raised the roof. Wiglaf pounded his fist against the arm of his chair along with the others, but inside it felt as if he'd swallowed live embers. Envy burned him from the inside out. Bjorn gracefully accepted his rewards from the Ring-Giver and Olaf clasped his arm.

As the warriors continued to hoot and cheer, Beowulf raised his arms and made "settle down" gestures. "I have one last honour to bestow, and this one gives me particular pleasure, because it concerns someone close to my heart."

Wiglaf's blood leapt, as if answering a rousing call. *Finally!*

"It is a great honour for me to make this lifelong dream come true," Beowulf said. He held out his hand and Olaf placed the magnificent sword, Hrunting, into it. The king held it aloft and turned to face the dais.

Yes, Wiglaf thought. It took a mighty effort not to leap from his chair and present himself to the king. *Yes.*

"Fryda," Beowulf said. "Come to me, please."

Wiglaf's breath seemed to stop. He watched, numb, as Fryda blinked in confusion and rose from her seat. She walked over to Olaf and the king, furrows between her brows and questions in her eyes.

For a moment Wiglaf's senses failed him. The light dimmed; all sound faded. Only the roaring in his ears and the rage in his breast kept him from pitching off his chair. He wanted to rip down the mead-hall. He wanted to tear it asunder and uproot its very bones. As anger consumed him, he longed to create havoc, to strike at the men and women who sat and grinned in delight at his sister. He wanted to tear them apart...destroy them... consume them until none remained and the hall stood empty, a deserted wall-stead bereft of all life.

The king's voice finally penetrated the fog of red rage and Wiglaf blinked, a little alarmed by the direction of his thoughts.

"...and she took up Nægling, my own sword, and struck the exile's head from his body," Beowulf was saying. "And thus, she saved me." He smiled at Fryda. He fingered his arm where Wiglaf knew a bandage lay under his sleeve. "Fryda of Clan Waegmunding, as King of Geatland I am happy to officially welcome you into Eceweall's sisterhood of warrior women. As of today, and for all the rest of your life, you are a shield maiden.

I wish you many years before a glorious death in battle stitches you forever into the tapestry of memory."

Fryda's embarrassed but joyful face was *almost* enough to make up for Wiglaf's disappointment. Beowulf held Hrunting out to her and Fryda hesitantly took it. Wiglaf could see she had difficulty gripping it with her damaged hand, but for once she didn't try to cover it up.

Beowulf passed an affectionate hand over Fryda's hair. "That's ceremonial nonsense, of course," he told her. "I very much hope you'll live to be an old, old woman with a dozen grandchildren, but even then, a shield maiden you shall be. Olaf will undertake your training himself."

Fryda held Hrunting reverently, and Wiglaf could see she struggled to contain her emotion. "I will endeavor to be worthy of this honour," she said, her voice thick. Wiglaf saw Beowulf put his hands over her trembling ones.

"Congratulations, sweet girl. No honour has ever been more deserved than this one." He leaned down and kissed her forehead.

Olaf grinned and bowed to her. "The honour is truly ours, my lady."

"And now," Beowulf said as Fryda made her way back to her seat, "I shall present to you your new lord and chief."

Wiglaf's chest tightened and he couldn't help but look at Olaf, who still stood at the king's side.

"The Waegmunding clan has a long and illustrious history," the king said, "and I know whatever fate has planned for us, your new lord will lead you into many glorious stories and songs. I know the grief he feels, for I, too, rose to chief and lord when my own father died. Weohstan was a noble battle-leader, and I know his son will follow in his footsteps. Wiglaf, please step forward."

Wiglaf's relief was so great it struck him like a physical blow. Olaf started with surprise, and Wiglaf guessed Weohstan had told him—but not Beowulf—of his plans. Olaf, however, could not contradict the king without seeming churlish and there were no other witnesses...

Wiglaf swore to himself as he stood. He looked at Fryda. She smiled at him, though she looked puzzled. She did not say anything as he made his way to stand before the king, but Wiglaf knew if Fryda and Olaf together went to Beowulf, they could convince him that Weohstan had not wanted Wiglaf to be chief.

The walls closed in and the beast within him stirred once more. He would have to do...something...about this. About Olaf. About her.

He shied away from his first unthinkable, impossible, monstrous idea.

No.

Beowulf interrupted his haunted thoughts. The king held out his hand and Olaf gave him the second sword. Wiglaf recognized Swicdóm, Betrayal, the sword that had hung at his father's waist for twenty years.

"Lord Wiglaf, as I pass your father's sword to you, so do I pass his title, his responsibilities, his obligations, and his duties. Your first duty must be to your people, and you must always do what is best for them. In your dealings with kings and princes, lords and chieftains, you must always first remember your people."

Beowulf put Betrayal in his hands. "Wiglaf, son of Weohstan, I name you lord of Eċeweall. I know you will do your father proud."

Wiglaf gripped the sword as a weak and tattered cheer rose from the crowd. He had done it. He was lord of the *burh* and now no one could ever treat him as unimportant or with disrespect again. He glanced again at Fryda, who did not look as happy as she should. She, a shield maiden and he, chief of the clan? She should be overcome with happiness.

Now he had to keep it all from falling apart.

★ ★ ★

Theow shivered as he watched Wiglaf accept the title of lord.

He had managed to secure a place inside the longhouse by pretending Moire had sent him from the kitchens to serve bread and mead. As soon as Beowulf started talking, though, he had faded into the background to watch.

Theow was pleased for Eawynn and Bjorn, but when Beowulf made Fryda a shield maiden he wanted to grab her and whirl her around the longhouse. The look of happiness on her face made up for a lifetime of indignities. He was glad, however, that she had not seen her brother's expression as she stood to accept her honour. Wiglaf's features had twisted into such ugliness, such malevolence, that Theow was transported back in time sixteen years, to when he was a boy.

He had seen that look on Wiglaf's face only twice before. The first instance happened before the sharp, leather lash had descended upon Theow's back. He remembered how Wiglaf had watched, his boyish face impassive but his eyes greedily taking in every detail as the thin strip of leather cut through Theow's back again and again, until the blood ran warm over his skin. Fryda, he remembered, had been ushered away and so never knew what happened, but Wiglaf just stood and watched.

In the weeks afterward, as Theow's wounds scabbed over and his skin knit itself back together, Wiglaf would often come up behind him and give him a "friendly" smack on the back. He would look contrite and apologize as Theow gasped, and as fresh blood seeped through his rough tunic. Wiglaf always claimed he'd forgot about Theow's wounds, but the next day he would do it again. And again the day after that.

He'd known, then, that Wiglaf had deliberately accused him of thievery and enjoyed seeing him whipped. Theow had always tried to convince himself he'd imagined that look, but seeing Wiglaf's expression now, he knew the truth. Fryda's brother was capable of unspeakable cruelty, and it froze him to the marrow to see him look at her like that.

The second time Theow had seen it was the previous night, during the funeral, when Fryda had recklessly thrown herself into his arms. That brief moment was going to cost them too much, he knew, and with Weohstan and Bryce gone, he had no more protectors in the *burh*. He wanted to talk to King Beowulf about Bryce's offer to buy his freedom, but he didn't know if the king would believe him.

He rubbed his eyes. He had planned to suggest to Fryda that she run away with him...that they go to Ériu to search for his family. But Theow had seen the joy on her face when Beowulf and Olaf made her a shield maiden, and he couldn't bear the thought of taking that away from her.

Theow watched as Wiglaf ascended to the throne and sat. He looked supremely pleased with himself, though he kept shooting troubled glances at Fryda. For her own safety, Theow had always tried to shield her from the knowledge of who and what her brother truly was, but he was beginning to worry he could not do so for much longer. Theow knew Wiglaf loved Fryda with an entirely selfish love, and so long as she provided her brother with the adoration he required and did nothing to endanger his ambitions, she would be safe. But Fryda was smart, and Theow feared she would not be safe much longer.

Fate

Time has become a dazzling confusion as past and present overlap. The Lone Survivor is here. And the hero who defeated him is here, but twice; split into young and old, man and woman. Stories written long ago are retold. Relived. Start over.

A great battle is coming, the second of three. Fýrdraca has seen it before. She knows the events that lead to it. There is a king, and a monster, and the gift of a sword. This same sword... Hrunting is its name.

It has passed from the hand of one who cannot fully know its power to one who can...and yet such knowledge will prove fruitless. Once more, the sword will fail, as such things always must when mortals refuse to trust in fate.

The events in play cannot now be undone...and Fýrdraca must play her part in them. The Lone Survivor, Grendel, the hero, the monster—all have their place, and the story calls to her, bringing her closer and closer to the surface of awareness.

She must wake.

The Lone Survivor's curse still chains her to every piece of gold, every gem, jewel, and treasure. And it is loath to set her free.

She will see the sword again, and all the characters in this drama. She knows it, because she trusts in fate. She trusts the story.

Twenty

"**W**HAT?**"** Hild stared at Fryda in disbelief.

"Yes!" Fryda's voice became high and squeaky. Hild had not seen such a happy, carefree smile on her friend's face since before Fryda's accident seven years ago. "Uncle Beowulf and Olaf gave Hrunting to me in a ceremony this morning. Look!" She pointed to an enormous, two-handed sword with intricate runes carved on the blade. Hild recognized it as the sword that always hung in the forge above the hearth.

The runed blade glinted in the morning light. They were in the field behind the forge and Hild could still smell the oily residue of smoke from the previous night's funeral pyres. Two great patches of blackened grass marked where the pyres had stood. Hild knew the ashes had been gathered and placed into ceremonial urns, which would later be buried in special barrows.

"Does that mean it's official?" Hild asked, staring at the beautiful sword. "I mean, I know he *said* it last night, but I wasn't sure…"

"It's official. I'm a true shield maiden now." Fryda bounced up and down on her toes.

"My lady, I'm so happy for you!" Hild saw the small frown Fryda couldn't quite hide, and knew it still bothered her that Hild would not use her name. "I know it's always been your dream to be a shield maiden."

"If it's still yours as well, I can speak to Olaf for you," Fryda said. "Without my father to object, he'd have no reason to say no."

Hild paused. She probed her heart, gently, carefully. It had been a long time since anyone has asked what she desired. Was that what she wanted? To fight for the people who owned her labour, owned her life? If she became a shield maiden, what would happen to the rest of her parents' time-debt?

Then she thought about the enormous pile of dishes in the kitchen waiting to be washed, of chapped, bleeding hands and Moire's fists birthing bruises under her skin.

"Yes." Hild said the word quickly, as if this chance might escape if she didn't grasp it while she could. She would rather die in battle as a warrior than live the next sixteen years as an indentured slave. "Yes, please. Go ahead and talk to him. He might still say no, of course, but I'm willing to work for the honour." She glanced down at her rough hands, chapped and scarred. "It would be better than working in the kitchens, that's certain."

Fryda looked at her for a moment, her expression sober. Finally, she sighed and tugged her sleeve over her hand. "I've spoken to Moire about that. I hope things will improve now. You must tell me if they don't." Her mouth twisted. "My father profited from buying and selling...*people*," she said, her voice tinged with disgust. "It has shamed me my whole life. Now that Wiglaf is lord of the *burh*, I hope I can convince him to change that, to free the slaves and forgive all years of indenture."

Hild snorted. "Well, that's not going to happen," she muttered.

Fryda frowned. "What?"

"Nothing." Hild silently cursed her flapping tongue. For all her idealism, Fryda was hopelessly blind to the faults in people she loved. Her brother spent a lifetime abusing his father's slaves and somehow Fryda managed to remain ignorant of his sadistic tendencies. Wiglaf was more likely to give up drinking mead and seducing the village girls than free anyone in Eceweall. "That's a very generous thought, my lady. I would be honoured to join you as a shield maiden."

Fryda smiled, clearly relieved. "I'll talk to Olaf."

Hild reached out and touched the ancient sword. "So…you really didn't know about Bryce? Being Unferth, I mean?"

Fryda sobered and looked at the sword. "No. I had no idea. I mean…" She tugged at her sleeve. "I knew he had secrets about his past, but…"

"I know. It's just…" Hild drew back her hand, as if the sword were a cursed thing. "I can't believe that *Unferth*, of all people, has been hiding out here for the past twenty years. All that time and he never said a thing to any of us."

Hild saw pain flash through Fryda's eyes. "I know. I can't believe he lied to me my whole life."

"My lady." Hild put her hand on Fryda arm. Her skin was cool and soft. "I'm sure he was trying to protect you. You know how much Bryce loved you."

"Yes." Fryda gave a small sigh and then smiled. "How about we honour his memory?" She lifted the sword, though she had difficulty gripping it with one hand. "Want to practice?"

"My lady, that sword weighs almost as much as you do," Hild laughed. "How could you possibly swing that at anything?"

"I'm stronger than I look." Fryda tossed Hild a practice sword.

Hild caught it and examined the flimsy wooden thing. "Then I suspect I'll be at a disadvantage from the start. Yours looks sharp as anything."

"Oh, don't be such a maggot in the meat. I'll be careful," Fryda said, and Hild laughed. She brought up her false sword and they began to spar.

It felt good to flex and stretch her muscles, but…the practice wasn't the same without Bryce, Hild realized with a pang. She missed his gentle, looming presence and his sharp, discerning mind. She missed the way he would correct her without making her feel as if she'd failed or lacked skill. The meadow seemed incomplete without his ready laugh and the smell of fire and smoke that seemed to cling to him like a lover. Fryda must have felt it as well. Her movements became more and more erratic as they fought, and her face twisted into a mask of grief.

Hild was about to call a halt to the exercise when Fryda gave a wild sob and swung the runed sword blindly. Hild, caught off guard, brought up her wooden one and blocked the blow. The practice sword shattered and Hild stumbled back. That movement was the only thing that saved her.

The tip of the sword scored her across the abdomen, slicing her tunic and carving a thin groove into her skin. Hild felt the burn of the cut, and then the warm trickle of blood. She gasped and Fryda dropped the sword with a cry of horror.

"Hild!" Fryda stumbled forward. "I'm sorry. I'm so sorry." Her hand fluttered over the flapping edges of torn cloth, unsure what to do.

"It's all right, my lady," Hild said. The cut stung, but it barely broke the skin. "I'm fine. It didn't go deep." She stared at Fryda. Now that she looked carefully, she saw the unnatural pallor of her cheeks, the shadows under her eyes. "Are…are *you* all right?"

Fryda sat abruptly, as if her legs could no longer hold her, and Hild followed her down with more grace.

"Yes." Fryda rubbed her head and a hairpin sprang from her thick curls and braids. "No. I don't know."

Hild reached over and took her hand. "Tell me."

Fryda sighed and gripped Hild's fingers. "Hild…something is happening to me. Something strange."

"What do you mean?"

"I've started to wonder if hanging in that chasm twisted my mind as much as my hand." Fryda said it jokingly, but Hild saw real fear lurking in her eyes as she rubbed her deformed fingers.

"Your mind is not twisted," Hild said. "Just tell me what's happened."

"It started the last time we practised with Bryce." Fryda proceeded to tell Hild about her strange bursts of energy, the uncontrollable surges of her blood, the heightened senses, her inability to control her strength...and her rage.

"It feels almost like someone takes over my body," Fryda said. "Like something from outside takes possession of me, and she is much stronger and angrier than I am. I haven't told anyone this, but I...I threw Bryce halfway across the meadow."

Hild laughed. "That must have startled him, a little thing like you being able to throw him down."

"No. Hild." Fryda caught her gaze and held it. "That's not an exaggeration. He came up behind me and grabbed me. It surprised me and my mind went blank. I don't remember what happened, but I remember the rage and the way my body burned, like I'd been hit by lightning. The next thing I knew, Bryce landed, hard, over thirty feet away."

Hild opened her mouth but couldn't think of anything to say, so she closed it again.

"It happened again during the battle," Fryda went on. "And again just now, when I hurt you."

"My lady, you didn't hurt me." Hild sat up straight and showed Fryda her stomach. "Look, you damaged my clothes more than you did me." She paused, and then blurted, "You didn't *really* toss Bryce thirty feet. Did you?"

"I did. I truly did. I also killed several exiles, both in my room and during the battle." Fryda dropped her head into her hand. "Hild, I don't know what to do. I'm not sure who...*what*...I am anymore."

Unease gripped Hild, like a cramp that pained her mind and heart. "Have...have you attacked anyone who didn't deserve it?" she asked.

"Bryce didn't really deserve to be thrown halfway across the meadow," Fryda answered. Hild saw she was deeply upset.

"But you said he surprised you. You would never have done it if he hadn't made you think you were in danger."

"That's true."

They fell silent. The sounds of the meadow that had gone into hiding during their sword practice gradually resurfaced. Sweet trills of birds and the rhythmic cadence of locusts kept time with the rush of the sea wind. Hild could hear distant voices from the *burh* as people went about their morning, and the muted noise was strangely comforting. After the exiles' attack, Hild felt a rush of affection for her fellow clan members. They had fought to keep the *burh* safe, as had she, and some of them had died for the honour of protecting her. They were as strong together as they were weak apart, and despite her situation, she loved being a part of something larger than herself. Weohstan and Moire treated her like property, as if Hild owed them something for merely existing, but Fryda treated her like a beloved friend, and that was enough.

"This thing that's happening to you," she said at last. "It cannot be madness. You're perfectly yourself in every other way. Perhaps Woden has bestowed some of his power on you. They say, once every generation or so, Woden and Frige choose a hero to perform great deeds in their honour. I've heard people in the *burh* say that Beowulf is one such hero." Hild smiled at Fryda. "Perhaps you are another."

Fryda's mouth twisted into a wry smile. "I actually wondered something like that myself..." She stopped. Shook her head. "I don't know. I don't feel very heroic."

A scream—raw, ragged, and steeped in anguish—cut through the morning stillness. The birds and locusts took refuge in silence once more as Hild and Fryda both looked up, startled. The scream came again, louder this time, and they scrambled to their feet.

"Come on," Fryda said, and started running towards the

longhouse. Hild followed. The screams cut off and were replaced by low, mournful wails. Hild and Fryda ran past the forge towards the main door of the mead-hall.

As they rounded the corner, Hild saw a beautiful woman on the ground, having fallen to her knees, her fists clenched and her head thrown back, her mouth open as if frozen in a rictus of pain. Lyset, one of the kitchen maids, stood beside her, looking upset.

"Gudrun!" Fryda dropped Hrunting and ran towards the grieving woman. "Lyset, what happened?"

"My lady." Lyset's voice was tearful and frightened. "I went to your rooms to clean this morning and I found...I found..."

The woman, Gudrun, wailed again and clutched her braids. Fryda dropped to her knees and put a hand on her shoulder. Hild put her arm around Lyset, who dissolved into incoherent sobs. Hild and Fryda looked at each other.

"We'd better go and look," Fryda said, her voice low. Hild nodded. She gave Lyset a little shake, and the girl gave a surprised hiccough.

"Lyset, listen to me," Hild said, trying to sound stern. Lyset blinked at her. "You need to stay here and look after Gudrun. Lady Fryda and I will go investigate her rooms."

Lyset's eyes grew huge and she shook her head in a panic. "No. No. You can't go in there. That place is cursed!"

Gudrun lowered her forehead to the path and made a noise that sounded like the lowing of a dying calf. Hild's heart twisted. "Lyset! Get a hold of yourself and take care of her. I don't want to hear any more curse nonsense. We'll be back as soon as we find out what's going on."

Fryda stood as Lyset pulled herself together enough to take Gudrun's arms. "Come along, my lady, let's get you on your feet," Hild heard her murmur as she and Fryda started to run.

They sprinted down the hill and through the green, past the righted standing stone and the barracks to the living quarters near the far wall. "My lady," Hild gasped as Fryda's house came into view. "Who is Gudrun?"

Fryda looked at her, worry painted across her features. "You've never met her?"

Hild gave Fryda a look. "Women like her rarely make appearances in the kitchens," she said dryly.

"Oh. Yes." Fryda blushed. Hild knew she sometimes forgot that she and Hild ran in very different circles. "Gudrun is Olaf's wife."

Hild's stomach lurched. They dropped to a jog, and then a walk as they approached the house, as if to delay the horrors they suspected awaited them. The front door stood open, and there were no guards in sight. Gudrun's screams had attracted attention, and most people moved towards the longhouse to investigate the commotion.

Hild followed Fryda inside. They moved through the large foyer towards the bedchamber. She caught a whiff of some foul smell that reminded her of the kitchens after a pig slaughter. Fryda hesitated at the doorway and then stepped through, Hild right on her heels. They both juddered to a halt as soon as they saw the grisly scene inside.

"Oh," Fryda whispered, and she put a hand over her mouth. "Oh no."

At first glance, the room looked normal. Bed, chest, table with a basin and pitcher of water. Firepit. All the trappings of a wealthy woman's quarters. But there on the floor, left in a huddled pile like discarded laundry, lay a man.

Olaf.

Hild heard a strangled noise emerge from her throat. Olaf lay face up, his eyes wide and staring. He wore no armour and the front of his tunic had been ripped open. His stomach and belly were torn open as well, and Hild could see his organs spilling out onto the floor. A great wash of red seeped into the rushes at his waist, but also at his head, soaking into his dark braids. Hild saw he had been stabbed through the neck and blood leaked from puncture wounds below both ears.

"Olaf..." Fryda's voice cracked on his name. Hild glanced again around the room, but saw nothing to indicate who had murdered him.

"My lady," she whispered as she stared at the mutilated body. "Who could have done this? More exiles?"

Fryda shook her head, apparently unable to speak.

A more chilling question surfaced as Hild stared at the mutilated corpse. "My lady. Why is he here?"

"What?" Fryda blinked and shook her head. "I don't know who would want to kill him."

"No." Hild gripped her torn dress. "I mean, why is he *here*. In your house? In your bedchamber?"

Fryda stood frozen for a moment, considering the question, and then her cheeks flamed scarlet. "Hild, you can't think...!"

"No, of course not." Hild gripped her arm. "But it is odd, is it not? Why would he be here? Has he ever been here before?"

"Just the night Theow and my brother..." Fryda's eyes widened and the hectic colour drained from her face.

Hild let out a tense breath. "Yes. No wonder Lyset was frightened. I don't know about any curse, my lady, but this makes me worried for you. It feels like..." Hild searched for the word. "...Like a warning. Or a threat."

A noise outside the room caught their attention. People were coming. Gudrun and Lyset must have managed to tell someone what had happened.

"My lady," Hild said in rushed undertones. "Don't answer any of their questions. We don't know who did this, so it's best not to say anything right now."

Fryda still stared at Olaf's corpse. "No," she whispered. "No, it couldn't be. He wouldn't."

Before Hild could ask whom she meant, Bjorn burst through the doorway followed by several of the *gedriht*. The young warrior made a pained noise when he saw Olaf and he glared at the two women.

"What happened here?" he barked. Hild saw he held Fryda's sword, Hrunting.

"We don't know," Hild said. She knew it went against convention to speak when in the presence of her superiors, but Fryda still stared in silent shock at Olaf's body. "We just got here."

Bjorn frowned at her and turned to Fryda. "How did you come to be here?"

Fryda looked up and Hild saw her face had turned practically green. "We heard Gudrun's screams, and Lyset told us something had happened here in Lady Fryda's rooms," Hild said, and put an arm around Fryda's shoulders. "My lady is understandably overcome. I must find a place for her to lie down."

Fryda swallowed and did not object. That's when Hild knew something was terribly wrong. Fryda did not take kindly to being treated like a fragile flower.

"Yes, of course." Bjorn pinned Hild with his intelligent eyes. He certainly was handsome with his brown braids and dark blue eyes, she thought. He studied her for a moment, his face inscrutable. She started to squirm under the weight of his regard when he said, "Where were you both before this?"

"In the meadow. I was picking herbs for the stillroom and Lady Fryda was helping me." That was only a half-lie—she could not very well tell the new chief of the *gedriht* that she had been sparring with the lady of the house.

Hild's stomach plunged, and she looked again at Olaf's body. The chief of the *gedriht* was dead. She wondered what would happen to her dream of becoming a shield maiden now.

"All right. I'm sure I'll have more questions later, but Lady Fryda does look like she needs some attention." He held Hrunting out to Fryda. "You dropped this, my lady, in front of the longhouse."

Fryda took the sword and clutched it in front of her. "Thank you."

Bjorn looked at Hild. "You may take her. But..." He frowned. "What is your name?"

She frowned back at him. "Hild."

"Hild." Bjorn seemed to study her. "But don't go far."

"I...I won't." Then, for some mad reason she could not immediately name, she said, "You can find me in the kitchens. Should you wish to." Hild grabbed Fryda's arm and hurried her from the house.

Once they were out of the house and a fresh wind had cleansed them of the smell of death, Fryda seemed to revive. She put a trembling hand to her head and let out a long, shaken breath.

"My lady." Hild stopped and looked at her with concern. "What is going on?"

"I'm not certain." Fryda looked troubled. "I...I need to talk to Wiglaf. Perhaps he can shed some light on the situation."

Hild raised her eyebrows. If Fryda thought her brother was somehow involved...well. No wonder it had hit her so hard.

Hild touched Fryda's arm. "I'm so sorry about Olaf, my lady. He seemed a good man."

Fryda grimaced. "He was. I was not close with him, but I liked him very much."

"The fact that he was murdered in your room still concerns me." Hild shuddered. That mutilated body and all that blood... this wasn't just a murder. This act spoke of unhinged rage.

"It concerns me, too. Don't worry, my friend. I'll be careful." Fryda looked down at the sword in her hands. "I think...I think I'm going to visit the forge. If Bryce were still alive, I'd be asking him for advice. Perhaps sitting in his special place will inspire me somehow."

Hild nodded and stepped away. The memory of the dead was very powerful, and sometimes they could even speak to the living if the need was strong. "All right. But you send for me right away if you need anything, all right?" Fryda nodded. "And my lady. I'm quite serious. Don't answer any questions about Olaf. I'm sure Bjorn is a very honourable warrior, but it feels as if someone is trying to connect you to the murder and sometimes men can't see what isn't right before their eyes."

They exchanged a sympathetic look, and Fryda nodded. "I promise. We were simply picking herbs for the stillroom."

Fryda raised her arm in farewell, turned, and headed towards the forge. Hild, thinking again of that pile of dishes, sighed and slowly made her way back to the kitchens.

Twenty-one

A short time later, Fryda found herself having her first quarrel with Theow.

"Please don't go back to the kitchens," she begged him for the third time.

"Fryda, I have to." Theow tried to walk past her. She planted herself in front of him and refused to budge. He gave her a frustrated look, but she would not yield. "If you take me away from the kitchens now, after what happened last night, people will talk."

"Nothing happened last night," Fryda insisted.

She knew it for a lie. At the funeral, she had flung herself into the arms of a slave, an act that spoke of more intimate things than a primal need for comfort and human contact. She'd felt open and raw, as if the skin had been flayed from her emotions and they kept seeping through her clothing like blood. She'd needed Theow last night and so had given in to that need, not thinking through the possible consequences.

They stood together in the field behind the forge. She had brought Hrunting with her, and she could not decide if she wanted to keep it for herself or hang it back up over the hearth. She thought it should belong to this place, in this building, but without Bryce the empty hearth lay cold, the anvil silent. The forge had lost its vigour and its voice with the death of its master, and somehow the sword did not seem to fit any longer. Theow had found her there some time later.

"Nothing happened," she repeated stubbornly.

"Fryda." Theow raised his eyebrows.

She gave a small huff. "Well, yes, a few things happened. My father died and my brother, who just sat there and watched it happen, became lord of Eceweall, and I learned that one of my dearest friends lied to me my whole life, and had a different name from the one I knew, and then he died, and you nearly died, and…"

"I did not nearly die."

Fryda returned Theow's sceptical look and reached out with one finger as if to poke his arm, where she knew a bandage covered a particularly nasty cut. He winced and backed away. "All right," he said, "perhaps I danced with danger yesterday, but I'm here and I'm well and so are you. But you have to let me go back to the kitchens."

"Moire *hit* you." Angry red flags rose in her cheeks, as if signalling her desire to march into the kitchens and do battle.

"You know that's nothing new, Fryda. She's been hitting us for years," Theow said.

His gentle reminder made her realize that anger could change the cadence of her heart and make her blood feel like molten lava and just-thawed river water at the same time. Rage bloomed inside her and she felt as if she could breathe fire. The first time she'd learned that the household slaves and servants sometimes suffered abuse, she had gone to her father with a righteous anger. He had brushed away her concerns and told her it was "normal."

Normal.

"I'm going to kill her." She started towards the kitchens. Battle? No. She would wage *war*.

Theow caught her by the shoulders. "You will do no such thing," he said, trying to soothe her. She nearly growled at him. She did not wish to be soothed. Her insides were wound as tight as harp strings and she thought at any moment they might snap and she would come undone. She struggled to regain control, but emotion swept through her like a raging river—fierce and unstoppable. She had buried both her father and the man she loved as a father the night before. Theow had kissed her after years of longing for him. Her brother was lord of the *burh*, and somehow that set her teeth on edge more than anything else. She felt abraded, as if scraped across rough stone. She could not bear the thought of Theow going back to the kitchens where he—and all the other workers—would be hurt and humiliated because he was a slave.

With a strength worthy of Weland the Smith himself, she wrenched herself back in control. "Fine. I won't kill her. But I am going to exile her from the *burh*," she said. "I dare anyone, even my brother, to try and stop me."

Theow bent his head over hers and gave her a gentle shake.

"Listen to me," he said. "You have to be careful, Fryda. I know a lot has happened in a very short time, but you need to realize everything has changed. Your most effective protector is gone. Weohstan may not have been much of a father to you, but no one would have dared speak against you while he lived. Now, I'm not sure we can depend on that any longer. Perhaps we would have been all right if we still had Bryce to speak for us. But we are alone, and with Olaf gone, I fear we have few friends in the *burh* who would be sympathetic to our...our situation."

The alien anger suddenly vanished, replaced by a subtle frisson of fear and a reawakening of the dull ache from her injured side. Fryda thought of Wiglaf, sprawled across their father's throne. She remembered his laugh when he told her Weohstan would die. Her eyes stung, and she knew Theow was right.

"What about Uncle Beowulf?" she said.

"He will leave in a matter of days. He has his own home and his own cares there. He may be able to help you for a little while, but eventually he will be gone, and you will be here—and you will be vulnerable."

"Oh. I see." Fryda bit her lip and then winced as the half-healed cut stung.

"He might not be able to protect you forever, but I do think we should talk to him." Theow twined a curl of her hair around his finger. "He might be willing to help us while he's still here."

"I want to talk to Eadith as well," Fryda said, looking concerned. "She was terribly upset at the funeral last night, and I want to make sure she's all right. I think…I think she and Bryce were lovers. Or maybe they were when they were younger." Her chest ached as she imagined the pressure of Eadith's grief at the loss of her love.

"I think they still were," Theow said. "I've seen them together in the forge on occasion, and they looked very close."

Fryda leaned against him. His wiry body felt so good pressed to hers, as if they had been designed to fit each other. "So, what do we do?"

"I don't know." Theow rested his cheek against her hair. "And until I do know, we must be very careful. We need to see how Wiglaf will take to being lord, and I need to ask him about something Bryce told me." He hesitated again, and she could feel the tension coil in his body.

"What is it?" She leaned back to study his face. "What did he tell you?"

Theow looked troubled. "He said…"

Before he could finish, a nearby voice interrupted them. "My lady!"

Fryda and Theow sprang apart. The voice had come from the other side of the forge. She peered through the open walls. Two guards in full armour and carrying spears waited in the doorway. "Oh, gods," she whispered. "They may have seen us. I'll go and see what they want." She gathered up her skirts and walked around to the front of the forge.

"Yes? What do you need? Do you have news about Olaf?" She tried to sound like the self-assured lady she ought to be.

"Orders from the lord," one guard said. His grim expression

gave her pause, but his next words chilled her. "You're to bring the slave called Theow to him at once."

Fryda frowned. "What does my fa…" She stopped, and an unexpected sadness washed through her. She cleared her throat and continued, "…my brother want with Theow?"

"He did not say, my lady. Just that you are to bring him to the longhouse immediately."

Fryda smoothed out her skirt. "Very well. Thank you."

The guards did not move.

Fryda raised an eyebrow. "Well?"

The second guard shifted. "Lord Wiglaf told us the slave would be with you, and we were to bring both of you in together."

The blood drained from her face. "Did he, now?"

"If you please, my lady." They waited.

She sighed. "Fine. I'll get him." She headed back to the field.

Theow did not take the news well. "What do you think he wants?" He rubbed his fingers along his scar. "And why did he send guards instead of a messenger?"

"I don't know," Fryda said. "Perhaps he wants to reward you for your bravery in the battle yesterday? It could be an honour guard."

Theow stared at her as if she had grown a second head. Her cheeks grew warm.

"It could," she insisted. "You saved my life yesterday. You saved *his* life yesterday! I can't imagine Wiglaf would make his first act as lord anything but uplifting and positive. I don't think we have anything to worry about." The writhing mass of butterflies in her stomach said otherwise, but she would not admit that to Theow.

"I think it's much more likely," Theow said slowly, "that he plans to accuse me of Olaf's murder."

Fryda's stomach lurched. "Surely not. You weren't anywhere near my quarters. There must be witnesses. People who know where you actually were."

"I'm not certain that's going to matter, Fryda."

And in that moment, Fryda knew her unthinkable fear was true. Her mind still shied away from naming it, but she could no longer deny it.

"We need to find Uncle Beowulf," Fryda said, her heart pounding. "He's the only one who can help us."

Theow glanced at the guards. "I don't think they're going to let us take off and look for him."

"I'll send someone to find him." She looked at Theow, feeling sick. He touched her cheek and gave a feeble smile.

"We could run," Theow said. Fryda suspected he only half-joked.

She shored up her own courage. "Let's go see what he wants."

★

They walked into the mead-hall, not quite at spearpoint, though it felt that way with the guards close on their heels as if wary they might try to escape. As soon as they entered, Fryda paused and whispered to one of the mead-hall warriors to fetch King Beowulf as quickly as he could. He nodded and left the hall while the guards nudged them up to the dais where Wiglaf sat waiting for them.

The longhouse looked its finest for the last night of the king's celebrations, with skins and furs and piles of gold coins and rings adorning every surface. The magnificent goblet, Beowulf's gift, sat at the centre of the room, and Wiglaf had draped Weohstan's chair in a sombre black cloth, a tradition borrowed from the Romans. The mead-hall was empty, however, except for Wiglaf, who sat in the shrouded ceremonial chair, and an arc of warriors that curved behind him, standing guard over their new lord. Bjorn, raised to be the new chief of the *gedriht* upon Olaf's death, stood off to one side.

Wiglaf looked better than she had expected, having had the night to sleep off whatever drugs he had taken the previous day.

His eyes were full of shadows and his mouth drawn with fine-lined tightness, but otherwise he seemed his usual self.

"We are here as requested, my lord," Fryda said with a brief bow. It felt strange bowing to her brother, but his new position demanded it. "May I take this moment to congratulate you, my lord?"

"Please don't," Wiglaf said, and she relaxed. He still sounded like himself—sardonic, self-deprecating, and irreverent. "I'm not sure I could bear that from you."

"As you wish. You may have my sympathies, then, on the loss of our father."

Wiglaf gave her a tired smile. "As you have mine." The smile fell away and Fryda felt a shadow pass over her. "As lord of Eceweall, I shall be making some changes, but I wanted to deal with the important and most immediate matters first."

"Changes?" She blinked. "It's been less than a day, Wiglaf. Shouldn't we slow down a little, work out what to do next together?"

Wiglaf scowled. "There is no *we* in this, Fryda. I know my own mind, and I've known for years what this stronghold needs. Believe me, I tried often enough to make Father see reason, but you know how stubborn he is. Was." Wiglaf shook his head, wincing. "He was so old-fashioned, you know. Especially in how he dealt with the household and the servants. And the slaves." His eyes moved to Theow.

Theow shifted next to her.

"Indeed." A sliver of hope pricked her. Perhaps he *did* mean to reward Theow for his part in the battle. Most landowners gave gifts to their slaves for outstanding work or great feats, even bestowing upon them land and wealth. Weohstan had always refused to offer any such rewards, but perhaps Wiglaf meant to change that.

That hope shrivelled and died, however, as Wiglaf looked at Theow and she saw the darkness in her brother's eyes. She shivered and tugged her sleeve over her hand. Wiglaf looked back at her, and the darkness did not dissipate.

"I'm told you know about what happened to Olaf," he said. He shot a glance at Bjorn, who stood silently beside his throne. "That you found him in your bedchamber."

Fryda's anger grew at the insinuation. This anger was no outside influence—this was wholly her own. "No," she said. "I was not in my rooms when Olaf was murdered. Lyset found him there when she went to clean."

"I do not think so."

"What?" Her heart was pounding so hard it filled her head with noise and she had difficulty hearing him.

"I think you were in bed with your lover," Wiglaf said, and glanced at Theow with an expression so malevolent she cringed. Bjorn's eyebrows shot up to his hairline and he stared at Wiglaf with a concerned intensity. "I think Olaf discovered you both and Theow killed him."

"*What?*" Fryda's voice echoed from the rafters. "That is ridiculous, Wiglaf, and you know it. I was…" She paused. "I was picking herbs with Hild in the back meadow. She will tell you if you ask her."

Wiglaf regarded her, his eyes darting over her face. "I'm sure she will," he murmured. "Hild would tell any lie if it would protect you."

Fryda stared at her brother as if she had never seen him before. Wiglaf had to know his story was preposterous.

Just then the corner of his mouth twitched and for one moment he looked insufferably smug. He quickly smoothed the expression away, but he had already revealed the truth—he knew he could lie to get what he wanted.

And Fryda's thoughts inexorably moved to the next obvious conclusion: if he could so quickly fabricate such a story, he most likely also knew the truth.

Which meant, she realized, that Wiglaf had probably murdered

Olaf, and he had left the body in Fryda's bedchamber in order to frame Theow.

Wiglaf's eyes held a kind of anguish as he gazed at her, as if he faced a decision that could only end in heartbreak. He looked away, as if he could not bear to meet her eyes.

"However, I have wonderful news for you, sister," he said, "and I'm certain you will be pleased."

"Will I?" Her head reeled.

"I very much hope so. You see, I have found a husband for you. You shall be married immediately."

Fryda jerked her head back as if Wiglaf had slapped her. "What?" Her voice sounded thin and shrill.

"Yes. Isn't it wonderful? Just this morning I have accepted Lord Ansten's offer for you. He has agreed to marry you and take you back to Sweden with him after the king's celebrations are over." He gave her a clear and level look. "Congratulations."

Fryda swallowed. She became intensely aware of Theow next to her, stiff and silent, and she willed him to hold his tongue. "Ansten?" she asked. "The man who offered two cows and a sunken ship for my bride-price? The man from Sweden, the nation whose king just attacked us in an unprovoked act of war?"

Where was that warrior with King Beowulf? Why didn't he come? She glanced at Bjorn but he still stood by Wiglaf's chair, looking straight ahead.

"The marriage shall be part of our truce agreement." Wiglaf sat back. She thought he looked a little lost. "A gesture of faith between nations and a promise of no further hostilities from either side. You will be playing an important role in the relationship between our people. You should be honoured."

"You're sending me away?" She yanked at her sleeve again and then clutched it, trying to stop shaking. "But Wiglaf, I do not wish to leave my home. I do not wish to marry. At least, I have no wish to marry Lord Ansten. I asked you to refuse his offer."

She conjured a vague memory of a man, not elderly but certainly not youthful, with light blond hair and a weak chin covered by a thin, straggly beard.

"I did refuse his first offer," Wiglaf said. "But he added another cow and ten cords of fine hardwood to the bride-price. I knew you could not possibly refuse."

Fryda stared, and her anger once again reared its head. Her brother knew such a paltry bride-price was an insult to her. "Wiglaf, I do not wish to marry Lord Ansten."

"The terms have already been set," Wiglaf said. "The betrothal is binding."

"But I did not agree to it!" Fryda cried.

"That is immaterial. Lord Ansten has agreed to it, and that is all that matters." Wiglaf glanced at her left hand, hidden in her sleeve. "He does not know you are a cripple, by the way, so please try not to let him see that before the wedding. We don't want a repeat of what happened with Dysg."

Fryda's jaw dropped as she stared at her brother. He had never been so deliberately cruel to her. "Wiglaf, please. I am your sister. Your closest family. We shared a womb. Do not do this to me."

"She has rights." Theow spoke up for the first time, and Wiglaf turned his dark gaze on him. "She has rights by law. You cannot force her."

"She is no longer your concern," Wiglaf growled. "In fact, she never was, and one of my father's great failings was allowing you to think you belonged with our family when we were children. He should have kept you in your place, down in the muck where you belong. But he could not say no to my mother, and she wanted you to be our playmates. Woden's beard, I have no idea why."

"Wiglaf!" Fryda wanted to clap her hand over Wiglaf's mouth to stop the ugly words.

"'No woman or maiden shall ever be forced to marry one

whom she dislikes, nor be sold for gold,'" Theow recited. "It's the law of the land."

"Theow, slave of Clan Waegmunding," Wiglaf said, ignoring his words, "you have been accused and found guilty of the murder of Olaf, chief of the *gedriht*, and of theft and the rape of Lady Fryda."

Fryda clamped her jaws shut. If she opened her mouth, she knew terrible and unforgivable words would spill out. The strange spark in her blood flared, and then ignited. She took a deep breath, and then another, trying to regain control.

"Who accuses me?" Theow asked with remarkable calmness.

"I do." Wiglaf smirked at him. "Do not think me blind to what is going on between the two of you."

"You know perfectly well that I did not kill Olaf," Theow said. "And what is going on between us is neither theft nor rape."

"It is if I say it is."

"It is not!" Fryda said, finding her voice. "I say it is not. *I* do."

"Again, what you say is immaterial," Wiglaf said. He looked at her with equal measures of incredulity and disgust. "Honestly, Fryda, what are you thinking? He is a *slave*."

Fryda gaped at him. "He is Theow," she said, amazed she had to state something so obvious. "He's a person."

"He is not a person, he is property," Wiglaf roared, slamming his hand down on the black-clothed arm of their father's throne. "And he has done enough damage to this family. You will marry Lord Ansten and I hereby sentence the slave to..." He paused and looked at Theow. His expression turned greedy and malevolent, and Fryda's fear grew. She must have made some small sound, because Wiglaf glanced at her and his face changed from cruel to reflective, as if considering the consequences of his next words. "...exile from the clan, and he is banished from Eceweall. He must leave immediately and never return on pain of death."

Fryda's senses sharpened as the wrath within her grew. She could suddenly hear the muted sounds from outside, could see sharply, more clearly than she ever had before. She looked around the mead-hall, listened for a familiar step. It did not come, but she did notice one incongruous sound. At some point during the argument, Bjorn had left his post by Wiglaf's side and Fryda heard his footsteps as he quietly left the longhouse through the great arched doors.

She was rapidly running out of potential allies.

"Where is Uncle Beowulf?" she asked. "I sent a warrior to find him. He should be here by now."

"Ah." Wiglaf shook his head. "He is not here, sister."

"What do you mean?" She began to feel real panic. "He would not leave before the final feast."

"Oh, no, it's nothing like that. He hasn't left the *burh*. I merely suggested to him this morning that he should visit the farmsteads and check on the state of the homes and buildings. See if everything is in good repair. Make a list of things he thinks I should do now that I am lord." Wiglaf looked extremely smug. "He'll be back later this afternoon."

Fryda's head swam, her thoughts scattered like leaves in the wind. She could not pin them down. Theow had been right. She would find no help here. "Wiglaf. How can you do this? Theow grew up with us. He is our friend. You used to play with him all the time. You liked him. He sat and ate with us only *three days ago*. You would not do that with someone you despised."

"I did not realize then that you had already defiled yourself with him," Wiglaf said. His voice turned rough and ugly. "Besides, you brought him there, not I. You've always insisted on treating him like an equal. It's because of you he never remembers that he's a slave who should know his place." Wiglaf glared at Theow. "But you never did, did you? Had you already spoiled her by then, or did you wait until she was hurt and grieving and vulnerable from her father's death?"

"Oh, you're a monster," Fryda whispered.

"No, I'm a lord exercising his legal rights," Wiglaf said.

"The two are clearly not incompatible. And this is not legal. Theow did not kill Olaf!"

She did not voice her next thought... *You did*... but she did not have to. She knew Wiglaf could read it on her face.

"I have another idea," Theow said, stepping forward. "One I think would work out better for all concerned."

Wiglaf sat back. "Oh, I cannot wait to hear this."

Theow looked at Fryda. "Just before the battle yesterday, Bryce... Unferth... told me he planned to buy my freedom from Lord Weohstan and make me his heir. He'd lost his own family years ago, and he loved Fryda as dearly as his own blood. He said he trusted me to protect her." He turned to Wiglaf as Fryda's throat tightened.

I loved you like a father, too, Bryce.

"You want Lady Fryda married and both of us gone," Theow said. "Let me have my freedom and my inheritance and I will marry her, if that is her wish. Then we will both be happy to depart and never return, if that is *your* wish."

Fryda blinked at Theow.

"Preposterous," Wiglaf snarled. "My sister is the most important person in the world to me, and I'd rather see her dead than shackled to a slave. Besides, I doubt Bryce said any such thing."

"He did," Fryda said, remembering. Bryce's cryptic final words suddenly became clear. "With his dying breath, he did. He said that he wanted to give everything he owns to Theow and me, and he said he wanted us to be free." She looked at Theow and everything fell into place. "He wanted to buy your freedom."

Theow nodded. "And he wanted you to have a choice."

Wiglaf frowned and shook his head. "Surely you don't believe that wild story the king told us last night. How could Bryce be Unferth, and have been in hiding here all this time? The warriors who went to Denmark with Beowulf would have recognized him."

"They knew each other more than fifty years ago," Fryda said. "Unferth was little more than a boy when Beowulf killed Grendel, and exile would have changed him." She looked at Theow. He met her eyes, his expression anxious, uncertain.

Her anger evaporated, and in its place came a happiness so profound it bordered on painful. It filled her, warmed her, and shone through all the parts of her. Theow saw the change of her expression, and he relaxed.

Silly man. He had been worried. Her entire body sang at the thought of living with him, of being his wife.

"All the more reason to be sceptical," Wiglaf said. "If he's changed that much, how did King Beowulf recognize him?"

"The sword," Theow said.

Wiglaf twitched and scowled. "Look, even if Bryce and Unferth are the same man, how much gold could he possibly have? His clan exiled him, and he worked as a blacksmith for most of his life."

"He said he had enough for two lifetimes," Theow said, "and that he wanted to spend one of them on making me a free man."

"Please, Wiglaf," Fryda said. Her injured side throbbed as she struggled to control her breathing. She was not above begging if it meant she would not have to marry Lord Ansten. "Please. This way would be best for everyone, including you."

Wiglaf stood. "It is absolutely out of the question," he said. "I've already given Lord Ansten my word, and I refuse to break it because you shagged a slave and fancy yourself in love. Or are you afraid he's already got you with child? Honestly, Fryda, I had no idea you had such low tastes."

"He has not touched me, you arsehole," Fryda spat. "And I don't think you have the moral high ground here, considering you've lain with every farmer's daughter and servant girl in the *burh*."

"Servant girls, yes, but never a slave. And *never* a barbarian from some savage land halfway across the world."

The naked contempt in his voice hit her like a slap to the face, and she knew there could be no convincing him of Theow's worth, of his humanity.

"Wiglaf," she whispered.

"Because Bryce died with no heirs or kin, by law of inheritance all his money and possessions revert to the clan," Wiglaf said. "Which means it's all mine now. Theow is exiled from this moment forward, and you *will* marry Lord Ansten if you know what is good for you. Guards, take him away. And hold her," he added as Fryda turned and launched herself at Theow.

He caught her and they managed one hard, desperate embrace before the guards pulled her away. She lost any semblance of decorum after that as she fought, screamed, clawed, and bit anything she could reach. Her cracked ribs protested, but she would not stop struggling. She reached for her strength, opened herself to its invasion and called to the gods to lend her that magic of fire and fury once more. But it refused her, obstinate, and she remained diminished. She was trapped within her own mortal, human strength, as if the disability in her hand had suddenly stretched and weakened her entire body. She watched, horrified, as a host of guards dragged Theow out of the longhouse, and she did not stop fighting until something hard and sharp crashed down on her head. The room went dark and she collapsed, insensible, to the floor.

Rejection

Fýrdraca struggles, fighting the Lone Survivor's curse to break the surface of sleep, to wake and live once more. Her connection with the girl-warrior helps. Fýrdraca channels her own power through their shared bond and with her sympathetic magic she can influence the world. Each time she does, it brings her closer and closer to full wakefulness.

In return, she gets to feel once more. She guzzles the shield maiden's pain and sorrow, drinks in her anguish like a drunk swallows mead. She fuels her anger and concentrates it, using the Lone Survivor's curse to make it powerful and strong. She feels, feeds the curse, and thrives.

But then the link between them is severed. Fýrdraca feels a sudden bolt of...something...from the woman-child, something that makes her flinch and recoil, as if from physical pain. It takes several moments for her to identify the feeling.

Happiness. Joy. And love.

The Lone Survivor's curse howls within her, and she feels its echo somewhere near the shield maiden. Fýrdraca's mind floods with images of the Lone Survivor kissing a beautiful woman, a wedding, a gold and silver goblet, the woman with a belly burgeoning with child. The pain is too much, and she breaks the bond.

She feels the shield maiden reach for her, desperate for her power. But, fearing the pain of her joy, Fýrdraca withdraws and settles back down into the stupor of cursed sleep.

Twenty-two

Theow shouted as the guards dragged Fryda from his arms. Two men grabbed him from behind as he surged after her. He struggled, but they had his arms locked in their strong grip. They pulled him backwards as he fought to get to Fryda.

She screamed his name and twisted and writhed against the guards who held her. She fought like a wildcat, trapped and frantic, while they hauled her away. One guard tried to slap a hand over her mouth to silence her, but he yelled and swore and snatched it away when Fryda bit him. Theow dug in his heels, but the guards simply lifted him from the floor and carried him towards the doorway. He kicked and bucked against their hands, but they were too strong for him. Just as they tried to force him over the threshold, he saw a guard raise his sword and bring the hilt down on Fryda's head. Her screams died and she crumpled to the floor.

Theow never could remember what happened next. A kind of madness took him, and the next moments were nothing but a blur of rage and fear. Some time later—mere moments or half a day, he did not know—the sound of distant voices brought him back, and he realized his legs had forsaken him and he hung limply between the two guards. Blood dripped down his face, his knuckles were scraped and torn, and a new ache in his stomach —about the size of a man's fist or foot—made him feel nauseous.

"...will take him from here," he heard a man say. He opened his eyes...odd, he did not remember closing them...and saw

Bjorn standing near the arched door, preventing exit. *Again odd*, he thought fuzzily. He thought Bjorn had left the mead-hall.

Theow heard footsteps approach and turned his head. Wiglaf stopped in front of him. Theow could not see Fryda, or the guards who attacked her.

"Pathetic," Wiglaf said with a sneer. "As if you could ever protect her like I can."

Theow managed to get his feet under him again. He licked his lips and tasted blood. "That's amusing, coming from the man who assaulted her." He glared at Wiglaf through narrowed eyes. "You're nothing but a menace to her."

Wiglaf's face underwent an alarming transformation, shifting from scorn and contempt to downright murder. He did not speak, but drew the *seax* at his waist—Theow dimly recognized it as Olaf's weapon—and lunged at him.

Raw fear stopped Theow's breath, and for one moment he stared his death in the eyes. But Bjorn leapt forward and knocked Wiglaf's arm away, and the blade went wide.

"My lord," Bjorn said as Wiglaf spun on him, furious. "I know you would not wish to spare him from the pain and degradation of exile. I fear, my lord, you would regret such an action later."

Wiglaf froze. For one, interminable moment he appeared to be at war with himself, wishing on the one hand to finish Theow then and there, and on the other desiring for him a lifetime of suffering. Finally, he dropped his arm and sheathed the *seax* in his belt.

"Yes." Wiglaf walked up to Theow until their faces were only inches apart. His breath smelled like stale mead and last night's meat. "Yes, he's right. This way is best. You'll know she's out there, somewhere. And you will never find her. You'll never see her again. You'll know she lives as another man's wife and you'll live with that for the rest of your life."

Theow pulled against his captors, but they only tightened their grip. Wiglaf laughed.

"You have no clan now, slave. You are worse than dead. You are...irrelevant. Alone. Unprotected. There is a reason exile is the worst possible punishment for a man." Wiglaf sniffed and gave a small, ugly smile. He leaned in and whispered into Theow's ear. "You are a lone-dweller, slave, and you will tread the tracks of this world in solitude until the end of your days. You must bewail your cares to the sea and the sky, for there is no person, man or woman, living who will now hear you. Sorrow will be your only companion, and your food and drink will turn to ash in your mouth because you will share it with no one."

Wiglaf leaned back, looking pleased with himself. Theow wrestled with his fear, but every word fell upon him with the weight of a standing stone. *Exile.*

"I may never see Fryda again," he growled, "but neither will you."

Wiglaf's face darkened once more and Bjorn put one large hand over Theow's mouth. "My lord," Bjorn said before Wiglaf could speak, "shall I remove him from the *burh* for you? I know you have important duties awaiting your attention."

Wiglaf's mouth worked and twisted, as if tasting bitter words on his tongue. "Get him out of my sight," he grunted. "He's to leave with nothing. No food, no clothing, no weapons." His eyes glinted as he looked Theow in the face. "Let him live out there like the animal he is."

Without a moment's hesitation, Bjorn took Theow from the two guards. "Back to your posts," he told them, and then pushed Theow out of the mead-hall.

Theow jerked away from Bjorn's hand. "Wait, what about..."

"Quiet. Not here." Bjorn shoved him down the path and past the green. As the young *gedriht* chief had just saved his life, Theow obeyed him and kept his mouth shut. Bjorn marched him through the *burh* and people stopped what they were doing to watch him. Such news travelled fast. People came out of their homes, the barracks, their places of work, and silently stared as

Theow was marched towards the western gate. Many of them turned their backs on him, denying his existence. He was no longer part of the clan.

Theow burned with humiliation and despair. For one moment, he wished that Bjorn had not stayed Wiglaf's hand. Death would be kinder than exile for a man with few skills beyond archery and servitude. But then he remembered that Fryda was—he hoped—still alive. If he could find a way back into the *burh* and sneak her out...perhaps something could be salvaged of this life after all.

If she would go with him. She'd smiled at him when he said he wanted to marry her, but that was before he became an exile.

Bjorn hustled him along the path until they reached the western gate. The wall that separated the *burh* from the farmsteads stood ten feet high and was built from the pale grey stone they dug from the quarry. Guards stood at the wooden gate and as Bjorn and Theow approached, Bjorn signalled for them to raise the lockbar and open the heavy doors.

As soon as the gates opened, Bjorn took Theow by the tunic and marched him through. He stopped and turned back to the guards.

"Keep it open," he ordered. "We'll be returning soon."

"Yes, chief."

"We will?" Theow asked, bewildered.

"Quiet."

They came through the gates near the edge of the cliff on the north side of the promontory. The land broadened towards the horizon until it connected to the mainland far to the west. Rich farms and pasture lay to the south and west. Crops, livestock, and the *burh*'s brewery dotted the landscape while copses of trees and orchards grew heavy with summer fruit. Bjorn pushed him towards one such cluster of trees, and soon he found himself in a dark, wooded area. The air was cool with an earthy, musky scent. Loamy ground gave slightly under his feet as Bjorn led him to a tiny clearing amidst the slender birch and beech trees.

To Theow's surprise, Hild stood waiting for them. She looked harried and flustered, her braids tangled and a sheen of sweat on her face. A basket covered with a piece of linen lay at her feet. As soon as she saw the two men, she rushed forward and threw her arms around Theow. He hugged her back.

"Is it true?" Hild's voice shook. "Bjorn said Lord Wiglaf exiled you and he's forcing Lady Fryda to marry some foreign lord?

Theow dropped his arms and stepped back and looked at Bjorn in astonishment. "You fetched Hild here?"

"I did." Bjorn regarded Theow with concern. "You should know that many of the warriors, especially the *gedriht*, do not look upon our new lord favourably. Olaf told us Weohstan had chosen him over Wiglaf to become the next lord of Eceweall, and…"

"What?" Hild stared at Bjorn. "If that's true, why didn't you say anything?"

Bjorn crossed his arms over his chest. "And what could we have said that Wiglaf would not deny? His words would carry more weight than ours, and that would cause a rift in the clan. Better to remain silent and plan from within. But then Olaf was murdered."

"You think Wiglaf did it," Theow said.

"I do not know." Bjorn passed a hand over his stubbled face. "I have no proof, and so could not bring an accusation. But as soon as he exiled you, I knew we had little time to act…and I knew Hild considers the Lady Fryda a friend. I thought she could help."

Theow raised his eyebrows. Loyalty to the lord was an important tenet of clan life, but a lord acting against the welfare of his people was the worst possible crime. If Wiglaf had, indeed, killed his rival for the position of lord, Bjorn and the *gedriht* would be fully justified in acting against him.

"I'll find out what happened to Lady Fryda once I get back inside," Hild said. Her words were rushed and urgent. She picked up the basket and handed it to Theow. "Here's a little food, a knife, some flint and tinder, and a few other necessities you might need. I couldn't get much without looking suspicious, I'm sorry. I'll try to bring more soon."

"I'll help," Bjorn said. "And I'll make sure she gets in and out of the gate again safely."

"Hild." Theow reached out and grasped her hands. "Please. You must find her. They...they hit her, and she...she..."

Hild's eyes widened with alarm. "I will, Theow. I promise. We'll get her out."

"You don't understand." Theow drew a ragged breath and tried to calm the panic licking at his insides. "I saw Wiglaf's face when he looked at her. He has murder on his mind..." He stopped. "If he thinks Fryda will in any way jeopardize his ambitions, he might..."

Hild shook her head. "No. Say what you will about Lord Wiglaf, but he loves his sister. He's always said she is the only person who truly understands him. He would never hurt her."

"I might have believed that some days ago," Theow said. "I'm not sure I do now. Trust me, I'm very aware of how cruel he can be." The gnarled, white scars on his back twinged.

"We'll find her." Hild looked at Bjorn. "Right?"

"Yes," Bjorn said. "But I also think we need to find King Beowulf and tell him everything that's happened. He's the only one who can truly help you now."

"That's why Wiglaf sent him away this morning," Theow said bitterly. "He knew the king wouldn't stand for any of this. Fryda is his favourite."

"All right. Theow, you need a safe place to hide out. If you head east along the cliff, eventually you'll come to the large crack in the ground. The one caused by the earthquake seven years ago."

"I've been there," Theow said. He had difficulty believing he had so recently been there with Fryda.

"Good. There's a cave in the cliff by the beach near there. It's used for storage. Do you know it?"

"I do." Sometimes Moire had sent him to the cave to bring supplies back to the kitchen.

"I haven't been there, but there should be a way for you to get down the cliff to the cave. See if you can find it, and then wait there. Hild will go back to the *burh* and try to find Lady Fryda, while I go to the farmsteads to find the king. I'll take him back to the longhouse and he can sort out this mess." Bjorn rolled his eyes. "I just hope Lord Wiglaf was telling the truth when he said he sent the king out there."

"What do I do when I find her?" Hild asked. She had wrapped her arms around herself, as if to keep from trembling.

"You'll have to smuggle her out somehow," Bjorn said. "Wait until the final feast is well underway, and no one should notice. If anyone stops you, tell them you're following my orders."

"And what happens if Lord Wiglaf catches us?" Hild's voice shook.

Bjorn reached out his hand and slowly, gently, put a single finger under Hild's chin. He tilted her face up until she met his eyes. "If that happens, then I will find you." He said it with absolute certainty, as if no other outcome were possible.

"Tell her to find Theow at the cave," Bjorn said, pulling his hand back. "I'm going to need you to stay in Eceweall and back up my story with the king, so once you get Lady Fryda out, send her to Theow on her own."

"Pfft." Hild's nervousness evaporated from the heat of her scorn. "As if the king would listen to me."

"He will listen." Bjorn gripped the hilt of his sword. "By Woden's strength, he will listen, and he will believe. Now go, and hurry."

Hild nodded and turned to go, but stopped. She looked at Theow and he saw a mischievous twinkle in her eye.

"Oh, Theow, I forgot to ask you something earlier."

Theow cocked his head at her. "What is it?"

"Just this. 'I am hard and sharp, strong in entering, bold in coming out. Sometimes he draws me out, hot from the hole. Sometimes I go back in the narrow place. What am I?' "

Bjorn threw Hild a startled look.

Theow groaned and put a hand over his eyes. "You are a terrible person, Hild. I got exiled today and you're trying to make me blush with dirty riddles."

Hild punched his arm playfully. "Blush? Why should you blush? It's a poker, you pervert."

Bjorn snorted with suppressed laughter and, despite the hardships of the day, Theow's lips twitched into a rueful smile.

"Hild," he called as she started back towards the *burh*. She turned and raised an eyebrow at him. "When you see her, will you please tell her..."

His throat closed over the words he meant to say, as if his body would allow him to say them to no one but Fryda herself.

"Tell her what?" Hild asked. Her voice was gentle and understanding.

"Tell her..." He swallowed. "...Tell her to be careful, and I'll see her soon."

Hild regarded him for a moment. Then she nodded, turned, and disappeared into the trees.

Twenty-three

Later that afternoon, Theow sat and stared into the jagged chasm that sundered the earth, but he did not really see it.

The past half-day kept running through his memory, and always it landed on his last glimpse of Fryda, crumpled on the floor of the mead-hall as the guards tried to pull him from the room.

If not for Bjorn, Fryda would now be alone and defenceless. Wiglaf would have buried Olaf's *seax* in Theow's belly and his corpse would have joined the other dead exiles on the rocky ocean shore below.

Other exiles. He was exiled. An exile.

Theow dropped his head into his hands. He saw Fryda again, face pale as mountain snow, lying in a heap on the floor. He stared into the deep gorge. Fryda had brought him here, and he had kissed her. They'd talked and she'd wept and they'd laughed here. In this moment when he felt the most separated, the most distant from everything he held dear, he could at least feel close to her here.

But he knew even that was an illusion.

Wiglaf's words echoed through his head, like the long, forlorn notes of a funereal horn. *I have found a husband for you. You shall be married immediately.*

Theow wondered what "immediately" meant. Would Wiglaf allow her to heal from the vicious blow to her head before he sold her into matrimonial slavery to Lord Ansten? Or would he wake her from her unnatural sleep long enough to force the marriage vows from her lips and then throw her on a ship to Sweden before she had a chance to recover? His scar twinged and he rubbed it.

Her brother would doom her to a miserable existence alone, without family, without love. Without Theow. Fryda would be as much an exile as he. Would Hild be able to find her and get her out?

He rolled over onto his back and groaned. He had no idea what to do next.

Unable to stay still any longer, Theow leapt to his feet and began pacing up and down the edge of the cliff. He braced himself as the salt wind buffeted against him, threatening to sweep him off the bluff and plunge him onto the rocks below. The sea was beautiful but restless, and the white-capped waves rolled in agitation towards the shore. Theow scowled, angry that such beauty could still exist when his life had been torn apart.

Movement from below caught his eye and he looked down at the beach. A small fleet of longships had recently returned from a raid, or a trading voyage, or a sea-hunt, and the long-necked vessels bobbed near the shore. He could make out a line of sailors heading over the rocky beach towards the cliff face. Their bodies were bowed under heavy burdens—barrels, sacks, crates—as they made their way inland. They would be headed for the storage cave Bjorn had mentioned.

The young, unweathered cave, a result of the earthquake seven years earlier, went deep enough into the rock cliff to work as a holding area for the *burh*. It kept items hidden, cool, and dry, as the tide never reached that far up the land. The sailors would stow the heaviest goods there, not wanting to lug them up the narrow, slippery stairs carved into the cliff face behind the longhouse.

But how to get to the cave?

Theow watched as several boatmen rolled large barrels down

the beach away from the cave. He frowned. Where were they going? Surely they weren't pushing heavy barrels all the way to the end of the promontory. Eventually, the sailors hefted the barrels upright and left them at the foot of the cliff. He saw one gesture upwards, talking to his boatmate, and after a few minutes they headed back to their longships.

Theow loped along the edge of the cliff until he came to a single tree growing at an extreme angle outward towards the ocean. The gnarled trunk looked sturdy and strong, and the thick roots entwined through the earth, anchoring the tree to the rock. Harsh winds had stripped away all the lower branches, so only at the very top of the tree did leaf-clad boughs stretch forward, as if longing to touch the sea. The tree looked wild, warped, and lonely, but had the air of a warrior determined to fulfil his duty. From this tree, positioned several feet from the cliff edge, a rope and pulley contraption descended.

He peered over the edge of the cliff and was not surprised to see the heavy barrels directly below him.

The hoist consisted of a series of ropes, pulleys, and a platform running down the cliff face. Theow lowered himself to his belly and peered over the edge of the cliff, careful to stay out of sight. Eventually the men emerged, empty-handed, and made their way back to the ships. Theow knew they would then sail to the permanent docks near the stairs where they would climb back into the *burh*.

Theow inspected the hoist. Next to the tree, someone had constructed a crude wooden frame and crank, several feet taller than himself, to house and coil a length of heavy leather rope. The rope ran upwards to the tree, where it looped through a pulley attached to the sturdiest branch and then dangled down the edge of the cliff. A few feet below the pulley, the rope tied off and separated into four parts, which were fastened to the corners of a small platform made of wooden planks that hung suspended in the air. A turn of the crank would move the ropes up or down, raising the wooden platform further up towards the tree, or lowering it down to the ground.

A long, *long* way down to the ground.

He could not ride the platform down—he had no one to stay up top and control the crank. He would have to lower the platform first and then climb down the rope.

He flexed his hands. He had no gloves. The rough rope would tear his skin to shreds.

Theow looked back at the water. The ships had left their moorings and were headed back towards the *burh*. He waited until all the longships were well away before he sprang into action.

First, he searched for a large rock and dug it out of the earth, splitting his nails and scraping the skin from his knuckles as he scrabbled at the dirt with his fingers. Once he could heave the rock up from its nest in the ground, he put Hild's basket on the platform and turned the crank handle until it descended all the way to the beach. He then wedged the rock against the handle, pushing the stone into the ground so it would prevent the crank from unspooling the remaining rope. Next, he stripped until he stood in the sun half-naked and, with the help of a sharp stone, tore the sturdy fabric of his undershirt into shreds. He wrapped the strips around his hands and fingers to protect them from the sharp edges of the ropes. They would not be as effective as a pair of falconer's gloves, but they would do.

He grasped the braided rope and slowly swung out over the cliff's edge. He lowered himself, hand under hand, down the rope. He descended easily at first, and he made it perhaps a third of the way down without incident. The wind buffeted him about a bit, but the cliff behind him provided some protection. The rope remained taut and did not have enough slack to bash him against the rock.

Slowly and steadily he climbed down the rope. After a while, his muscles burned and his hands began to cramp, but he was wiry and strong. He blinked sweat from his eyes and his tunic clung to his back like a second skin, but still he descended. At least the cloth wrapped around his hands soaked up the sweat from his palms, keeping him stable. He began to think he had chosen an easier route than navigating the slippery, windy stairs behind the—

The rope gave a shudder and a lurch, and then it dropped Theow down the side of the cliff.

The rope caught him again almost immediately, but the drop lasted long enough to make his stomach lurch. His arms snapped up as the rope stopped falling and his shoulders screamed in protest, but he did not let go. He gripped the rope and braced his feet against a spur of rock on the cliff face. From up above he heard a faint creak and a groan, and the rope again shuddered under his hands.

Panic churned in Theow's stomach as he scrambled down the braided leather, careless of either good sense or safety. He tried not to look down, but he kept glancing at the ground, estimating how far he had to go before he could survive the fall. The rope jerked and dropped. Stopped. Jerked again.

Down…down. With single-minded focus, Theow climbed down. A sudden, cruel gust of wind snagged the slack in the rope and crashed him into the cliff, and he turned just in time to shield his face and hands. The back of his left shoulder and buttock bore the brunt of the blow. Theow felt a sharp sting and then warm blood seep through his tunic at his shoulder as a sharp fang of rock tore his skin. But he did not stop climbing.

Don't look down, don't look down…

The rope plunged again. The wind stole his yelp of fear as he fell, and real dread gripped the pit of his stomach. After about ten feet of freefall, the rope caught again, but he could not maintain his grip and it tore from his grasp. He continued to fall, this time with no anchor to stop him.

He made a frantic grasp for the rope, but the wind teased it away from his hands. The ground came up fast. With one last, mighty effort, Theow forced his body to tilt forward just as the rope swung back towards him. He seized it and this time held on. He fell too fast, and so his hands slid down the rope as he tried to control his descent. The sharp edges of the braided leather tore at the bindings around his fingers and cut into him where it found little bits of skin between the wrappings. When he slowed enough to stop without dislocating his shoulders, less than ten feet of air lay between his feet and the ground.

Shaking, Theow managed to peel his aching fingers from the rope and climb the rest of the way down. As soon as his feet touched the ground, he collapsed next to the basket on the wooden platform and lay there, struggling for breath and amazed he had survived.

After a while, his body calmed, and the trembling receded. He took stock of his injuries. His cut shoulder hurt, but nothing seemed broken. It would heal, he decided, though it might leave an impressive scar. He would have an enormous bruise on his arse and his hands stung with a dozen shallow cuts and burns, but the cloth from his undershirt had saved him from losing all the skin and flesh from his fingers and palms.

Theow looked back up the cliff. The rope had got twisted in the roots of the tree, but the mechanism was so unstable it would not take much to bring the entire thing crashing down. Bjorn would have to smuggle him back into Eceweall by way of the cliff stairs.

Theow decided he would think about that later.

He shook out his arms and staggered to his feet. He grabbed the basket and made the short walk along the cliff to the cave on a path well-worn from years of foot traffic. After the earthquake had shaken loose the stones from the cliff, a dozen men had cleared them, leaving a space inside about thirty paces deep and twenty paces wide. The cave boasted a narrow entrance— little more than the width of a doorway—but as soon as Theow entered, the cave opened out and he could see the silhouettes of crates and barrels against the rough-hewn walls. Someone had fastened torches high up on the rock and left some flint and a steel striker hanging from a nail. Theow checked one last time to make sure the ships were well out of sight before he used the flint to light the torches.

The flames cast eerie, flickering shadows across every surface and the cave glowed with soft orange light. The air smelled musty, a combination of briny sea-salt, stale smoke, and whatever lichen or fungi called this cave home. Crates were stacked to the height of two men against the back wall and barrels had been grouped in clumps based on their contents. Piles of neatly folded cloth sat on benches to keep them off the dirty floor—silk, linen, and fine woollen fabrics ready for a needle and thread, which, he thought, were probably around here somewhere too. A trestle table held a stack of expensive treated hide and fur pelts, including a very fine blanket made of sea-otter fur. On two smaller wooden tables were roughspun sacks and leather bags. Weapons, shields, and armour had been stacked on racks. He saw barrels of grain, potatoes, onions, and other foodstuffs that could last the winter in a dark, dry place, including, he was happy to see, a large sack of dried caribou meat. He would not starve.

He searched the contents of the cave, leaving anything too heavy or worthless behind and putting the smaller, more valuable items into the basket. He had collected a sizable stash of food, clothing, light weapons and jewellery when he realized he would need a small axe to build a fire and some rope and netting to catch fresh fish for his supper. He couldn't survive for an unknown number of days on dried caribou alone.

He found an axe but didn't see rope anywhere. He searched in corners and behind crates and barrels. He looked under the tables and checked to see if any ropes hung from the walls, but found nothing. He had nearly given up when he noticed the stack of crates against the wall farthest from the entrance. The runes for "farm equipment" had been scratched into the wood, and one crate, labelled "horse tack," sat near the bottom of the stack. There would be leather strips and straps enough to make some netting for fishing.

Theow shoved a large cask of honey close to the stack of crates. He clambered up on it and, careful of his precarious balance, started to lift the top crates down. Fortunately, they were small, only a few handspans wide and not heavy. It did not take him long to get to the crates containing the horse tack. He cracked them open with his axe, and had begun pulling out long ribbons of leather, when a strange glimmer caught his eye.

It came from the wall he had just uncovered—or, more accurately, from behind it. Theow straightened and moved forward to examine the wall. He could see a narrow gap, still partially covered by another stack of boxes, which seemed to open out into a cavernous space, as if the earth beyond the rock cliff had been hollowed out in ages past. The light from one of the torches had snagged on something that sparkled on the other side of the broken wall.

Theow shifted his barrel and removed another stack of boxes, this time not bothering with their contents. The cave floor became cluttered with scattered crates as he revealed a complete passageway in the back wall. It was deep and narrow—too narrow for most men. But the life of a slave had kept Theow a touch too lean, and he thought he could make it through.

He yanked one of the torches from its holder. Whatever glittery thing had caught his eye lay well back from the broken wall. If more treasure hid back there, perhaps he could find enough to buy his way back into the *burh*, or maybe King Beowulf could be persuaded to grant his freedom and allow him to buy some land where he and Fryda could start a new life.

Theow pushed the thought out of his mind. If he started thinking of Fryda now, and her pale face as she crumpled to the floor, he would shatter into pieces. He stretched the torch through the rift in the rock and winced as his wounded shoulder rubbed up against the rough-hewn surface. He sucked in his stomach and pushed himself through the gap with the sacrifice of a few inches of skin across his chest. He emerged on the other side and slipped as the floor shifted under his feet, as if the solid stone had turned to scree. He lifted up the torch and looked around.

He stood not on scree, but on gold. Thousands, tens of thousands of gold coins lay piled around a cavern so large that the light from his torch did not reach the far wall. A huge mound of treasure rose into the middle of the black, enclosed space, filling most of the room. Gems, jewellery, gold ornaments; weapons and armour chased with gold and silver; coins and rings, plates, statues, and every conceivable valuable object had been piled into this cavern. Theow had not known so much treasure existed in all the world.

He whistled as he turned in a slow circle. The cave held enough treasure to last a hundred lifetimes. A thousand.

A sudden shower of coins sliding down the mound startled him. It sounded like music, and reminded him of the noise he and Fryda had heard the day before, when they had come to the chasm together. It felt like a lifetime ago.

A single shaft of light filtered in from the ceiling far above. He must be close to the fissure, he realized. Lying in the puddle of sunlight lay a goblet. Theow tilted his head and squinted at the object as he moved closer.

It was the extraordinary goblet Beowulf had given Weohstan. Theow blinked and examined it closely. It had the same dimensions, and in the flickering firelight he could see intricate carvings of a hunting scene, with forest trees and animals etched in silver over rich, shining gold. Small gems glimmered from wolves' eyes and an owl's talons.

Theow remembered the story King Beowulf had told when he presented the goblet to Weohstan. *No one knows what happened to the second brother, and so the other goblet fell out of time and memory.*

It had been right under their feet all this time. He reached down and hefted the goblet, amazed again by its weight. This one seemed heavier than the other, or perhaps he simply missed the feeling of Fryda's hands under his own as he'd lifted the goblet with her. Dark stains covered the inside of the cup, as if it had been tossed into the cavern filled with wine or mead that had dried to a thin film over the years.

If he could prove to Wiglaf that he knew of a treasure hoard so rich it would make him the most powerful lord in the known world, Wiglaf would have to accept him back and acknowledge him as a free man. He would be a slave no longer. And Wiglaf would have to free Fryda from the betrothal contract to Lord Ansten, he thought. Otherwise, Theow would take the location of this secret hoard with him to the grave and Wiglaf could spend the rest of his life searching for it on his own.

Theow grabbed the goblet and filled it with as many jewels and coins as it could hold.

He squeezed back through the gap in the wall. He had some trouble holding the goblet, the treasure, and the torch, but he managed it. He fixed the torch once again to the wall and restacked the crates to cover the gap. He tossed the treasure and the items into the basket, doused all the lights in the cave, and headed back out to the beach. He thought he heard the musical chimes of tumbling coins again as he hurried along the shore towards the stronghold and wondered what force had caused them to move in the first place, as he had felt no breath of wind or stirring of air inside the cave.

Twenty-four

Fryda opened her eyes. She instantly decided that was a grievous mistake and closed them again.

Her head throbbed. Her lips were cracked and her throat ached with thirst, which brought back unpleasant memories of broken bones and dangling in chasms. Her ribs felt as if a dagger had slid between them and lodged there. Her body ached and her left shoulder felt stretched and painful. So painful, in fact, that she forced her eyes open once more to examine the problem.

Oh, bollocks. She closed her eyes again.

Someone had chained her left hand to the wall. That explained the feeling of cold metal against her wrist and the insistent pain in her shoulder.

She had seen enough to know that she lay in her own bed, at least. She still wore the red-dyed linen dress she had donned that morning, though someone had removed her slippers and her feet were bare. A manacle circled her deformed wrist and a chain trailed from the clunky iron hoop to a thick ring fixed to the wall above her bed.

Fryda opened her eyes again and stared at the ring in the wall. When had *that* appeared, she wondered. It had not been there that morning.

Azure-blue light seeped in through the window and she estimated it must be late afternoon. Everyone would be gathering in the great hall for the third night of the feast. She wondered if Uncle Beowulf would notice her absence; if he would worry about her. But no…Wiglaf would have some plausible story for him, and the king would believe it without question.

"You made me do this, you know."

Fryda jerked her head towards the voice and winced as pain lanced through her skull. When she opened her eyes again, she saw that Wiglaf sat on the trunk at the foot of her bed.

★ ★ ★

Wiglaf watched as his twin sister's eyes widened and then went dark. She had purple circles, like bruises, under her eyes and she looked unnaturally pale. Her hair had become a maelstrom of wild curls and she had an ugly wound on her lower lip from the night Fægebeorn had assaulted her.

He burned again with rage, seeing that split lip, and spared a curse for Theow for killing the scoundrel before he could.

"I made you do this." Fryda's voice was flat, not a question. "I made you attack me and chain me to the wall." She shook her left arm, making the heavy chain jangle. "Wiglaf, take this thing off me right now."

He looked at her with regret. "I can't do that, Fryda. I need you to see reason, and that won't happen if I let you out."

Fire sparked in her stormy grey eyes. "How is any of this possibly my fault?" she demanded.

Resentment burst inside him, like a lanced boil. "Because you chose *him*!"

Her eyes grew huge and a look of horrified disgust replaced the anger on her face.

He huffed with frustration. "I don't mean romantically," he said. "Woden's beard, you're my sister. I'm talking about loyalty. I'm talking about family and trust and…" He clenched his fist and lifted it, trying to control emotions that galloped away from him like a runaway horse. "By the gods, Fryda, you were the only thing I had, and you abandoned me."

Fryda stared at him. "Have you lost your wits?" she asked.

"Our entire lives, you've had everything I did not. You were born first. You had tutors paraded before you your whole life and you took no interest in their teachings, while I had to scrape and scrounge to find people willing to teach me the things I was so desperate to learn. You had Father's ear, but you never used it. He couldn't even look at me without seeing both Mother and the person who killed her. King Beowulf asks your opinions on affairs of the clan and nation and he listens to you. He loves me, yes, but he pats me on the head and treats me like a pet he's fond of." She sat up on the bed and Wiglaf frowned with concern when he saw her wince with pain and rub the back of her head with her free hand. "You've had everything handed to you on a platter, but you threw it all back at those who wanted to help you become a better man. You preferred to drink and whore your way through life instead."

Wiglaf shook his head in disbelief. "You really don't see it, do you?"

She blinked at him. "See what?"

"You had Bryce, who at least treated you like the father you deserved. You even have the love and respect of the king, and you brush it away as if it means nothing." He clenched and unclenched his hands. "I had you, Fryda. I had *only you*."

Fryda looked bewildered. "First of all, that's not true. How many chances did Father give you that you just threw away? How many times were you given opportunities to prove yourself in raids when you sailed with the longships?"

Before he could stop himself, Wiglaf drove his fist downward into the lid of the trunk he sat upon. Pain jolted up his hand and arm, and he heard a *crack* as the wood splintered under his knuckles. Fryda jumped and shrank back against the wall.

"We are twins!" he thundered. He was so angry he could not think straight. "We are two halves of one person. If you forsake me, you forsake yourself. You forsake our family. You forsake our ancestors!"

Fryda's jaw hung open. She stared at him in obvious astonishment.

"You are supposed to choose *me*! You are supposed to be on *my* side. You are supposed to depend on *me* and support *me*. But it seems lately you have time and attention for everyone *except* me." Wiglaf wiped his mouth, which was wet from flying spittle.

Fryda closed her mouth. She took a deep breath and looked at the bed. Wiglaf had a moment to hope she was too ashamed to look at him, but then she raised her eyes to his and he saw the truth.

She was *furious*.

"Wiglaf," she said in a low, tight voice. "I am not half a person, and neither are you. I am certainly not half of you. Yes, we are all part of the family, the clan—and I honour that. But the whole clan deserves my attention and loyalty. Not just you."

He started to speak but she raised her hand to stop him.

"Also, you could not expect us to remain the way we were as children forever," she went on. "Yes, I'd hoped we could always be close as brother and sister, as twins, but it has always been known that we would live our own lives. Marry. Have children. Things could never have stayed the same."

Wiglaf's face twisted into a snarl. "That would be fine," he said, his words clipped, "if you had chosen a worthy man for your mate. Instead, you…you debase yourself with a slave." Bile burned in his throat. "You turn to him for protection. You turn to him for comfort. You turn to him for affection. Not to me. And everyone saw it." The bile crawled into his mouth and he swallowed. "Fryda, he's a slave who could never be worthy of you, or of anyone. Slaves are not deserving of love."

Especially that one, he thought.

Fryda's eyes burned with a vivid and passionate fury, but now that he'd started, he could not stop.

"I've always done everything for you," he said. He launched himself to his feet and paced up and down the room. "I defended and protected you when we were children. I convinced Father to save your hand after you fell."

That was not strictly true. Wiglaf had been so frantic at the thought of losing his sister that he had been more than willing to sacrifice her hand to save her life. However, she didn't need to know that, and the lie he'd told her for the last seven years would never hurt her if she never learned of it.

"I stood up for you when Dysg abandoned you right before your wedding," he continued. That, too, was a bit shy of the truth. He had secretly encouraged Dysg to break the betrothal contract. If Wiglaf could not bear the thought of losing her to death, he had not wanted to lose her to marriage, either.

Now, however, that might be the only thing that could save her.

"And when everyone called you *brytan byrde*, even our father, I was always there for you."

Fryda barked a laugh. "You mean you were there for me the times you weren't drunk? Or with your women? Or gambling and playing at games with the farmers?" She shook her head. "We have two very different memories of our lives, Wiglaf. For most of mine, you have felt very absent." Her eyes darkened again. "Theow, on the other hand..."

Wiglaf whirled to face her. "Do not speak his name! He is not worthy of it."

"It's because of us he has no name," she retorted. "We stole that from him, along with his freedom. You complain about obligation and duty...you know *nothing* of these things. Theow is twice the man you are, even if he is a slave." She glared at him, defiance written across her face.

Wiglaf stared at her, breathing hard. "Well. I am lord now, so it is up to me to decide what is best for the *burh*, and everyone in it. That includes you."

Fryda looked up at the chain holding her to the wall.

"You are lord now," she repeated. She looked at him then, and he saw something new in her eyes.

Fear.

"Wiglaf. I need to know. Were you working with Eadgils? Did you have a hand in our father's death? Did you betray him? Betray us?"

Wiglaf dropped his eyes and his jaw clenched. "I can't believe you could even ask me such a thing."

That was not a lie. He could not lie if he did not answer her questions.

"The thing is," Fryda continued, "the night I was attacked, everyone was drugged. No one heard me scream except Theow… and you."

"For the same reason, obviously. I didn't drink the drugged mead."

"But you were drinking all night during the feast. Out of everyone, you should have been affected the most. Yet you said you heard me scream and came running soon after Theow got there."

Wiglaf stayed silent.

"Did you take me out of the feast for our little picnic because you didn't want me to drink the mead in the hall?" she asked. "You gave me mead from your own flask, and so I didn't drink any more when I went back inside. Not until I retired to my rooms, and I took a small cup with me. Is that why you were so angry I brought Theow? Because you wanted him to drink the drugged mead?"

"I was angry because I wanted to talk to you about private matters *privately*," he said, aggrieved.

"And then there was the battle. You weren't anywhere to be seen when it began, and by the time I got to Father's house, you were already there. You were clearly not in your right mind, but you seemed to be there by choice." Fryda did not drop her gaze.

"Eadgils had no guard on you, as if he knew you would not try to get away."

"I remember very little about that night," Wiglaf said truthfully. His palms began to sweat.

"And then there's Olaf." Wiglaf went very still. "He knew our father had replaced you as his heir, that Father wanted him to be lord of the *burh*. Olaf was killed the same way you killed the exile in my room. Stabbed sideways through the neck." Fryda's voice caught. "Wiglaf. Were you behind the attack on me the night of the first feast?"

Rage stampeded through him and he stormed to the side of the bed. "You ask me that?" he shouted, clenching his bloodied fist. "You ask if I arranged to have you beaten and cut with a knife? If I planned for Fægebeorn to rape you?" He turned away. Fryda may as well have plunged a *seax* into his heart for the pain her question caused him. "How can you think that of me, Fryda?"

She again looked—pointedly—at the manacle that chained her to the wall. "Right now, brother, I have no idea what you might be capable of."

"This is for your own good," he yelled, and began pacing again. "This is to protect you from yourself. I would never... *never*...do something to hurt you like Fægebeorn did. I cannot believe you would think so little of me."

"You must admit, the circumstances were suspicious," she insisted.

"No! They were not! Eadgils obviously planned the attack on you, but only to use you in his plot against Father. Fægebeorn decided to indulge in revenge for how you humiliated him at the feast."

Fryda's jaw dropped. "How *I* humiliated *him*?"

"Yes, yes, I know." Wiglaf waved a hand. "But from his perspective that's what happened. I had nothing to do with any of that. And, if you'll remember, I was happy to help tear Eadgils' corpse apart for the role he played in hurting you."

That part, at least, was true. Eadgils had neglected to mention to him that he'd planned to use Fryda in his plot to kill Weohstan.

Wiglaf rubbed his eyes and sighed. Eadgils had proven to be a treacherous ally indeed, but at least he'd accomplished what Wiglaf did not have the means—or stomach—to do. Eadgils had been a quick and convenient path to his goal. He had become lord of the *burh* at age twenty.

And, he assured himself whenever inconvenient twinges of conscience might bother him, his father would not have wanted to grow old and feeble. He would have found the weakening of his body and mind humiliating, and Eadgils had at least spared him that. It had just happened a little sooner than anticipated, due to his father's unexpected decision to make Olaf lord of Eceweall.

"All right," Fryda said. "I'm sorry. I believe you."

Wiglaf turned to look at her. She looked so small on the huge bed, unable to cover her mutilated hand as she always did in the presence of other people. It made her look vulnerable and fragile.

"Look, Fryda." He once more sat on the wooden trunk. "Everything has changed. Father is gone and I am lord now."

"Why didn't you tell Beowulf that Father intended Olaf to be lord?" Fryda asked.

Wiglaf regarded her steadily. "Why didn't you?"

She remained silent and Wiglaf nodded.

"So, if you are not willing to stay here and support me... unquestioningly and completely...then you'll marry Lord Ansten and he'll take you to Sweden. He at least is worthy of you, unlike..." Gall once again filled his mouth and he swallowed down the name. "The marriage will also help the political situation between our countries, so you'd be helping your clan instead of chasing your own foolish and selfish desires."

"Never." Her answer was immediate and adamant. "I will never marry Ansten. You cannot force me. And once the king gets wind of all this, he just might have your head for trying."

Wiglaf stood up and walked to the door. "He already knows," he said, pushing it open, "and he approves. Did you think the king would let you marry someone so beneath you?"

Fryda looked stricken. "There is no way Uncle Beowulf would condone this," she said, rattling her chain once more.

Wiglaf smirked. "You would be surprised what King Beowulf would condone. He is hardly the hero you think he is," he said. "The great stories don't always tell the truth, you know. Gods, you've always been so naive. By all accounts, Beowulf ruined King Hrothgar's marriage, he was responsible for Unferth's… for *Bryce*'s exile, and he helped our father steal King Eadgils' own lover away from him. Oh yes," he said as Fryda's eyebrows soared. "Mother was Eadgils' lover first. Did you think Eadgils hated Father and Beowulf just because of his brother Eanmund? No. Father abducted Mother when he was in Sweden, and Beowulf hid the two of them until they could marry." He looked at his twin sardonically. "It's a good thing I look so much like father, and you so much like mother. Otherwise some might question our legitimacy."

"Surely Mother had some say in all of this," Fryda said, but he could see she was stunned by his words.

"Whether she did or no, Beowulf helped them. He gave them this land and this stronghold and betrayed one of his oldest and closest friends as he did it. I would not look to him to rescue you." He stepped through the doorway. "I'll give you some time to think about your options."

"You aren't going to leave me here like this!" Fryda cried. He heard a note of panic in her voice. "Wiglaf, this is my injured hand and arm. It is very painful to be chained like this."

"It won't be for long," he assured her. Privately, he thought she deserved to suffer a little for all the hurt she had caused him. "Ansten is eager to fulfil his part of the bargain, and I don't want to make him wait too long. I wouldn't want him to change his mind."

"Wait!" Fryda leaned forward, as if she would have run to him if she could. "Theow. What happened to him?"

Anger and resentment went from a simmer to a full boil. He was tempted to tell her the slave had resisted so much the guards had been forced to kill him, but he knew he would get caught out in that lie. She would learn the truth eventually.

"Exiled. As I decreed. If he shows his face in the *burh* again, he'll be killed on sight."

He smiled at her horrified expression, then closed the door and locked it. He pocketed the key and made his way towards the longhouse and the third and final feast for the king. Fryda would eventually reconcile herself to her situation. She would come to see he was doing what was best for her. Of course, he wanted her to stay with him, but more and more he was seeing that she would be a liability rather than a comfort. She was too clever for her own good, and it would tear his heart from his chest if he had to silence her forever to protect himself.

Twenty-five

Fryda stared at the door for several long moments after Wiglaf left her.

The various revelations of the day, coupled with a debilitating head wound, made her feel sick and dizzy. She did not for a moment doubt Wiglaf had lied through his teeth for much of the conversation, but she'd been able to pick up several truths from his evasions and fabrications. At least she knew he had not been behind her assault. He could not have feigned such fury when she'd asked him about it. She also believed the extraordinary tale he'd told her about their mother. She remembered Eadgils' words as her father slowly bled to death on the floor.

He took her from me, you know. Your mother.

Every mention of her, uttered with reverence, and his anger at Weohstan for Ielfeta's death spoke of the truth. Fryda was surprised she'd not seen it earlier.

And Theow. Wiglaf had exiled Theow. Theow needed her, and so she needed to get out of these chains and this room. As she looked at the iron band around her wrist, the reality of her situation hit her fully for the first time. Her own brother had attacked and imprisoned her. Something inside her broke, permanently this time, for she knew nothing could redeem him. There would be no forgiveness. Nothing he could do or say would erase the harm he had done.

Clearly no help would be coming. She would have to get out of these chains herself. She thought about shouting for help, but reconsidered. What could she do if someone came? Beg them to let her go? They would not. Demand to see her brother? He would either refuse, or decide to ship her off to Sweden right then and there. Attack them? They had chained her to a bloody wall. Bryce had not taught her how to attack someone from that position.

The thought of the blacksmith seemed to twist the knife in her chest, but it also made her smile. She wondered if a time would come when she could think fondly of him without pain.

Careful of her head, Fryda turned and examined the ring fastened to the wall. Someone must have put it in that morning when they replaced the broken door. The ring was mounted on an iron plate bolted to the hardwood planks of the wall. She picked at the bolts with her nails, tried to prise the plate away from the wall, attempted to twist the ring off the plate, but neither would budge.

She braced her bare feet against the wooden slats of the wall, gripped the chain in her good hand, and pulled as hard as she could. She levered her body backwards, bending her spine in a desperate arch as she tugged and pulled at the chain. But the iron ring did not move. She tried again, coiling the chain around her good wrist and pushing her feet against the wall with all her strength. Her body lifted off the bed as she braced herself and pulled. She groaned, growled, and cried out as she heaved all her weight backwards...but the ring in the wall remained fast.

Panting, she gave up and examined her lopsided wrist, now red and scratched from her struggles. The shackle was wide and thick and stoutly made—she could not break it. It occurred to her that Bryce had probably made it, and her anger doubled in size. Bryce would have broken the chain right off the ring if he were here now. He would then punch her brother through the wall and Woden take the consequences. Her chest tightened again and her eyes prickled, and for a moment she felt a physical pain where the large blacksmith's death had torn a hole in her life.

She pulled and yanked and picked at the chain links until her fingers were bloody. She tried to break them by striking them against the wall, but she only succeeded in damaging the wall. The chain did not reach the floor, or even the wooden frame of her bed, so she discarded those as potential tools. She thought of the poker she had used during the battle with the exiles. She would have made short work of this chain if she still had it.

After what seemed like hours of struggle, she slumped in defeat. She would not be able to free herself by breaking the manacle. She knew of only one way she could be certain of escape. Her mind reeled away from the thought, but it kept forcing itself back in.

She would have to break her hand.

Her entire body rebelled against it. She huddled on the bed for a time, cold sweat dampening her dress and her body shaking, knowing what she would have to endure. Knowing intimately, because she had endured it before, and the memory of it nearly broke her resolve.

She remembered certain moments of that night vividly. She was thirteen years old and her mangled hand throbbed with unendurable pain. She could hear voices arguing around her as she lay in her bed, her father's voice rising above the protestations from the healers. In that moment, she remembered, she almost wished he would let them take her hand. She felt so tired, so thirsty, though they had already given her water, and she hurt so very much. Amputation would at least lessen the pain, she reasoned. A hand could not hurt if it was not attached to her body.

Eadith, who had nursed her share of warriors through the severing of a limb, told her later this was not always true, but she did not know that at the time.

The argument ceased. Her father had won. A healer put the lip of a bowl to her mouth, urging her to drink. She swallowed the bitter *dwale*. As she waited for the drug to take effect, her father came to stand over her. She knew he despised her for her disobedience, for the choices she had forced him to make, and his eyes accused and censured her. Even so, he reached down and took her good hand. She could not remember when he had ever willingly touched her before.

It will hurt, he had said. *Be brave.* And he gave her no other comfort before the healers started to pull and twist her swollen fingers, trying to piece together the shattered bones, and she screamed and screamed and screamed...

Fryda shook her head, chasing the memory away. *Theow*, she told herself. *Think of Theow.* She had to get to him. But even more than that, she had to get away from her brother. She would not allow herself to be bound and gagged and shipped off to Sweden, married to some insignificant stranger just because Wiglaf considered her inconvenient. With Wiglaf as lord of the *burh*, she truly would become *brytan byrde*—the "lord's burden."

Her mouth begged for water. Her arm, held in suspension by the chain, spasmed and ached, and her shoulder sent echoes of its old pain through her chest. If she closed her eyes, she could almost believe she relived that day seven years ago, hanging by one hand inside the chasm, waiting for death to take her.

Well. She was thirteen no longer. She had grown into a woman, the lady of the house. An extraordinary man with eyes full of stories loved her—even if he had not said the words yet —despite her mangled hand. Or perhaps because of it, or maybe because of the strength she'd cultivated to survive it. She would have to rely on that strength now.

She examined her left hand. Whoever had chained her chose that one deliberately. She could have slid her slender, undamaged hand out of the iron circle without any injury whatsoever. But the odd angle of her wrist, the bent middle finger, and the bulbous thumb-joint all conspired to keep her chained.

Three breaks, then. Just three. Finger, thumb, wrist.

Her right hand trembled as she reached for her middle finger. She grasped the knuckle and extended the finger as far as it could go. It would not go far.

She looked around the bedchamber, searching for something heavy. The table with the pitcher and bowl of fruit was out of reach. She slid to the edge of her bed and leaned over as far as the chain would allow. *Ah*, she thought. *There*. The women who had cleaned her room missed a hefty piece of wood from her broken door, which had slid under her bed.

She stretched and strained and finally managed to hook the slab of wood with her toes. Back on the bed, she lay her hand as flat as she could on the hard surface of the wall. Her breath came in short, sharp gasps. She sat there, unmoving, for a long, long time. She squeezed her eyes shut and sour sweat soaked through her clothes, but still she could not move. Tears ran down her cheeks and she could not stop trembling.

She thought of Theow and remembered how he had touched her hand, kissed it, and told her it did not disgust him. She took a deep breath and trapped it behind her sore ribs. Before she could change her mind, she slammed the heavy wooden board down onto her middle finger, forcing it straight.

Her screams covered the loud *snap* of the bone. After a moment her raw cries dwindled to a series of whimpers as she grew weak and dizzy and struggled to stay conscious.

After many long moments, Fryda opened her eyes. Everything looked blurry until she remembered to blink the tears away. She couldn't seem to stop making small noises in her throat, pathetic little bleats that somehow made the burden of pain easier to bear. She looked at her finger. It looked straight, but as soon as she let it go, it flopped down. She had no control over those muscles, but that didn't matter right now, she thought. As long as it didn't prevent her from getting out of the manacle.

After she got her breathing under control and the dizziness receded, she turned her attention to her thumb. The lower joint had healed so the large pad covering the joint bunched and pulled the thumb inward. She could extend it slightly, but a large, bony bump prevented the manacle from slipping over her hand.

Sweat poured down her face. She realized that strangled, involuntary noises still leaked from her throat and she wondered why no one had come to check on her when she screamed. Oh yes, she remembered, through the buzzing in her brain. The feast. And why would Wiglaf waste guards on her when she could not escape from the room on her own?

She was stalling, and she knew it. Her heart raced and she felt the echoes of its limping rhythm in her broken finger. She concentrated on her breathing, braced herself against the wall, and brought the board down hard on the joint of her thumb.

Lightning pain shot through the palm of her hand. Fryda cried out and let go too soon, and her thumb sprang back into its original position. She had not broken it. This bone had fused in the joint, she realized, and would resist more than the first. She wouldn't be able to break it with her own strength.

She wiped sweat and tears from her face and tried to breathe through her nose. She braced her left forearm against the wall with her knee and looped one of the links of the chain over her thumb, pressing it as far down as it would go, like an unwieldy ring. She twisted her right hand into the rest of the chain and leaned all her weight upon her forearm. She tensed the chain until her thumb extended as far as it would go and again paused, eyes closed, breathing heavily. She pressed her knee against her arm, took three harsh, short breaths, and pulled as hard as she could on the chain.

A wild, animal cry tore from her throat, but this time it could not mask the resounding *snap* of her broken bones as her thumb burst from its housing and ground against itself. She wailed, cradling her hand against her chest while sparks danced across her vision. She rocked back and forth, back and forth, and waited for the world to become bearable again.

It eventually did. Her head cleared, and the initial jolt of searing agony settled into a constant but tolerable thrum. She again opened her eyes and examined the results of her work. Her thumb still bulged, but it was now mobile and she would be able to fold it in to get the manacle off...oh, she didn't want to think about that.

Fryda wondered if she could remove the manacle without having to re-break her wrist. She moved the iron band up and tried to angle it so that she could slide it around the awkward crook between her wrist and her hand. But no. She would have to remove her pinky finger entirely in order to make that work, and she would be mad to attempt it. She had no knife, for one, and she certainly did not want to bleed to death.

Mercifully, when she would tell this story to others later, she'd find she could not remember the details of the third bone break. She remembered wrapping the entire chain around her palm and pushing at her wrist with her foot, but the particulars of the procedure eluded her. Perhaps she did lose herself in a swoon that time, or perhaps her mind simply cast a protective veil over those memories. Whatever she did must have worked, though, for when Fryda's mind cleared and she became aware of her surroundings once more, she found herself in the middle of her room, the manacle still secured to the wall but she, herself, free and unfettered.

She blinked. Her hand and forearm were on fire, but a quick glance showed no blood. The bones had not broken through the skin this time. It began to swell, however, so she quickly moved to her clothes chest. She knew she needed to wrap it as soon as possible. Seven years ago, the swelling had made it impossible to set the bones straight and she did not want to make the same mistake this time. Fryda opened the chest and selected the thinnest, flimsiest garments she owned and nabbed one of her thick leather belts.

Using only her good hand, Fryda awkwardly tore the clothing into strips with her teeth. She then sat on the bed, put the leather belt between her teeth, bit down hard, and set to wrapping the bandages around her fingers, thumb, and wrist.

She had to stop several times and wait until her breath returned and the tears slowed, but eventually she bound her hand. She made sure all the bones were as straight as she could make them, grinding her teeth against the leather belt as she moved broken edges and shattered joints into alignment. She then wrapped the cloth around the injuries. She tucked the ends of the bandages in and tied off the knots with her teeth. All in all, she thought she made rather a good job of it. Her hand throbbed, but the support from the wrappings calmed the screaming pain to something bearable. As long as she didn't try to move or bend it, she could tolerate it.

She did wish she had some *dwale*, though, or a draught of simple white poppy syrup to dull the pain. But that would dull her mind and senses as well, and she could not afford that right now. There would be time later, she hoped, to medicate her broken body and soothe her wounded spirit.

Fryda stripped off her sweat-soaked clothes and changed into a white underskirt, shift, and a plain, clean blue dress with long, flowing sleeves to cover her hand. She wrapped the belt around her waist and found another pair of shoes, these made of leather and much stouter than her delicate slippers. She poured water from the pitcher into the basin on the table and drank and drank and drank until her unbearable thirst abated, and then she washed her face with the rest of the water. She needed to look as normal and unconcerned as possible for her plan to work.

Through it all, her hand sang its terrible tune, pulsing in time with her heartbeat and making it difficult for her to think and act. It overshadowed all her other hurts—her head, her ribs—until she nearly forgot about them.

There, she thought. *Ready.* She moved to the door, new and sturdy, and tried to open it.

It would not budge.

Disbelieving, Fryda tried again. Nothing. Outraged, she pulled and yanked and rattled it with all her might. The door refused to yield. Then Fryda noticed the lock. Wiglaf must have ordered it and she burned with resentment. The lock and the manacle told their own sordid story. Her brother had known she would not go willingly with Ansten.

Before she could pluck a hairpin from her braids and pick the lock, she heard a key rattle in the door. She lurched back, thinking Wiglaf must have returned, and spun around searching for some heavy object with which to hit him. She grabbed the water pitcher and flung it just as the door flew open and Hild entered the room.

Fortunately, Fryda's aim was anything but true and the pitcher shattered harmlessly against the wall next to Hild's head. Hild flinched and ducked back behind the door.

"It's only me, my lady," she cried in a low voice. "I've come to get you out."

"Hild!" An entirely inappropriate, hysterical giggle bubbled in the back of her throat. "I'm so sorry. I thought you were Wiglaf."

"My lady, stay your tongue," Hild said, her face screwed into a mask of distaste. She silently slipped into the room. "He is at the feast. I made certain of it before I came."

"Hild!" Fryda clutched her friend's arm with her good hand and her words tumbled over themselves in her haste. "Oh, Hild, I am so happy to see you. I must get out. I must find Theow. He's been exiled. My brother exiled him, and I don't know…"

"I know, my lady," Hild said. She laid her own warm hand

over Fryda's pale, cold one. "He's at the cave down the beach. Bjorn got him out of the *burh* and I took him some food and supplies. He will wait for us at the cave while Bjorn goes to the farmsteads to find Beowulf and I help you get out of the stronghold."

"Theow." Fryda felt hope flare. "He's all right?"

"Yes." Hild led her through the front rooms of the house to the door. "He's unharmed. He will wait for us there until King Beowulf has fixed this whole mess with the lord."

Fryda looked back at the unlocked door. "How did you get the key, Hild?"

Hild's eyes twinkled. "Do you know how Toland survived before Eadith found him starving by the docks?" she asked.

Fryda shook her head. The boy had either been lost or abandoned, and she remembered when Eadith had brought him to the kitchens to nurse him back to health.

"He was a very accomplished pickpocket." Hild grinned at her, and waggled the key before dropping it into her dress. Fryda managed a feeble smile back. Oh, her brother would be so angry when he tried to find his key.

Her hand throbbed, and she tried to ignore it. "Are you coming with me, Hild?"

"No, I have to stay here. Bjorn said he might need my help."

Hild poked her head out the doorway. After a quick, furtive look, she said, "All right, my lady, it's clear. Come on."

They slipped out of the house and made their way towards the eastern cliff. As they emerged, however, the king's festivities spilled out into the open, grassy areas of the *burh*. Men and women milled about the raked pathways, drinking and laughing and making merry while children scampered across the grass. Several people surrounded the standing stone on the green, which had been righted after the battle with the exiles. Others wrestled or sparred while onlookers shouted for their favourites and made bets on the outcomes.

Hild cursed under her breath, and Fryda looked at her, startled. "Apologies, my lady," Hild said, looking sheepish. "But we won't get through this without someone seeing us."

Fryda scanned the crowd, alert for either her brother's dark head or Beowulf's white one. "The cliff stairs," she murmured.

Hild nodded. "There's no other way. Keep your eyes open for Lord Wiglaf. Follow me, my lady."

They crossed to the edge of the stronghold and skirted along the fortifying wall, slipped behind the longhouse, and headed for the cliff stairs.

Two guards stood watch near the edge of the cliff. Fryda took a deep breath, made sure her sleeve covered the bandage on her hand, and strode forward with Hild, hoping they both looked confident and normal. She also hoped Wiglaf had kept her imprisonment a secret. If he had not, this would end quickly. However, he would surely not jeopardize his newfound authority by announcing to the entire *burh* he had locked up his sister against her will.

She breathed quickly as they approached the men, but the two guards' expressions changed only to polite respect when they saw her. Fryda relaxed. They did not know.

"Not going to the feast, my lady?" one asked as she drew near.

The second guard peered at her. "You look fearsome pale, my lady. Are you feeling all right?" He glanced at Hild. "Should you perhaps take your lady back to her rooms?"

Fryda's hand gave a swell of pain, like a wave that rolls and gathers force until it crests and crashes. She clenched her teeth. "I'm going down the stairs to the shore," she told them.

The first guard frowned. "Why are you going down there, my lady?" he asked. He glanced at Hild. "Surely you could send your servant or a slave for whatever you need. Those stairs can be treacherous and in truth, my lady, you do not look well."

Fryda arranged her features into what she hoped resembled an offended, haughty expression.

"Are you questioning my actions, guard?" she demanded. "Do I need to fetch my brother to teach you how to show respect?"

Both guards straightened and looked alarmed. "No, my lady," the nosy one said. "My apologies, my lady."

Fryda smiled at them. "Thank you. Now, please let me through."

They stood aside. Fryda nodded and she and Hild headed for the edge. Though her neck prickled and she knew they were watching her, she did not look back. At the top stair, she turned to Hild and drew herself up. "You are dismissed," she said.

"Yes, my lady." Hild bobbed a bow, and Fryda caught her significant look as she raised her head. She nodded, and Hild turned and headed back towards the kitchens. Fryda calmly set her foot to the first step and began to wind her way down the cliff.

Broken

As much as the Lone Survivor's curse recoils from joy, it rears its corrupted head to fierce attention when presented with pain. And Fýrdraca feels so much pain. First, the exquisite agony of physical pain. The woman-warrior lights up with it, as she did when she was but a child trapped in the chasm over the dragon's cave. It becomes her second heartbeat, thrumming through her like a plucked string that strikes a sour note. Fýrdraca rouses to this music. She wishes to dance with the wind, her wings spread wide as she did when she was free.

But the wounds on the spirit are far graver than any bodily harm the girl might suffer. Even now Fýrdraca can feel the cracks splintering across the surface of the shield maiden's soul, like fissures threading through thin ice under her feet. When it broke, she would be plunged into the icy depths of pain to suffocate and drown.

The Lone Survivor's curse quickens in Fýrdraca's blood, as if in anticipation of such an event. And as the curse wakens, finding kindred and familiar spirits in the world to strengthen and entertain it, it brings Fýrdraca with it. The stronger her shield maiden becomes, the closer the dragon gets to wakefulness.

Soon. Soon she will meet her warrior-woman, and then Fýrdraca will truly be allowed to rest. Her struggle shall be over, and the earth trembles at the power of her desire for such oblivion.

Twenty-six

Theow had underestimated how difficult it would be to walk on an uneven, rocky beach carrying twenty pounds of treasure and other goods, with an injured shoulder and an enormous bruise on his arse.

The small but alarming earthquakes that trembled under his feet from time to time didn't help matters either.

He had decided to take his chances with the cliff stairs. If he could convince the guards not to skewer him with an arrow until he explained about the treasure, he could possibly get back in to see Wiglaf. He also knew that trying to climb back up the cliff face would kill him faster than the guards. So he found himself trudging beside the cliff and frequently laying down his burdens so he could rest. Strangely, the carved goblet seemed to get heavier the longer he carried it.

He hadn't moved far from the cave when he set his sack down for the third time. His hands were raw and sore from his descent down the leather rope, the wound on his shoulder kept cracking open and welling with fresh blood as he moved, and he felt battered and abused by life in general. He put down the goblet and settled himself on a flat rock to catch his breath.

A gull screamed above him and another, far down the beach, answered. The sky deepened, creeping up on night. Not darkening, not yet. The light lingered for hours during the summer months, but the quality of the light changed; became more saturated with colour and intensity as the twilight hours approached. The ocean wore grey that day, as if in mourning for those they had lost.

Theow shivered, and the earth once more shivered with him.

The gull screamed again, and again came an answer. The second gull seemed closer this time, with an oddly human-sounding, thin-pitched tone.

"Theow!"

Strange, Theow thought. The gull's scream almost sounded like his name.

"THEOW!"

His head jerked up and he looked down the beach. A small, lithe figure in blue hurtled towards him, careless of the slippery, jagged rocks beneath her feet. Her legs pumped hard, her butter-coloured hair flew behind her, and before he could think, Theow surged to his feet and ran to meet her.

Fryda leapt, her arms outstretched. Theow caught a glimpse of something white on her hand before he seized her and pulled her against him. She wrapped her arms around his neck and clung to him, feet dangling, her chest labouring and her gasps stirring the hair at his neck. He clasped her tight, his hands fisted in the back of her dress, and buried his face in her hair.

They stood that way for a long, long time. Theow forgot his aches and pains in the pleasure of feeling her body against his, her arms tight around him. Fryda, however, soon became distracted by his injuries and drew his attention back to his discomforts.

"You're bleeding," she said, her voice muffled against his neck.

"It's nothing." Theow refused to loosen his grip.

"No, really," she said, her voice laced with concern. "You're bleeding quite a lot back here." She probed his wounded shoulder with a gentle finger, and Theow flinched. "See?" She lifted her head to look at him. "We need to clean that and perhaps stitch you up. Your tunic is going to stick to your wound otherwise."

Theow lifted his head and gazed at her. He kept one arm around her waist and raised his other hand to her face. "You're here." He stroked her cheek with his thumb. Her face was so pale it alarmed him. "Tell me what's happened."

Fryda's expression shuttered, as if she did not want him to know what she felt in that moment. "I managed to escape," she murmured. "Hild came to let me out. She told me Bjorn smuggled you out, and I was to meet you at the cave."

"Your head." Theow passed a hand over her hair. "They hit you...are you all right?"

Fryda smiled, though it did not reach her eyes. "Oh yes," she said. "Just a bit of a bump. There is an advantage to having all this hair after all."

Theow put her down but kept her close. "You'll have to tell me all about it."

"Later. Right now, I need to look at your shoulder."

She released his neck and slid her hand down his arms. He caught her left elbow and raised it before she could stop him. Her sleeve slid down and he saw the makeshift bandages around her hand and wrist.

"Fryda." His voice shook.

"No." She tried to twist away from him. Her voice held a note of panic.

Theow eased her back to him and examined her left hand. Strips of cloth that looked like they used to be undergarments swathed her fingers and hand. The strips wound around her wrist as well, but even so, he could see an angry red circle on her skin that told the story eloquently enough. She had been cuffed and restrained and had somehow...somehow...

He stared at her hand in horror. The middle finger that had curved under against her palm now stood outward, rigidly straight, and her wrist no longer crooked to the side. He looked at Fryda, but she stared at his feet, refusing to meet his gaze.

"Fryda." He couldn't seem to say anything but her name. "Fryda."

"I had to," she whispered. "I...I had..."

Her face crumpled. Theow lifted her up as her legs seemed to give up their strength and he held her as she let out a broken, feeble keening sound that went straight through him like an arrow. Fryda drew in a ragged breath, buried her face against his chest and screamed, screamed, screamed...her voice tore from her throat and fluttered away on the wind, only to be pulled back by her inhale for another cry. Again and again she howled against him, mouth open, nose running, breaths ravaging her throat. She made the most rending, disconsolate sounds Theow had ever heard. He scooped his arm under her knees and sat, nestling her in his lap. Careful not to jostle her newly injured hand, he rocked her back and forth, back and forth, as she sobbed against him.

"I have you," he whispered to her, his cheek pressed against her hair. "I have you, love. I have you."

She clung to him, weeping. She had endured so much in such a short time, Theow thought. Her father's murder. Bryce's death. Her brother's betrayal. His own exile. Inflicting such pain on herself, knowing what it would feel like. He had never known anyone with her strength.

After a while she quieted. She cried still, but not the wild, savage weeping of an inconsolable heart. Theow held her and rocked her and whispered love in her ear, telling her she was safe, he would not leave her, he had her, he loved her.

Eventually, Fryda sniffled and heaved an enormous sigh.

"I've ruined your shirt," she said, her voice thick and watery.

Theow gave a puff of laughter against her hair. "I'd already ruined it," he told her. "Blood, remember?"

Fryda pulled back from him, her expression dismayed. Her eyes were red and puffy and her cheeks blotchy from crying. He wiped her wet face and runny nose with the sleeve of his tunic.

"I'm sorry." She sputtered as the cloth of his sleeve got into her mouth. She got to her feet and pulled him up with her. "I shouldn't have..."

The earth shuddered beneath their feet and Fryda stumbled. Theow held her upright and they looked around, startled.

Fryda blinked up at him, her golden lashes darkened with tears. "I haven't felt anything like that for seven years," she said.

Theow raised his eyebrows. "They started a little while ago. Did that earthquake feel like this one?"

"No, mine was much stronger. It threw me to the ground."

Another tremble made Theow feel as if stood upon a cascade of pebbles, and then the earth grew quiet.

"Oh," Fryda said, once they had steadied themselves. She touched his bloodied shirt. "I'm sorry, I should have seen to this right away, instead of...of..." She wiped her eyes.

"Hush." Theow leaned forward and kissed her on the mouth. She tasted of salt tears, sorrow, and her own sweetness. "I won't hear it, Fryda. No apologies for that." He glanced at her bandaged hand. "So...did you do that yourself?"

Fryda nodded and scrubbed her face with her own sleeve. "I couldn't think of any other way to get out of the manacle."

Theow froze. "Manacle?"

"Wiglaf had me locked in my room and chained to the wall."

Theow could not speak for a moment. He stared at her, his gaze travelling over her face. She raised her eyebrows questioningly.

"Would you mind terribly," Theow asked, "if I killed the bastard?"

She sniffled again and gave him a wobbly smile. "Only if you let me help," she said. Then she blinked at him. "Wait. Did you say you love me?"

Theow tamped down his unquenchable fury. He would revisit that later. "I did," he said. "Several times, in fact."

A slow smile bloomed across her face and Theow gripped her a little tighter. He had a sudden urge to slip his tongue inside that sensuous mouth, to lay her down and give her a true reason to smile.

"Say it again?" She traced his lower lip with a fingertip.

Theow leaned forward until his forehead pressed against hers. "I love you."

Fryda sighed and closed her eyes. "And I love you."

Theow kissed her, tender and slow, and when he lifted his head, she nestled against him. "I'm so sorry you had to suffer so much," he said. "*Again*. Especially after..." He shook his head and looked at her hand. "We'll have to make sure it heals well this time. Do you feel feverish?" He put the back of his hand up to her face.

"No. The bones didn't break the skin so...no blood. Maybe there won't be a fever this time?" She sounded uncertain and hopeful. "It really hurts, though."

"We need to get you some medicine."

"And we need to get you stitched up." She sat up and smoothed back her hair, pulling herself together. "Though I'm not sure how we'll manage either of those things if we can't get back into the *burh*."

"Ah." Theow grinned at her. "I have something to show you." He took her good hand and led her back to where he had dropped his things.

"I think we can get back in with this." He bent down, opened the basket, picked up the goblet filled with treasure, and held it up to show her.

Fryda gaped at him. "You *stole* it?" she said, her voice loud and pitched high.

"What? No!" Theow threw her an exasperated look. "How would I have managed that? No. I found it in a cave not far from here. It must be the second twin's goblet from the story King Beowulf told us. The younger brother's, the one permanently exiled who disappeared."

Fryda leaned in close to examine it. "It's amazing. It looks exactly like the other one, only dirtier." She reached out a finger to trace the outline of a silver stag with brown topazes for antlers. "Same animals, too."

"Fryda, you should see all the treasure in that cave." Theow tilted the goblet towards her. Her jaw dropped as she saw the gold coins, gemstones, and other small ornaments he had taken with him. "I thought if I promised to tell Wiglaf about the treasure, and show him where it is, he would let me come back. That's why I didn't wait in the cave. I was coming to get you myself. I hoped the king might let me buy some land and my freedom with this. He might...might let us get married?" It ended up sounding more like a question than a claim.

Fryda's eyes shone as she looked at him. "I hope that, too," she said. "I hope that very much."

"Really?"

It was Fryda's turn to look exasperated with him. "Theow. Yes, really. I already said, *in front of Wiglaf,* that I would."

"So you really..."

"Yes."

"But wouldn't you rather..."

"No."

Despite everything, Theow thought he may never stop smiling again.

Theow put the goblet back in the basket, slipped his hand inside his shirt, and drew out the rich gold ring King Beowulf had given him at the feast—his prize for saving Fryda from public humiliation. Since that night, he had worn it about his neck, hung from a thin leather cord like a talisman, a promise of future hope and happiness. He unfastened the cord and lifted Fryda's right hand. He slid the gleaming ring over her middle finger.

"We'll have a proper ceremony later," he said, "with music and a feast. But for now, this will have to do."

Fryda lifted her hand and stared at the gold band on her finger. A brilliant smile flashed across her face and Theow's chest loosened. "This will more than just *do,*" she said. "And I don't need an elaborate ceremony. I just want Wiglaf to lift your order of exile and dissolve the betrothal contract with Lord Ansten. Then we can take a ship and start our lives anew, somewhere we will both be safe."

"Do you think we have enough to bargain with?" Theow looked at the goblet and its wealth of gold and jewels.

"Yes, I do," Fryda said. "Though I'll have to be the one to bring the goblet up the stairs. We can't take the risk that they would impale you on sight if you tried it."

"I don't like the risk of you ending up in a locked room again." Theow frowned.

"That won't happen. Bjorn will be there with the king, and I'm sure Uncle Beowulf won't let anything happen to me." She tugged at his shirt again. "Are there bandages in the cave? Needle and thread?"

"I think so. It's very well stocked. I'm sure there's something in there for patching up wounded seafarers."

"Let's head that way, then. We can get ourselves cleaned up and figure out what to do next."

★ ★ ★

"Take off your shirt," Fryda said as Theow relit the torches along the walls. "I'll see if I can find something to stitch you up with."

"It will be tricky to do it one-handed."

"I'll manage. I've done it before. Remember when Hild cut herself in the stillroom and I had to put six stitches in her finger?"

Theow dragged a sturdy crate to the centre of the cave and sat. Fryda stared around her, marvelling at the wealth of supplies and items stored in this lonely cave. It looked like enough to outfit an entirely new stronghold.

"I had no idea all this was here." She chucked off her shoes to ease her sore feet as Theow dragged his tunic over his head and tossed it to the side. Fryda caught a glimpse of a smooth, white, freckled chest and lean muscle layered over a slender frame. She averted her eyes, suddenly feeling shy.

"Wait until you see what's beyond the back wall," Theow laughed. "It makes all this look like a drab pebble on a vast beach of jewels."

Fryda inspected a pouch on the trestle table and discovered a handful of dress fastenings. Another held small ivory carvings, exquisite in their precision. A third, however, held bone needles and linen thread. She would prefer silk, but she'd take what she could find.

"I'll need something to serve as a table beside you," she said, and Theow stacked a couple of crates next to him and then threaded the bone needle for her. She rummaged through a pile of tools and found a file, and Theow used it to file the needle to a sharp point. When all was ready, she plucked a candle from a large pile by the entrance and lit it from one of the torches. She put the candle along with a flask of mead and extra thread and needles on the crates and moved behind Theow to assess his wound.

As the flickering candlelight rippled over his skin, Fryda gasped and dropped her needle. The golden light brought out in stark relief a lattice of old, white scars layered across his back. The thin lines went from his shoulders, now smeared with red blood from his fresh wound, to the narrow plane of flesh above his drawstring trousers. They looked like a handful of loose straw tossed carelessly across his body. She stood, frozen, staring at the dense forest of pain and mutilated flesh until Theow shifted under her horrified gaze.

"That bad, hm?" Theow asked. "I just knocked my shoulder. Surely amputation isn't necessary."

Fryda reached out and touched a shaking fingertip to one straight scar on his shoulder blade. It had healed flat against his flesh, but it had a strange, tacky texture unlike his healthy skin. Theow twitched at her touch, and then stilled. She traced the scar down to the small of his back as a half dozen unfamiliar emotions clamoured for supremacy in her breast.

"These are not burn scars," she whispered. She glanced at the stripe of mottled, puckered flesh above his right ear. It had an altogether different composition and colour.

Theow did not move. "No."

She traced the scars with trembling fingers. There were so many. Someone had cut his skin open again and again. These wounds had bled. They looked old, so he had most likely worn them since childhood. Fryda felt sick as she laid her palm against them.

"Who did this to you?" she whispered.

Theow turned to face her and took her hand. He looked hesitant and unhappy. "Does it really matter?" he asked.

She looked at him in astonishment. "Theow. If I'm to be your wife, then yes...it really matters that I know and understand everything about you. Including the painful parts." She touched his cheek. "I understand if it's difficult for you to talk about..."

"That's not it." Theow dropped his head in his hands. "I didn't tell you before because it will be painful for *you* to hear."

"Your pain will always trouble me." Fryda shook her head, bewildered. "That doesn't mean you shouldn't tell me."

"No, you don't understand." Theow took a deep breath. "But you're right. I should have told you before this, but considering the circumstances, you should know."

Theow proceeded to tell her about what happened that day years ago after he, Wiglaf, and Fryda were caught with stolen food from the larder. She had been bundled away, protected, but Theow had been whipped to within an inch of his life because her brother had lied and accused Theow of the theft. She listened in silence, her eyes clear and dry. When Theow finished, he looked at her with concern.

"Are you angry with me for not telling you sooner?" he asked. He rubbed a thumb over her knuckles.

"No." And it was the truth, she discovered. "If I had not recently seen what Wiglaf is capable of myself, I might not have believed you. But Theow." She passed her hand over his autumn-coloured hair. "I knew you didn't steal the food. I could have told father and spared you so…so much pain." Her voice caught.

Theow bowed his head. "I only wanted to spare you pain," he whispered, and pressed a kiss against her palm.

She slid her hand under his chin and raised his face to look at her. "Theow, you don't have to protect me from the ugly truths of this world. I'm stronger than I look."

Theow smiled. "I'm starting to realize that," he said.

Fryda took a deep breath and let it out. "I'm actually a little relieved," she said. "When I saw the scars, I thought my father had given them to you after he caught us with those practice swords when I was ten years old. I'd already concluded that my brother is a villain, but I couldn't bear the thought that I might have been the cause of so much of your pain."

"Never." Theow tugged her down and kissed her. "You are my light and joy, always."

Fryda nuzzled her nose against his, and then straightened. "All right. I still need to stitch this new wound. I was going to warn you about the nasty scar it will leave, but…"

Theow sputtered with laughter and turned his back to her once more. She picked up her bone needle and said, "This will sting a bit." She pushed her left forearm behind the cut, raising the lip of the wound enough to catch her needle, and carefully pushed the tip into the edge of the cut, first one edge then the other.

"Ouch!"

"I'm sorry." Fryda said, contrite. She dabbed at his shoulder with her sleeve. "Here we go. Needle again."

She heard Theow take a breath and he tensed as the bone needle slid through his skin, first one side of the wound and then the other, and the tug of rough thread pulled his flesh together.

"This would be a lot easier if I could use both hands." Fryda's voice shook. "I'm so sorry I'm hurting you."

"You're doing fine." Theow winced as she made another stitch, and then another.

"I'm afraid I'm not doing a very good job," she said. "You really tore yourself up back here."

"Well, you're the only one who will see it. If you don't mind, I don't."

Fryda's hand stilled on his skin. She smiled and once again feathered soft little strokes against his skin as she ran her fingertips over the cords of muscle strapped about his bare back. Goosebumps broke out all over his body and she smiled. She traced the white scars that tracked across his skin, reminders of old treachery and misplaced trust. Where Wiglaf's hatred had tried to take him apart, Fryda's love would stitch him back together.

"I won't mind," she said, and then got back to business. "Two more."

She put in the last two stitches. Theow uncorked the flask of mead and she poured a small trickle of the liquor over his wound. Theow hissed and dug his fingers so hard into his thigh she feared he would leave bruises.

"Sorry." She winced. "I thought this would be better than saltwater since I couldn't find any fresh. Maybe not, though." She patted a cloth over the wound to dry it and stepped back.

Theow swivelled around on the bench to face her. "Your turn," he said. "Let's take a look at that hand."

Steeling herself, Fryda offered it to him. He carefully unwrapped the cloth from her fingers, cutting away the knots and trying not to hurt her. Her hand still throbbed with pain, but she did not cry out at his ministrations. Underneath she could see some swelling, but it did not look as bad as she had feared. The breaks were clean and she had done a passable job of setting the bones straight.

Theow made some clean bandages from a pile of fabric that had been stowed away in a dark corner of the cave and dug out some small, stiff pieces of leather. He rewrapped her hand, splinting the breaks with the leather so they would not pain her so much.

"How's that?" He tied the last knot.

"Not bad." She flexed her arm, testing out the bandage. It still hurt, but the splints reduced the throbbing considerably. "That feels a lot better."

"I don't know how you managed to wrap yourself up one-handed," Theow said. "You did a good job, but this should help."

Fryda smiled. Theow could not seem to stop touching her, which secretly delighted her. He put a hand on her hip and the other on her ribcage and gave a slight squeeze. She gasped and flinched as he pressed against her injured side and he snatched his hands back.

"Your ribs?" he asked. Fryda nodded. "All right, then. Let me see."

Fryda looked at him and her face turned pink. "You want me to take off my dress?"

She nearly laughed when his blush matched hers. "Just so I can look at your ribs," Theow said. He cleared his throat.

Not if I have anything to say about it, she thought.

Fryda met his eyes and became quite still. Without breaking his gaze, she tugged at her belt, fumbling at it with one hand until she managed to loosen the knot and remove it. Taking her time, she reached for one of the brooches that held her dress together. She drew it off and tossed it to the ground. One by one she undid the fastenings of her dress until she could slide the cloth from her shoulders and step out of it.

Fryda tried to control her breathing. *He is hurt*, she reminded herself. His body needed care, not her clumsy fumbling, so she must proceed carefully. Theow, however, objected not at all and watched as she lifted her shift over her head and let it fall from her fingers until she stood in nothing but an underskirt.

He gasped at the vivid, purple bruise that spread across her ribs under her left breast. It looked particularly lurid compared to the paleness of her skin, and at first drew attention away from the spattering of golden freckles that dotted her chest like constellations in the winter sky. The freckles had always embarrassed her, but Theow seemed to delight in them. They congregated across her breasts and trickled down her body, spilling here and there across her belly and leading his gaze below her navel. He snapped his eyes back up to hers and she warmed at the desire she saw in them.

It matched her own.

"It looks worse than it feels." She moved closer to him, within touching distance. "It hurt much more yesterday."

Theow swallowed. "Tell me if I hurt you." He raised a hand to her ribs, warm and impossibly gentle against her skin. He leaned in, examining the bruise and her ribs beneath it. He probed the primary injury site and she winced, but did not jerk away.

"No loose ribs," he murmured. "Does this hurt?"

"A little," she admitted. "But not nearly as much as it did at first. I thought that warrior broke them when he kicked me."

"Bruised," Theow said, sitting up, "and perhaps cracked, but not broken." He swept his fingers up her ribcage but stopped before he brushed the underside of her bare breast.

He sighed and moved his hand away.

Fryda gulped and moved in closer.

Theow looked up at her. Her cheeks felt fire-red now. She reached down and took his hand. She could feel it trembling.

She did not speak. She placed the flat of his hand on her breast and pressed it against herself.

Theow raised his eyebrows at her, an unmistakable question. Fryda nodded.

"Touch me," she whispered.

"But your hand...your ribs..."

"We can be careful. Unless...oh." She put her hand over her mouth. "Your shoulder pains you. I'm sorry, I didn't think..."

Theow slid his other hand around to her back and drew her between his knees. He leaned in and pressed his lips against her abdomen and her apologies stuttered to a halt.

That felt...extraordinary.

He touched her with his lips again and again, light kisses, exploring, worshipping as he stroked her with his hands. He mapped her freckles with his mouth and let his tongue glide against her skin. She twined her hand into his hair as he kissed the shallow, healing cuts that Fægebeorn had left on her body. He laid his cheek against her stomach and inhaled the sweet, musky scent of her.

Fryda giggled. He raised his head and looked at her.

"Your whiskers tickle." She ran her fingers across his stubble. He grinned at her.

"Maybe there's a razor in here somewhere," he said. She laughed.

Her laughter died as Theow leaned back and looked at her... really looked at her. Slowly, giving her time to stop him or back away if she chose, he reached out and nudged her underskirt down over her hips until it puddled on the ground at her feet and she stood bare before him. Despite her cuts and bruises, his eyes caressed her, moving slowly over her hips, her belly, her chest, the springy thatch of yellow hair between her thighs. He read her body like lines from a lyric poem. Her nipples tightened as he looked at them and she suddenly felt powerful. He hadn't even touched her there and her body responded to him. She wanted him. She could see his desire...she grew giddy with the scent of her own.

As Theow's eyes tracked over her body, Fryda inched her injured hand behind her back, ashamed to let him see it. It was the unthinking movement born of seven years of hiding, and she felt more vulnerable exposing her hand to him than she did her naked body. Theow put his fingers on her shoulder and swept downwards, exerting a soft pressure on her elbow to draw her arm forward. Fryda stiffened but let him reveal her hand, and her entire body clenched as he ran his fingertips over the bandage on her palm in a barely-there touch.

"You don't have to hide from me." Theow pressed a kiss to the inside of her wrist above the bandage. "You don't have to be ashamed."

"I know." Fryda's voice trembled. "It's just habit."

"You are beautiful." A kiss on the inside of her elbow. "Everywhere." A kiss across her linen-bound knuckles. He looked up and grew still when he saw tears tracking down her cheeks.

"Did I hurt you?" He started to lean away, but Fryda tangled her fingers through his hair and pulled him back. She did not hide herself again.

"Don't stop," she whispered. "Please."

Theow dipped his head to her once more and his lips wrote their own verses across her skin, encomiums to her body and heart. She made music, too, with her sighs and gasps and that startled little "Oh!" when he drew the tip of her breast into his mouth, and when his fingers and tongue searched for the hidden secrets of her body. He reached out and pulled a blanket of silky sea-otter pelts to the floor. Careful not to put pressure on her ribs or to jostle her hand, he folded her into his arms and rolled her onto the fur, his body hovering over hers. She ran her hand over his bare chest, down to his belly, hesitating at the waist of his roughspun trousers.

"Fryda." He moulded his lips against hers. "I love you," he whispered against her mouth.

She inhaled the words into her body and breathed them back into his mouth. A sense of desperation gripped her, subtle at first but quickly mounting to a frantic need as she forgot fear and pain and betrayal in a maelstrom of sheer sensation. Theow caught her urgency. In two breaths he stripped himself naked. In three he was inside her. They clutched each other, his hand in her hair, hers digging into his back, until the cave echoed with the sounds of the comfort and pleasure they found in each other.

Desire

Fýrdraca stirs, roused by a shift in the curse. The treasure-song has changed. She hears strange noises in her sleep...the strike of a stone, a spark of fire, the scrape of something soft and fleshy against rock, a whistle. She shifts and moves and her treasure slithers and falls from her pile, and she realizes then that the gold has gone out of tune.

Time passes, or perhaps it stands still. Again she hears voices, and this time the smell of blood and the taste of pain invade her quiet space. She soon senses something else...something so powerful it reaches through her cursed sleep to rouse her. Not waken her entirely. Not yet. She rises just to the surface of understanding and sensation. And there is such sensation, the likes of which she has not felt in a thousand years. But she remembers.

The languid slide of skin against skin. Bodies overlapping, coming apart, weaving together. Breaths and moans and singing pleasure. The perfect glide of hardness against a surface unendurably soft. Welcoming wetness and a quiver deep within the bones.

She can taste the salt and strange, luxurious savour of pleasure. The tightening, the urgency. A moment of pain, a careless knock against broken skin, broken bone. Broken serenity. Concern and care...and then the laughter.

That laughter...she remembers it. It fills her with unimaginable rage, that carefree, happy sound. She moves again and the gold *strikes its sour note once more. Something is missing. Something is wrong.*

The Lone Survivor's curse has consumed her for an age. She knows every angle of it, every flavour, every facet. The curse feels different now, and that sudden knowledge overshadows even the first cresting pleasure-tide that rushes in, sudden and shocking, to steal the breath, and then the second some minutes later.

The heart. Fýrdraca rouses more, searching for that one bit of gold, the cup filled with an ancient man's shattered heart and the one thing keeping the Lone Survivor's curse from overwhelming the world. For that heart had once loved, had known tenderness and joy just as fully as it knew despair and hatred. Without the heart, the curse runs unchecked, and pleasure turns to terror-tide as Fýrdraca...

...wakes.

Twenty-seven

Getting back into Eceweall proved something of a challenge the next morning. Theow scowled at Fryda and said, for the second time, "You cannot go up by yourself. I'm not certain Wiglaf will let you live if he sees you've escaped."

"I'm sure he's discovered I'm gone by now," she said. "Besides, he's much less likely to kill me than you. You're an exile. If *anyone* sees you in the *burh* you'll be killed on sight."

Theow rubbed the scar over his ear. She was not wrong, but that did not change the problem. "Well, we can't stay here forever. One of us needs to go up and find Hild or Bjorn. And we need to find you some *dwale* as soon as possible." Fryda had woken up in terrible pain that morning, though she was trying to hide it.

They stood at the foot of the easternmost cliff, where stairs carved into the rock would take them back into Eceweall. The rocky beach stretched to the water where a system of wooden docks secured a dozen or so longships. Theow felt exposed enough already with the men and women milling about the ships, cleaning the hulls, repairing sails and rigging, and generally keeping busy. So far no one seemed to have noticed them, but Theow felt twitchy. He was putting Fryda in danger just by being there.

"My lady?"

Theow whirled towards the voice. Fryda gasped and started back and he caught her by the shoulders.

"Eadith!" Fryda sagged against him in relief.

Eadith, perched on the cliff stairs with a large basket in her arms, stared at them. She glanced wildly around and scurried down the remaining stairs.

"What are you doing here?" she hissed, as she dropped the basket and dragged the two of them into the shade of a hardy tree growing between a cluster of boulders. "My lady, Theow has been exiled. It is a death sentence for him to come back here."

"Eadith," Fryda said again, and threw her good arm around the bony woman. Eadith patted Fryda fondly.

"Now, now," she said, setting Fryda upright. "It's all right, child. We can work all this out."

"Actually…" Theow looked at the housekeeper thoughtfully. "You could help us. Listen." And as briefly as possible, he told her what had happened. Olaf's murder, Wiglaf's treachery, Fryda's escape…everything. Eadith's eyes grew wide as he spoke, but by the end of his story she peered at them with pensive concentration.

"Wiglaf?" she asked, staring at Fryda. "Your brother Wiglaf. He did all that?"

"Yes."

Eadith scowled. "That boy needed a strong hand when he was a child, but never got it." She grunted. "Like to give him a smack myself next time I see him."

"Is King Beowulf at the longhouse?" Fryda asked.

"He is." Eadith nodded. "He came back with Bjorn a short time ago."

"Oh, thank Woden." Fryda yanked her sleeve over her bandaged hand. "Eadith. We desperately need to talk to him, to tell him what's happened. Only he can save Theow now and convince my brother to drop this ridiculous betrothal contract."

Eadith regarded Theow for a moment, and to his surprise her eyes filled with tears.

"Bryce was so fond of you," she said. "He told me about his plan to buy your freedom and make you his heir."

Theow's chest tightened. Bryce had talked to Eadith about him?

The housekeeper touched her gnarled fingers to his cheek. "He wanted a life with purpose for you, and…" She glanced at Fryda. "…perhaps even happiness. And he loved you so very much, my lady." She dropped her hand. "If Bryce were here, he would do everything in his power to help you. As he is not…I will do it instead. I'll get you to the king."

★ ★ ★

Fryda burned with anger as Wiglaf glared at Theow and then shot an accusing look at the cliffside guards who had escorted them into the longhouse.

"Tell me again why you didn't just shoot him?" Wiglaf demanded. To a man, the guards ducked their heads and tried to look innocent. True to her word, Eadith had smuggled them into the longhouse, though it had taken her some ingenuity and powerful help to do it.

King Beowulf, who stood beside Bjorn, held up one enormous hand. He wore the look of a man who had celebrated hard, as he must have done at the feast the night before. His blue tunic and grey trousers were plain, though still of fine quality, and he had braided his white hair and beard. Despite his humble clothing, his air of command was absolute. Gone were the broad smiles and booming laughter, the jocular gibes and avuncular storytelling. Beowulf the king and warrior faced them now.

"The guards acted on my command," he said. Fryda saw him glance at Eadith. He nodded to the old housekeeper. She bowed to him and left the longhouse, throwing Fryda and Theow a concerned look as she went.

"I gave direct orders," Wiglaf said, his voice plaintive. "It seems to me a lord's will should be considered first in his own stronghold. And where is my drink?" The new lord of Eceweall looked petulantly into his empty cup.

"The situation has changed," Fryda snapped, stepping out from behind the guards and moving up to the dais. Wiglaf's face turned dead white as soon as he saw her. His jaw dropped, and she felt a small, vindictive pleasure in his shock. He had clearly thought her still locked away and chained to the wall of her room.

"Enough." Beowulf turned his serious gaze to Fryda and his eyes widened. "Sweet girl," he said. "Your hand."

Fryda glanced at the bandage as she again became aware of the pounding pain through her hand. The *dwale* Eadith had given her helped, but could not entirely mask the throbbing of her damaged bones. Wiglaf's complexion went from milk-white to green as he stared at her hand and understood the implications. Hild appeared at his side with a pitcher of mead and filled his cup. He drank it down in one gulp and held it out again, demanding more. Hild poured the golden mead again. She met Fryda's eyes, gave the barest smile, and Fryda relaxed. Wiglaf did not know Hild had helped her.

"Surprised to see me, brother?" she asked. She winced as Beowulf took her bandaged hand gently into his enormous one.

"How did this happen?" The king's voice was deceptively soft and mild. And now...even now...she hesitated to tell the truth about what her brother had done. Why, she wondered, was she so quick to protect him when he made it clear she could not expect the same courtesy from him?

"Wiglaf locked her in her bedchamber and chained her to the wall." Theow, obviously, suffered from no such compunctions. "She had to break her own hand again to get free."

Beowulf became unnaturally still. Fryda saw her twin close his eyes and his knuckles went white on the arms of his throne.

The ground gave a massive shake under Fryda's feet, as if the king's wrath was so fierce it could uproot earth and stone. A great rumble filled her ears as everyone staggered and tried to remain on their feet. Furniture skidded across the floor and the original goblet teetered on its plinth, but did not fall. The earth quickly settled, and the noise faded away.

Even the earthquake could not distract the king from his wrath. "Is it true?" he asked, ignoring the murmurs of the guards who straightened themselves and glanced around uneasily. To Fryda's surprise, Beowulf aimed the question, delivered in a level, controlled voice, to her and not to her brother.

"Yes." Without thinking, she pulled her sleeve over her bandage.

Beowulf looked at Wiglaf, his hard blue eyes the colour of slate. For a long time he said nothing, and a breathless silence hung over the room.

"Explain." He flung the word at Wiglaf like a spear, and her brother flinched as it hit its target.

Wiglaf's mouth worked as he searched for the words he wanted. Finally, he shrugged, flung himself back in his seat, and muttered, "She was being difficult. I had no other choice."

Fryda stepped forward. "Did you decide to lock me up before or after you betrayed our father and did nothing to stop a madman from murdering him?"

Beowulf's eyebrows nearly soared right off his forehead.

Wiglaf surged to his feet. "As you no doubt both saw for yourselves," he snarled, including Beowulf in his glance, "I was drugged. I was out of my mind."

"So you did not willingly conspire with Eadgils against our father?"

"Of course not!" Wiglaf dropped his gaze and sat once more. He did not meet King Beowulf's eye. "I don't remember much about that night, I admit, but I certainly was not in any state to come to our father's aid. Or yours."

Fryda did not flinch from his glare. "I think you revealed a great deal about yourself that night," she said, "whether you meant to or not."

She felt a twinge of satisfaction when her brother's face turned dark red. She thought of the white scars on Theow's back, the pain her brother had caused him, and felt as if another quake had shaken her to the core.

"Enough of this," Wiglaf said. "I'll not have you questioning me, especially in front of a *slave*."

"That's enough." Beowulf's voice snapped like a whip. "Wiglaf, you'd best hold your tongue for now. It seems to be running away with your sense."

Wiglaf subsided with a resentful glare at her, as if he lay the blame for his predicament squarely at her feet.

"Now." Beowulf turned his attention back to Fryda and Theow. "Eadith told me you have something to show me?"

"We do." Fryda nodded to Theow, who put Hild's basket on the floor and opened it. Eyes on the king, he brought out the second goblet and held it up. Instantly, six guards raised their spears to his throat. Theow froze.

Fryda saw the exact moment her brother and the king came to the same erroneous conclusion she had. Wiglaf's eyes darted to the stand that still held King Beowulf's original gift.

Beowulf, however, was not quite as quick to understand. He saw the gold and silver goblet clutched in Theow's hands, and his face fell in disappointment.

"Ah, my thane-for-a-day." The king sounded mournful. "I had not thought you would come thieving for what does not belong to you. I thought more of your mettle."

"No, Uncle," Fryda said. "Do you assume just because Theow is a…a slave, he would resort to thieving?" She frowned at the king, his easy prejudice irking her. "Theow did not steal the goblet. Look, your gift still stands in its original place."

Beowulf looked at the plinth and the shining goblet on top of it. He looked at the other cup, astonished. "What...? How?" he sputtered.

"Theow discovered an enormous hoard of treasure, Uncle Beowulf. He found the second brother's goblet from the story you told."

Wiglaf's eyes gleamed. "You will take me there." He started towards Theow. Even before Beowulf could move, Fryda stepped in front of Wiglaf and blocked his way.

"First," she said, her voice soft, "we will come to an understanding. Will we not?"

Wiglaf looked at her, and his cold, calculating eyes made her shiver. She wondered how she could have been so wrong about him all these years. She always believed he could be a better man if he wished it. Wiglaf had called her naive, and she had to admit the truth of his words.

"What do you want?" Wiglaf's tone rang hard and brittle. The opposite of conciliatory.

Fryda glanced at Theow who still stood, unmoving, at spearpoint. They had agreed she would do most of the talking, because Wiglaf would never bow to the wishes of a slave. Theow, still holding up the goblet despite the half dozen spears pointed at him, smiled at her. Her insides lurched and her body rose to the memory of their stolen night in the cave.

Fryda grinned at him, ignoring her brother's scowls.

Beowulf shoved guards out of his way as he stepped to Theow's side. They all moved back and let their spears fall. He lifted the goblet from Theow's hands and inspected it.

"Astonishing." He turned the cup in his huge hands. "It's the exact same workmanship, the same artistry, the same designs." He looked at Theow with approval. "Well done, my boy! Well done indeed! You shall be rewarded for this find."

"Yes, about that, Uncle," Fryda said before Wiglaf could interject. "We were hoping that Wiglaf, my lord and brother, would accept this treasure as a gift and rescind his order for Theow's exile."

"Exile?" Beowulf frowned at Wiglaf. "Why did you exile the lad, since he obviously did not steal from you?"

Fryda pressed her throbbing hand to her stomach. Eadith must not have had time to tell the king everything about their situation.

Wiglaf flushed. "He importuned my sister." He snapped off each word like a dog biting at a bone offered and then withdrawn.

Fryda stepped forward. "He did not, in fact, do any such thing," she said. "I'm afraid my brother was misinformed, and he did not give me the opportunity to set right the truth before he ejected Theow from the *burh*." She turned to Beowulf, her eyes wide and innocent. "However, now that we are here, and you are witness to my testimony, surely there can be no objection to Theow's return? I assure you, Uncle, he in no way acted as he has been accused."

Beowulf looked at her, his expression fond. He took her hand and the rich gold ring Theow had given her glowed and shimmered in the flickering candlelight. Distracted by the silky reflections, Beowulf glanced at her finger, and then looked at Theow. A line appeared between his brows.

Fryda held her breath. They could not have announced their intentions more clearly if they had stood upon a table with a ceremonial cord wrapped around their hands and shouted their vows for all the stronghold to hear.

Beowulf turned back to her. He looked thoughtful and serious as he studied the ring. Then, he looked up and cocked an eyebrow at her.

She knew what he wanted to know. She smiled and nodded. Beowulf squeezed her hand.

"And the goblet?" Beowulf turned to Theow and Fryda let the breath trickle out between her lips in silent relief.

"A peace offering." Theow bowed to the king. "A gift, to show there are no hard feelings for Lord Wiglaf's mistake. In truth, my king, I found a great deal more treasure than this. I would be happy to reveal its location if a few considerations could be made."

"Considerations." Beowulf took the goblet and looked inside. He tipped it over and poured a stream of riches into the basket. He sounded amused. "What sort of considerations?"

Fryda saw Wiglaf's face tighten. She knew he boiled with rage as he watched his control and authority slip out from under him.

Theow bent his head. "Before he died, Bryce...Unferth...told me that he planned to speak to Lord Weohstan to purchase my freedom. He wanted to make me his heir and leave me his fortune so I could buy some land and...and perhaps even have a family one day." He did not look at Fryda, though the king flicked her a quick glance. "I would ask that Unferth's wishes be respected, my king, and have my freedom granted, my inheritance bestowed upon me."

"What utter codswallop," Wiglaf snarled. "The slave is obviously lying."

"He is not," Fryda said. She kept her voice quiet, so all had to settle down to hear her. Beowulf looked at her questioningly. "With his dying breath, Bryce told me his wishes. He wanted Theow to be free, and named him his heir."

"Convenient that no one else heard that," Wiglaf said, crossing his arms over his chest.

Fryda met his eyes and did not flinch. Her hand throbbed and she relaxed her clenched muscles. "I am certain you mean no insult to my character by calling me a liar in front of the king, brother."

"I..." Wiglaf glanced at Beowulf, whose face turned thunderous and troubled. "I'm merely suggesting that perhaps you were mistaken."

"I assure you, I am not."

"My second condition," Theow said, "is that you free Lady Fryda from the betrothal contract with Lord Ansten. That contract was made without her knowledge and against her wishes, and you will not malign her character when you break it. You will tell Lord Ansten that *you* were mistaken...not that Lady Fryda 'changed her mind' or went back on a vow she never even made."

Fryda loved Theow in that moment more than ever before. Trust him to think about her reputation, even at a time like this.

"Betrothal contract?" Beowulf again looked at the gold ring on her finger, bewildered. "But I thought..."

"I'll explain later," Fryda whispered to him.

Wiglaf growled. "Absolutely out of the question. I will not risk war with Sweden when our nations are already..."

Beowulf interrupted. "Enough. I have heard enough." He gave Wiglaf a wry, sympathetic smile. "My boy, you are the lord of the *burh*, I know. But it took your father many, many years to gather all the wisdom that burned with him on his funeral pyre. He made many mistakes in his life." He shook his head with deep, heavy regret. "Many mistakes. And I did not act when perhaps I should have to prevent them. The events that occurred here two days ago, the attack on the *burh* and the death of your father, were partly a result of my folly. I feel somewhat responsible for what happened."

Fryda stayed silent, biting her lip as Wiglaf clenched and unclenched his fists. She could see his internal struggle. On the one hand he did not want to give Theow the dignity of making him a free man—and a free *rich* man at that. On the other, Wiglaf could not deny the wishes of his king, though Beowulf had scolded him like a child in front of his men.

"Wiglaf," Beowulf said as the silence stretched like a drawn bowstring. "Don't be a fool, boy. This deal benefits you more than anyone else."

"I will see this treasure first," Wiglaf said through clenched teeth. "If it is sufficient to cover the loss of Bryce's inheritance, I will fulfil the blacksmith's dying wish. If it is not, however, Theow will have to work off the difference until I am satisfied."

Theow grinned. "Oh, I think you will be satisfied," he said, and Wiglaf scowled. "And the betrothal contract?"

Wiglaf had the look of an animal caged or cornered—panicky and desperate for any way out. "She must go to Sweden with Lord Ansten," he said. "The truce…"

"Pah." Beowulf swept his protests aside with one enormous hand. "After what Eadgils did, Sweden will do anything to regain our trust…and most importantly, our trade. Their wrong far outweighs yours, even if you do break the contract." He eyed Wiglaf beadily. "And if what Theow says is true, that Fryda does not want the marriage, then I suggest you find a way to make Ansten adequate compensation for his loss."

Fryda held her breath as Wiglaf hesitated, and she let it out the moment she saw him give in.

"Very well." Wiglaf clamped his lips tightly shut, as if trapping dangerous words behind them.

"Excellent!" Beowulf said, his sombre humour forgotten. "We shall all go and see this wondrous treasure. I'd planned to go out hunting this afternoon. I've been feeling a bit restless with all the feasting and celebrating, but a treasure hunt will suit just as well. Lead the way, my thane-for-a-day, and show us where you found this remarkable artefact." Beowulf looked at the goblet in his hands. "Though you may want to have someone give this second one a polish," he remarked. "It looks a bit worse for wear." He set the goblet down next to its twin, and the two cups gleamed in the firelight.

A curious humming filled the longhouse. Fryda looked around in confusion, unable to pinpoint the origin of the sound. Then a flash of light caught her eye and she looked at the two goblets.

She gasped. A golden aura surrounded the cups, a glowing

light that increased in intensity as the humming sound grew louder. Beowulf stepped away from the goblets and Fryda felt Theow's hands close around her arms and draw her back. The gemstones set in the twin cups flashed with impossibly bright, rich colour and Fryda had to shield her eyes as the longhouse was suddenly bathed in a rainbow of jewelled tones and gold.

And then the lights went out.

Fryda blinked and, along with everyone else in the room, leaned forward to examine the goblets. She was astonished to see they were both full to the brim with liquid. The polished goblet, the gift from Beowulf, contained a clear pale gold fluid that smelled sweet and fresh. The goblet Theow had found, with its tarnished surface, held a murky brew smelling faintly of decay and death.

Beowulf's face was a mask of wonder and delight. Before Fryda could protest, he dipped his finger into the pale golden liquid and popped it into his mouth.

The king's eyes grew wide, and he stared at his finger. "That," he said, "is the finest mead I have ever tasted."

Fryda gave the second goblet with its dubious contents an uneasy look. "Please don't drink from that one, Uncle Beowulf," she pleaded.

"Ah. No." Beowulf stared at the goblets and shook his head. "I guess the stories were true. When placed together, the goblets fill themselves by some magic."

"How...?" Wiglaf stared at the goblets. "How is this possible?"

"I have no idea, my boy," Beowulf said, his voice booming. He threw an arm around Wiglaf's shoulders. "Perhaps we are seeing a return of magic to our lands. Wouldn't that be a marvellous thing?"

Fryda glanced at the foul, corrupted brew in the dirty goblet and shivered. She was not so certain that *marvellous* was quite the right word for it. She looked at Theow, relieved his exile was over and her contract broken, but frowned as she saw his face lose all its colour. His eyes widened and turned black as his pupils dilated in unreasoning fear.

And then she smelled it, just as a scream reached them from somewhere in the *burh*.

Smoke.

Fryda looked up and gasped. Great tendrils of silver-white vapour curled around the rafters and the beginnings of molten red embers crackled through the thatched ceiling.

The longhouse was on fire.

Awake

The barrier between the earth and sky, the dark and light, the cursed and exalted, disintegrates under the force of Fýrdraca's powerful wings and her even more powerful wrath. The earth ruptures, tears, giving birth to the monstrous form that blackens out the eternal summer sun as it rises into the sky.

She is awake. She is free.

Nearly a thousand years of dreams weigh down upon her, but she shakes them off like water droplets after rain. She feels the distant presence of the dragon-touched shield maiden, the heartbeat that batters her senses with pulses of magic, like meteor strikes. After so many long years of cursed sleep, she finally opens her eyes.

With difficulty, as if a thousand chains hold her fast to the ground, she works her feet under her and pushes herself out of the pile of riches. The treasure-song squeals at her, discordant music that sets the Lone Survivor's curse humming through her blood once more. The coins and jewels cascade down her scales in a glorious shower, and though no light penetrates the barrow, Fýrdraca can see everything.

Everything except the Lone Survivor's heart.

Enraged, she flings herself against the walls, the ceiling, the floor of the cavern. The earth shakes under her ruthless onslaught as she feels the curse break through the bonds of the world. The gold and silver threads fused to her hide soften with the raging heat of her blood. They move with her, pliant, like living armour, *and the blackness of her scales shows between them. Curse-mad, Fýrdraca scrabbles through the treasure with her great claws, searching for the goblet. The heart. But it is no longer in the cave.*

And so she tears it asunder.

The cliff and the beach become unrecognizable. Rock and rubble litter the ground and the headland collapses, creating an enormous divot carved into the cliff. The chasm that split the earth disappears within a gaping crater that obliterates the features of the landscape.

She stretches her wings luxuriously, glorying in the vast expanse of space the sky offers her, and beats them against the salt-touched wind.

Whump. Whump.

White smoke trickles from her mouth and her slitted nostrils as she draws in a deep breath, stoking the great hearth of her chest. The smoke turns silver, then ash-grey, and finally black. Her mouth opens…her cambered fangs emerge…and then the slick-skinned dragon vomits streamers of fire, an embrace of red and orange flame licked with blue and white. The air shimmers with intense heat as the flames roll over the ruined landscape. Rocks hiss and break open and grasses wither, and then blacken and crumble into ash. The dragon's fire melts much of the silver and gold that tumbles from the treasure hoard, and it flows over the beach like spilled mead. It cools and hardens into a vast carpet of precious metals. Every rock, every grain of sand, every sliver of driftwood in its path now wears a robe limned with golden glory.

Fýrdraca screeches again and circles the ruined headland, casting all the land into shadow. She turns to the east and raises her head, sniffing the air. She pauses, suspended for a moment as if immune from the physical laws of mortal creatures, and then flies off with unnatural speed towards Eceweall.

Twenty-eight

Fryda ran to Theow as flaming scraps of straw and ash rained down upon them. He had the paralysed look she'd seen in the kitchens when Hild had burned the bread. She reached up and put her uninjured hand against his cheek, running the tips of her fingers gently along his mottled scar. She stood on tiptoe and pressed her lips against his.

He started, and a moment later he drew in a deep breath and kissed her back. She forced herself to pull away.

"Theow, I truly do love you. But the building is on fire. We have to get out."

He blinked at her, still breathing too fast. "Out. Yes." He flinched as a smouldering ember landed on his cheek and she brushed it off. "I love you, too."

Fryda, her anxiety already stretched thin, gasped a laugh. "Yes, I know, but you have to move, love. I think we're being attacked again." She grabbed his hand and they joined the others, who were already running for the door. Wiglaf, she knew, had seen her kiss Theow, for he looked at her with such disgust she thought he might vomit. But then Beowulf grabbed him by the shoulder and shoved him through the arched doorway.

"You're the lord now, lad!" she heard the king boom. "Time to earn your keep. You'll never forget your first raid as a lord... if you survive it!" And they were swept away with the crowd.

A raid? Fryda and Theow locked eyes and she knew they

both had the same thought. More exiles? Reinforcements from Sweden? But how, she wondered, would they get past the wall?

More screams, shouts, and the desolate lowing of horns greeted Fryda and Theow as they ducked out of the burning building. Fryda, blinking smoke from her streaming eyes, spun around, trying to identify the danger, but she saw only her father's warriors—her brother's now, she supposed—scrambling to arm themselves with a fear so frantic it invaded her own body, even though she could not see the new threat.

Then her eyes cleared and Fryda stared, horror-struck at how her world had changed in just a few moments. The stone wall that surrounded the *burh* had a gaping hole knocked into it, and the strong wooden gates had been reduced to a pile of splinters. All the buildings on the green lay in piles of ash and timber, and on the circle of grass, the clean-raked paths, a number of corpses burned still. The menhir, which had been erected centuries before Fryda's ancestors had brought war and conquest to Geatland, lay in two shattered pieces on the smouldering ground. Some of the barracks, which stood in straight lines between the green and the farmsteads, seemed intact while others burned. The farmsteads, which spread out towards the mainland, remained untouched.

But she could not see the enemy.

Charred bodies lay everywhere. Brave men and women bearing bows and spears and wooden shields leapt over the corpses of their fallen companions to enter the fury of a battle Fryda could not see. Bryce's forge was in flames and Fryda cried out in distress as it collapsed upon itself in a pile of ash and burning rubble. As she watched in mounting horror, a fireball streaked though the sky and hit the kitchens, which went up like an inferno.

"Hild," Fryda gasped.

Theow gave her a squeeze. "She was in the longhouse," he reminded her. "She got out. She's all right."

A shattering sound, alien and strange, rent the air—a screech so high and loud it cracked stone and shot pain, like lances, through Fryda's head. She clapped her hands over her ears, wincing as her damaged fingers and wrist throbbed, and looked up towards the sound.

Her jaw dropped. She watched as the shape of her fear took an incomprehensible form in the sky, and then her knees truly did forsake her. She was looking at...

A dragon.

Fryda's mind blanked, as if refusing to believe her own eyes. Theow, wearing an expression of the same disbelief she felt, reached down and pulled her to her feet. She clutched at him and he held her tightly to his side.

The beast was enormous—longer than the mead-hall and taller than an ash tree. She had small scales that covered her like a sleek skin, ink-black, as if she'd stolen night itself and left the northern summer bereft of darkness, even at midnight. Her scales would suffer no light to shine upon them, no reflections, as if her hide soaked up the light and killed it. She might have been nothing more than a shadow, a hole cut in the fabric of the sky, if not for the glints of gold and silver that ran between her scales. The metal moved with her like a living thing.

She reared her dreadful, wedge-shaped head and bugled her strange call again. Two magnificent ebony horns swept back from her temples and a number of shorter, razor-sharp spikes grew away from her face. Her sinuous neck writhed back and forth, as an adder might approach its prey, and her mighty black wings stretched impossibly wide as she wrapped them around the wind to raise herself into the sky.

Her great shadow fell over Eceweall as she rose. More horns sounded and a great shout went up and the air filled with spears and arrows. Fryda watched as one small boy, a child perhaps five years old, hurled a rock at the beast. It soared less than three feet and fell back to earth.

The spears left no mark on the dragon. By the time they hit

their target, they had lost all their power. The arrows fared better —Fryda could see several protruding from her body. However, they did nothing to slow her down. Fryda spied King Beowulf and Wiglaf marshalling the troops and shouting orders to the warriors near the smoking longhouse.

The dragon extended her neck and belched out bright ribbons of flame. The homesteads burned and the people screamed as they fell beneath the fierce heat of angry fire. Fryda gasped as Theow lifted her off her feet and sprinted to the cliff stairs while, with one breath, the dragon immolated the archers, the pikemen, the shield maidens…and one brave, tiny warrior hurling his rocks at the sky.

Fryda struggled out of Theow's grip and hit the ground running. They sprinted past the remnants of the forge towards the cliff stairs as chaos continued all around them. They stopped at a safe distance and Fryda tore her eyes from the abomination in the sky, looking at the ruin of her world.

She saw with relief that both the king and Wiglaf had so far escaped the scourge. The two men stood near the longhouse, which appeared intact, if slightly charred around the edges. It seemed a stray piece of fiery debris had ignited the thatched roof, but it had not fully caught. Movement from the undamaged barracks distracted her from the carnage.

The *burh*'s warriors spilled from the buildings to face the ebony sky-menace. Most of the warriors and honour-guards who had come for the king's celebrations were dead—they burned with the guest houses and the barracks on the green. Those who survived, however, leapt into the fray to protect the king and his kin.

The dragon screamed again, circling the sky, and Fryda flinched at the sound. Another volley of arrows darkened the air. Again, the dragon appeared unaffected, as if the barbed broadheads were nothing more than flies that nipped at her scales. With another ear-bleeding shriek she raised her wings and dipped her body, undulating through the air towards the longhouse…and towards Beowulf and Wiglaf.

The two men bolted, each running in opposite directions. Fýrdraca stretched her wings, the sails thin as spider-silk and opaque as coal, and hovered over the mead-hall with its intricate dragon carvings and ivy-covered walls. With one swipe of a clawed foot, she tore the charred, thatched roof off the building and flung it away. The debris narrowly missed Wiglaf, who kept running without looking back, but it flattened one of his remaining guards.

Deprived of structural support, the longhouse walls began to cave in. Ivy snapped and tore as the walls buckled, and the great arched doors slipped their moorings. The fire-dragon lashed her tail whip-fast and one wall of the longhouse shattered into kindling. Fryda screamed and ducked as pieces of wood sailed over her head. The dragon landed another blow and the entire structure collapsed.

The beast landed, the green summer grasses withering black and putrid beneath her taloned feet. She plunged her head and rooted through the rubble of the longhouse, moving debris with her snout and claws while she propped herself up with her wings. After a moment she pounced, like a cat with a string, and the warriors who had crept up behind her for a concentrated attack scattered and fled. The beast lifted something from the remains of the longhouse with her mouth. Fryda squinted but was too far away to identify it. The dragon paused for a moment, and then tossed the object away. She let out an angry shriek, and Fryda clapped her hands over her ears. The earth trembled as the sound died away, though her ears continued to sing its tune.

The dragon went back to her search, pawing and snuffling through the ruins.

A soft lick of wind blew smoke into Fryda's face. It burned her eyes, as if she'd walked into a mist of acid, and she smelled something sulfurous, sickly, like rotten eggs soaked in poison.

She coughed. The dragon...Fryda's mind stuttered on the word, still unable to take in the enormity of what she saw...the *dragon* paused and raised her head, sniffing the air as if she sensed something familiar. She turned and stared straight at Fryda.

A jolt of recognition shot through her and she felt strength surge through her blood and bones, as if those obsidian eyes contained lightning and thunder, coastal storms and tidal waves. They stirred up her blood, filled her with tumultuous energy. She gasped. The dragon...her strange new powers were somehow connected to the dragon. Those fathomless eyes sparked the power within her—the dragon the hammer and Fryda the blade, shaped blow by blow against the anvil of the world. Fryda gazed into those knowing eyes and a longing, sharp and potent, tugged so strongly at her heart it felt like pain. The dragon blinked at her, and turned back to the longhouse.

Fryda staggered and would have fallen if not for Theow's steadying arm. That yearning...it was not for the familiar things, like love or riches or anything she knew and desired.

The dragon longed for death.

With the warrior-power burgeoning within her, Fryda thought she could singlehandedly deliver that wish. In fact...

She broke from Theow's embrace and ran towards the ruined longhouse, his startled exclamation and shout of warning fading as her pumping legs ate up the distance towards the dragon. Witnessing the ruin of her home ignited a deep anger low in her belly. Fryda leapt over a blackened, smoking corpse and, without slowing, reached down and snatched up a long spear mostly untouched by fire. The fearsome beast loomed impossibly large as she ran closer, and for one moment Fryda's heart nearly faltered. But the magic within her grew the nearer she came, and it wove bands of iron through her body. She gathered it close, breathed it in, felt it twine through her flesh, blood, and bones. She drew her arm back and, on a burst of inhuman strength, let the spear fly.

At the same moment, Fýrdraca turned and snatched up another object from the ruined longhouse with one clawed foot. The spear arced through the air, and the dragon's shriek of triumph turned to outraged pain as the fire-hardened tip punched through the scales of her flank, and buried half of itself deep in her flesh.

Fýrdraca screeched again, making Fryda wince, curved her snake-like neck alongside her body, and gripped the spear with her fearsome mouth. Without any hesitation she yanked it out, spat it on the ground, and peered at the thing still clasped in her talons. Fryda, trembling and dizzy as the tidal wave of preternatural strength collapsed back into passive ripples, saw a glint of golden reflected sunlight from the object.

Apparently satisfied with her prize this time, she sat back on her haunches and prepared to launch. Her leg muscles tightened and bunched, and she gave a mighty push to the earth, her wide wings outspread. The fading sun glinted off her rich armour, but still the unrelieved black of her scales reflected no light. She spun upwards, writhing and whirling around the wind, and then headed northwest, back towards her ruined treasure cave.

Fryda watched the dragon wing her way towards the horizon. The beast had not spent all her anger, however, for she let fly streams of liquid fire as she flew over the farmsteads, and the survivors all looked on as the outlying homes, fields and livestock met the same fate as the men and women of Eceweall.

Twenty-nine

"**W**e have to kill it."

Fryda watched, numb, as Wiglaf turned to stare at King Beowulf. "And how do you propose we do that?" her brother demanded. "You saw how it destroyed our warriors. You saw the arrows and spears bounce off its scales. It's impervious."

Fryda sighed. Her father, despite all his flaws, would have been knee-deep in plans by now, not wringing his hands and whining that the task could not be done.

"Not entirely impervious," Theow said, glancing at Fryda. "You all saw what Fryda did."

Heat stained her cheeks. She had no idea what had possessed her, but in that moment, she'd known the dragon could not hurt her. She was invincible. Immortal. Unbeatable.

A bloody fool.

"Yes," Beowulf drawled. "Your bravery was inspiring, sweet girl, but please, have a care for my old heart. It nearly stopped when I saw you run right at the beast." Fryda saw his eyes flick to Wiglaf, who glowered back at him. "Aside from that, you may have a point, Wiglaf, which makes it all the more important we come up with some sort of plan."

The survivors of the dragon attack had all removed to one of the only buildings left standing, a large, sprawling structure of hard stone near the barracks, which had resisted the dragon's flame. Eceweall was a wasteland, a charred and blackened graveyard. The walls had finally been breached and its people conquered. Bryce's forge had fallen, all his beautiful creations either melted or scorched. The longhouse—the heart of the community—lay in splinters. Nearly all the warriors and shield maidens were dead; only a scant handful remained, huddled around the firepit tending their own and each other's wounds. Hild passed around mead from a cask that had escaped the dragon's fire in the single cup she managed to salvage from the wreckage of the kitchens. Fryda noticed that Bjorn stayed close to Hild's side, and she was glad they had both survived. This stone building would outlive them all. It had once been used as a strongroom to store treasure and coins and valuable objects, but in recent years it had fallen into disuse and now housed bits of broken armour, rusted weapons, and damaged furniture.

Beowulf turned ice-blue eyes on Wiglaf. His face was grave. This Beowulf was all sharp-minded warrior, protector of his people.

"Uncle Beowulf, in all your travels and battles, have you ever seen a dragon before?" Fryda asked, as Hild brought Beowulf a mug of mead and checked the arrow wound on his beefy arm. She *tsk*ed, gathered fresh bandages and medicines, and went to work.

"Can't say that I have," Beowulf answered, looking at her with affection. "Though I've heard about them in songs and stories, of course." He looked out on the blackened landscape. "I never in my life expected to see anything like this, though. A winged beast straight out of legend."

Wiglaf, however, seemed to take the dragon's attack as a personal insult. "That thing destroyed my stronghold," he said, his voice pitched much higher than usual. He looked around at the ragged remains of Eceweall's citizens and threw his hands in the air. "How are we supposed to defeat a dragon with a handful of farmers and servants? Most of the warriors are dead."

"Several of the *gedriht* have survived," Fryda said as Hild tied off the bandage. She did not mention that Wiglaf had hidden himself like a coward while she had actually managed to wound the creature.

"The dragon destroyed the forge and the armoury," Beowulf said, flexing his wounded arm, "but we have three legendary blades that should serve. My own sword, Nægling, given to me by King Hygelac." He drew the long, narrow sword from a scabbard at his waist and held it up. The blade glinted silver-grey in the shaft of late afternoon sunlight that streamed through the hole in the roof, and the hilt glittered with gold and gems. "It belonged to his father, Hrethel, and has never failed in battle."

He laid the sword on the table.

"Then we have Swicdóm." Beowulf gestured to Wiglaf, who unsheathed the sword and handed it to him. Fryda raised her eyebrows. She had not realized Wiglaf had taken to carrying their father's sword. "An aptly named sword. Betrayal. An ancient blade, said to have been forged for Woden himself, but the god gifted it to his favourite mortal and so it passed from father to son until your father killed Eanmund and took it for himself. Legend says it was named by Woden's *völva*, the seeress who predicted the creation and destruction of the world." He put Swicdóm on the table next to Nægling.

"And finally, there is Hrunting," Beowulf said. Fryda lifted the rune-kissed sword, grateful she had decided not to put it back in the forge, and gave it to the king. He raised it and traced the pattern of the blade with a thick, scarred finger. "I had never thought to see it again," he murmured, turning it to catch the light. "I returned this to Unferth after it failed me in my fight with the bog-witch. To think he'd kept it all these years."

Fryda was startled to see tears glisten in the king's eyes. He looked at her and for the first time she saw shame in his expression. "I wish I could tell him how sorry I am for my part in what happened. Had I known he would be exiled…"

Fryda squeezed his massive hand. "He did not blame you," she said. "I'm certain he only worried that you believed the stories of his evil intentions."

"And for that alone, I cannot forgive myself." Beowulf stood up straighter and Fryda let him go. "But we know the dragon can be hurt, thanks to our fierce shield maiden." He looked at her and smiled. "Believe me when I tell you we will have a talk about your impetuous nature one day soon. But if the arrows and spears could pierce its hide, perhaps with these swords we can kill it." He put Hrunting on the table beside the other two blades.

Fryda remembered that moment when she, bursting with strange magic, knew she could kill the dragon. The problem wasn't her strength or her resolve...she'd simply had too weak a weapon.

There was one problem with Beowulf's plan, however.

The four of them stared at the blades. Fryda took a deep breath. "Three swords," she said. "To kill a dragon."

"One for each of us." Beowulf's voice was laced with iron and purpose. "We must all prepare to face the beast together."

Fryda coughed.

Beowulf smiled at her and ruffled his hand in her hair. Pins sprang in every direction and her heavy curls fell down her back. Fryda sighed again. "Not this time," the king said. "This time you stay safely away from the fight."

"Have you forgot, Uncle?" she asked, her voice sweet. "I'm a shield maiden now. You proclaimed me so yourself. My place is in the fight with you."

Beowulf opened his mouth as if to protest, but snapped it shut again.

"Besides, I don't think there is such a place as 'safe' right now," Fryda continued. "In case it escaped your notice, the dragon can fly. Rather quickly."

"I don't think your poker can do much good against a

dragon," Theow said. He smiled, clearly trying to take the sting from his words.

"And you think with these you can?" Fryda gestured to the three swords. She suddenly found herself in the grip of an incandescent rage. She looked up at Theow and he blanched at whatever he saw in her face. "These are *swords*." Her voice rose. Across the room, Hild raised her head and looked at her with concern. "That is a dragon. A rutting *dragon*, Theow!" She was shouting now. "Do you have any idea how close you have to get to a *bloody dragon* to stick it with a sword? Do you think the dragon will let you get that close? That she won't see you coming? She can fly! All she has to do is sit on the wind and pick us off with her flame-breath one by one and we can never touch her."

She glared at Beowulf, who stared at her in alarm. "And you!" she cried, pointing at him. Beowulf eyed her finger as if it were an adder that might bite him. "You are *seventy-six years old*. I know you've been hearing stories about how marvellous and brave and strong you are for the past fifty years, and I've seen you fight, so I know you still have skill and stamina, but this is a *dragon*. All she has to do is breathe on you and you are dead. And you are not the young man you were when you fought Grendel and Grendel's mother."

She whirled and fixed her furious scowl on Wiglaf. The image of him standing over her while she was chained to the wall rose in her mind. "And you haven't held a sword since you were fifteen years old," she thundered. "For the last five years you've been wallowing in women and liquor and your own cruelty, trying to live up to Father's bad opinion of you and you think you can just pick up a sword and kill a *dragon*?"

"I have not..." Wiglaf began, but Fryda cut him off.

"I know what you did to Theow," she yelled at her twin. "I know how you had him tortured when we were children. You can never...*never*...convince me you are a good man again, but that doesn't mean I want to see you being *eaten by a bloody dragon*."

Beowulf blinked and looked back and forth between Wiglaf and Theow.

"What…?" he began, but Theow caught his eye and shook his head. Beowulf subsided, looking troubled.

Fryda refused to be distracted and scowled at all three of them. "You saw what that beast did. You saw her kill dozens of people with one breath, and they didn't even get close to her. She destroyed Eceweall in moments. You may as well go out there with stalks of wheat in your hands instead of swords. You'll end up dead either way. You need a better plan."

The men stared at her, silent. Her cheeks flushed and she pulled her sleeve over her bandaged hand.

Theow shuffled his feet. "Well," he said to Beowulf, looking abashed. "She's not wrong."

"I ripped Grendel's arm off without any weapons at all," she heard Beowulf mutter under his breath.

Wiglaf threw Fryda a resentful glance. "At least the dragon solved one of your problems," he sneered at her. "Your betrothal to Lord Ansten is null and void, now that he's most likely smouldering in a pile of bodies down on the green."

Fryda gaped at him. "You think I rejoice in any of this?" she whispered. "You think I celebrate his death because it makes things easier for me? By the gods, you do." She shook her head in disbelief. "Because that's how you would feel, isn't it? I knew you were selfish, Wiglaf, but I had no idea how much."

"So, let's hear your great plan then." Wiglaf crossed his arms over his chest.

Fryda closed her eyes and pictured the destruction of Eceweall —the dragon spitting fire, her graceful aerial acrobatics, people screaming, arrows flying, the buildings burning.

The buildings burning…

"What did she take from the longhouse?" she asked.

"The goblet," Beowulf said. "The second one, I mean. The one Theow brought."

"The one I stole," Theow corrected. "From the treasure pile." His face paled. "*Her* treasure pile, I'm guessing."

"Ah." Comprehension dawned on the king's face. "So that's what she came for."

Wiglaf rounded on Theow. "So, you are to blame for all of this," he snarled. "All these deaths. All this..."

Fryda opened her mouth to protest but Beowulf shot her a quelling look and put a heavy hand on Wiglaf's shoulder. "That's enough, lad," he said, and his voice was laced with iron. "It's not the boy's fault."

"I didn't know there was a dragon in that cave," Theow told the king, his voice steeped in regret.

"I know, my lad." Beowulf ruffled Theow's red hair. Fryda blinked. She had never seen the king give that gesture of affection to anyone but herself.

"She found something else first and tossed it away. The other goblet?" she asked, looking at Beowulf.

He nodded.

"So Theow's goblet was her target." Fryda stroked a finger over her chin. "And she didn't burn the longhouse like she did the other buildings. It caught on fire from burning debris. Why didn't she use her flame on that one, too?"

Beowulf looked blank. Wiglaf looked bored. Theow looked impressed.

"She didn't want to damage the goblet," he said.

"Exactly. She wanted that goblet." As soon as she said the words, she knew the truth of them. Somehow, the dragon and that goblet were connected. "We need to get it back. With it, we can lure her anywhere we want."

"Somewhere closed in." Theow clearly saw the direction of her thoughts and arrived there first. "Somewhere she cannot fly."

"If we can keep her on the ground, I think we can defeat

her." Fryda bit her lip. "The chasm might work. If we go further inland, the crack opens out into the rock quarry, which is wide and spacious enough for a fight, and there is a rock overhang that would prevent her from taking flight. She'd be too big to squeeze past it. We may be able to fight her there."

"And how do you propose we do all this?" Wiglaf asked, his lips set in a sneer. "How will we get the goblet away from her?"

"We need some bait." Theow's voice was steady. Fryda glared at him.

"No." Her injured hand throbbed as her pulse raced. "Absolutely not."

"I can draw her out," Theow said. "And, well…I'm the one who stole it."

"That makes no sense whatsoever."

"One of us has to distract her. It might as well be me."

Fryda growled in frustration. "She'll kill you outright!"

"Not if we're smart about it," Wiglaf said, his tone thoughtful.

Fryda rounded on him. "Oh, you would *love* a chance to throw Theow in front of a dragon, wouldn't you?" she snapped, and to her horror tears pressed against her eyelids.

"No, child," Beowulf said. He looked at each one of them. "Theow is right. And I have an idea how to kill the dragon and maybe keep all of us alive."

Fryda sighed. "All right. Let's hear it."

"In a moment. First, I have an announcement. I was going to wait, but I'd better say this before another dragon attacks us." He raised his voice so everyone in the stone building could hear him. "Survivors of Eceweall…hear me!" Heads rose and chatter dwindled off. "Your losses have been grievous. You have lost your lord, your blacksmith, and now your *burh*. You watched your warriors and shield maidens fall beneath the dragon's breath, and yet we are still here."

He looked at each of them, and the men and women straightened under his gaze, finding their pride beneath their sorrow and exhaustion. "But I shall help you rebuild. We will find a way to defeat this scourge, and you will once again have peace in your home. In the meantime, I want to assure you that even if I should perish in dragon-fire, the kingdom will remain in good hands.

"As you know, I have sired no son. I have not known the joy of having a daughter of my own." Fryda smiled as he glanced at her with affection. "However, this does not mean I've given no thought to naming my heir. After all, I've travelled well past my youth and I have a responsibility to see the nation is in good hands."

Fryda saw Wiglaf tense and go still.

"Therefore," the king proclaimed, "I say to you now, and I charge you all as witnesses, that I have chosen my heir."

Fryda could swear Wiglaf wasn't even breathing.

"When I am gone, I hope many, many years from now, Geatland will need a strong leader. A strong warrior. Someone who runs towards a dragon when all others run away." Fryda heard his words, but at first she did not understand them. Then his meaning hit her.

"I name as my heir Fryda of Clan Waegmunding. After my death, she will be queen."

After one stunned moment of silence, the room erupted in cheers and shouts of joy and approbation. Fryda stared as King Beowulf beamed at her, pleased by the effect of his announcement. Her stomach plunged and her extremities went cold.

Queen. She would be queen.

She looked at Theow, instinctively seeking his calming presence. He looked stunned, and then, as his eyes caught hers, his entire face lit up with joy. His broad grin did much to thaw the icy fear that gripped her, and she remembered she would not have to stand in the longhouse alone. They looked at each other for a long moment, and Fryda felt a different sort of power flow through her body—this was not the invasive battle-strength that gripped and shook her like a furious fever, but rather it warmed and lifted her from the inside out.

But that warmth turned to frost and her lightness became iron that weighed her down and brought her crashing to the earth when she saw her brother's face. Malignant fury twisted his features into something monstrous, and for a moment he resembled a bestial creature warped into the shape of a man. His eyes spoke of hatred, and murder, and the feral forgetting of a brother's love.

Fryda shivered, as if reading her own fate in Wiglaf's venomous look, and she knew she would never feel safe or easy with her twin again. He had already imprisoned her and chained her to a wall simply for defying his will and daring to love a slave.

What might he do if forced to acknowledge her as his queen?

She turned away. She would worry about that later. Right now, they had larger problems to deal with, and if she was to become queen, she would start by doing whatever she could to keep her people safe.

The dragon had to die.

Thirty

Beowulf looked at Theow questioningly as he ground to a halt. They had come about halfway down the shore towards the cave, and despite his wound and his weakness, Beowulf's body awakened as his nerves began to dance in anticipation of a mighty fight.

It had been too long since he pitted himself against a mythic creature.

"I've changed my mind," Theow said. "This is a terrible idea."

Beowulf grinned at him. "Isn't it, though? Most fun I've had in years."

Theow stared at him, and Beowulf suddenly remembered their circumstances. "Well," he amended. "Except for all the deaths. That part is most regrettable."

"This plan is insane," Theow said.

"I know. But that's why it will work."

"That makes no sense whatsoever."

Beowulf fairly vibrated with anticipation. "I know. I just said it to make you feel better."

Theow stared at him for a moment, and then began walking again. "I sure hope you live up to all the stories," he muttered.

Beowulf didn't respond as he fell into step beside the boy. Of course he didn't live up to the stories. That was the whole point of stories. They took the mundane and ordinary and transformed them into legend.

But then, sometimes legend took everyone by surprise by flying and breathing fire and being terrifyingly real.

He surreptitiously flexed his bandaged arm. The wound troubled him little, but he could not stop thinking about that moment after the dragon attack when his battle-power seemed to desert him. He remembered, too, the image of Fryda pelting across the *burh* to hurl a spear into the dragon's side, as if she'd siphoned off his strength and used it herself.

Beowulf thought of his battle with Grendel so many years ago…how strong he'd felt when he tore the creature's arm clean off his body with his bare hands. He wondered what would happen if he faced Grendel today. A cold wind swept through him. A premonition of his own death, perhaps.

Well. His mortality had to catch up to him some day. There were worse ways to go than in glorious battle with a legendary dragon.

He shook his melancholy thoughts away and concentrated on their plan. After the four of them had spent several hours strategizing, Beowulf and Theow climbed back down the cliff stairs and made their way towards the treasure cave—the most likely location of the dragon's lair. Wiglaf, who remained up on the headland, travelled with Fryda and the other warriors to the quarry. If Beowulf and Theow could lure the dragon into the quarry, they had a good chance of victory this day.

They walked for a while in silence, until Beowulf could contain his curiosity no longer.

"So," he said to Theow. "What's all this about Lord Ansten?"

Theow clenched his fists. "I think it's time I told you the whole story," he said. "Everything that has happened. You need to know what Wiglaf has done."

And so he proceeded to tell Beowulf about the assault in Fryda's room the night of the first feast, and how Wiglaf had insisted he take the credit for the kills. He talked about the conversation

Fryda overheard in Eadgils' rooms and the events leading up to the Swedish king's betrayal. He related the circumstances of his exile, how Wiglaf imprisoned Fryda and how she had broken the bones in her own hand to escape captivity and a forced marriage to Ansten. He even told Beowulf what Wiglaf had done to him when they were children, about the white scars on his back from a whipping he had never earned. Through it all, Beowulf stayed silent, listening, while rage gathered in his belly, white-hot, like lightning.

When Theow finished, he glanced at Beowulf and blanched at what he saw in his face.

"Do you think Wiglaf will be a danger to Fryda," Beowulf asked, his voice soft but backed with iron, "now that I have announced she is my heir?"

He heard Theow inhale sharply. "This does worry me, yes."

Beowulf spared a moment to be grateful that Theow, not Wiglaf, walked beside him at this moment, for if the new lord of Eceweall were within his reach, he would have wrung him by his neck until his spine snapped. He took some deep breaths and tried to calm the violent anger that gripped him.

"I'm sorry, lad," he said at last. "That is a great deal for two people to suffer. I will make certain that Fryda is protected." He slid his eyes to Theow without turning his head. "As, I suspect, will you."

"My lord," Theow ventured after a brief, awkward silence. "Why did Weohstan warn you against making Wiglaf your heir?"

Beowulf rubbed his face and grimaced. "It was foolish of me to even hint that I had considered it," he said, "but I was flush with drink and feeling regretful I never sired a child of my own. I should have known even then that Fryda was the better choice."

They walked a few paces on and Beowulf tried to marshal his thoughts.

"Weohstan made many enemies during his lifetime," he said

after a while. "His decision to support Onela against the Geats created a rift between Weohstan and the other clans that could not be mended. The only reason no one has attacked Weohstan before now, before Eadgils, is because they did not wish to incur my wrath. Weohstan was my kin, and such an act would have started an endless blood-feud against me that they could not win."

Theow thought about that for a moment. "But Eadgils…" he began.

"Eadgils was an old man," Beowulf interrupted. "I don't think he had any expectation of surviving that battle. He knew he had nothing to lose, so he took his chances."

"I see."

"Do you?" Beowulf studied him.

"I think so," Theow said. "If you die, and Wiglaf becomes king, there is nothing to stop the clans from declaring war on the Waegmundings and then going to war with each other to take over the throne. It would destroy the nation."

"That's exactly right." Beowulf nodded with approval.

"But how will that be any different with Fryda as queen of Geatland?"

"Fryda actually has a chance to unite the nations, which is something Wiglaf could never do. They perceive Wiglaf as weak. A drunken womanizer. But as soon as they hear Fryda ran towards a dragon and managed to wound it…? They will recognize my own power in her and respect her."

Theow nodded and looked relieved. The more time Beowulf spent with his thane-for-a-day, the more he approved of him. Fryda had chosen well for herself. They were silent for a moment, and then Beowulf added, "And I think Wiglaf's father was not so deceived as to his son's character as I have been. Wiglaf seems to have a streak of cruelty in him that he lets slip the leash far too often."

They continued to walk, and as they neared the cave, Theow

kept reaching up and rubbing the scar that trailed from his right eye to the patch of hairless scalp over his ear. Beowulf cast about for a subject to ease his anxiety. His mind caught on a memory and he grinned.

"That ring on Fryda's finger," Beowulf said. "Is it the one I gave you?"

Theow shot him a wary look and seemed surprised to see him smiling. "Yes." Theow looked away. "Do you disapprove, my lord?"

"Disapprove?" Beowulf frowned at him. "Why would I disapprove? You are a free man, and a rich one at that. I believe you love that woman beyond reason and would protect her with your life. I can't think of anyone I would rather give her to." He snorted with derision. "Certainly not Lord Ansten, all bland milk and sour mead!"

Theow blinked. "I'm…free?" Beowulf regarded him and was relieved to see a smile spring to the boy's face. "I'm free," he whispered.

"You are free," Beowulf agreed, smiling back at him.

"But I have spent my life as a slave," Theow said. His voice was tight, as if it was difficult to push the words past his throat. "And now Fryda shall be queen. Surely you think she deserves a better man."

Beowulf shot him a level look. "And you think birth determines the goodness of a man?" he asked. "Do you believe Wiglaf is a better man than you?"

Theow remained silent.

"Mmm. I thought so." Beowulf stroked his beard. "Birth does not make the measure of a man, and I never thought it did. My own father was a nobody who rose in King Hrethel's estimation and eventually married his daughter. If we survive this day, I plan to make you my thane in earnest. No," he held up a hand to forestall Theow's objection, "it is no pity offering I make you. You've earned it, and I would like to see my kin well taken care of. I have a deep fondness for Fryda and would be happy to see her settle down in a *burh* of her own, and I can provide that for you both. Oh." Beowulf ground to a halt as they rounded the curve of the cliff and came in sight of the cave.

Or, what used to be the cave.

Where once the cave had burrowed into the cliff, a massive crater now dominated the landscape. Rocks and rubble littered the beach and a carpet of melted gold and silver spread out from what used to be the enormous pile of wealth. The dragon had clearly let fly her flame over her precious treasure, which had turned to liquid and flowed from the crater like a golden river. It had then hardened, and upon this priceless blanket the dragon slept.

Beowulf gripped Theow's arm and pointed. "There's the beast."

She was no less intimidating for being asleep. She curled around herself, like a dog lying in front of a fire, her tail wrapped around her thick body. Her ink-black scales still reflected no light, and she radiated a chilling malevolence.

As they drew closer, now creeping low to the ground, he noticed that within the curve of her body, protected by her spiky tail, lay the magic goblet.

"She's taking no chances with that, I see," Beowulf murmured.

"Can we get to the quarry from here?" Theow whispered. His face had gone very pale.

"Yes, look." Beowulf pointed to the back side of the crater. "You can see an opening to the chasm behind her. We run down there, and it should lead us straight to the quarry. Sit yourself down, lad. We now wait for Wiglaf's signal."

Theow sat behind a large boulder, out of sight of the dragon, shifting his long sword out of the way.

"Have you ever used a sword before?" Beowulf asked. *Perhaps*, a small voice niggled inside his head, *you should have asked him that before you suggested he face a dragon with it.*

Theow shrugged. "Practice swords, yes. Nothing like this, though. It feels a bit awkward." He tugged at Hrunting, moving it away from his waist. "It drags at me, makes me feel off balance. It's constantly reminding me of its presence, like a piece of clothing that doesn't fit."

"You'll grow into it, lad," Beowulf said. He hoped the boy would have the chance, at least.

As if reading his thoughts, Theow said, "Let's hope I live that long."

They waited until the tide began to crawl back up the shore. Then, from above, came the single blast of a horn.

Beowulf and Theow leapt to their feet. Beowulf's eyes darted to the dragon, but she did not rouse at the noise.

"They've arrived at the quarry," Beowulf said. He felt the flex of his courage and the rush of his blood as he quivered in anticipation of a mighty battle. Theow, on the other hand, paled and looked slightly sick.

He had to admit, however, the boy had valour. Beowulf grinned as Theow squared his shoulders, took a deep breath, and stepped forward to meet his fate.

★ ★ ★

Wiglaf dropped the horn from his lips as the wind caught its forlorn cry and swept it out to sea. He chewed his lip, staring at the gaping corridor that led from the beach to the quarry. He almost wished the passage had been blocked off. It would have been so easy to blow the horn and lead that *sott* of a slave into a dead end with an angry dragon blocking his only exit.

Of course, the king would be with him, but after what Beowulf did this afternoon...

Wiglaf felt the familiar fury boil in his belly. The king had out-manoeuvred him once more. By naming Fryda his heir...his *heir!*...Beowulf had forced Wiglaf to give up any plans to marry her off to a foreign lord or king. That meant she would stay in

Eceweall, in a position of extreme power and authority, where she would be a constant threat to Wiglaf's safety and freedom. He knew she suspected him of…his mind shied away from the memory of his many misdeeds…of *certain things*, and so he would never be safe while she remained in Geatland.

…*Alive*, the insidious voice within him whispered.

He twitched the thought away as he would a fly and glanced at the warriors who stood beside him, awaiting his orders. He felt a twinge of guilt, as if they could read his thoughts, and his eyes sought out the small but sturdy woman clutching a poker with a wild puff of butter-blonde hair bunching out from under her helmet. Fryda stood beside the servant girl Hild and regarded him without expression, as if trying to divine his intentions.

Wiglaf whirled away and moved to the hoist mechanism built into the lip of the chasm wall. The large platform was already down at the bottom of the quarry and the winch and pulley seemed in good repair. It would be faster for the warriors to slide down the rope than to ferry them up and down the wall on the platform. However, as much as he tried to concentrate on the situation, he could not tamp down his feelings of betrayal at the king's words that day.

Had Beowulf not made him lord of the *burh*? he thought angrily. And was not the lord the most exalted status beneath the king? Certainly higher than a mere shield maiden, anyway. How could Beowulf have insulted him by choosing Fryda, *of all people*, as his heir? A crippled girl given a trophy position out of pity! Wiglaf flinched, pained at the direction of his thoughts, but he could find no lie in them. Fryda hadn't even hurt the dragon, for all she ran at it, he argued bitterly to himself as he tugged on the rope to test its soundness. A knot of rage, like a smouldering ember, flared in his chest and made it difficult to breathe. He had not been the only one who had fled the dragon's wrath, but had it really been necessary for Beowulf to point out the difference so starkly between his behaviour and that of his sister?

Wiglaf glanced down into the quarry. It was a broad, expansive space, closed within the rock walls—more than enough space to fight the dragon. His breath caught at the thought. Any number of things could go wrong down there, he thought. One blast of fire, one unescaped claw or tooth or sweep of the tail, could erase all his problems without any sibling blood on his own hands.

He glanced at Fryda again. She and Hild were laughing at something...the type of nervous laughter fuelled by anticipation and battle-fear. His thoughts slid away from the viper stings dripping poison into his mind and he raised his hand, commanding the attention of all who waited his instructions.

"Warriors!" he called out, his voice fighting the wind and the sound of the crashing surf. The company shifted, like horses awaiting the command to run. "For today you are warriors, whatever your customary position or station. Make yourselves ready, for this will be the fight of our lives. The fight of legends!" He took a deep breath, his words steadying him with their promise of fame and fortune. "Our names will be spoken alongside the greatest heroes of the ages—Widsith and Weland, Breca and Hygelac. And especially our own beloved king, Beowulf. If your death finds you today in glorious battle, know you'll live on in our memories, and we'll meet with you again in the revered mead-hall of the gods. If we prevail, those who survive will be enshrined in the halls of heroes for all eternity. So raise your swords, ready your fire-tipped spears and your lindenwood shields and prepare to fight for your king and country!"

A rousing cheer rose from the meagre company and Wiglaf felt a flush of pride at the bravery of his people. The sound rained down like gold and covered his dark thoughts until he nearly convinced himself he had never thought them at all.

★ ★ ★

The dragon would not wake.

Theow stood nearby, hands on his hips, wondering what to do next. He had shouted, jumped up and down, and waved his arms in the air, but she had not moved. At this point, he thought he could just clamber over the coils of her tail and snatch the goblet right off her body, but that would still leave the problem of the dragon herself. They needed to lure her into the crevice, but she blocked the way. They could not let her live, knowing she would rain death and destruction down upon some other hapless village. Theow was at a loss.

He cast about, looking for something he could throw. The wind shifted and carried the scent of rich earth, warm stone, sun-kissed grasses, and a hint of rotten leaves and cinnamon from the dragon's lair. He kicked at a gold-clad rock until it broke away from the lake of metal that had turned the beach into a glimmering pool of melted treasure. He leaned down and hefted it in his hand.

Theow moved a few steps closer, edging his way along the slippery golden curtain. He drew his arm back, gathered his strength, and heaved it as hard as he could right for her head.

It struck her on the end of her nose. For a moment, nothing happened. And then…

…her eyes opened.

Theow cursed and turned to flee. His feet slid out from under him and for a moment he flailed impotently on the slippery surface in his desperation. As the fire-dragon unfurled, he scrabbled forward on hands and feet and finally righted himself —and then he ran like he had never run before.

He could hear her behind him, heaving her enormous bulk upright. Theow sprinted down the beach, yelling curses and screaming to Beowulf to hurry and finish his part of this insane plan. The hair on his neck prickled as he heard movement behind him, and he did not dare look back.

Whump. Whump.

She had taken to the sky. Theow swore again. Then the dragon screamed, and he thought about nothing at all. He ran on pure instinct.

A deep shout behind Theow brought him back to himself, and he swerved in a broad semicircle to run back the way he had come. Fýrdraca wheeled overhead, watching. Beowulf stood in the centre of the dragon's nest and held the golden goblet aloft. He shouted again and this time the dragon saw. She looked at the goblet in his hands and abruptly coiled her body, as if wracked with a deep spasm of pain.

Then she shot towards the courageous king.

Their roles reversed, Theow now chased the wind-walker as she folded back her wings and dived straight for Beowulf. The king turned and ran towards the back of the basin, heading for the wide chasm that cracked through the headland like a wound. Theow hoped the dragon would not risk fire around her precious goblet. Beowulf would burn, but the goblet would melt with him.

Theow held his breath as Beowulf scrambled over piles of rock and the slippery hills of gold coins and riches that had escaped the dragon's fire. He launched himself over the far side of what had been her cave and landed within reach of the channel that split the land. Beowulf slid down the final wall of treasure and snatched a large, ancient metal shield from the pile as he passed it. Fýrdraca unleashed herself, swaddled in gold and silver armour, and she came gliding and flexing towards her fate.

As Theow dashed over the carpet of gold and into the dragon's lair, he wondered why she did not bathe them in deadly fire. Perhaps, he thought, she had used it all up when she incinerated Eċeweall. Did dragon-fire need fuel? He hurtled after her, hoping Fryda and the others were in position at the quarry and Beowulf would make it to the chasm before the dragon caught him.

He did, but it was a near thing. With the goblet tucked under one arm and the shield looped over the other, the king ran over the rough ground into the wide gap, the two tall walls on either side of him rising up like tidal waves threatening to crash down upon him.

Thirty-one

Fýrdraca *watches as the mortal hero disappears into the rock. He has the heart; carries the Lone Survivor's curse. She is bone-tired but she must follow, must bury the curse in deep sleep until the world's end.*

She shrieks and the ground shakes, but the walls stand firm. She longs for the freedom of true release from this curse that keeps her beating heart chained to a life of pain and loneliness.

Fýrdraca spreads her wings and tucks her back legs up to her belly, braking hard in the air before she collides with the rock. The curse runs before her—she can see its light like a small sun.

She must follow. She must take up the challenge.

★ ★ ★

Fryda looked nervously at the rope contraption, staying far back from the lip of the quarry wall. Her heart pounded and she felt little beads of sweat on her forehead and upper lip. She would have to slide all the way down that rope into the chasm. She looked down at her twisted hand and felt her stomach clench.

What if she fell again?

No, she thought. She looked at the set of stairs that were carved into the quarry wall. The ropes were much quicker, but the stairs would be safer.

She looked up and caught Wiglaf's eye. His expression made her freeze, as a deer might use stillness to escape a hunter's notice. His eyes glittered, as if touched by fever, and his mouth had an ugly twist. In that moment, she did not recognize him, or the emotions that leaked through his customary control. Her hand throbbed as she thought of how he had chained her to the wall and, looking at him now, she wondered what else he might be capable of.

Wiglaf suddenly whirled away and began fussing with the rope. Theow and Beowulf would arrive at the quarry soon, she knew, and she would have to jump down and join them. To fight a dragon.

Fryda glanced again at her brother and hoped the dragon was all she would have to fight.

A low throb beat through her body, echoing the painful pulse in her hand. She had felt it since arriving at the quarry. It strengthened and grew, and she felt again the quicksilver sharpening of her mind and the iron-bound vigour of her blood.

"My lady?"

Hild's voice at her side startled her and she jumped. Hild gave her a sympathetic smile.

"The waiting is almost worse than the actual battle," her friend said.

Fryda laughed, her tone a little higher pitched than usual. "It is. I feel like I'm going to burst if I don't hit something soon."

Hild regarded her with serious, dark eyes. "Is it happening again? The feeling you told me about?"

Fryda nodded. "It was faint at first, but it's getting stronger and stronger. Almost as if..." She glanced towards the sea where a dragon was presumably making its way towards them at that very moment. "...As if reacting to some threat that draws near."

And yet...Fryda's eyes wandered back to her brother. She could not shake the suspicion that the stronghold faced a far greater peril, and that within its broken walls a malevolence lurked that, left unchecked, would eat them all alive.

The tension within her built, pressing against her insides, testing her fear, her courage, her resolve. If she could figure out how to channel it—control it—she thought she could tear any danger limb from limb to keep her people safe.

"Warriors!" Wiglaf's ringing tones turned her attention back to the situation at hand. As her brother embarked on a rousing speech, filled with words of encouragement and bravery, Fryda thought of Theow. He was not a warrior, yet he threw himself into battle for her, for the clan. She took a deep breath. She was a shield maiden. It was time she began to act like it.

Wiglaf finished his speech and the survivors of Eceweall cheered and clapped resoundingly. He basked in the noise for several minutes, his pleased smile erasing the dangerous, calculating look from his face until he simply looked once more like her familiar twin brother.

Finally, Wiglaf lifted his hands and raised his voice over the din. "Remember the plan," he called as the warriors went quiet. "I go down first and see what's going on. When we need you, I'll signal you by tugging three times on the rope. If the situation is hopeless, however…" His eyes swept over the ragged company. "Then you stay up here and do whatever you can to survive. I have no doubt we will triumph this day." His eyes found Fryda's, but she looked away. Wiglaf paused, and then grasped the rope and swung himself into the chasm.

The amateur warriors ran to the edge of the cliff and peered over, watching him descend into the quarry. Fryda alone stayed well back, but it suddenly occurred to her that leaving Theow alone with her brother in an enclosed space while King Beowulf battled a dragon was probably not the best plan. She caught Hild's eye and cocked her head, beckoning her over.

It was time to make some plans of her own.

★ ★ ★

To Theow's relief, the dragon had to land and go after the king on foot, just as they had planned.

The beast was so large she had to fold her wings across her

back to get through the wide passageway, and in places her flanks scraped against the rough rock sides. She lumbered on her two hind legs, awkward and graceless, which gave Beowulf the advantage of speed and agility. It did not take Theow long to catch up with the dragon. She let fly another scream, and the closeness of the walls amplified the sound. Theow winced, clutched his ears, and waited for the pounding in his head to subside.

Maddened by rage, the dragon roared forward.

Beowulf pulled further and further ahead of the dragon until nothing remained of his footsteps except the faint echoes wafting back to Theow's ringing ears. The dragon waddled forward and Theow matched her pace, keeping a safe distance behind her. The ground here became level and grey, layered and striated like slate, but as they moved further inland, he had to skirt more cracks, rocks, and fallen boulders. Soon, the passageway widened and Theow emerged into a large clearing, like a hollow bubble in the earth. The rock walls bowled out and then came back close together at the top, creating a partial canopy above their heads that would prevent the dragon from taking flight. The walls bore the marks of hundreds of cuts where the labourers from Eceweall had carved stone from the earth, and Theow recognized a much larger, sturdier rope-and-pulley contraption for lifting men and stone in and out of the quarry. The large wooden platform rested at the bottom near some boulders and abandoned tools—axes and buckets—littered the ground.

A series of long, thick ropes woven of linden *bæst* dangled from the pulley above and were fastened to the platform below. Wiglaf was about halfway down the *bæst*, already on his way to join them. Theow thought of Fryda and her wounded hand, thought of her having to lower herself into the quarry, and a stab of fear more potent than even the dragon evoked made him tremble.

Beowulf stood at the far end of the quarry. He had tossed

the goblet behind him and now awaited the dragon, ready with Nægling and shield in hand. The dragon raised her head, bowing her long neck, and issued a heart-rending shriek. Theow winced as the echoes bounced around the quarry, and unsheathed Hrunting as the dragon tried to follow her cry up through the crevice ceiling.

She could not fully extend her wings in the enclosed space. Wiglaf landed near Theow just as the tip of a wing caught the rope and tore it from his hand. Wiglaf swore and let go, but not before the rope had peeled the skin from his palm. The platform spun away and shattered against the rock wall.

"Wiglaf!" Theow cried as the dragon flew towards the opening above them.

"I'm fine," Wiglaf called back. He tore a strip from his shirt with his teeth and wrapped it around his hand. Theow noticed Wiglaf's skin was covered in a sheen of sweat, and only then did he realize how warm the quarry had become. The dragon's body heated the air, like a forge stoked with peat and charcoal.

The beast limped upward on cramped wings and hit a ceiling of rock with only half her strength. She had broken through dirt and loose rocks to escape her earthly prison, but here she was trapped by ten feet of solid stone. She screeched as the earth refused to yield and she collapsed back to the ground.

The dragon landed directly in front of King Beowulf. She shook herself and inspected the king with eyes full of black fire. Beowulf stood resolute and brave before her, and the dragon lowered her head as if to sniff him. *Or eat him*, Theow thought with a wisp of panic. Beowulf held fast as she brought her head level with his body, and she peered at him, as if attempting to define such a puzzling creature, while pure white smoke leaked from her mouth and nostrils. Then, with a roar, the mighty king raised Nægling high and brought it down on the dragon's head, throwing his whole strength behind the sword-stroke.

And Nægling snapped.

Theow blinked. He did not know if the dragon's hide was too tough or if the weapon could not withstand Beowulf's strength, but the blade shattered into a dozen pieces. Fýrdraca bellowed again and shook her head, but Nægling had not even broken through the matt-black scales layering her head and face.

Beowulf staggered, thrown off balance by the force of the blow. "Aim for the more vulnerable spots," he called as he tossed away the glittering, useless hilt and regained his feet. "Joints, belly, wings."

"Right," Theow muttered. He gripped Hrunting with both hands as the beast advanced on the king. The temperature in the wide, open space became nearly suffocating as the heat from the dragon shimmered like an evil miasma around her. Theow let out a hoarse cry. The dragon turned to look at him, and he charged forward, blade raised.

She twitched, flicked one wing, and Theow went flying.

He crashed against a boulder and grunted as he hit the ground. The smell of hot rock, dust, and the hint of rotting leaves and cinnamon assailed his nose. He looked up and saw Wiglaf facing the king, Swicdóm in his uninjured hand.

Theow groaned and tested his limbs, checking for broken bones. He had bruises and perhaps a few torn muscles, but his body remained sound. He staggered to his feet. Beowulf, now unarmed, held his purloined shield in front of him as the dragon turned her head back to him.

Where were Fryda and the warriors? They weren't going to last long against this beast without help.

"Toss me the sword," Beowulf roared at Wiglaf. The dragon lunged forward, snapping with her great jaws and the king sprang out of the way. "Hurry, lad!"

Wiglaf stood still and clutched Swicdóm to his chest, favouring his wounded hand. His face became twisted and ugly as he bared his teeth and snarled at the king. "Go on, then, Beowulf," he shouted. A bilious fluid dripped from the dragon's mouth, sliding down her enormous fangs and dropping onto the rock, where it sent up thin wisps of smoke. "Do everything the legends say you did when you were young. Fight the beast without sword or armour. Tear its limb from its bone-lappings and hang it from the ceiling of the mead-hall. Cut off its head and put it on a pike. Save us all with your heroic deeds."

Theow gaped at the naked hatred in Wiglaf's voice while the dragon opened her mouth and pawed at the ground. The temperature rose even higher.

"Wiglaf..." Beowulf's voice betrayed his disbelief, and a touch of desperation. He stood between the dragon and the goblet and she flicked her wing once more, trying to brush the king out of the way. But Beowulf was quicker and his reflexes more practised than Theow's and he managed to evade the attack. Sweat trickled down Theow's face and his shirt was plastered to his chest. Despite everything he had heard that day, Theow could not believe Wiglaf would betray the king so thoroughly. The heat continued to mount as the dragon's breath turned silver in the dusty air.

★ ★ ★

Beowulf, still holding up the silver shield, stared at Wiglaf. The young man, Swicdóm clutched in his bloody hand, stood across the quarry and glared at him with eyes full of anger and hatred. Beowulf could practically see wrath lashing through him like tongues of flame flickering in his eyes with feral fire.

"Wiglaf..." he said, and then stilled as his voice drew the attention of the dragon. The monstrous beast—blacker than the night sky, than Unferth's fate, than Grendel's heart—seethed and rippled under her lightless scales as she lunged and snapped at him with her poison-slick fangs. Beowulf lifted the shield and ducked out of the way, the shock of Wiglaf's traitorous words thawing in the dragon's oppressive heat.

Movement across the quarry momentarily distracted him,

and Beowulf saw Theow clutch his shoulder and shake off the brutal blow the beast had dealt him. He felt a rush of relief to see the boy still lived. He did not wish to tell Fryda that a dragon killed her lover because her brother betrayed them and her king had become a blithering *sott*.

Beowulf had not understood the magnitude of the danger he had put them in, even after seeing the dragon destroy Eċeweall. It was not until he stood before Fýrdraca that he realized how foolish he'd been to think he could grapple the beast by himself, as he had with Grendel and his monstrous mother. His pride had blinded him to the truth. He looked back at Wiglaf.

In more ways than one, apparently.

The dragon raised her head and gave a long, guttural screech. The sound scraped against Beowulf's ears, causing him to wince, and she struck with the quickness of a snake. She flicked her wing towards him, as if to swat him away from her goblet, but his aged bones answered the call of his youthful strength once more and he dodged out of the way.

Without Nægling he was helpless, and Wiglaf still stood, holding hostage the sword that might save them.

A wild noise spawned from above, and Beowulf saw Theow jerk his head upwards. The sound distracted even the dragon, and Beowulf breathed with relief, but he refused to look away from Wiglaf's hateful gaze. They stared each other down, as if each waited for the other to act. Beowulf saw Theow run towards the quarry wall and disappear from view behind a cluster of large boulders.

Beowulf was suddenly overwhelmed with the sense that he had been here before, standing in front of a monster bent on his destruction. Wiglaf had the same hopeless hatred he'd seen in Grendel's eyes just before he tore the creature's arm from the trunk of his grotesque body. Beowulf nearly forgot the dragon hulking over him, ashen-grey smoke trickling from between her huge, curved fangs. With her attention focused on whatever caused the howling and shrieking noises from the top of the quarry, the dragon seemed the lesser danger.

Wiglaf finally broke eye contact and turned the full force of his attention back on Beowulf.

For the first time in his long, battle-hardened life, Beowulf felt a quiver of fear that threatened to turn his bowels to water. A premonition shivered through him and he inhaled deeply, as if he could anchor his life into his body with just his breath.

Wiglaf adjusted his grip on the sword and started towards Beowulf. He held his hands up in a conciliatory manner and waggled the sword back and forth.

"Is this what you want, king?" Wiglaf asked, his voice mocking. The dragon shifted, as if agitated by Wiglaf's approach. Wiglaf's expression was mild, but Beowulf was not deceived. He spun around, searching for something that might help him, but he saw only the shield already in his hand and the gold and silver goblet lying on the ground behind him.

Beowulf took another breath and turned to face the fate that came to him, be it glorious victory in battle or a final dance with the death that had stalked him for so long.

★ ★ ★

For a moment it seems the Lone Survivor stands once more before Fýrdraca, his heart a wasteland of anger and pain, his soul riddled with the same injured pride at what has been taken from him. He holds a legendary sword in one fist and pulls out a stolen dagger inscribed with another man's name with the other.

The Lone Survivor approaches.

Fýrdraca sees Betrayal.

And then she sees the betrayal.

Thirty-two

Fryda watched as Eċeweall's remaining warriors, clad in leather and mail, leapt into the chasm. One by one they grasped the rope and slid down until nine in all dropped into the earthen hollow. They bristled with swords and spears and short knives, bows and arrows and all the instruments of death. As they each neared the bottom they sprang from the rope towards the dragon. They moved like lightning, howling and filling the air with their battle-cries, until Fryda alone remained atop the promontory.

She looked at the shallow stairs etched into the quarry wall. It would take her far too long to make her way down the winding steps, and there would be no rope to help her if she slipped and fell.

And by then, Theow could be dead.

She stowed her iron poker in her belt, took a deep, shaking breath and gripped the thick *bæst* with her good hand. She hooked her other arm around the rope and briefly closed her eyes, tamping down the panic that buzzed under her skin. She would not fall, she told herself firmly. She opened her eyes and looked down. The warriors had swarmed the beast and targeted her wings, slashing at the gossamer sails and rending them from her bones. The dragon screamed as deep, purplish blood welled from her wounds and splashed against stone.

Fryda winced, feeling the dragon's agony as her own. With a muttered invocation to the gods, she jumped from the edge of the cliff and slid down the rope into the quarry.

She made it to the ground without mishap and pulled the fireiron from her belt. The dragon, confused and overwhelmed by the sudden onslaught from above, spun about and her tail crashed through boulders, reducing them to broken rubble. The echoes of war-cries, breaking rock, and the mayhem of battle rang through the quarry and made Fryda feel disoriented in the rising heat. Ash-grey smoke dribbled from the dragon's nose, and she knew that the instant it turned black they would all be dead.

Fryda bit back a shout of relief as she saw Theow running towards her. His fire-red hair was mussed, there was blood on his shirt and face, but he looked otherwise unharmed.

"Theow," she said as he skittered to a halt by her side. In her unbandaged hand she clutched the long, iron poker, and Theow's mouth twitched as he looked at her.

Fryda cocked her head at him. "You have blood on your face."

"That happens when you fight a dragon," he said, and she heard some of his frustration bubble out with the words. "Fryda, where have you been? Why didn't you arrive with Wiglaf?"

"He was supposed to signal us when wanted us to come down, but he never did. So, we just came down anyway." She looked at the warriors as they battled the dragon and grinned at him. "I see you've made some progress on your own, but it looks like we got here just in time." She ran her eyes over him, cataloguing every scrape, cut, and bruise. "I'm so happy that you're still alive, though you look a little banged up."

Theow grabbed her and clutched her tightly. She let out a startled squeak.

"If we make it through this and you become queen," he muttered into her neck, "I'm going to expect you to outlaw all dragons from Geatland."

She laughed against his hair. "And you, my king" she whispered, "can make certain my laws are enforced."

Theow released Fryda and she wiped the sweat from her eyes. The air in the quarry felt like the hearth in Bryce's forge. The dragon released another ear-shattering screech and the warriors paused, stunned and disoriented by the sound. The smoke leaking through her curved, pointed teeth turned dark grey and her chest began to expand, fuelling the fire within. The warriors, already suffering in the oppressive heat, redoubled their attacks. Fryda saw Hild manage to wedge her sword under the joint of the dragon's wing and slice it open. The strange, amaranthine blood obscured the gold running through her scales, and her anguished cry tugged at Fryda's heart. But the smoke kept coming and she knew she could not get everyone out of the quarry fast enough to save them. And Theow...

She thought of Theow's dreams of flaming embers, of his old burn scar, and his face white with panic from a bit of burned bread.

No. Determination stiffened her spine.

Theow would not die in fire.

A throng of warriors clambered onto the dragon's back and began to hack at her scales with their weapons. Hild grasped one torn and flapping piece of wing, but immediately snatched her hand back. "Don't touch her with your bare skin!" she called out to the others. "She'll burn you...we have to finish her before she goes off!"

The dragon leaned forward and attempted to shake the warriors off, and as she raised her tail to keep her balance, her soft underbelly became exposed.

Without thinking, Fryda leapt forward. She heard Theow gasp something as he reached out to stop her, but she could not catch the words, and he could not catch her. She sprinted across the quarry and ducked under the dragon's tail right where it joined with her back end. Fryda clasped the sharp poker in her uninjured hand and drove the hooked point upward into her body. She aimed for a space between trickles of melted gold and buried the iron deep.

The beleaguered beast made a noise like nothing any human

had ever heard. Her rage and pain and fear seeped into their blood and bones, and every person in that quarry would carry a piece of it with them from that moment to their dying day. With a burst of strength, Fryda yanked the poker down, catching the tip on the dragon's flesh and elongating the wound. She dropped the poker and backed away from the beast, but not before she was bathed in a fall of hot amethyst blood.

★ ★ ★

The heart. Fýrdraca can still see the heart, though her own heart slows as her blood spills onto the ground. The wound, however, is not a mortal one, she knows. Not yet. The shield maiden must do more to unchain Fýrdraca's life from this world. The Lone Survivor's curse would not relinquish its hold on her so easily.

Fýrdraca is pain.

She is death.

She is dying.

She cannot stop the flame. She cannot stop the curse. With her little remaining strength, Fýrdraca channels magic, like a gift, into the girl…the woman-child. Her dragon-warrior.

★ ★ ★

Fryda had not delivered a death blow. The dragon angled her vulnerable back end away and the smoke dissipated, as if she used her breath now only to remind herself to live. The warriors, sensing her growing weakness, rushed to attack with relentless force and distracted her attention away from Fryda and Theow. Fryda wiped dragon's blood from her eyes and backed away.

Theow ran to her and pulled her to the side, away from the battle and the blood. "Woden's beard, Fryda," he muttered, clutching her tightly to him, "would you please stop running *towards* the bloody thing?"

Fryda's body thrummed with magic and energy. She returned

Theow's embrace, careful not to crush him with her dragon-sized strength. "Where are Beowulf and Wiglaf?" she asked.

Theow drew away, now sticky with dragon's blood. "By the head." Theow looked down at Hrunting and then glanced towards the far side of the quarry. "Nægling broke, so I think Beowulf needs a sword. Let's go."

Fryda followed as Theow took her hand and led her towards the dragon's head. As they skirted the beast's broad body, the king came into view. He lay crumpled on the ground, limp and writhing, with Swicdóm near his hand as if the sword had fallen from his grip. His eyes moved, scanning the quarry as if unable to fix on any single feature, and his mouth opened and closed around a bright river of blood. Wiglaf crouched over him, holding Olaf's *seax*.

Theow skidded to a halt and clasped Fryda to keep her behind him. Fryda saw Wiglaf rise and stare at Theow. Beowulf gasped and gurgled as more blood poured from a wound in his throat— a gaping hole torn through the width of his neck.

Theow stared back at Wiglaf.

"The dragon bit him," Wiglaf said. He still clutched the *seax* in his uninjured hand. "Fang went right through. I managed to stab it through the neck, though, as it did."

Fryda looked at the *seax*. Drops of fresh blood, red as rubies, fell from the tip and spattered on the ground at Wiglaf's feet. She looked back up at her brother and their eyes met.

Wiglaf averted his gaze first.

Beowulf twitched, and with a low cry, Fryda dropped her poker, dodged around Theow and flung herself on the ground next to the king. She tore off her helmet and tossed it aside, calling his name, and for a moment Beowulf's eyes focused on her.

"No," she whispered, laying her bandaged hand over his heart. "Please, no."

Beowulf reached up one shaking hand and swiped it over her

hair, as if she were a small child, and left streaks of red blood on the unruly curls. He mouthed two words at her, and though he could make no sound beyond the bubbling of his blood, she could read his last words on his lips.

Sweet...girl...

Another scream rent the air and a warrior flew past them, his limp body falling into unnatural angles of broken bone and spine. The dragon, weaker now but still fighting, swivelled as another warrior sank a spear into her flank. An archer shot an arrow through her eye and the beast wailed and cried and tossed her head.

Theow leaned down and swept Swicdóm into his free hand. Fryda saw a brief spark of fear flare in Wiglaf's eyes, as if he thought Theow would use the sword against him. Instead, Theow tossed it to Fryda, who caught it with her good hand, and he held Hrunting at the ready.

Beowulf's hand fell from Fryda's hair, slack and bloody. She gazed at him for a breath or two, her chest tight and tears locked behind her eyes, before she clambered to her feet and turned to face Theow. They looked at each other, and in their gaze they exchanged a lifetime's worth of words in a single moment. She saw in Theow's eyes his promise to tell her all the stories he'd hidden for so many years. Then together they turned and ran across the stone quarry towards the flailing beast.

The sword, Swicdóm, felt heavy in Fryda's hand, as if it were burdened with the lives of every man it had ever killed. Theow, having longer legs, got to the dragon first. The beast, broken and bleeding, blinded in one eye, still fought, though her strength was clearly waning. Theow raised Hrunting high.

"We almost have her!" Fryda heard Hild shout. "Keep away from her teeth and tail and we can take her!"

Theow buried Hrunting to the hilt in the dragon's flank. Fryda beamed with pride as she ran to catch up. But she was still too far away to do anything but scream when the dragon swung her head around, whip-fast, and knocked Theow off his feet. His head hit the stone floor with an audible *crack*. The dragon, ignoring Theow's limp body, gazed balefully at Wiglaf, her head cocked to one side as if confused by what she saw. Wiglaf froze, as if held in thrall by the worlds that swirled in her eye, and he didn't even flinch as she snapped her teeth into his shoulder and tore his arm off like a haunch of meat.

★ ★ ★

Fýrdraca revels in the taste of human flesh once more. She feels her magic waning, leaving her body with her leaking blood. But she also feels it growing, burgeoning, in the warrior-woman as, now a true shield maiden, she loses her control. Fýrdraca sees her own death coming.

She turns to face it.

She rejoices.

She rejoices.

★ ★ ★

Swicdóm dropped from Fryda's nerveless hand. She stared as the ebony beast tossed Wiglaf to the side, like a sack of rags. He tumbled across the floor and came to rest against a boulder where he screamed and writhed in agony. Blood pooled beneath him. Theow, lying motionless nearby, did not move.

Fryda's mind went blank. Words and thoughts disappeared like chalk swept from stone. She breathed in, and as she did, her insides expanded, enlarged past the physical limitations of her body. A fire ignited in her gut and spread outward…down her legs, out to her fingertips, to the crown of her skull. She was suddenly flooded with a heat so volatile it could destroy the world.

She looked at the dragon, the creature that had hurt—perhaps killed—her love and her brother…and decided to destroy her instead.

* * *

*One eye is extinguished and the other flickers, falters…fails.
Fýrdraca can see only the heart now…her heart.*

* * *

Fryda kept inhaling, and the fire within her grew. She gathered it close into a ball, a centre of fury and power inside her body. Sparks crackled at her fingertips as she lifted her arms, and her hair rose around her head like a sun-coloured halo. She drew even more heat into that centre, and it lifted her up to her toes…and then the earth fell away from her feet entirely. She rose, hovered in midair, and all activity ceased as humans and dragon stopped what they were doing to stare at her.

The dragon regarded Fryda with her one good eye, and then the beast bowed her head—mouth still stained with Wiglaf's blood—as if acknowledging defeat.

* * *

Fýrdraca touches the shield maiden with her cursed music and suddenly they are one. The dragon opens her mind, and her pain becomes the woman-child's pain.

* * *

A black light sparked in the dragon's eye and Fryda gasped, suddenly seeing what the dragon saw, feeling what she felt. She knew the beast recognized Fryda's right to her blood, and she offered up her own life to pay the *wergild* for the lives she had taken. The ancient creature *wanted* to die. And Fryda, cold and desolate despite the heat flooding through her, accepted the invitation. This did not feel like the lash of power she'd unleashed on Bryce when he startled her in the meadow. It was unlike the burst of strength she'd felt in the battle with the exiles.

This felt like a choice. She could use this power within her to do anything, and it would obey.

* * *

Fýrdraca begs the shield maiden to end her. She pours her own pain into the goblet as well, and it fills to the brim, mixing with the Lone Survivor's curse. The hearts are no longer in exile; are no longer alone.

* * *

Fryda lifted her hands and released a pulse of magic so strong it knocked her backwards to the ground. She heard a few shouts and a scream as she watched the dragon's chest burst apart and her heart spill onto the floor.

* * *

She can rest.
She can sleep.

* * *

The dragon faltered, then fell. She canted to one side, her ruined wings twisted beneath her heavy body. Her head hit the ground with a resounding thud, and the jet fire in her remaining eye flickered and went out.

A loud *crack* reverberated through the enclosed quarry and the faint smell of residual smoke wafted up into the warm air. On the floor, near King Beowulf's cooling body, the gold and silver goblet split and shattered into two pieces.

* * *

Fýrdraca falls away to the comforting sound of the treasure-song, the music that sustained her for so many centuries.
It sings sweetly now, the gold tuned back to true.
It follows her down, down...and she is not alone.

Thirty-three

Silence descended for the space of a breath as everyone stared at Fryda and the dragon, and then a mighty cheer went up from the victorious warriors.

Fryda lay where she had fallen, silent and wondering. As soon as the dragon died, all her magic and power surged through Fryda, causing a riot of sensations throughout her body. All her aches and pains vanished. Her mind became sharp and clear and her senses heightened to fine sensitivity. She felt strong, alert... almost invulnerable.

She sat up and looked around. The dragon lay in a heap of black scales and purple blood, her chest cracked wide open and her heart splayed on the floor. Her remaining eye, which had once held such fire, was dull and filmy, and no smoke trickled through her nostrils or mouth. The dragon was dead.

Be at peace, Fryda thought. *You will live on in our stories, in songs and poetry, in myth and legend and memory.*

Next to her body lay another, much smaller bundle of cloth and blood. *Theow.* Fryda scrambled to her feet and ran to Theow. Hild was there before her, carefully turning him onto his back so she could examine his wounds. There was blood on his face and soaked into his fiery hair.

"He's alive," Hild said, her voice tense and short. "I'll tend to him. Go look to Lord Wiglaf."

"Will he...?" Fryda could not even finish the question in her own head. Everything in her rebelled against it.

"I don't know." Hild's face was fierce with concentration. "I need to examine his head wound. Go, quickly, or your brother will die, if he hasn't already."

Fryda forced herself to turn away and ran to where Wiglaf lay. He was still now, his eyes closed, and for one moment she was certain he had died. But she saw his chest rise and fall as shallow breath still fuelled the forge of his body, and she dropped to her knees by his side.

His shoulder was a ruined mess. The dragon had not bitten cleanly through his limb, but had ripped it from his body. His bloody flesh hung in tattered scraps and splintered bone. Fryda pulled off her leather belt, wrapped it around the small stump that remained at his shoulder, and pulled it tight, being careful to control her new dragon-strength. The bleeding slowed, and then stopped. Wiglaf's face was white as a summer cloud, but still he breathed.

Bjorn came running to her. His armour was stained with purple liquid, and his own red blood adorned his face and neck. He did not seem to notice his wounds, however, as he knelt beside the lord.

"Excellent work, my lady," he said. "You've stopped the bleeding in time. He might yet live. I'll make sure he gets to the surface safely." He then turned to the other body lying nearby.

Fryda looked at Beowulf and the sight sent through her a jolt of pain so acute she immediately turned away. The king's eyes were open and staring, but they had seen their last. He had spoken his final words and his life had fled from his breast, transforming him from man to memory.

Her eyes fell on Wiglaf's severed arm, which lay near the dead king, still clutching the *seax*. She saw the bright red blood on its blade, saw the gaping wound in Beowulf's neck, and knew the unthinkable truth.

She thanked Bjorn and stumbled back to Hild and Theow. He

remained still and senseless, though Hild had cleaned much of the blood from his face.

"He still lives, but we need to get him out of here as soon as possible," Hild muttered. "I need my herbs. We'll try the hoist. The dragon destroyed the platform, but we can rig some armour to act as a pallet."

As Hild called for Bjorn to help her with Theow, the warriors around Fryda took up their weapons again and worked the enormous beast's corpse with their knives and daggers, chipping away at her scales, talons, and teeth for war-mementos. Fryda understood their delight in such a victory, but the sight of the mutilated creature, and the smell of blood, cinnamon, and rotting leaves made her stomach churn.

Eventually the chaos calmed, and the warriors began tending to the wounded and caring for the dead. Fryda watched as a few hardy warriors shimmied up the rope and then cranked first Wiglaf, then Theow up the hoist to the top of the quarry, followed by King Beowulf's body. There were no cheers or celebrations then, but a sombre mood settled over the survivors and they performed their melancholy duties in silence.

Fryda jumped when Bjorn unexpectedly appeared again at her side. He held a small object in his hand and looked at her with a wariness that confused her... until she realized that, with the exception of Hild, not one person had spoken to, or even looked at her since she had somehow levitated herself into the air and torn the beating heart out of a dragon's chest without even touching the creature.

That... might take some explaining, if she managed to find the words.

"Bjorn," she said. She took a deep breath and rushed on. "Thank you so much for what you did. For Wiglaf and Theow, I mean. Getting them out so quickly."

"Of course, my lady," Bjorn said. "It was my honour to help."

He held out his hand to her, and she saw he clutched a sliver of something so profoundly black her eye nearly skipped over it, as if it were not there. It was one of the dragon's scales, Fryda realized. She hesitantly reached out to take it, and Bjorn slipped it into her hand.

"You saved us," he said. "I...I saw what you did. I don't understand it, but I saw it. It was like watching the king himself fight a monster from an epic poem."

Fryda suddenly wondered if anyone would ever write epic poems about her.

"Thank you," she said, staring at the scale. It was the shape of a chicken's egg, but as thin as her fingernail with a hint of a curve on the surface.

Bjorn lifted his other hand and held out another scale. "For Master Theow," he said.

Master Theow, she thought, and took the offering. That would amuse him to no end. Now he just had to wake up so she could tell him about it.

Bjorn shot a glance up at Beowulf's body, which was nearly halfway up the quarry wall. "Anyway. I wanted to thank you for your bravery and let you know the way up is clear...my Queen." He bowed to her and hurried away.

Fryda stood there a moment, stunned, before remembering to close her mouth.

Beowulf was dead. She was queen.

Queen, she thought. *Woden's beard, what have I got myself into?*

A glimmer on the ground caught her eye and she blinked. Something beside the far stone wall shimmered in the late-morning sun. Fryda tucked a wayward curl behind her ear and padded over to investigate.

It was the goblet, the one Theow had taken from the dragon's hoard. The one that filled with corrupted mead when placed alongside its mate. It was a charred and twisted ruin now. Somehow during the battle, the bowl and stem had split in two, the ragged edges blackened and melted, the gems cracked and devoid of lustre. Fryda picked up the pieces of the cup. It felt lighter than she remembered.

As she walked back to the stairs that would take her to Theow, she held up the dragon's scale. She blinked in surprise. There, on the surface that refused to reflect any light, she saw her own face mirrored back at her.

*

Two days later, a newly dug barrow stood open, high above the Baltic Sea.

Fryda asked to see it before her coronation. She did not feel she could take the title of queen until she had said her farewells to King Beowulf. Theow stood beside her and clasped her hand in his as they both paid their respects to the fallen hero. The mound rose high above the headland and overlooked the turbulent waters. The men and women of Eceweall filled it with gold rings and rich jewels, torques and crowns, and many other treasures that had survived the dragon's hoard, as befitted the heroic and kingly warrior. An alabaster urn stood in the centre of the death-house, marbled and crafted with care, and within this urn the bereaved had placed the ashes from King Beowulf's funeral pyre.

Beside the urn stood a goblet forged by Weland the Smith, son of giants. Trees of gold and silver hid bejewelled forest animals, and intricate vines ran up and down the stem. On the other side of the king's final resting place lay the ruined second goblet, its two pieces charred and twisted, yet somehow still noble. Fryda had brought it back from the quarry and put it with its brother in King Beowulf's barrow, for he had told her their story. The moment she lay the broken cup down, the pristine goblet filled with golden mead that never soured, and from the broken one dripped perfect, sweet droplets, constant and pure.

Fryda inhaled deeply, as if she could trap her emotions in her chest with her breath. In front of the urn she placed a single dragon's scale, blacker than soot. It threw off no light, but instead gathered up the darkness and hoarded it like treasure. Fryda knew, because she had asked him, that Theow saw nothing reflected in the scale, yet she still saw her own face whenever she looked at it. Next to the scale lay all the shattered pieces of Nægling, loosely reconstructed to imitate the original shape of the sword.

After the battle with the dragon had ended, Fryda had jumped into action. She issued orders for an honour guard to bear the body of the king and his fallen warriors back to the *burh*. She oversaw the disposal of the dragon, watched as she was hacked and hewn with axe and sword and thrown into the sea, piece by piece. She instructed the warriors to lay out Eceweall's dead, and she grieved to see Eadith, Lyset, and young Toland amongst the slain—though she could not bring herself to feel much sorrow at the loss of Moire. Theow was under orders to recover from the knock to his head, so Fryda and Hild had helped build the funeral pyres and called for memorials to be built for the king and his fallen. They collected food, raised tents, and established a temporary campground where the clan could regroup, and Fryda sent off messengers with requests for aid. And, of course, she had asked the *scops* to write the glorious—if somewhat expurgated—story of Beowulf and the dragon.

Fryda let out the breath, and with it came tears. She squeezed Theow's hand. "All right," she said. "I'm ready."

All the survivors of the *burh* waited for them in the meadow behind the burnt-out forge, which she was determined to rebuild immediately after they finished the new longhouse. All the survivors but one, Fryda silently amended. Wiglaf still lay limp and senseless in the strongroom, the stump of his shoulder bandaged and his belly full of white poppy syrup to ease his pain. She had taken the precaution of giving him the same treatment he had shown her, and chained his remaining arm to the wall.

He would live...but he would not have much of a life.

She raised her hands and the people stilled, hushing their voices to hear what she would say. Their small sounds of movement blended with the music of the meadow and soothed her with its life and vitality.

"This has been a time of sorrowful endings and hopeful beginnings," she said, her voice strong against the breezes that tried to whisk it away. "We have said goodbye to our beloved king who loved us and served us all so well." Her throat tightened and she cleared it. "Without him, we would never have triumphed over the dragon so bent on our destruction."

Over the past two days, Fryda had been constantly aware of the dragon-power that thrummed through her body. It flitted through her, surprising her at moments as it moved from her chest to her fingers, and then, perhaps, to her head, like a bird looking for a comfortable place to perch. Eventually, however, she felt the magic settle into her bones, her blood, her flesh, as if it at last accepted her body as its home. She finally felt comfortable with the power and believed that, as she learned to use it wisely, it would become like a sixth sense she could control. This, she suspected, was the origin of Beowulf's legendary strength.

"Therefore," she continued, "I am humbled and honoured to accept King Beowulf's wishes to take his place as his heir, as was heard and witnessed by many of those present here today."

"Heard and witnessed," the people murmured, including Theow, Hild, and Bjorn, who all stood near her in steadfast support.

Bjorn, newly chief of the *gedriht*, stepped forward. He held a golden circlet in his hands, a wide band studded with many jewels. Blue, green, and red gems glowed in the sunlight, and pink and white pearls gleamed richly in their settings. This, too, had escaped the dragon's fire in the treasure cave.

Bjorn stopped in front of Fryda and smiled at her. He lifted the crown and placed it on her head. He had to exert a fair amount of force to squeeze it past her thick mane of curls, but eventually it rested snugly against her forehead. Somewhat red in the face, Bjorn stepped back, and a cacophony of cheers rose from the small crowd.

Fryda raised her hands until the noise subsided. "I have three proclamations to make," she announced. "My first three acts as queen. These decisions have given me both sorrow and joy, which seems fitting because ruling a nation is both a heavy burden and a great honour." She saw approving nods in the crowd.

She swallowed. "First the sorrow, and I know you will believe me when I say this is truly an arrow to my heart. My brother, Wiglaf…"

She stopped. His name tasted bitter in her mouth. Theow stepped closer and she took comfort from his nearness.

"My brother, Wiglaf, has proved himself a traitor to his people and his king," she said. A shocked murmur went through the crowd like a wave. "I do not say this lightly. But he imprisoned me, wrongly accused Theow, and…and he murdered King Beowulf."

Silence rocked through the meadow.

"Therefore, it is my sad duty to strip Wiglaf of Clan Waegmunding of his lands, titles, and properties, and to exile him from Geatland as soon as he has strength enough to travel and survive." It was not enough, Fryda and Theow had decided, to exile him from Eceweall. Theow still feared for her safety and she admitted she would feel more secure if they banished Wiglaf from the country entirely. She looked at Bjorn. "He is clever and wily. I will need the *gedriht* to watch over him until he is fit to leave."

"Of course, Lady Fry…I mean, my Queen," Bjorn said, stumbling over her name.

"But this leads to my second proclamation, which is much more pleasant." Fryda beckoned to Hild, who looked surprised but came to stand before her. "Uncle Beowulf believed that a person is not defined by birth or status, but by deed and what lies in the heart. I mean to begin my rule by honouring that belief."

She smiled at Hild, whose eyes grew huge. "With my brother's exile, Eċeweall will need a new chieftain. I can think of no better choice than the valorous Hild, who showed her bravery both in the battle with the exiles and with the dragon."

Hild's jaw dropped and Bjorn's face broke into a grin.

"Hild, I induct you into the ranks of the shield maidens and name you chief of Eċeweall." Fryda smiled impishly at her friend. "As such, you will be working closely with the chief of the *gedriht* in the course of your new duties and training."

Hild bowed and shot Fryda a speaking look as she straightened. Unrepentant, Fryda took her friend's hand. "As chief, it is your duty to rebuild our home, protect it, and help it grow. You will have help from our allies and neighbouring *burhs*, as well as your queen...who will remain in residence."

"I am honoured, my...I am honoured, Fryda."

Fryda grinned at her friend as a flash of happiness lifted her heart. Hild grinned back, and Fryda knew her friend had meant her name as a gift. She released Hild's hand, and the new chief stepped back, unable to hide her pleased smile.

"This brings me to my third proclamation," Fryda said, her voice carrying to every ear. "As Beowulf's heir I have inherited his lands as well as his title. Therefore, while we work to rebuild Eċeweall, we shall relocate the residents to Beowulf's castle, *Wlwulf-Edor*, where we will find homes for you. We shall also erect a camp here for people who want to remain and help with rebuilding our home. All are welcome in both *burhs*."

Fryda pushed down her worry that Beowulf's people might not be quite as welcoming as she might hope of their new queen and her bedraggled band of refugees. She would spend the next days sending many, many messages. But today...

"I stand before you a woman of many names. I am Fryðegifu,

daughter of Weohstan. I am Sunbeam, friend of Bryce. I am 'sweet girl,' kin of Beowulf, and I am Fryda, Shield Maiden, sister warrior." She looked at Hild, who had tears sparkling on her cheeks. "I am Queen, protector of Geatland. And now..." She turned to Theow, who stood and smiled at her, his green eyes warm and loving. He still had a bandage on his head from his battle-wound, but it was healing well and Hild was confident he would make a full recovery. "...Now I become Fryda, wife of Theow."

She heard gasps and exclamations as Hild stepped to Fryda's side with a sword in her hands and Bjorn stood next to Theow, also bearing a weapon. Hild gave Fryda Swicdóm and Bjorn passed Hrunting to Theow. They bowed and moved back.

"It is our people's custom to have the ritual exchange of swords," Fryda said, "And I cannot think of two more appropriate gifts than my father's sword..." She held up Swicdóm. "...and the sword owned by the two men who loved me like fathers, Beowulf and Bryce." Theow held up Hrunting. They passed the swords to each other and sheathed them in the empty scabbards at their waists. There were more cheers and hoots as Theow brought out a golden cord and wrapped it around their joined hands. Fryda could not imagine where he had found it, but as soon as she felt it against her skin, the dragon-magic rippled through her body, as if in approval of their union.

Theow blinked at her and leaned in to whisper in her ear. "You're glowing, love."

Fryda breathed in his scent—grass and smoke and something spicy—and whispered back, "I'm happy, love."

He carefully took her bandaged hand, and for once Fryda did not try to hide it. The healers had told her that she would never regain full use of it, and that her newly broken bones would not do much to repair her deformity, but in that moment she did not care in the least.

They spoke their vows, brief and heartfelt, and after they were married, the hunters roasted a deer they had killed that day and the warriors broke open the last casks of ale and mead that had survived the dragon's assault. Stories were told, songs were sung, and life settled back into something like normality.

For one shining moment, Fryda felt peace, and hope, and a frisson of excitement at the thought of embarking on a new adventure. She was the mistress of her own fate and had linked her life to this remarkable man. And anyone...*anyone*...who tried to bring her down, or to interfere with her *burh* and her people, would learn the dangers of provoking a dragon-touched shield maiden.

Glossary

Ælfgifu (ELF-yee-foo)—Bryce's daughter. Her name means "gift of the elves" in Old English.

Aegan (AY-gan)—One of Eadgils' exiles. His name means "youth" or "young man" in Old Irish.

Aesc (ASK)—One of Eadgils' archers. His name means "ash tree" in Old English.

Ansten—A minor Swedish lord.

Arleigh (AR-lee)—Bryce's wife.

bæst (BEHST)—A plant fibre collected from the inside of tree bark, used to make many items, including rope.

barrow—A grave dug into the ground and covered with a large mound of earth.

Beowulf (BAY-oh-wolf)—King of the Geats. His name means "bee-wolf" in Old English, which is another word for "bear."

Breca—Beowulf's friend and swimming competitor.

Bryce (BRY-cheh)—Blacksmith at Eċeweall. His name means both "peace" and "breakable" in Old English.

Brycg Stowe (BRIGH-sk stow)—Old English for "Bridge Settlement." The Old English name for modern-day Bristol, famous for its slave markets and a main trade centre with Ireland.

brytan byrde (BRY-tan BEER-deh)—Old English for "lord's burden."

burh (BURR)—The Old English word for "burg," it is what Old English speakers called their fortresses and keeps in the tenth century.

Byrhtnoth (BIRTH-nohth)—The Saxon lord who fought and died at the Battle of Maldon in 991 CE.

dwale (DWAYLE)—An anaesthetic and sleeping potion used by the early medieval clans, made of opium and other ingredients.

Dysg (DISK)—Fryda's ex-betrothed. Old English for "foolish," "weak" and "ignorant."

Eadgils (EYED-gills)—Beowulf's advisor, he is the son of Ohthere, brother of Eanmund (killed by Weohstan) and nephew of Onela (killed by Eadgils himself).

Eadith (EYE-dith)—Chief housekeeper at Eceweall.

Eanmund (EYN-mund)—Son of Ohthere and nephew of Onela. Weohstan killed him in battle.

Eawynn (EYE-win)—One of Weohstan's warriors.

Eceweall (ETCH-way-ull)—Weohstan's stronghold. The name means "durable wall' in Old English.

Ecgþeow (ECK-thee-oh)—Beowulf's father.

Ériu (AY-roo)—The Old English name for Ireland.

Fægebeorn (FEH-geh-beh-orn)—A warrior in Weohstan's army. His name means "doomed man" or "doomed warrior" in Old English.

Frige (FREE-yeh)—Early English medieval goddess of the home and marriage.

Fryda (FREE-dah)—Fryðegifu's nickname.

Fryðegifu (FREE-dah-YEE-foo)—Wiglaf's sister, daughter of Weohstan and Ielfeta. Her name means "gift of peace" in Old English.

fuþorc (FOO-thark)—The Old English runic alphabet, used until the eleventh century.

Fýrdraca (feer-DRAH-cah)—The last dragon, guardian of the Lone Survivor's treasure hoard. Her name means "fire dragon" in Old English.

Geatland (GEET-land)—Most likely the land that is now southern Sweden, where this story takes place.

gedriht (yeh-DRICHT)—A chief's most prized warriors in an elite warband.

Grendel (GREN-del)—A monster in Denmark, killed by Beowulf in his youth.

Gudrun (GOOD-rune)—Olaf's wife.

hægtesse (hig-TESS)—an Old English female witch or magician.

Hild (HILL-d)—A slave in Weohstan's house, descended from Roman slaves taken from sub-Saharan Africa. Her name means "battle" in Old English.

Hrethel (hr-ETH-l)—Hygelac's father and King of Geatland before him.

Hrunting (hr-UNT-ing)—The sword Unferth gave to Beowulf to kill Grendel's mother. It failed, and so Beowulf returned it to Unferth after the battle.

Hygelac (HEE-yuh-lahk)—King of Geatland before Beowulf.

Ielfeta (eel-FATE-eh)—Weohstan's wife, mother to Wiglaf and Fryðegifu. She died at Fryðegifu's birth. Her name means "swan" in Old English.

Iorlund (ee-OR-lund)—A lord from Denmark.

Lyset (lee-SET)—A kitchen maid.

Mjolnir (MYOL-neer)—The name of Thor's hammer in Norse mythology.

Moire (MWUAR)—Mistress of the kitchens at Eċeweall. Her name means "bitter" in Old English.

Nægling (NAY-gling)—Beowulf's sword, a gift from Hygelac for killing Grendel and Grendel's mother. It originally belonged to Hrethel, King of Geatland and Hygelac's father. The name means "little nail" in Old English.

Olaf (OH-luff)—Chief of the gedriht at Eċeweall. Originally Danish, he came to Geatland with Beowulf after the battles with Grendel and Grendel's mother.

Olaf Tryggvason—The King of Norway in the tenth century.

Onela (AHN-eh-lah)—King of the Swedes, killed by Eadgils, uncle to Eadgils and Eanmund.

Panta River—Now called the Blackwater River in Essex, England, it was the site of the Battle of Maldon in the year 991.

pintel (PIN-tell)—Old English word for "penis."

ráth (WRATH)—A ringfort, or walled enclosure, built in Ireland during the Iron Age.

Rawald—A lord of Frisia.

Roman foot—11.6 inches.

scop (SHOPE)—An Old English bard or storyteller.

seax (SEEKS)—A knife, dagger, or short-sword, often engraved with the names of the maker and owner.

sott (SOHT)—Old English for "dullard" or "fool."

Swicdóm (SWEEK-dom)—The name of Eanmund's sword that was awarded to Weohstan when he killed Eanmund in the Swedish–Geatish wars. Its name means "betrayer," "treachery," or "treason" in Old Norse.

Theow (THEE-oh)—A slave in Weohstan's house. His name means "slave" in Old English.

Toland—A kitchen boy. His name means "mighty" in Old Irish.

Unferth (UN-firth)—Hrothgar's thane, who doubted Beowulf's boasts and deeds before his battle with Grendel.

völva (VEL-vah)—A Viking witch.

Waegmunding (WAYG-mun-ding)—The Geat's clan name.

Wealhtheow (WAIL-thay-oh)—King Hrothgar's wife.

Weland (WAY-land)—An Old English and Old Norse legendary blacksmith.

Weohstan (WEE-oh-stahn)—Theow's master, regent and landlord of Beowulf's lands, husband to Ielfeta and father to Wiglaf and Fryðegifu. His name means "sacred stone" in Old English.

wergild (WEAR-gild)—The monetary value determined to be equal to the value of a person's life.

Widsith—A traveller and poet in Old English tales.

Wiglaf (WEE-luff)—Son of Weohstan and Ielfeta, Fryðegifu's brother.

Wlwulf-Edor (WOLF-ay-dor)—The name of Beowulf's stronghold and castle. Old English for "warrior-protector."

Wyrmsele (WEERM-say-leh)—The early English medieval equivalent to an underworld, like Tartarus or Hell.

Woden—The principal god in early medieval religion, the All-Father, analogous to Odin from Norse mythology.

Acknowledgements

I must first acknowledge Seamus Heaney's translation of *Beowulf*, which I consulted extensively in the crafting of this book. I used Stephen A. Barney's lovely dictionary, *Word-Hoard*, for the snippets of Old English that appear in the characters' mouths and names. I would also like to thank Dr. Aaron K. Hostetter from Rutgers University for giving me permission to reference his lyrical translation of "The Battle of Maldon" that appears in this novel. Perhaps most importantly, I wish to thank my amazing agent, Kristina Pérez, and my extraordinary editor, Rosie de Courcy, for believing in this project enough to help me get it out into the world.

And finally, I would like to thank the people without whom this book would not exist in its current incarnation. My professors and mentors in the University of Alaska Anchorage MFA program: David Stevenson, Rich Chiappone, Daryl Farmer, Ed Allen, and Valerie Miner. Thank you also to my cohort, to everyone who read and critiqued chapters of this book as part of residency workshops. Thanks to Janet Lee Carey, who helped solve some thorny problems with the beginning, and to Jamey Bradbury, my writing buddy extraordinaire. Thanks, also, to my valiant and generous beta readers: Muff Hackett, Cammy Vokits, Rebecca Deisher Coffin, Dave Dannenberg, Michele Kinsey Roszell, Kat Crosthwaite, and Rebecca May Mouser. And finally, to my tireless and unflagging cheerleaders, Kate Holloway, Roberta Alexander (yes, the opera singer), Jennifer Stone, Amanda Keiter Rosenberger, Amanda Sprochi, Mum and The Daddy Person, Big Bruddah and Liz-in-Law—I could not have done any of this without you.

Meet the Author

Kevin Hedin Photography

SHARON EMMERICHS was born in Sweden to American parents and grew up in Wisconsin, near Lake Michigan. She has been a writer all her life, from the time she scribbled "words" and pictures on pieces of paper, stapled them together, and called it a book. Her love of stories later translated into an English degree, and then she went on to get her MA and PhD in medieval and early modern literature...and because she collects degrees the way some people collect stamps or baseball cards, she graduated with her creative writing MFA in fiction in 2021. She is an Associate Professor of Shakespeare and medieval literature in beautiful Alaska, where she lives with Juneau, the goofiest Siberian husky ever.

Interview

What first drew you to medieval and early modern literature, and to Beowulf *in particular?*

It all started with Shakespeare. When I was seven, my mother took me to see a performance of *Romeo and Juliet*, and while I didn't understand everything, I was utterly entranced. That started my lifelong fascination with early British literature. And *Beowulf* is itself such an amazing story with its heroes and monsters—I loved it from the first time I had to read it in freshman English in high school! John Gardner's *Grendel* was also a huge influence on me. So when it came time to choose what literature I wanted to study/teach, the choice was easy!

What was the most challenging part of writing Shield Maiden?

Well, that would be...me! I had this story in my head for about fifteen years, and I tried to write it many times, but I kept getting in my own way. My insecurity, my lack of experience and skill, and my busy life as a professor kept me from getting very far. So finally, I applied for an MFA program, knowing I needed to learn, I needed guided feedback, and I needed the motivation to actually write the book. And it worked!

Shield Maiden *weaves together history, myth, and of course, the unique story you've crafted. How did you incorporate the former into the latter?*

This was one of my biggest challenges! I wanted to write a *Beowulf* book, but also to write a book that a reader who has never heard of *Beowulf* could read and enjoy. This meant I had to use history and myth in a way that worked seamlessly with my story as well as with the source material. So for history, I concentrated on "daily life"— what would life in an early medieval clan actually be like? What would they wear, what objects would they use? And for myth, I focused on the dragon, which was a huge part of the original poem, but also a recognizable creature for most readers, whether they'd read *Beowulf* or not.

What's one thing you invented for Shield Maiden *that you wish was true?*

I actually wrote a poem in the Old English style that was edited out of the final version—I worked so hard on that poem, and it was something of a pang to remove it! But I think my favorite invention was the story of the two brothers and the two goblets. I love the idea of having some sort of magical object through which we can connect to those we love the most, even over vast distances. (If only cell phones existed in the early medieval era!)

At the heart of Shield Maiden *is a touching, sweet romance between Fryda and Theow. How did you decide on this central relationship?*

I needed a reason for Theow to be exiled. The original poem states that the nameless slave who wakes the dragon was exiled from his master's house, but it never explains why. I figured, well...maybe he got a little too frisky with the lord's daughter. And boom, Fryda was created. I did not anticipate then, however, that she would ultimately become my main character!

How did you approach writing Fryda as a disabled heroine?

It was difficult. I have really terrible rheumatoid arthritis, so my own hands are disabled and I often have to wear braces on all my fingers and thumbs. I wanted to represent that in the book. However, I had a *really* hard time writing her disability. Often I would have to rewrite her scenes because I'd neglected to show the disability of her hand realistically, but more often, I'd have completely ignored the emotional and psychological impact her disability had on her everyday life. It wasn't until I took Neil Gaiman's masterclass on writing and got to his lesson on honesty that I realized I wasn't representing her disability honestly at all—I was playing it safe and hiding her vulnerability. I'd glossed over all the shame, the frustration, and the way others viewed or treated her, so I had to go back and add all that in.

Who are some of your favorite authors and how have they influenced your writing?

Oh, there are so many! My very favorite from the time I was small was Patricia A. McKillip. I was always entranced by the poetic lyricism of her writing—she is why I became a writer, really. Dorothy L. Sayers, Neil Gaiman, and Jasper Fforde taught me that writing can be both humorous and emotionally wrenching. Recently I've made an effort to read more women, queer, and BIPOC writers, so I've thoroughly enjoyed getting to know Octavia E. Butler, Rebecca Roanhorse, R. F. Kuang,

Erin Morgenstern, and Samuel R. Delany. Right now, I'm inhaling *everything* written by N. K. Jemisin! I'm a huge fan of old-style gothic romantic suspense novels, so my shelves are full of Elizabeth Peters and Mary Stewart. I will automatically one-click buy anything from Deanna Raybourn and Courtney Milan to satisfy my mystery/romance itch, and Marissa Meyer, Veronica Roth, and Kristin Cashore for my YA fix.